Ironroot

by

S.J.A.Turney

I would like to dedicate this book to my son, Marcus; born April 2010, the light of my life. May he grow to great things.

Also, to all the people who have helped and supported me over the last two years; friends I have made that I hope will last a lifetime: Jules, Prue, Robin, Simon O, Ted and Liviu most of all.

Published in 2010 by YouWriteOn.com

First Edition

Published by YouWriteOn.com

By the same author:

Interregnum (2009)

For twenty years civil war has torn the Empire apart; the Imperial line extinguished as the mad Emperor Quintus burned in his palace, betrayed by his greatest general. Against a background of war, decay, poverty and violence, men who once served in the proud Imperial army now fight as mercenaries, hiring themselves to the greediest lords.

On a hopeless battlefield that same general, now a mercenary captain tortured by the events of his past, stumbles across hope in the form of a young man begging for help. Kiva is forced to face more than his dark past as he struggles to put his life and the very Empire back together. The last scion of the Imperial line will change Kiva forever.

Marius' Mules (2009)

It is 58 BC and the mighty Tenth Legion, camped in Northern Italy, prepare for the arrival of the most notorious general in Roman history: Julius Caesar.

Marcus Falerius Fronto, commander of the Tenth is a career soldier and long-time companion of Caesar's. Despite his desire for the simplicity of the military life, he cannot help but be drawn into intrigue and politics as Caesar engineers a motive to invade the lands of Gaul.

Fronto is about to discover that politics can be as dangerous as battle, that old enemies can be trusted more than new friends, and that standing close to such a shining figure as Caesar, even the most ethical of men risk being burned.

Available from all good online stores.

For more information visit www.sjaturney.co.uk

Author's Note:

This book picks up around two decades after the events of Interregnum, though it is not a direct sequel and stands alone as a tale. For those who have read Interregnum, some names and locations will be familiar and some new. For those who are new to the tales of the Empire, I hope you enjoy Ironroot and perhaps it will lead you to revisit the earlier story.

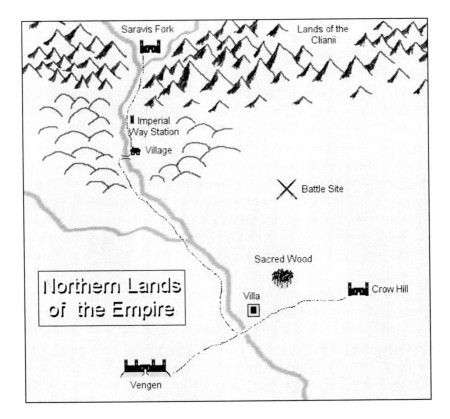

By moonlight white, portentous sight...

I remember that night.

I remember it as though it happened yesterday.

I always take a walk the night before a fight; always have. Helps clear the mind and lets you focus on the job at hand. Some people drink; some make love. I walk. Of course, it helps that I'm an officer and I can leave the camp any time I like.

Where we'd camped that night there was a small river a little to the north. Not much of a river really; more of a stream, but it ran down into a deep copse of copper coloured beech trees. I strolled from the north gate out into the moonlit night and wandered aimlessly in the general direction of the copse.

I had my armour on and my sword with me, partially because over the years it's become such habit I often forget I'm wearing them, but also because I was leaving the camp and there were barbarians out there. To the south, for sure, but you never know.

The peace out there on the blasted moonlit heath was a balm and a blessing once you left the echoes of the raucous and nervous men in the camp far behind. The only sounds were the wind blowing through the heather and the long grass, the occasional rustle as something nocturnal scampered away from you, and once or twice the eerie, haunting call of an owl.

I'd no need of a torch or lantern. A lantern would have guttered and died in the moorland winds anyway, but the moon was full and white and shone with the aura of the Huntress. It was almost as bright as day. And I descended the slope toward the stream, my boots beginning to make sucking sounds as I stepped into the soft peat on the hillside. Reaching the stream, I stopped for a moment, trying to decide which direction to take. I may have been drawn toward the copse, or perhaps I later imagined that, given the events that unfolded. For whatever the reason, I turned and followed the babbling brook into the trees.

There everything was dark; a sort of primal darkness, such as must fill the endless halls of the underworld. I almost turned back; should have really. I'd walked far enough and needed to be among the men before we turned in. Something made me go on; again I'm not sure whether it was mere curiosity or something more. Sounds mystical and strange, I know. I'm not really a very religious man. Like most of us brought up in the chaos of the Imperial Interregnum, I paid lip service to the Gods of the Empire while maintaining my own private belief in the ability of a man to control his own destiny.

The Gods may have had other ideas. You see there are many other Gods that aren't commonly prayed to in the Empire, but that are held in equally high esteem by the peoples on our borders. I'd been fighting the northern barbarians long enough to become quite familiar with some of these fringe deities, such as the wolf of battle, Hrogar and, of course, Cernus.

And as I stumbled along in the claustrophobic darkness of the trees, I stumbled upon a slope; almost tumbled rather than stumbled, I should say. I reached out and grasped the rough bark of a tree and regained my footing. A single animal track, probably a badger, led away and down to my right and curiously I followed it into a dell; a shallow depression sheltering a pool. It was a small pool, still as glass and reflecting the bright moon on its dark surface, framed by wavering branches. It was so still and peaceful as I wandered down through the trees to the water's edge.

And saw the truth of these 'fringe Gods'. I saw Cernus.

Across the water, on the far shore he stood. Among the shadows but bathed in silver moonlight, the great white stag watched me calmly. I've met ordinary low barbarians who became chieftains and led armies into battle just because they'd seen Cernus in the flesh. To see the Stag God by the light of the full moon is one of the tribes' most powerful portents, though at the time I was blissfully unaware of this. I felt something that I find difficult to describe; as though I had been skewered by a thought. A single consciousness had passed from the great Stag across the water and entered my eyes, filling me with a silvery certainty. Something vast and important had just occurred that was not for me to yet fully understand. All I knew for certain was that this creature was no forest game, but a spirit of the most powerful and profound sort. And I still feel that there was no accident involved; no coincidence.

Cernus drew me to that wood. Over the coming weeks it was an opinion shared by two others.

For that moment, I stood rigid, my mind filled with the shimmering light of the lake and the God that stood beside it.

And suddenly I was dismissed. My mind cleared and I actually staggered a little. A sceptic would say that a cloud drifted across the moon and shattered the silvery reflection on the water's surface, and this is indeed true, but *that* was the coincidence. The stag let out a deep breath, a cloud of steam whisked away by the low breeze in the dell.

I felt in some way hollow; as though I'd just lost something truly important from my being. And yet, at the same time, I felt a certainty; a surety that something important had just transpired, but that something of even greater import lay ahead. One thing of which I was certain was that the battle the next morning held no fear for me. I would survive the following day.

I bowed once; quietly and with military precision and with an almost imperceptible acknowledgement, Cernus turned and strode silently away through the dark hollow beneath the trees. With a sense of purpose, I turned on my heel and picked my way up the difficult badger track and along through the copse to the point where the stream entered. Climbing the sucking, peaty slope once more, I set my gaze on the distant flicker of torches and made my way back to the comfort and human warmth of the camp.

Chapter One

Lucius Varro, captain of the second cohort of the fourth army, tightened his grip on the large, heavy shield covering most of his body. The knuckles of his right hand whitened as he held fast to the short sword by his side, watching the ragged line of the barbarians only a hundred yards away, taunting their enemy, chanting unintelligible war cries and howling. Such behaviour may frighten their neighbouring tribes but it would take more than a few grunts and screams to turn the hearts of the Imperial army. Glancing down, he carefully memorised once more the ground beneath his feet.

A low grassy slope leading up to the enemy line; not the best terrain. There had been a strategy meeting in the command tent yesterday and Varro had been only one of several arguing over the need to make the terrain work with the army, but the prefect had been adamant that the incline be granted to the barbarians in order to keep the sun behind the imperial line. The discussion had raged on into the late afternoon, the Commander waving aside all suggestions regarding archers, slingers and artillery. This would be an easy fight, after all. Prefect Cristus had a disconcerting habit of ignoring the best tactical advice of his officers, yet had a track record of glorious successes regardless. But then the prefect would not be there to see the effect of his decisions, travelling to Vengen for a staff meeting as he now was. And though Varro had taken a long walk last night before the battle, it had done little to calm him. His eyes refocused on the grassy incline.

Only a couple of feet ahead lay what looked like a rabbit hole. Better be careful of that. One slip and he'd be delivered back to the fort in the dead-wagon. He shrugged his shoulders and felt the interlocking plates of his armour settle slightly as the weight distributed, eradicating that annoying pinch in his shoulder. He smiled.

Glancing to his left, he saw the standard bearer holding aloft the magnificent raven banner with the image of the emperor and the ram with a lightning bolt, symbol of the Fourth. Belianus glanced back at him and grinned.

"I wish they'd just charge. My feet ache."

Varro laughed and returned his gaze to the enemy, whose blue-painted faces twisted with violent lust. Someone behind him began to whistle. He began to drift into a reverie once more, his mind tracking back through nineteen years in the Third and then Fourth Northern Armies, and five years of the civil war before that, serving in the private army of Velutio. Things had changed so much in his short time in this world. Shaking his head slightly, he returned his focus to the enemy line and saw some of the warriors in the centre lurch forward. Their companions remained in place, howling, and the bulge soon flattened back into the line. Stupid! How could anyone fight a battle without tactics or direction? Still, the barbarians were getting twitchy and any moment now that line would break as they surged down the hill towards the waiting steel line of the Empire. The second cohort, along with the first and the third, held the centre of the Imperial line. It was here the charge would hit hardest. He cleared his throat.

"Steady lads. They're coming any moment now."

Behind him and along the front line he heard the clink and rattle of his men settling into their stance, prepared for the force of a barbarian charge. Risking another glance away, he gazed far along to the right, past the infantry line, to the small cavalry force hidden behind a line of trees. If you knew they were there you could see movement, but the enemy had neither outriders nor scouts. They were blissfully unaware of the horsemen waiting for the opportunity to sweep behind them and cut them down from the rear.

There was a faltering in the cacophony up the slope and, returning his gaze once more, he saw weapons being raised by the more important looking warriors. The din fell to a low rumble and then rose once more into an ear-splitting crescendo as the line of filthy, hairy, leather-clad warriors began to pour down the slope.

"Lock shields!" he cried, as the men to his sides set themselves to receive the charge. His knuckles tensed again and he clenched his teeth in a snarl as the barbarian force flung themselves against the wall of Imperial iron. He was almost knocked from his feet with the initial impact, but held the line as the tribesmen began to swing wildly overhead, raining down blows upon the shield wall. As the line to both sides braced once more following the initial collision, the short swords of the second cohort began to lance out between the shields, carefully marking targets and delivering precise blows. The barbarians' one great hope had been that a strong charge would break the line, but now they had failed and the Imperial force would hold for a moment and then begin their inexorable slow push forward. The front row of savages began to thin out almost immediately, their companions to the rear climbing over the fallen in their lust for Imperial blood. With an almost contemptuous flick, Varro thrust his blade through the narrow gap afforded in the shields and dug deep into the side of the man before him, who stiffened for a moment, his raised sword faltering and then falling loosely away. Withdrawing his blade for another thrust, the captain gritted his teeth and then called out along the line.

"Advance!"

The front line took one step forward slowly and carefully, navigating the fallen barbarians and various undulations of the ground instinctively. As the barbarians rallied and hit the line again, this time ragged and in small groups rather than one heavy charge, the men of the Fourth Army kept their shields close in a wall, stabbing purposefully with their short swords.

A series of crashes and screams rang out along the line as, with a steady and measured pace, the entire cohort took another pace forward, stabbing and slashing at their shabby opponents. Another step and more carnage, and the line had begun to falter. The advance was difficult over the corpses of their enemies and at irregular points along the line men of the Fourth had succumbed to the occasional well-aimed or lucky blow, the second line rushing forward to plug the gap. Still, Varro mused, as he drew his shoulder back and thrust the blade once more through the shield wall and bit deep into flesh, the enemy line had become a total shambles by now. With a glance over the heads of the opposition, he noted the cavalry wing now harrying the rear of the enemy force. This was the time. He drew a deep breath.

"Melee!" he cried over the sounds of steel and butchery.

Immediately the Imperial wall broke. Those men already engaged with a warrior continued to fight, while those with a clear field marked a target among the rabble and made for them, some lending aid to their more beleaguered companions as they surged forward. There was a note of panic in the unintelligible shouts of the enemy now. They were no longer advancing, but being forced backwards, while their rear ranks had turned as best they could to deal with the fast-paced cavalry. They were trapped.

Paying no heed to his men, who knew well enough how to proceed, Varro stepped forward, eyeing a short, yet heavy-built man clad in furs and leathers and a chainmail shirt. Nimbly stepping over the body of one of the fallen men, the captain raised his shield, staring out over the rim at his opponent. The man had clearly marked him. With a loud cry of challenge, the warrior strode forward, contemptuously knocking aside the blade of one of the Imperial soldiers and driving his own sword deep into the man's ribs. The soldier collapsed with a shout, falling back among the melee and the barbarian let go of his hilt, allowing the blade to fall with the body. Smiling grimly, he drew a second sword from his belt and came on, sparing not a glance for his victim. With surprise, Varro noted that the new weapon was an Imperial blade of some quality. The hilt was bound in red leather and the pommel formed into the shape of the raven. This bastard had stripped an Imperial officer of his fine weapon in some previous engagement and the fact incensed Varro. With a growl, he stepped further forward from the now broken line and hefted his shield, changing his grip for comfort.

"Come on then, you son of a diseased dog!" he shouted at the stocky barbarian, momentarily loosening the grip on his sword hilt to beckon the man on with three fingers.

The man raised a small, round shield of bronze embossed with some bearded visage, presumably a depiction of one of their Gods Varro didn't know, his own face fixed in a rictus of brutal lust. He closed the gap and leapt into the fray with agile enthusiasm.

Varro lifted his own shield a little and blocked the first blow, an over-arm thrust aimed above the shield, straight for his neck. The screech of the barbarian's blade scraping along the shield's bronze edging made Varro's teeth vibrate and the weapon continued its descent to cut a large gash in the wood and leather. Varro reared back and retaliated with his own sword, jabbing sharply around his shield and aiming for the kidney, only to be blocked by the bronze shield in a surprisingly swift reaction, leaving a deep groove across the embossed face.

Again and again the two hammered at each other, their shields blocking every blow. The shriek of Varro's sword against the bronze disc continued to grate on the captain as wood chips and scraps of leather showered away from his own rapidly-disintegrating shield.

And suddenly the barbarian was gone. One of the advancing infantry had lashed out with his shield as he passed and knocked the man from his feet. Varro glared at his underling irritably; even in the midst of battle there was a certain etiquette to be maintained. He didn't have time to ponder however, as another barbarian leapt forward and faced off against him. The captain spared a brief glance at his erstwhile opponent who was trying to regain his feet as one of the Imperial soldiers battered against his bronze shield, trying to put him down for good. Returning his gaze to the new enemy before him clad in ragged furs, he raised his battered shield to ward off a sweeping blow from a long northern sword. With a crash the two met and began to hack and swipe at each other. This man was weaker and less prepared and, as the idiot swept his sword far too wide for a good strike, Varro flicked his blade out once, catching the man's upper arm, just above the elbow. The warrior grunted, his sword falling away from suddenly spasming fingers, and Varro took advantage of his distraction, slamming his huge shield forward into the face of the surprised barbarian. The solid bronze hemispherical boss at the centre hit the man square in the face and filled the air with the sound of splintering bone. The man tried to scream but the sound came out a throaty gurgle as he gagged on his own blood.

Even with uncouth enemies, that battle-etiquette bred into the Imperial army held true. With a smile, Varro thrust his blade out once more straight at the heart, sinking his blade in deep and swiftly ending the man's agony. Satisfied, he stepped around the falling body, trying to identify his next target. He squared his shoulders again, his grip tightening once more on sword and shield, as he felt a sudden pain in his side. His head shot round in surprise to see the stocky barbarian with the imperial blade rising from a crouch. The warrior had quickly despatched his infantryman and had taken the opportunity of Varro's distraction. As the man withdrew his blade for a second strike, Varro turned, fiery pain lancing through his left side as he did so, and placed his shield firmly between them.

Feeling the warm blood pooling in his tunic above the belt and running in rivulets down his thigh, he ground his teeth and squared off against his opponent. As the barbarian drew back his blade for a second thrust, Varro slammed his shield down to the floor with all the strength he could muster. Even above the din of battle he heard the bones in the warrior's foot smash beneath the bronze rim of the heavy shield, and the man faltered.

Grimly, Varro lifted his shield once more and pushed at the man, knocking him backwards. As the barbarian staggered on his crippled foot, Varro lanced out with his straight blade and bit deep into the man's gut, the point ripping through the chain mail, severing links and scattering fragments of iron around. The man staggered again and stared down in surprise as the captain withdrew his blade and a gobbet of blood gushed from the wound. Giving him no second chance to rally, Varro thrust again, his sword plunging into the neck just above the collar bone. The barbarian's eyes widened and he lurched back once more, stumbling. Dropping the stolen Imperial blade, he clutched at his neck, blood spraying finely between his fingers. He was done for. The captain grunted as he watched his opponent fall away onto his backside, clutching his neck and rocking gently back and forth as the colour drained slowly from his face.

The captain turned to move forward, and his left leg buckled. Perhaps the wound in his side had been worse than he thought. He glanced down to see his leg, soaked in crimson, shaking wildly. Damn that ignorant savage and his stolen blade. Cursing gently, Varro sank to his knees as his leg gave way again. With a growl, he toppled gently to the blood-soaked grass.

The second wave of infantry passed by, stepping carefully around him. The battle wouldn't pause for a fallen man, whether he be soldier, captain or even the prefect himself. That was one of the great advantages of the Imperial war machine. Everyone knew his place and his task so well that when battle was joined the whole affair could continue smoothly even with a loss of command. He watched with growing annoyance as the second cohort passed their captain by, moving swiftly to support the first line in the carnage. The crash of steel on steel and cries of victory and agony swept over the battlefield like a blanket of sound as Varro pulled himself upright to look at the hill. It would soon be over.

Tentatively he prodded his side where the blow, either lucky or very well aimed, had slid between his skirt of leather strops and the lowest plate of his body armour. His eyes filled instantly as the pain lanced through his body once more.

"Damn it! A portent of great things eh?" he snapped.

And then somebody pushed his hand away from his side and he glanced round to see one of the field medics crouched beside him, rummaging in his bag. With a wave of his arm the medic called over two orderlies with a stretcher.

"Lie still, Captain," the man uttered in a low voice as he quickly and efficiently packed and bound the wound. "You're losing quite a bit of blood, but you're very lucky. A few weeks and you'll be out front again. An inch higher and I'd be putting coins on your eyes now."

Varro struggled for a suitable reply, but the medic stood as soon as he'd tied off the bandage and disappeared across the field. With a sigh, Varro gave up on conversation, gritting his teeth against the pain while the two orderlies lifted him as gently as they could onto the stretcher. Glancing once more at the wound, the captain noted in irritation that the medic had snipped away three of the leather strops to bind him. That was going to cost.

As he was hoisted to shoulder height, the captain lifted his head a little to glance across the battlefield. The barbarian army had been boxed in and was shrinking by the minute. The whole thing would likely be over before he'd even reached the makeshift hospital at the camp. He clicked his tongue in irritation.

"Busy day for you gentlemen?" he enquired of the two stocky orderlies bearing him away from the field.

"Every day's a busy day sir. If we're not in battle, you'd be surprised how often we deal with frostbite and infections and all sorts. Wish they'd post us back down south where it's warm."

The other orderly gave a gruff laugh.

"Then there's the *other* kind of infection too. We get a lot of that."

Varro smiled. At least he could be proud of his scar. He rolled his head around and craned his neck awkwardly to see in the direction they were taking; it was making him irritable watching the battle progressing so well without him. He saw the two units of archers attached to the Fourth as he passed and they looked glummer than he. Command instructions had determined that the deployment of missile troops and artillery today would be unnecessary and wasteful, as the odds were so favourable anyway; and everyone knew Cristus had a certain mistrust of indirect warfare. The unit looked as bored as the artillery engineers who stood behind them, chewing on their lips as they watched the distant action.

With another smile, he beckoned to one of the engineers as he passed.

"You there!"

The engineer, startled at the unlooked-for attention from a senior officer, saluted and then ran over to the bobbing stretcher.

"Sir?" He looked nervous.

Varro hoisted himself as best he could onto his side, eliciting groans of discomfort from the two men carrying him.

"Go and find me a flask of something alcoholic and bring it to the hospital. I don't mind what it is so long as it's alcoholic. I'll pay you double what it cost you when you get there."

The engineer's eyes lit up and he nodded and saluted before scurrying off to find his prize. Varro leaned back again to find one of the orderlies watching him with a raised eyebrow.

"Something you want to say, soldier?"

"Not me sir," the orderly replied, "but probably the doctor will."

"You let me deal with the doctor."

He lay back again and groaned at every slight shift in the stretcher. He'd been wounded plenty of times of course, in almost twenty five years of service. Indeed, his first major wound had come in the civil war and he'd been quite lucky to live long enough to see the new Emperor installed at Velutio. But still, every wound was a fresh worry. He wasn't as young as he'd been then, and he was taking longer to heal these days. And however lightly the field medic's tone had been, he knew the feel of a more major wound and he'd be damn lucky to be in combat in a fortnight. Maybe a month or two.

His face turned sour at the thought of two months' enforced convalescence; he'd never make it. He was still grumbling to himself about the stupidity of allowing distractions in battle to take his mind off the target when he realised they'd passed into the camp and were approaching the huge leather hospital tent. The smell was foul, but they'd only be here until the morning, then they'd all be heading back to the fort at Crow Hill to await the return of the prefect and inform him of his glorious victory.

He watched with some distaste as they passed the first wave of wounded who'd been brought in from the initial charge. Surprisingly light casualties, he supposed, but a grisly sight nonetheless and precious little consolation for the infantryman sitting outside the tent waiting for attention while he held his severed left arm in his right. Damn that Cristus for denying the archers and artillery. The man may have been a war hero, but whether he distrusted missile units or not, he should have taken every opportunity to thin out their ranks before the fight. The prefect may be lucky and with a record of victories but he was certainly no great tactician.

Mulling over what he perceived as the prefect's mistakes and what he would have done differently, he issued another grunt as the two orderlies laid his stretcher inside the doorway of the huge tent. He spent long minutes listening to the groans and general hubbub of the hospital until one of the attendants strode over to where he lay.

"Captain Varro. You'll have to bear with us for a minute, I'm afraid. Scortius is dealing with an amputation, but he'll be free shortly."

He crouched and examined the captain's side, gently lifting aside the temporary dressing. With a nod he stood once more. "You'll be fine."

Varro grumbled and winced as he shuffled slightly on the uncomfortable stretcher.

"So long as I don't spend an hour lying in a doorway I will."

The attendant smiled and strode across to the line of wounded stacked along the outer facing of the huge leather tent. Varro watched him probing wounds and marking a I, II or III on them with a charcoal stick. The order of severity of their case; he'd seen it often enough to know his wound would rate a II at best, possibly even a III. Privilege of rank made him a I though.

"Varro?"

The captain turned to see Scortius, Chief Medical Officer of the Fourth, standing above him with blood-stained arms folded and an amused expression on his hawk-like face.

"Are you trying to get out of the paperwork?" the doctor barked. "How in the name of four hells did you manage to get yourself stabbed in the first five minutes? When are you going to learn to stand at the back?"

Varro grunted. Scortius knew full well why an officer led from the front, but over two decades of service together the pair had come to know one another very well and Scortius never passed up an opportunity to poke fun at the captain.

"Just shut up and stitch me, Scortius. I haven't the time to lie in your doorway and bleed to death."

The doctor laughed and craned his neck to glance across at the attendant, kneeling with the wounded.

"So what d'you think? A III?"

The attendant smiled back at them and cocked his head to one side. "Perhaps we should start using a IV, sir?"

Varro growled and Scortius gave a deep laugh. "Alright, captain. Don't get yourself stressed; you'll aggravate your wound." He turned to look inside the tent and spotted two more orderlies.

"Get captain Varro here to the back room carefully and put him on the table."

As the two orderlies ran out to collect the wounded officer on his stretcher, Scortius raised a hand to shade his eyes and gazed out across the open space to the battle raging on the opposite slope. The figures swarming along the hillside were predominantly in green now, giving a fair indication that the battle was all but over. He nodded to some internal question and then turned and followed the captain as he was borne aloft through the hospital tent and out to the back room, reserved for the most violent or most important cases.

Varro grunted once more as the orderlies lowered him gently to the table. His gaze lingered for a moment on the small desk to his right, covered with nightmarish instruments, as yet unused. Well, he shouldn't need any of them poking in his side anyway. Turning his head again, he caught a dark, bleak look pass across Scortius' face.

"You're not about to tell me it's worse than I thought, are you?" he enquired, only half jokingly. Scortius shook his head, apparently more to clear his gloom than to answer the question. Then he smiled and the smile was not a particularly inviting one.

"Oh you're not going to die, Varro. Don't be daft. But this is going to hurt rather a lot and you know I can't give you mare's mead since the general ban. Sorry. Battles make me... I don't know, but not happy anyway. I know that's a bit of a setback for a serving officer, but you know why. Now lie still."

Scortius gestured to his two orderlies and they approached the table, gently lifted Varro's torso until he half sat, half lay. There one held him, grunting with the effort, while the other unlaced the plated body armour and finally swept it out from beneath him. Relieved, the orderly let Varro fall slowly back to the table. Varro watched the two rubbing their arms after the strain and groaned, shifting his shoulders slightly, now free of the armour.

"I said lie still, Varro."

The captain lay as rigid as he could as the doctor began to carefully remove his temporary dressing. It was in the nature of doctors to abhor battle, of course. A captain saw only the glory of the charge, the melee and the victory, or if he was unlucky, the defeat and the rout. The nearest he came to the true loss involved was the interminable casualty reports to be delivered to the staff the next day; the head-counts, hoping that old friends called out their names. But to a doctor the first five minutes of battle were spent preparing the facilities and the rest was an endless sea of blood and screaming. The captain's brother, a civil servant in Serfium, had always lauded him, congratulating him on the bravery it took to charge headlong into a fight with barbarians, but Varro knew different. Battles were fought largely on adrenaline, and bravery wasn't always a requisite. But he could never be a doctor. He didn't envy Scortius the job.

Varro's attention was brought rudely back to the present as a lance of white hot fire ran through his side. He gave a strangled cry and turned his head to focus on the doctor. Scortius merely clicked his tongue in irritation and used his free hand to gently push the captain's head back down to the table.

"Do shut up, you baby. I've had to deal with amputations that caused less fuss. It's only a damn probe."

Varro growled as the fiery pain subsided. The doctor withdrew his nightmarish implement and wiped his hands on the towel beside him, already stained pink. Reaching over to the back of the desk he withdrew a flask and held it in front of Varro's face.

"Mare's mead," he whispered in hushed tones. "Don't overdo it as I'm going to be putting you on other medication in a minute and for Gods' sake don't tell anyone. This stuff is concentrated and I want you happy and quiet when I sew this up."

Varro grunted again and took the proffered flask, lifting it gingerly to his lips and taking a swig.

"By the Gods that's strong", he choked in a hoarse voice.

"I warned you. Now shut up and go numb while I work."

The next quarter hour or so passed in a haze for the wounded captain, who watched with placid and euphoric interest as metal objects and swabs were thrust under his ribcage and a surprising quantity of his lifeblood sprayed out and ran down the table leg. He later vaguely remembered chuckling at something, though the first thing he truly recalled was the sting as Scortius slapped him several times across the cheeks.

"Come on, wake up you old goat. All done and I need the table. I've just had the standard bearer of the sixth cohort brought in." He patted his apron." Can't find my needle. Oh well; if you feel anything sharp when you bend in the middle, we've found it. Come on," he urged, gently shaking the captain's shoulder, "look lively."

As Varro gradually emerged from the swimmy effects of the drug, he glanced at his side. A fresh bandage covered his wound with a small red stain blossoming.

"Should it be leaking?" he asked absently.

Scortius shook his head as he rummaged on his desk for something.

"It's only a little seepage; no harm. It'll stop within the hour."

The captain swung himself around on the table and dropped his feet over the side. The sudden movement pulled at his wound and he winced. Scortius tutted.

"Don't be stupid. Do everything carefully for at least a few days. No duties of any kind. See me every day for the next three days and after that only when you feel the need."

"Here;" he said brusquely, thrusting out a hand. Varro peered myopically at it, his sight still a touch blurred. A small pouch sat in the open hand. He raised an eyebrow and looked quizzically up at the doctor, who sighed.

"I know you well enough to know you're not going to lay off the booze while you heal, so I'm a bit limited with what I can give you that'll work well. Let one of these dissolve in liquid and then drink it when you get up and in the mid evening. It'll lessen the pain and hopefully stop any infection. If it doesn't do enough for you, you'll just have to lay off the drink and I'll give you something better. Now be a good chap and disappear; I've plenty of other patients waiting."

Varro slowly slid from the table, almost collapsing in a heap as his feet took his weight.

"Want me to get an orderly to help you back to your tent?"

Varro grunted and waved a hand, not trusting himself to speak without whimpering. Steadying himself against the table, he waited a moment for his head to clear a little further and then took a tentative step toward the open flap into the main hospital tent. As his leg straightened and he moved forward, pain rushed up and then down his side, a pain so intense he almost cried out. Gritting his teeth, he took another step, making sure to balance most of his weight on the good side. Less pain this time; good. He took a deep breath and then realised that someone behind him was clearing his throat. He turned and almost lost his balance again as the white fire exploded around his body. Scortius still had his hand extended with the bag of herbs and a maddening smile. Varro grunted again, snatched the bag and turned as fast and purposefully as he dared before limping painfully out into the main room.

The scene here was blood and chaos. He tried not to actually see too much detail of the activity and was immensely grateful that his mind still seemed to be stuffed with something fluffy. Turning slightly he spotted the main tent doorway and the bright sunlight beyond. Being careful not to slip in the various nauseating pools inside the hospital, he straightened himself as much as he could, as befitted an officer, and tried his best to stride from the tent. In all, he managed seven purposeful steps before he had to stop, his teeth clenched and eyes shut tight against the pain. At least he'd reached the doorway. He realised as the pain subsided, that the thing he had gripped in his painful moment had not been the tent frame as he'd thought, but the shoulder of a soldier.

He stood for a moment, letting his eyes focus and gradually a smile crept across his lips. The eager face of the young engineer regarded him with concern, but Varro's smiling countenance passed that and his eyes fell on the bottle the soldier was holding tightly.

"You found something? Out here? Well, well, well. Help me back to my tent and I'll pay you for it."

Without a word, the engineer ducked to one side and grasped Varro's wrist, draping the arm across his shoulder. Slowly and with great care, Varro and the young engineer picked their way through the viscera, blood and piles of used bandaging and out into the open, past the lines of wounded waiting their turns. The first waft of fresh air hit him and, as the wind changed again bringing with it the sickly-sweet smell of the hospital tent, the captain stopped, bent forward as far as his pain would allow, and vomited copiously onto the grass.

"Come on sir," the engineer said comfortingly, "let's get away from this."

Varro nodded, wiping his chin with his wrist, and the two slowly wound their way through the supply and fabrication tents and off into the main part of the camp, away from the grisly sights, sounds and smells of the hospital. Along the deserted lines of identical bleached leather tents they staggered, through the quarters of the second cohort and finally, at the end of the ordered rows, to the command tents. Here, larger campaign tents had been pitched for the senior officers of the cohort, the largest being Varro's own, subdivided by an interior wall and serving as both quarters and headquarters.

The captain limped straight through the main tent and into the private quarters, where he slowly and carefully lowered himself onto the bunk with the young engineer's help. The soldier, satisfied that his superior was safely settled, placed the bottle on a small three-legged stool and slid the makeshift table in front of the officer. Varro smiled and reached out to the desk nearby for a goblet. The sudden careless action brought a fiery, white blinding pain that almost caused him to topple forward off the bed. The engineer rushed forward and grasped Varro's arm, steadying him. The captain breathed in shallowly, little more than a gasp, his eyes watering and, not trusting himself to speak, he pointed, wincing, at the tray of goblets on the desk and held up two fingers.

The young soldier raised his eyebrows.

"Are you asking me to join you sir? My sergeant'll be wondering where I am."

Varro winced again and bit his cheek, pushing the pain down and away to where he could deal with it. A handy little trick a Pelasian mercenary had once taught him.

"It's all in the mind," he muttered to himself, and then looked up at the engineer and smiled. "Pull up a seat and get two goblets. If your sergeant has anything to say, send him to me. I might be wounded worse than I thought and I'd rather have someone with me right now. Besides, drinking alone is for sad old men and lush women; not for soldiers."

As the engineer collected two goblets and placed them on the small makeshift table and dragged a small chest across for a seat, Varro tentatively prodded his side and winced once more.

"Usually my second in command's here with me. Missed his support on the field today. I daresay *this* wouldn't have happened if he'd been there."

The young engineer nodded uncertainly. Sitting in the presence of such a senior officer seemed unthinkable, let alone speaking to one in such a familiar fashion. He cleared his throat.

"Sergeant Corda wasn't here today sir?"

"No. He was given the dubious honour of commanding the prefect's guard. He's been gone since yesterday morning delivering Cristus to the command meeting at Vengen. Typical High Command, to draw an army's commander in chief away during a campaign for mindless bureaucracy, though I can't imagine the day would have turned out any different if he'd been here."

The young engineer scanned the face of the captain, wondering how he had become involved in such a personal conversation with the most senior officer in the cohort. There was a misty film across Varro's eyes, attesting to both the seriousness of the pain underlying his light conversation and the lingering effects of the doctor's concoction. While every ounce of his training told him that this was wrong and he should make his excuses and respectfully bow out of the command tent, how could he leave the captain right now when he stood a very real chance of falling over at any moment? The young soldier swallowed nervously and gave the conversation a gentle prod.

"I've heard tell that sergeant Corda is the longest serving non-commissioned officer in the fourth army, sir."

Varro shook his head, fuzzily.

"Still feel groggy. That M…" He paused and corrected himself quickly. "Scortius' concoction must've been strong."

The engineer nodded respectfully. "That's probably a good thing sir," he replied quietly.

The captain sat for a long moment, focusing on the young man, shook his head once again, and waved his hand in the direction of the small stool bearing the goblets.

"You do the honours while I start as I mean to go on," he rumbled, as he fished in the small pouch Scortius had given him and dropped some of the contents into one of the goblets.

The engineer carefully filled the goblets, pouring the dark wine across the medicinal herbs in one and, replacing the wine bottle, reached up for the jug to water down the heady liquid. Varro lunged forward, gently knocking aside the water jug and wincing with the sudden sharp and violent pain that lashed him. As he slowly and carefully let out a measured breath and the pain subsided, he noticed the look of concern on the young soldier's face. He waved his arm dismissively.

"Smells like good wine. Don't waste it with water. B'sides, I think the stronger the better right now."

The engineer nodded uncertainly and replaced the water jug.

"Perhaps I should go, sir? You need to rest."

Varro frowned and, moving as slowly and carefully as possible, leaned forward, bringing his face close to his companion's.

"Frankly, soldier, I'm groggy, in pretty constant pain, daren't stand in case I topple and can't reach out for fear of opening the wound up, so you stay. Where were we? Mind's getting a little hazy."

The young man nodded. "Sergeant Corda, Sir."

"Ah yes. Known Corda since before there was a regular army; back in the days of the private armies. We were both on the field when Darius took the throne. Hell, I got splashed with Velutio's blood when his head came off. 'Course we were both non-commissioned then. There's not a man in the army, nay the Empire, that I trust more than Corda."

He reached down gingerly and took a deep pull from the goblet, wiping his hand across his mouth. He eyed the young engineer from beneath arched brows.

"How old are you lad?"

"Nineteen sir."

Varro smiled. "You won't really remember the chaos, do you? Before the Emperor?"

The young man shook his head.

"Actually sir, I was born to one of the tribes on the border. We weren't really counted as part of the Empire then. It's only since the borders have been settled we've even been allowed to enlist again."

The captain continued to nod slowly, mulling back over the last few sentences when a thought struck him and his brow furrowed. He took another sip and shuffled back onto the bunk.

"You're from one of the tribes up here?"

The young engineer looked up at the captain, his face worried. "Yes sir. I'm totally committed to the Empire, though. I…"

Varro waved aside the boy's uncomfortable defensiveness.

"I'm not suggesting anything, lad. I've some questions, though."

The young man nodded nervously and Varro continued.

"My knowledge of the Gods of these tribes is fairly limited, but I know a little. The white stag is Cernus, yes?"

The engineer nodded. "That's right sir. Cernus of the beasts; Lord of the woodlands and more. He's a symbol of nobility and pride."

Varro squinted through the growing haze in his mind. He stared down into the almost empty goblet where the dregs of the wine lapped at the bedraggled remnants of the herbal mixture. Perhaps he'd underestimated the effects of Scortius' medicine? Once more he forced himself to focus on the young man. Couldn't afford to fall asleep quite yet. He was on the edge of something… something important. If only he could think what it was.

"Cernus. He's connected with chieftainship, isn't he?"

"Yes sir," the young man took a sip of the wine and tipped his head to one side, unsure of the direction the conversation was taking. "He's a God of portents and change. Just seeing him can alter a person's life. Some see him on more than one occasion, but still not often. There's the tale of Faenn An Ghalaeg who was visited by the Stag Lord each full moon, but then that's just a legend and he ended up becoming a God himself."

He noted the look on his commander's face and swallowed nervously. "Of course, it's all just barbarian folklore, sir."

Varro shook his head. "Don't put your origins down, lad. Only a fool believes he knows everything about the world. In some places the Imperial Raven and Wolf still hold little sway."

The engineer continued to watch the captain carefully. The older officer's eyes were starting to glaze and were already half closed.

"I think it's time I went sir. You need to sleep."

Varro nodded, his eyes flickering a couple of times and then focusing once more on his companion.

"You're probably right, soldier. I want to speak to you again. Tell your sergeant that you're excused departure duties in the morning. Report to my tent at reveille." His eyes flicked closed once again, and it took the young man only a second to realise his commander was already asleep. He leapt forward and caught the captain, allowing the goblet to fall away and roll under the bunk while he gently lowered Varro down to the soft pillow.

Bending, he replaced the goblet on the tray, corked the bottle and quietly backed out of the tent, closing the flap as he left.

Chapter Two

Varro was awakened by the jarring blare of the horns calling reveille though, truth be told, he'd spent several hours drifting in and out of consciousness during the night through discomfort, so the interruption was not entirely unwelcome. The captain hauled himself very slowly and carefully from his bunk, still fully dressed in his bloodied tunic and the leather vest worn beneath the armour to prevent chafing, the sheets stained pink with the leakage from his wound. Wincing and gritting his teeth, he pulled himself slowly upright and reached out to the cupboard to steady himself. A little further movement brought on a wracking cough that threatened to floor him.

There was a respectful knock at the door and a voice called out.

"Are you alright sir? Can I help?"

Varro stood a moment, shaking, disconnected thoughts flittering around him like the memories of dreams. Slowly he focused on the tent flap and recalled the young engineer. Ah yes. He'd told the lad to come at reveille, hadn't he?

"I'm ok lad. Come in. Is my body servant out there?"

The soldier lifted the heavy leather tent flap with one hand and poked his head through.

"He was here a few minutes ago, sir. He left toward the laundry tent saying something about your uniform."

Varro nodded. Martis, his ever-efficient servant would be preparing clean clothes for the journey back to camp. He turned, staggering slightly, and the engineer was there in the blink of an eye, supporting his commander's shoulder. Varro smiled a weary smile and, as he sat to regain his balance and began to unlace the boots he'd slept in last night, a thought welled up and he eyed the engineer speculatively.

"What's your name, lad?"

"Salonius, sir," the young man replied, stamping his feet and coming to a perfect salute.

Varro finished unlacing his boots and stood, allowing Salonius to take the brunt of his weight as he swayed slightly. Two steps forward and he swept aside the tent flap and gestured at one of the two soldiers on guard outside, bearing the white horsehair crest of the command guard.

"Send word to the sergeant of engineers that I'm seconding one of his men. Salonius is being reassigned. And get him a white crest and pass the details along to my clerk."

"Sir!" barked the guard as he snapped a salute and jogged off toward the engineers' compound, visible above the lines of tents as a collection of tall, oak-beamed siege engines and plumes of smoke, accompanied by the sound of smiths hammering iron. Varro glanced round at his newest guard.

"Go and get your personal gear. Ignore the tent or any shared equipment and report back to here in an hour to help take the headquarters tent down. We'll be moving out just after lunch."

Salonius was still blinking in shock, but pulled himself together sharply, saluted his captain and ran off toward the lines of tents that lay outside the engineers' compound.

As the young man left, a thought occurred to Varro, and he called after him.

"Salonius! Go by the hospital on the way back and pick up my armour."

The soldier spun on his heel, almost losing his footing and saluted before turning once more and disappearing among the tents.

Varro watched him run out of sight and then turned to the other guard, standing at attention beside the tent flap.

"Break him in, but gently. I might need him."

"Aye sir," the guard saluted.

Varro retreated inside the tent and let the leather flap fall. For a moment, he staggered, and then sank onto the edge of the bunk once more, letting his unlaced boots fall away. One of his woollen socks was crusty and dark red from where his lifeblood had pooled in his boot. That was going to take some cleaning. He briefly scanned his breeches and tunic and realised the job wouldn't stop at his ankle. He felt unpleasant. Sleeping in his sub-armour had given him aches and pains that only added to his general discomfort, and the clothes soaked with sweat and blood had given him a smell that, he was sure, would be noticeable from a considerable distance.

Slowly and with care, he removed the leather vest and let it fall to the floor with a thud, tiny droplets of sweat bouncing as it landed. Gently he lifted the shreds of his tunic to one side and tugged at the dressing. The sudden pain and the smell from the wound almost made him vomit and he gently toppled backward onto the bunk.

This was no good. He couldn't disturb the wound, but he was going to have to clean himself up and get rid of this mind-rotting smell. He began to force himself slowly upright again, when he noticed the figure standing just within the tent flap: Martis, his body servant. Relief swept across the captain.

"Oh good. Martis, I'm very much going to need help cleaning up. I need to wash down properly without touching my dressing and wound. And I might need a bit of help getting down to the wash tent too."

Martis, a short and stocky bald easterner, frowned and shook his head. He was a man of few words, but as efficient and careful as they came. He'd been the most expensive servant available at the Vengen markets five years ago, but had been worth every corona over those years, and probably more. Soon Varro was going to have to raise his wage, or he'd leave for a position more sedentary and considerably less dangerous. Yes, a raise was definitely due.

The servant pointed to the rear of the tent and, turning gingerly, Varro noticed for the first time a low steel bathtub, wisps of steam rising gently from it.

"Prepared it while you were sleeping sir."

Reaching out, he gently took his master's arm, helped him across the tent to the tub and began to remove the grimy and bloodied clothes. Varro moved as much as he dare, but in the end resigned himself to luxury and allowed Martis to finish undressing him and help him step into the tub.

"I have to be careful not to soak my wound."

Martis nodded and produced a square of leather, smeared around the edge with a dark shiny substance. He slowly and carefully removed the captain's dressing and placed the patch over the freshly sealed wound, very lightly but firmly pressing down at the edges to form a water-tight seal.

"Propolis and waxed leather; watertight as long as we're careful, sir", he said quietly.

Varro smiled and nodded. Where had Martis found bees' glue in a temporary camp? The man really was a marvel. With gratitude, he sank slowly into the warm water and allowed himself finally, properly, to relax. He was dozing gently as Martis took away his bloodied clothes and left a fresh set on the stool nearby before retiring to the corner where he began the laborious job of repairing the three leather strops on the armoured skirt as seamlessly as possible.

For a moment Varro panicked and splashed, and then suddenly two stocky arms were around him, gently hauling him upwards. The panic quickly receded as the captain remembered where he was and allowed himself to be helped out of the now lukewarm tub. Though he'd fallen asleep before he could scrub himself clean, the difference the hot water had made to him was tangible. He felt fresher, cleaner and considerably more relaxed.

"Thank you, Martis. I'm actually going to attempt to dress myself, if you could just unstick this pad and put my dressing back on."

The body servant nodded curtly and very carefully and slowly peeled the edges of the patch away from Varro's wound. As the skin pulled slightly taught with each gently tug, the captain clenched his teeth and grunted. He looked down at the wound as the last of the bees' glue came away. The mark was now a straight line of purple and grey with some ancillary bruising. It looked so innocent and belied the intense pain and complication it was causing. And then it was covered with a fresh pad and linen. Somehow, Martis had also found fresh dressing material too.

As the linen was tied off, Martis went back to his leatherwork as the captain slowly dressed, keeping every movement as slight and gentle as possible.

As he finally settled his tunic into place and shuffled round to the bunk to take a seat and lace his boots, there was another knock on the tent frame.

"Enter," he called.

Salonius, the young engineer, pushed the heavy leather flap aside and entered in full kit, sporting a white horsehair crest and his dress cloak. In his arms he carried the captain's plated armour, recently polished. Varro smiled and reached out to his body servant for the leather under-vest. Martis stood with it, but Salonius cleared his throat and stepped between them.

"Doctor's orders, Sir," he said quietly. "The chief medic gave me strict instructions that you were to travel today on one of the carts, rather than horseback, and on no account are you allowed to wear body armour."

Varro growled.

"I'm an officer, boy. I need my armour to keep this rabble in line."

Salonius nodded slowly. "I understand that, sir, but the sergeants can get us de-camped and on the move, and you need to put as little strain on your side as possible. Doctor's orders, sir: tunic and cloak only."

Varro glared at his newest guard for a moment and then seemed to arrive at a decision.

"Very well. Let's go out and tour the cohort while they decamp; make sure they know I'm still alive. Leave the armour. It can be packed away with the rest of my things now we're heading back to the fort."

Salonius placed the armour gently on the bunk, and turned to escort his commander from the tent. As they exited into the crisp morning air, the young soldier thought he saw, just for a moment, a flicker of emotion pass across the face of the guard beside the door. Dislike, he thought; or possibly even hatred. Have to be careful around that man, he noted, memorising the guard's face with its flinty eyes and lantern jaw.

Taking a deep breath, Varro strode out with as normal a gait as he could manage, and began the walk down the slight incline to the tents. Salonius stayed to one side and slightly to his rear, enough to display the respect due a senior officer, yet close enough to grasp the captain should he suddenly falter.

Varro cast his experienced gaze across the commotion as they walked. Everywhere they went, soldiers would immediately stop what they were doing and salute their commander. The more veteran among them had long since perfected the art of straightening the back and saluting with one arm whilst continuing to grip the tent rope with the other. To the untrained eye it would appear to be chaos, but to Varro all was clearly proceeding according to cohort standards. They would be ready to move within the hour. The captains would all be required to attend the post-battle meeting in the command tent, along with all the auxiliary unit commanders and the adjutants of the general staff. Injured officers would not be required to attend, for which Varro would be grateful enough to make a little libation on the altar back at the fort.

A little further and they passed the entrance of the engineers' compound, a palisade ring full of burly soldiers hauling ropes or carrying timber to the wagons that would transport it back to the fort. Once more, Varro clicked his tongue in irritation. Such a waste, hauling literally tons of siege equipment forty miles from the fort and not even deploying it. Shaking his head sadly, the captain turned, looping slowly round the farthest tents, and began the more exerting climb back up the slope towards his tent.

Not far from the command tents, Varro spotted his counterpart from the third cohort observing preparations among his own troops. Turning to Salonius, Varro gestured towards the captain of the third. "You can leave me now," he told the young guard. "I'll be fine from here. Go help with packing the headquarters tent and my gear."

Salonius saluted and began to stride off between the last of the tents to the captain's at the summit, while Varro slowly and carefully made his way to his comrade. The standards outside the tent had already been taken down, Salonius noted as he approached, and a number of the ropes had been unfastened. Ducking beneath a remaining line, the young guard pulled aside the leather flap and, leaning into the darker confines of the Headquarters tent, suddenly found himself dragged bodily inside.

He took a moment after he was released to regain his footing. Glancing quickly around himself, he caught the heavy-set faces of three men, including the memorable square jaw of the guard from earlier. Yanking himself back, he pulled his tunic out of the grip of the man who had hauled him in and stood as straight as he could, raising his arms and clenching his fists tight.

"Alright. Let's get this over with, then."

Varro arrived at the muster area for the wounded. The carts were full, noisy and gave off the sickly-sweet stench of wounds, sickness and decay. One of the medical orderlies waved him over respectfully. The captain walked carefully across to him, took one look at the meagre space in the cart and shook his head.

"There is not a hope; not a chance in three hells of you getting me on that cart. Scortius or no Scortius, I'm taking my horse."

He turned his back on the protesting orderly and strode away from the carts to where the Fourth were busy performing their last minute checks before the return journey began. He strode over to the collection of white crests gathered around the horses at the head of the column. A quick head count revealed the command guard of the second cohort to be a man short. As he approached, they moved fluidly into two lines of seven, came to attention and saluted in unison. Varro nodded his acknowledgment and scanned the lines for Salonius. Perhaps he was attending to something before assembly and… no; there he was. So who was missing?

The captain glanced once more up and down the lines and allowed his gaze to settle on his newest guard, noticing for the first time the faint purple and brown of a sizeable bruise blossoming slowly around his left eye. With a frown, his eyes wandered among the other guards, this time paying close attention. Two more of them sported facial bruising.

"I'm not going to ask what went on, but I'm a man down, and I want to know where he is."

There was a moment's silence, then someone from the second row cleared his throat.

"Gallo had to go see the medic, sir, for stitches. He'll be back in a few minutes"

Varro grumbled and allowed his frown to deepen.

"As if there aren't enough barbarians out there waiting to give you all a damn good thrashing, you have to go beating your own to a pulp. Get your horses saddled and ready. We leave in ten minutes, with or without Gallo."

Still grumbling to himself, the captain spun and headed for his own horse, already saddled and being tended to by his servant who would travel with the baggage train at the rear. As soon as their officer was out of sight, the guards stood at ease and the man beside Salonius turned his head slightly, giving the shorter, younger recruit a sidelong glance up and down.

"You fought off three of them?"

Salonius nodded, concentrating on a point in the middle distance.

"Maybe you do deserve the crest." The soldier turned away, his plated torso armour scraping Salonius' as he went.

"Short and young does not necessarily mean weak and frightened", Salonius grumbled to himself under his breath and from between clenched teeth. The engineers were happy enough with new recruits as long as they could handle a mallet and haul on a rope, but the command guard were supposedly the cohort's best, and were paid accordingly. It would take some time to settle in here and turn their resentment into respect.

With a sigh, he turned and looked at the horse he'd been given. He'd ridden a horse a few times, years ago, but not since joining up; engineers used horses for transporting equipment and for labour, not for riding. It was already saddled and waiting. With a disbelieving shake of his head, Salonius walked over to the horse.

The column had been rumbling across the landscape for half a day, the immense cloud of dust thrown up into the air by an entire army on the move making the beautiful azure blue sky somewhat difficult to see. The adjutant and the senior staff, along with the flag and standard bearers, rode as the vanguard, in the clear and open air. Behind them came the various ancillary officers, camp staff and the like, followed by the six cohorts themselves in numerical order and finally the engineers and the baggage train, slowly grinding away the miles.

Some half a mile behind the column came the army's provosts with the prisoners taken the previous day, staggering along in three lines, chained together to be ransomed, sold or executed at the marshal's whim later.

Varro sat astride his horse at the head of the second, blinking regularly to keep the dust from his eyes and wincing with every step of his horse. After only an hour of travel, he'd realised why Scortius had wanted him in a cart. By the second hour, his wound had begun to leak again slightly and, though it was a seep rather than a flow, by now, nine hours into the journey, his left leg was soaked with crusty dried blood and coated with dust. When they finally reached the fort it would take more than a quick dip to clean all this off.

He glanced over his shoulder at the command guard of the second, fifteen now off-white crests in three lines of five, riding silently behind him. With a quick motion to the guard to continue on as they were, he wheeled his horse and gently walked it out of the column, continuing a hundred yards or so until the cloud of disturbed dust swirled behind him and he could breathe fresh, untainted air. The summer sun shone down on a verdant green landscape, quite beautiful even with the disturbances of thousands of marching boots; a landscape most of the column would barely see through the dust.

Stopping his horse, the captain took several deep, clean and satisfying breaths. Perhaps he should request a break in the march? As he sat astride Targus, his bay colt, scanning the hills to the west, his eyes caught a brief sign of movement. Suddenly alert, he strained and focused on the shapes and slowly they swam into focus: perhaps a dozen or so riders. Some were clearly armoured, glittering in the sun. And then he saw the flag being borne by one of the riders, and recognised the black banner with the silver ram and bolt of lightning. With a sigh of relief, he kicked his horse into a trot once more and set off at a tangent to intercept the approaching riders, safe in the knowledge that no barbarians would be stupid enough to try a ruse against such a large armoured column. Besides, they'd broken the back of the local tribes yesterday.

As the party of a dozen riders slowed to a trot and hauled on the reins to pull alongside Varro and his mount, he recognised the pale face of Corda, his second in command, covered by his helmet and partially hidden behind the bandana pulled up across the lower half and hiding the thick, black beard. The dozen men were the second cohort's contribution to the prefect's honour guard. As Varro drew his steed to a halt, the riders also stopped, saluting their commander wearily. Varro grinned as his second in command untied the bandana, revealing the yet paler skin of his lower face, framed with his dark beard and untouched by the dust of travel. Corda, never a man given to frivolity, displayed his usual scowl, which deepened as he spotted the dried blood encrusting his superior's leg.

"Sergeant," Varro greeted him happily, "a sight for sore eyes, if ever there was one."

Corda's intense pale blue-grey eyes bored into the captain's, carrying an air of disapproval.

"Captain," he said at last, his voice surprisingly low and soft. "What the hell have they done to you?"

Varro shook his head. "It's not bad, Corda. Scortius has sorted it, but I've sort of bounced it open on the horse."

The sergeant opened his mouth to speak again, his eyes flashing angrily, but Varro interjected before he had the chance.

"Scortius did a good job, Corda, and I know I should be in the wounded carts, but I'd rather this than have to sit among the stench of serious injuries for a day or two, so forget about it."

The sergeant sat still and silent for a few seconds, his eyes locked on his commander's, until he was sure his point was made and his opinion noted.

"Very well sir. Permission to dismiss the guard?"

Varro nodded, and the sergeant turned and waved at the other riders, who saluted once again and then rode off past their officers to join their companions in the cohort's cavalry squadron. As soon as they were out of earshot and sight of the two commanders, Corda's attentive position relaxed and he slumped wearily in the saddle.

"Ok, Varro. Tell me everything, including how the hell you ended up in this state."

The captain sighed. Corda was the quintessential sergeant among the cohort and the linchpin around which the unit moved, but on a personal level, the two had come up through the ranks together so many years ago that it was impossible now to feel any level of superiority over him when the two were alone. And, of course, Corda knew him perhaps better than he knew himself.

"I was unlucky. That's all there is to it. I saw some barbarian bastard with a nice sword he'd stolen from an Imperial officer and I took it personally. Seems he did too. The doctor wasn't concerned and the medics all reckon I'll be fine in a few weeks. Now you need to tell me what you're doing here. You're supposed to be in Vengen with the prefect."

Corda nodded wearily and shrugged his shoulders, allowing the interlocking plates of his armour to settle into a new and slightly more comfortable position. The standard Imperial kit was highly protective and certainly better than the chain mail the army had once worn, but it left a great deal to be desired when on horseback.

"We're all on the way home," the sergeant replied, rubbing the dusty upper half of his face with his bandana. "The prefect doesn't particularly need his full honour guard to protect him on the way back."

Varro raised an eyebrow questioningly.

The sergeant let his bandana fall back down to his neck and took a deep breath.

"Marshal Sabian's coming with him."

"The marshal?" Varro whistled through his teeth. "I suppose this latest round of victories has earned the prefect more attention and honours. I wonder if he's just going to hole up at Crow Hill with the staff, or whether he might want all the unit commanders involved."

Corda nodded. "That's why the prefect sent me on ahead. He wants to make sure the entire army's spick and span when they arrive at the fort and everything's organised for a high command visit. I'm not sure it's really necessary. You know Sabian. He'd rather things worked well than looked nice."

"What else?" Varro narrowed his eyes.

Corda shifted uneasily.

"Sorry?"

"I said what else?" Varro growled. "You're avoiding telling me something."

The stocky sergeant cleared his throat and sighed.

"Catilina's coming with him."

He watched his captain intently, but Varro merely sat astride his horse for a moment and then shrugged.

"It's been a long time. She might not even remember me."

Corda smiled a rare smile and gave his superior a light punch in the upper arm.

"You're a hell of a sight better at fooling yourself than me, so don't even try. This is what we're going to do: Firstly, you're going to go to either the engineer or quartermaster sergeant and travel on one of their wagons. Not comfortable, but at least you won't shake yourself to bits or be jammed in with the wounded..."

Varro waved a hand to interrupt, but Corda knocked his gesturing finger aside and continued, raising his voice slightly.

"When you're settled, I'm going to have a medic sent back to you so he can get that wound fixed back up and sort you out. I'm quite capable of leading the cohort back to the fort and you know that. I'll go find the medics and deliver my message to the adjutant, then I'll take command."

Once again, Varro opened his mouth to speak, but Corda pointed purposefully at him and went on.

"And when we get back to the fort, you're going to head straight off to the baths and get yourself clean and tidy, while Martis goes to sort out your dress uniform. We'll only be a few hours ahead of the marshal, even if we rush, and you need to look commanding and a little bit dangerous, if you know what I mean."

A low rumbling growl rose in Varro's throat.

"I am not primping for a visit from the high command. I'm not a young social climber."

"Not for the marshal, you idiot!" Corda laughed. "For his daughter."

Varro furrowed his brows but said nothing for a long moment. Finally he sighed. "Well I suppose you're right about my wound and the cart at least. Let's get back to the column."

The two wheeled their horses and rode back toward the line, slow and noisy and choked with dust. As they approached, Corda turned and headed for the vanguard while Varro rode toward the engineers with their great wooden constructions, rumbling along the dusty trail dragged by teams of sweating oxen, the engineering teams of all six cohorts travelling together. The engineers in the army usually held to their own company anyway, having much more in common with each other than with the rest of their own cohorts. But the sense of unity among the engineers of the Fourth Army had been further enhanced by the prefect's distrust of missile warfare and the fact that he plainly considered them superfluous to requirements on campaign.

As the captain pulled alongside the head of the group, the various sergeants of engineers glanced at him in surprise before saluting. He waved the gesture aside and pointed at his discoloured leg.

"Mind if I hitch a lift on one of your wagons?" He could have demanded or ordered, but when dealing with such an insular bunch it was always worth politeness and consideration, as he'd learned time and again over a twenty-five year career.

The sergeant of the second cohort's engineers whose name, Varro realised to his disappointment he didn't even remember, hauled his horse to one side and rode out of the column to join his commander.

"I'll escort you to our supply wagon, sir. You'll find it the most comfortable."

Varro nodded and rode alongside the sergeant, back along the slowly rumbling column of catapults, bolt throwers and other more arcane engines of war. As they trotted, he noted with a professional eye the care and attention with which the machines had obviously been treated and, equally obviously, the lack of use to which they had been put.

The supply wagon of the second cohort's engineers was equally well maintained, pulled by two horses, covered over with a waxed protective sheet that was carefully anchored with ropes to hooks drilled into the wagon's side, and driven by a big soldier with a shaved head and a thick beard who looked, to Varro's mild amusement, as though his head had been placed on his shoulders the wrong way up.

The wagon driver and his superior exchanged brief words, and then the sergeant saluted and rode back to join his companions at the head of the engineering column. The driver untied the bag of goods strapped down to the seat next to him and hauled them into the back of the cart with one enormous arm while continuing to steer with the other. He turned back and grinned at Varro, revealing a wide mouth and large square teeth, two of which had been replaced with what appeared to be iron facsimiles. Glancing with a sort of horrified fascination at the man, Varro couldn't decide whether he looked more like a blacksmith or a pit fighter.

Matching his horse's pace with the roll of the wagon, Varro slipped out of the saddle as gracefully as he could, wincing and emitting a small, involuntary squeak, and planted his feet on the board below the wagon's seat. Still holding the reins, he slid onto the seat and then tied his horse off to one of the many hooks on the wagon's side. A quick glance and the captain was satisfied that Targus was happily walking alongside.

With a groan of comfort, he lounged back on the wagon's seat and stretched languidly. Reaching into his pouch, he withdrew his flask containing a mix of one part wine with five parts water.

Tipping some of Scortius' herbal pain mixture into the almost empty flask, he shook it to mix and dissolve the medicine before taking a long swig. The relief began to trickle through him even before he returned the flask to its pocket. Closing his eyes, he raised his face skywards. While he knew he was still surrounded by the immense cloud of dust thrown up by marching feet, walking horses and rolling wheels, with his eyes closed he could feel the heat of the sun beating down on him, even through the muck. If he concentrated on the idea and turned his thoughts inwards, he could almost drown out the cacophony going on around him and imagine he was somewhere peaceful and pleasant. Almost. Ah well. Peace was not a soldier's lot, he thought to himself humorously.

He opened his eyes and started. His travelling companion's bearded and shiny head was only a foot away from his own, peering at him with that increasingly disturbing grin. Varro returned the smile weakly, and then closed his eyes again and began to drift off into thoughts; a stream of consciousness.

What the hell was Sabian doing coming to the fort? True, it was well known that Cristus was Sabian's favourite prefect, but that was based on events decades ago. Oh certainly Cristus was an adequate commander, but the captain had served under some of the best, including Sabian himself before the reconstitution of the Imperial army, and the prefect was far from that league. His flat refusal to place any reliance on archers or catapults had cost them dearly today, and had done in several previous engagements. In fact, his decision to surrender the terrain in favour of some largely-imagined lighting advantage gave Varro rise to question whether the commander should have been involved in planning the strategy of the battle at all. The officers could have altered the battle plan once he'd left without him ever finding out.

But still, it was a captain's job to command his men and to carry out the orders of his prefect without calling the man's ability into question. There was no doubt at all that Cristus was lucky, and likely that luck had carried him throughout his career. And yet he must have been a hell of a commander early on in his career.

"What, sir?"

Varro stirred from his reverie, opening his eyes suddenly and blinking, the effects of Scortius' drug now beginning to draw a cloth of hazy whiteness across his mind. He turned his head to find the bulky engineer peering at him questioningly with his brown furrowed.

"Sorry?" said the captain in confusion. "What was that?"

The big man frowned. "You said 'lucky bastard', sir. Sorry if you was asleep. Din't mean to wake you. Just thought you might been talkin' to me."

"Ah, no soldier. Just ruminating aloud."

He looked at the deepening look of confusion on the big man's face and adjusted his thinking once again.

"Just thinking on things; on the prefect."

"Ah," replied the engineer in a flat voice, "the prefect sir. Yes sir."

"You don't approve of the prefect, soldier?"

The big man rumbled for a moment, his expression changing several times in the process.

"Not my place to say, sir."

Varro nodded. It certainly wasn't, but whether because of the effects of the medicine, or purely due to his own need to vent his feelings, he found himself sympathising with the quiet giant beside him on the wagon seat.

"Tell you what, soldier," he said, settling back into a relaxed posture and closing his eyes, partially due to the slight haze that seemed to have settled over them, and partially because of the ever-present dust. "There's only you and me in earshot and I'm wounded and drugged and tired and I just can't be bothered to stand on ceremony. I give you permission to freely speak your mind. Even if I remember this, I'll not report anything."

The engineer cleared his throat nervously.

"Well sir... I don't think the prefect likes us, sir." The big man recoiled slightly as though expecting a blow, but the captain merely opened one eye and scrutinised him briefly before closing it again.

"I think you're right. He's never trusted missiles of any type. And before you say it, yes, I think that's short sighted, wasteful and probably just plain stupid."

The big man frowned again.

"But why would someone so important throw away good men because he don't like a catapult, sir?"

Varro shrugged as best he could, given the limitations imposed by his wound and the plain wooden bench.

"Some people are set in their ways, and not all of them are good ways. In one respect we're lucky. The prefect may create strategies or make decisions we don't agree with, but he's got the luck of the Gods. I can name at least three engagements we've been in over the years that we should by all rights have lost, but he's managed to pull out of the fire at the last minute and turn it around."

"Yessir," the big engineer nodded, "but maybe he shouldn't 've put his men in that shit in the first place, sir?"

Varro opened his eyes again and gave the man a flinty look.

"Speak freely, but be careful. That's still our commander you're talking about. Respect where it's due..." he growled, "even if it isn't."

The engineer nodded.

"'Course sir. Never meant anything by it."

Varro laughed a short and sharp laugh.

"Whatever you say, soldier. Just remember, the man's a war hero. And the marshal's favourite."

The big man scratched his beard reflectively with his free hand.

"War hero sir?"

Varro blinked. "You don't know the history of your own prefect?"

"Only been serving five years sir, and the engineers... well we don't really get to hang around with the rest, sir. Camp regulations keeps us in our own stockade. Where we can't do no harm, so my sergeant says."

"He does, does he?" Varro smiled coldly.

"We engineers is kind of second class soldiers in the Fourth, sir. No use denying it. We all know it. But we're happy anyway."

Varro shook his head irritably.

"Shouldn't be like that. Maybe the prefect was better cut out to be a captain. He was a damn good captain. Won his reputation at Saravis Fork over a decade ago."

The burly man raised his eyebrows but said nothing.

"The Clianii are the big tribe up there" Varro said wearily. "Back... what fourteen? Fifteen years ago? Something like that...

there was a series of invasions by northern tribes. Cristus was a captain in the Second Army under Sabian at the time. He was sent to Saravis Fork to relieve the garrison of the fort there."

The captain turned his head and looked at the big man who was regarding him with rapt attention. For all gruff look and massive frame, he was still a young man when one looked closer. He'd probably have only been ten or eleven years old at the time. With a slightly sad smile, Varro closed his eyes and leaned back as he resumed his tale.

"When he got to the fort, he found they'd been under attack for weeks. Their captain was dead and they were running at about a quarter strength; a totally hopeless situation. He took command and sent out harrying and distracting strikes for a day while he rebuilt the fort."

"Must've had engineers with him then, sir."

"Don't believe so," Varro mused. "Never thought of that before. Never heard about engineers there, but still, I guess any soldier can pile rocks, eh?"

The engineer nodded, his expression clearly registering other thoughts on the subject."

"Still," the captain went on, "he got the fort to a defensible state again. He held on to that fort for another four days before they were overrun and had to pull back down the pass. Impressive, regardless of whether it be brilliance or luck. Just to have tried makes him one of the bravest men I've known."

The engineer gave another nod; this time genuine, if given grudgingly.

"So what happened, sir? I've not heard of these Clini or whatever they're called."

Varro shook his head slightly.

"Not surprised."

He shuffled into a new position and looked up at the burly engineer, squinting with the sun almost directly in his eyes.

"Cristus had given the Clianii such a mauling they didn't dare come down out of the pass. Basically, he averted an invasion. He and his men rode back to Vengen and delivered their report to Sabian. The marshal made him a prefect on the spot and gave him command of the Fourth that had just been raised, in order to go back and finish the job."

"Back to Saravis Fork, sir?"

"Yes. And beyond. He went through the mountains like the wrath of the Gods and wiped the Clianii from the world of men. Killed everything in those mountains that moved, walked and talked."

The engineer looked momentarily taken aback, a strange look on the brawny giant.

"That's not right sir."

"Maybe not," agreed the captain, "but he got his revenge, and after that the other tribes sued for peace. It was more than a decade before any of them dared cross the mountains again. A bloodthirsty bastard he might have been, but he saved the northern provinces."

Varro sighed as he settled once more into his cloak.

"War hero, as I said. I suppose the day we've saved a province from a barbarian invasion we'll have the right to criticise Cristus. Until then, he's our prefect and we do what he tells us."

The big soldier nodded and let out a gentle sigh.

"It'll be good to get back to the fort, sir."

"Oh, yes."

The engineer cleared his throat. "Do you think…" But as he turned to look at his travelling companion, the captain was already fast asleep.

Chapter Three

"Fort's up ahead, sir."

Varro desperately tried to remember where he was before he opened his eyes. The pain medication Scortius had given him must be potent stuff. A lot of hours must have passed since he'd taken the damn powder and his brain still felt as though his was trying to think through a linen sheet.

Rumbling.

Yes, he was on a cart. On the engineering wagon, with the bearded giant. Oh yes, and he was wounded.

"Ow!"

The captain sat up with a sharp motion, causing his head to swim slightly. The field medic, who had joined the wagon shortly after Varro and had stayed aboard ever since, gave him the despairing look that doctors reserve for a difficult patient, and pulled a dressing tighter round his middle.

"Captain, you really have to sit still."

"What the hell are you doing?" Varro asked.

The medic sighed and directed a level glare at the captain.

"You gave me so much trouble last time I changed the dressing, I thought I'd try again while you were asleep. You wouldn't have needed all these changes, sir, if you'd not tried riding your horse until the wound was fully sealed."

With a last tug, he tied off the dressing.

"I'll not bother making a neat job of it, captain. You'll be in the camp in five minutes and then you'll need to go and clean up properly. Be very careful and I need you to go and see doctor Scortius at some point before sunset tonight."

Varro grumbled something that could have been an agreement and prodded at his side.

As the medic clambered down from the wagon and hurried alongside the column, stuffing his kit back into the medical bag, Varro leaned to one side and saw through the dusty haze the familiar and welcome sight of the great, heavy grey stone walls of the Crow Hill fort and the large oak gates standing wide open to admit the column. The vanguard were already inside and dispersing. Corda and the Second would be inside in a few minutes, but despite what the medic had said, it would be at least fifteen minutes before the slow, lumbering carts and wagons of the engineers crossed the threshold. With a sigh, he leaned back and drifted away into comfortable sleep once more.

"Sir."

Again Varro stirred with difficulty and took a moment to focus his gaze on the great, bearded young engineer sitting beside him.

"Mmmph?" The captain wiped his mouth with the back of his wrist and pulled himself a little further upright.

"We're here sir. Thought you might wanna get down 'fore I head to the compound?" the engineer said quietly. "You sure you're alright sir? You've slept most of the day away."

Varro nodded wearily.

"Just the medication. Thanks for the lift lad. And thank your sergeant for me."

The big man smiled. "I'll do that, sir."

As the captain climbed down and unhooked his horse's reins from the wagon, the engineer sat patiently and, as soon as Varro and his mount were free, he saluted, shook his own reins and trundled slowly off toward the engineers' section. The captain stood for a moment, getting his bearings, and then realised the soldier had brought the wagon round half the camp and deposited him about thirty paces from his house.

"That's what a little courtesy gets you" he muttered smugly to himself as he led his colt to the one-horse stable that formed the rear entrance to his abode. Every fort, Empire-wide, followed the same rough plan as Crow Hill, but in these days of relative stability, the four great armies rarely moved from their base for any length of time, preferring to send out small sub-units on six month tours to man smaller forts on the frontiers. The centre of the fortress held the great headquarters building with its fine arcade, the prefect's house with its peristyle garden and three wings, and also those small, yet still impressive, abodes of his adjutant and staff officers. Behind them stood the temple to the Imperial Gods in white marble, the shrine to the Emperor Darius with its gilt statue and the many facilities the fort required, from the enormous vaulted bathing complex to the contained rows of shops staffed and run by civilians from the local area. Then, fanning out from the centre like the rays of the Sun God depicted on Pelasian temples, the rows of barrack blocks, each with a sergeant's small house at the end. And at the near terminus of each street of barracks, the houses of the departmental sergeants for each cohort. Finally, between them and the central area: the houses of the six cohort captains and the other two mid-ranking officers in charge of the camp and the stores.

These houses, eight identical buildings standing facing one another along the near end of the four streets that cut the fort into quarters, were well-appointed as befitted a cohort's commanding officer. Essentially a two-storey town house with a garden and stable at rear, they towered above the barracks and were, in turn, towered above by the headquarters and command area.

Fastening his horse in the compact stable he noted that Martis had run on ahead and filled the feed rack with hay. With a weary smile, he closed up and headed through the interior door into his house, already glowing with the light of small oil lanterns and slowly beginning to warm through with the crackle of fire from the hearth on the main room.

"Martis?"

The stocky manservant came sauntering slowly from the kitchen, a large knife in one hand and a fresh half-plucked game bird hanging from the other. "Sir?"

He shook his head.

"Never mind, Martis. You keep preparing dinner. Best prepare a good amount too. I'll likely have Corda round for the evening. If anyone calls for me, I'll be in the bathhouse for the next forty five minutes or so."

Martis nodded. "I anticipated a larger gathering, sir. I've also placed another waterproof pad on the table by the door, along with your dress uniform. It will save time if you dress fully before returning from the baths."

Varro laughed loud. "Martis, I need to give you an extra corona a week. Are you content with that?"

"Most assuredly, sir." The servant bowed slightly and then spun and returned to the kitchen with his goods.

Varro, still smiling, collected the neat pile of green tunic and breeches, his cloak and other accoutrements, along with the waxed and treated leather pad, and made his way out of the house and along the busy street in the rapidly diminishing daylight. Even after a day of relative rest, twice on the short journey he had to stop at the side of the street and lean on the wall, clutching his painful side while he regained his breath and each time, concerned soldiers would ask him if he needed help. As he once more pushed himself away from the wall in the direction of the baths, waving aside offers of assistance, he made a mental note to ask Scortius later about the possibility of different medicine. Something that lasted longer but allowed him to think a little straighter. This felt like the time as a newly-commissioned captain he'd caught some Gods-awful fever in the swamps near the northwest coast.

Finally arriving at the baths some minutes later, he passed beneath the great arch and made his way to the changing room. Leaving his clothes in one of the alcoves under the watchful eye of the civilian attendant, he carefully removed the temporary dressing the field medic had applied on the cart. Wincing as the last of the pad came away where it had stuck to the blood, he slipped a robe over his shoulders, carefully pressed the treated leather patch to his side, and entered the central area of the bathhouse. Within minutes he had been oiled, scraped and rubbed down and was sinking gratefully into a small, private, warm bath. Fortunately, while most of the army would be desperate to get to the baths after the day's travel, the majority of them would have innumerable tasks to perform before they had the chance; even the non-wounded officers, who would be required to settle their units and report in before going off-duty.

Leaning his head back on the tiled edge of the semi-circular bath, he allowed himself to doze lightly for a while.

A half hour later, cleaner if not refreshed, the captain walked out of the baths and into the dark street, the dying embers of the day casting an orange glow on the dark cerulean horizon and lending the shadowy street a strange glow. His head still hazy and his sight slightly blurred, presumably from the mixture of the dull pain, the after effects of the drug and the steam heat within the baths, he walked directly into the soldier before he saw him.

"You alright, captain?" the soldier asked with concern, grasping him by the upper arm and holding him.

Varro shook his head slightly, startled. The lower ranks didn't treat their seniors like this. He squinted in the low light and the figure swam slowly into focus. The neat uniform and shiny armour, the black crest and cloak and the white baldric bearing the raven and the wolf; the uniform of the marshal's personal guard. Even the lowest member of that honoured unit might argue seniority over a cohort captain. Varro steadied himself and nodded, as though to an equal.

"Just suffering a little after effect from the battle. Apologies."

"No apology necessary, captain, as long as you're alright", the man replied sincerely.

Varro stepped back and straightened a little. The cooler night air was beginning to clear his head a little and his focus was sharpening. The man was not alone, but indeed part of a squad of six guards, all in the marshal's guard dress uniform, and betwixt them stood a slighter, shorter figure wrapped tightly in a lustrous dark blue robe against the chill of the night air. Varro frowned as he caught sight of the pale, slender hand holding the robe closed, and the two white gold and amethyst rings on the hand.

"Catilina?"

The captain stepped back and straightened, a dozen emotions fighting for control of his face. He suddenly felt quite ill.

"Catilina…"

The lady let the hood of the robe fall back to reveal her delicate porcelain features. Her prefect brow and the tresses and curls of her ebony hair gave her an austere and otherworldly appearance in the strange, waning sunlight. Catilina had been renowned as a beauty from a very young age and many a courtier had been deceived by her looks into believing her to be flighty, weak or even vapid. Nothing could be farther from the truth and, given her parentage, there was no surprise in that. marshal Sabian had built the modern Imperial army back up from scratch, and the Lady Cassida had survived twenty years of civil war as mistress of her own estate, purely through nerve and insight, while many a powerful lord had fallen.

"Captain Varro, you should address me as Lady Sabianus." The primness of her words caught Varro off guard and he stood dumb, weighing her words and trying to decide whether she was truly serious or playing some game with him. This was not a simple woman, even in simple conversation.

She waited a moment, watching the uncertainty on Varro's face. "Has the constant drudgery of battle finally driven your Godsborn manners from you?" she enquired in a flat tone.

The captain remained still. When he opened his mouth to reply, all that came out was a choking, stuttering noise. He felt a slight flush rise in his cheeks and damned himself to more than one hell for showing such childish weakness in front of professional soldiers. He was a longstanding and decorated veteran and yet, faced with a dozen words from Catilina he fell apart like a fresh faced boy. A low growl of irritation or anger began to well up deep in his throat.

"Varro," the woman laughed lightly, her eyes suddenly sparkling in the moonlight, matching the amethysts on her fingers almost perfectly. "I do believe you are blushing!"

Before he could react, for which he was truly grateful, Catilina's smile warmed and she tilted her head slightly to one side.

"But I see you've been wounded again, my dear captain."

Varro's hand went to his aching side in an involuntary movement.

"Yes."

The lady locked his eyes with her own for a moment and a look of concern passed briefly across her face before being replaced once more with a visage of good natured elegance. Her eyes bored into his.

"You're not yourself, Varro" she stated as a matter of fact.

He shook his head and gave a weak smile, but Catilina tapped her cheek with a slender finger, her gaze never leaving his face.

"You've no banter and no quick wit. Most unlike you. Your eyes seem hazy and they wander while I speak." To emphasise her point, she held up her index finger and moved it slowly from side to side while her eyes remained locked on his face.

Varro found with great irritation, that he was watching her finger and shaking his head like an idiot. He growled and waved a hand at her irritably, dismissing the conversation, but her look hardened.

"You've been on mare's mead," she said with a note of accusation. "Or something stronger, possibly. Whatever it is, you don't look well."

Finally Varro found his voice. It wasn't as strong as he'd like, but still clear enough in the cool evening air.

"I'm fine, Lady Sabianus." He stressed the title a little too much. "A little battered, but I'm fine. I'm due to see Scortius sometime today…" He looked around the street, now almost dark with the sun fully set. "Tonight, I suppose."

Catilina glared at him.

"You need to see him now, Varro. Not later. I'll have two of the guard escort you."

Varro waved his hands at her in a way he hoped looked pleasantly admonishing and shook his head, which threatened to send his brain spinning once more. The queasiness came again in a sudden blast but was, fortunately, gone in a flash.

"I'm going to see him later," he replied flatly. "Right now, I'm going home for a while. I haven't eaten for a year or so, my stomach tells me."

For a long moment the two held each others' gaze, locked in a battle of wills, until Catilina looked away, folding her arms indignantly to indicate to all present that she had decided the captain's decision was wrong but was willing to watch him fail to prove her point.

Varro ground his teeth in frustration. No matter how he dealt with Catilina, in every argument, every conversation and even every minor exchange of greetings, he had always left feeling that he had lost the debate and she had let him go.

"I'll no doubt see you shortly, Lady Sabianus. I expect your father and the prefect will want to see me tomorrow."

Catilina regarded him with an unreadable expression.

"In this world, Varro, all things are possible."

She gestured at the man Varro had bumped into.

"Crinus, take two others and make sure the captain gets back to his house safely."

She looked at him and smiled mischievously.

"If, that is, he can remember where he lives."

Varro continued to grind his teeth, unable to form a suitable reply. His mind was feeling surprisingly clouded, even here in the late evening breeze.

"Come!" Catilina waved to her retinue and swept away past the captain toward the grand headquarters building at the centre of the fort.

The captain watched her go with a curious mixture of desire and relief. The three remaining guards exchanged a look that Varro recognised in irritation: soldiers that had been assigned a duty they felt was beneath them. Baby-sitting. He grinned a wicked grin.

"So, lads. Who's for a jug of good wine?"

The senior of the soldiers regarded Varro with something akin to disdain, as though he were some sort of carrion, and returned the captain's smile with no warmth.

"Home, Captain."

The other two guards reached for Varro's elbows as if to support him, and he pulled away indignantly with as much pride as he could muster.

"I'm quite capable of walking, even if the Lady feels I need an escort," he narrowed his eyes at their leader. "So let's just go."

The group of four walked purposefully along the street toward the officers' quarters as the arteries of the fortress gradually filled with off-duty soldiers on their way to the baths, taverns, gambling pits, or to the other dens of pleasure that were to be found in the civilian settlement just beyond the fort's massive walls. As he walked, Varro found he had to concentrate with every step to prevent himself staggering.

As they rounded a corner, sergeant Corda strode into view, still in his armour and coated in the grime of travel. Varro nodded a professional greeting as he came to as steady a halt as he could manage.

"Corda. Would you care to join me this evening? Martis is making something fowl."

The sergeant smiled a rare smile at the pun and nodded.

"I'd be glad to, sir, but I must settle in and bathe first. I'll join you shortly."

With a salute, he strode off toward his quarters while Varro made for the welcoming lights of his house. At the door, he thanked the marshal's guards with mock extravagance and entered, closing the door behind him. He leaned on the door jamb for support for a moment, breathing heavily, and then turned and walked into his main room.

"Good evening, captain Varro," the marshal said from his seat beside the fire.

Varro stopped in his tracks and swayed for a moment before recovering himself as best he could and coming to a surprisingly smart salute. The sudden movement certainly made his head swim a little, but he snapped his arm back down by his side and stood as straight and as still as he could, a gentle sweat beginning to glisten on his brow.

Marshal Sabian, tall and imposing with his iron grey hair and his handsome, yet lined and careworn face, sat with his legs crossed and his black-plumed helmet on his lap. The fact that the marshal already held a crystal glass of what was clearly Varro's best wine and a small platter or cold meats lay on the table beside him made it plain that Martis had been as diligent and efficient as ever in dealing with the man who was, after all, the second most powerful man in the Empire.

The captain smiled weakly.

"Marshal, you honour my house."

Sabian waved his hand, brushing aside the compliment.

"Gods, Varro, I have more than enough obsequious sycophants hanging around me at Vengen; I don't need the same here. Sit down before you fall down. I sent your servant out for a short while. I don't want us to be disturbed." He reached and took a neat slice of chicken from the plate, rolling it and dipping it in the accompanying pickle before popping it into his mouth. His eyes swept the room, taking in its austere appearance, almost entirely lacking in decoration, and that which could be seen was clearly of military origin: a worn pennon here, a scabbard with a telling dent there. Clearly the home of a career soldier.

Without a word, and quietly grateful, the captain made his way to a seat close by; close enough for low conversation, but not close enough to seem discourteous.

"It's been a long time, marshal," he replied, being careful to keep his tone slightly familiar and yet thoroughly respectful.

"Long indeed," Sabian replied quietly, his gaze slowly wandering down to rest on his boots. "Always knew you'd be commissioned, Varro. Even in the old days, I mean. I suspect if I hadn't given command of the Fourth to Cristus, it would have wound up with you, sooner or later."

Varro blinked a few times, gently shaking his head. Likely it was the fault of the drugs and the drowsiness, but his mind seemed to be refusing to work correctly. He was suddenly entirely unsure of the situation around him and the scene felt increasingly unreal to him.

Here was the second most powerful man in the Empire, a close friend of the Emperor himself, speaking to him as though they were campfire companions on campaign in the wilderness; suggesting that he could be a staff officer in the right circumstances. Oh, not that he hadn't considered that himself from time to time, but had never thought to hear it from above. And perhaps he hadn't done. It wouldn't entirely surprise him to find his mind was playing tricks on him. He focused once more on Sabian, aware that the marshal had continued to talk, long after he'd stopped listening.

"…and so you might still get that chance, Varro; probably will in fact."

The marshal raised those insightful eyes, 'a window onto genius' as some poet had once written of him, and rested them on Varro.

"But for that to happen," he said with surprising force, "I need you to do something."

Varro blinked in alarm. He'd missed something. Trying not to sound panicked, he settled slightly in the seat and gave a reassuring smile.

"Can you just repeat that, sir?"

Sabian gave him an odd look; disturbingly reminiscent of the one Catilina had given him in the street outside the bathhouse.

"Prefect Cristus will, tomorrow, be formally announcing his decision to step down from command."

Again Varro blinked and Sabian's eyes narrowed.

"You are taking all this in, aren't you Varro? If I didn't know better I'd say you were topped up on Mare's Mead." His eyes narrowed and he leaned forward in his seat.

The captain shook his head.

"Sorry sir. Strong medicine our cohort doctor put me on. Took a stab wound in the side yesterday and it pinches a bit."

Sabian smiled.

"I expect it does, Varro; I expect it does. Still, it'll be towards the end of the year before Cristus can actually fully step down. He's plenty to do before then, but he'll be looking at a position on the Imperial Council in Velutio. And that's where I need to strike a bargain with you, Varro."

"Sir?" The captain's brow furrowed. Taking this in at face value was hard enough. Digesting the details and trying to read between the lines was positively crippling in his current state, though with the marshal it was always worth checking.

Sabian sighed and leaned forward over the plume of his helmet, resting his elbows on the knees of his black breeches and steepling his fingers.

"Catilina."

"Catilina, sir?" replied Varro, thoughts rushing around his head and refusing to settle. For certain Sabian had known of their dalliance; Varro would never have been foolish enough to tangle with the marshal's daughter in secret. But that had been over for years now, hadn't it? And yet the marshal had come to his house; the house of a lowly captain, to speak of her?

"Yes Varro," Sabian continued, his voice clear and suddenly much less familiar, "Catilina. I know the two of you had something together; a few years ago, back in Vengen. I might have been busy, but I couldn't miss my daughter fawning and swooning over a scarred captain on a furlough. Besides," he continued, "my son knew well enough. And he and I talk."

A momentary panic seized Varro but faded into disbelief. Catilina was not a woman to whom anyone would apply words like 'fawn' and 'swoon'.

"It was truly nothing sir. We never…"

Sabian stopped him with a hard look.

"She was sixteen and headstrong," the marshal interrupted. "She's always known exactly what she's doing and I trusted her judgement even then; even with you."

His look softened once more.

"But the problem is this: Cristus has asked me for permission to court her."

Varro leaned back heavily in the chair. He tried to find his voice, but nothing seemed to be coming out, no matter how hard he tried.

Sabian continued to stare directly at him.

"Cristus will be one of the most powerful politicians in the Empire. Very suitable as a match for Catilina. But the problem is: I am very much afraid she still carries a torch for you. A worryingly bright torch. I almost had you broken when you went back the next month. You left her a mess, though she would have no one tell you of it. A father knows, though."

Again Varro's mouth moved with hardly any sound emerging.

"I won't have her marry a soldier, Varro. It's a dangerous profession, no matter how good at it one is. I love my daughter and I won't have her destroyed because the man she loves is lying face down in a mountain pass with a spear in his back. Do you understand me?"

Varro nodded and managed an affirmative sound. He really was having trouble now. It was one thing to be feeling light headed and woolly, but he was now having real difficulty forming words in his head, let alone voicing them.

Shaking his head again in a vain attempt to clear it a little, he squinted and focused on his commander.

"I understand that sir. Catilina's n'extraordinary woman sir, but I never expected her to…"

Again he fumbled with his words.

"I wouldn't…"

He was saved any further attempt as Sabian nodded.

"Calm yourself, Varro. I'm not here to rake over the past with you. My visit here concerns the future. All I'm asking you to do is keep my daughter at arm's length and, if she insists on being near you, to try and put her off; to dissuade her from pursuing this. She doesn't know about Cristus' troth yet, but she will do so before we return to Vengen at the end of the week."

Varro nodded uncertainly.

"This may sound a little unfair to you, Varro," the marshal continued. "But I've watched both you and Cristus. He's moderately ambitious on a personal level and actively seeks a lifestyle that I'd like him to be able to provide for Catilina. You are an outstanding field officer. I've said as much many times. You may even be a truly great officer. But one thing I'm also certain of is that you will live and die a soldier. I've known your sort many times. Many of my closest friends fit that very mould." He sat back once more.

"But that's just not for my daughter."

Varro shook his head again. Nothing he tried was clearing the fog that continued to settle on his mind. He smiled weakly at the marshal.

"So," Sabian went on, "the fact remains that when Cristus steps down at the end of the year, the fourth will need a new prefect. By general right of seniority, I should give the position to the captain of the first cohort, but you know Parestes as well as I do."

Varro nodded and cleared his throat.

"He's 'by th' book' sir. Good enough, but no 'magination." Why the hell wouldn't his tongue work properly. Surely the drugs must be wearing off by now.

"He hasn't an imaginative bone in his body, Varro. Moreover, though he's commanding the senior cohort, you actually have more years' active service than he. You were just held back by that incident at Fallowford. My doing, I know, and probably unfair, but necessary at the time." The marshal smiled.

"So I'm going to name you. It's my prerogative, and I really don't think Parestes will be put out over the matter. He knows you have more 'time-in' than him."

Varro nodded again, and then shook his head.

"Thank you sir."

Sabian flexed his shoulders and pulled himself upright.

"Very well, Varro. I'll see you at the headquarters tomorrow morning. Get some rest. That wound's clearly taken a lot out of you."

"I will, sir" the captain replied and hauled himself out of the chair, wobbling slightly as he came upright.

"Goodbye, captain." The marshal inclined his head slightly and, turning, left the room.

Varro saluted as his superior departed, and then staggered slightly.

He turned to find the chair he'd been in, and as he spun, noted with fascination the way the light from the oil lamps in the recessed alcoves streaked along, like a greasy stain on a pane of glass. He smiled at that, or at least he thought he smiled. His mind didn't seem to be functioning properly at that moment. He spotted what could well have been the expensive, carved oak chair with the leather padding and reached out to grasp the handle and sit while the feeling passed.

Varro pitched forward with all his weight, unconscious even before he fell through the oak chair with a crash, splintering the finely carved legs and coming, after a brief roll, to a halt amid the wreckage, viscera leaking from his reopened wound and fresh blood seeping from half a dozen new cuts.

When Varro awoke it felt as though his body were pierced through in a dozen places with jagged knives. His head felt heavy and thick and he had a headache that threatened to break through his skull, but the uncertain fluffiness of before seemed to have retreated. His eyes flickered open. The light immediately made his head thump all the louder, but he was grateful to note that after mere moments a dark wooden beamed ceiling swum into view. At least he could see.

With a groan he began to rise to a seated position and suddenly hands were on him, gently pushing him back down. In a minor panic, he turned his head, sending fresh thumping beats and waves of nausea through him. Two medical orderlies were performing some menial task over by the side bench.

The hospital then. He'd been here before often enough.

Very slowly and carefully rolling his head the other way, two more figures came into view.

Corda, clad in his dress tunic and cloak, stood beside the table, a look of great concern on his pale features. With a start, Varro realised his second in command was covered in dried rivulets and pools of blood. Varro's blood, plainly.

Standing behind Corda was another figure in white. Even with his back to Varro, the captain recognised the low rumble of disapproval that was a trademark of Scortius, the chief doctor of the second cohort. The man was hunched over something on a table. Varro looked weakly up at Corda.

"Am I…"

The sergeant reached out a hand and clasped Varro's in a time-honoured fashion.

"I found you on your floor. Don't know how long you'd been out, but there was quite a pool of blood. You're looking quite pale and Scortius had to take a chunk of chair out of your back. Another wound, sir, I'm afraid."

Varro tried to lift his head from the table, failing drastically. There was so little strength in his body and the muscles refused to obey. Breathing deeply and collapsing back he closed his eyes. Corda cleared his throat.

"Your other wound opened right up again too. Scortius has been having a good look inside you."

"Has he," gurgled Varro with an edge of resentment. "And did he find anything he liked?"

Slowly the doctor turned and approached the table.

"Varro," he said quietly, "lie still. You're putting too much strain on what's left of your body."

"Nice." The captain rolled his eyes. "At least I feel better."

The doctor cleared his throat and leaned closer.

"You only feel better because I've filled you so full of pain-killing remedies that you probably couldn't stand straight even if you were in full health." He sighed. "I've got to tell you something; something you're not going to like."

Varro merely nodded as best he could.

"I'd a feeling something was wrong. I've been wounded many times, but it's never hit me like this. Even worse-looking wounds I've suffered. But surely I can't die from this? I mean; it's not that bad a wound, surely?"

Resting the heels of his hands on the side of the surgical table, Scortius leaned over the captain and Varro felt his heart skip a beat when he saw the look in the doctor's eyes; the same look that crossed them every time the man thought of his long-gone son, Terentius; a look that carried loss, and despair and utter hollowness. A look that frightened Varro to his very core.

"What...?" The captain's voice came out little more than a croak, or a whisper.

"There's nothing I can do, Varro."

The captain's eyes closed for a moment and then he frowned deeply before opening them once more.

"Would you just care to run that by me again, Scortius?"

The doctor sighed and, reaching out, pulled a basic wooden chair across to the table and took a seat.

"It's not the wound. The wound is alright. It's nasty, but it'd heal, as would the new furniture wound in your back."

"So..." Varro's frown deepened, "what are we talking about then?"

Scortius rested his elbows on his knees, clasped his hands together and raised his sad eyes to Varro.

"Have you ever heard of Ironroot?"

Varro shook his head, pensively.

The doctor pinched the bridge of his nose.

"I can't say I'm really surprised. Ironroot is the Imperial name for a substance the Pelasians know as Sher-Thais. It's harvested from the seeds of a plant the locals call the 'suicide tree'. I've seen it used in the eastern provinces as both a poison and a pesticide, but never this far north or west."

Varro stared at the doctor, confusion and panic fighting for control of his expression.

"I'm sorry," Scortius shook his head. "There's no cure." He sat back with a flat look on his face.

Varro tried once more to raise his head, growling.

"How can this happen?"

Scortius pinched his nose again and frowned.

"There appears to be some discoloration of the organs and flesh around your wound. At this point, I'd say that the blade that cut you was coated with the stuff. Very nasty. And curious..."

"Curious?"

Varro's growl deepened.

"Curious? That's all you have to say?"

The doctor sat back slightly. "Curious that a hairy, unwashed barbarian from the northern mountains would have a sword coated with an exotic and expensive poison from the other side of the world? I'm sorry this has happened Varro, and if I could stop it, I would, but I can't help being curious as to how he got it."

"How long have I got?"

Scortius shrugged slightly. "He's obviously used a strong dose. And straight into your body. Normally I'd expect a few days at most, but I think I can give you things that'll keep you going longer than that. A week? Maybe two? I'd have liked to see that sword. Perhaps we could have learned more."

Varro collapsed back, exhausted and stunned, as the doctor gave a weak and sympathetic half-smile.

"I'll go see what I can mix up for you." The doctor shuffled off among his bottles and bags in the corner, muttering "for pain, stimulation, retardation and blood. Hmm…"

Varro blinked and turned his head to look at Corda, clearly stunned, his face bleak, but showing the first signs of anger. The sergeant leaned down toward his officer and growled.

"I take it the bastard's dead? We'll not be able to find out."

Varro's eyes narrowed.

"The barbarian's dead alright, but I don't think he was the problem."

"What?" Corda frowned and leaned closer. The captain closed his eyes and the veins on his temple pulsed as he tracked back over the last two days.

"The sword." Varro's hand reached up and grasped his sergeant by the shoulder. "The bastard that stuck me had an Imperial sword; a nice one too. A proper officer's sword. That hairy piece of shit didn't get the poison at all. This is someone else's doing! One of our own, for Gods' sake, Corda… one of our own!"

Corda's expression hardened.

"I'm going to go see the quartermaster and go through the loot; see if I can find an Imperial sword." He looked up at Scortius as the captain sank wearily back to the table. "You get him up and about. I don't care how you have to do it. Just get him moving."

Corda gave his captain a last determined glance, grasped his shoulder, and then strode out of the tent as though he'd do battle with the Gods.

Varro watched Scortius approaching the table once more, his soul hardening like baked clay as he lay there. There was more to this than simple chance. Someone had engineered Varro's death, and that made him angry. Hopefully angry enough to stay alive long enough to settle this. Someone was going to pay for this. Someone would pay.

And cleft in two does history lie…

I opened my eyes. It took a few moments for me to place myself and my surroundings, but after a minute or so I remembered being helped back to my house by two medical orderlies. Scortius had given me some compound that quickly begun to clear my head and return the strength to my body. I know I was still feeling a little strange and confused as I woke, but some of that could well have been natural grogginess on waking from deep sleep.

I wasn't prepared for what happened.

Clearly I was still hallucinating. Of course, a few hours later I began to doubt that, and in retrospect I'm now totally convinced of the reality of the situation; or at least the reality of it to me. But nothing prepares you to wake from fuddled sleep and find yourself staring deep into the eyes of a stag.

Needless to say, my first reaction was to turn my head this way and that, convinced that this was some trick of the light or reaction to Scortius' medicine in my brain. Evidently the early morning sunlight streaming in through the glass panes of my room, squeezed to a sliver by the heavy drapes, was colliding with the many dust motes and creating a vision my battered subconscious had forced into the shape of a stag.

Yet as I turned my head and squinted, the creature was still there. I think I chuckled to myself as I struggled off the couch and my feet touched the tiled floor, sending a cold throb through them. I pulled myself upright with little pain and stood, swaying slightly. I remember the smell. I didn't notice it at the time, but later conversations brought it flooding back to me. The scent of a forest. The mulched leaves and pine needles.

I reached forward, fully expecting either for my hand to pass through the beast like a fog, or to wake with a start and realise that I'd still been asleep. I felt a shudder pass through me as my fingers brushed the fine white hair of the creature's nose. I had read stories of unwary hunters being gored by the antlers of even small stags, and yet this was no ordinary stag and no ordinary circumstance. In fact, this was impossible, I told myself again.

And yet for some reason it felt right. And more important than that, whereas the previous day I'd felt panic and horror, fear and anger, at that moment I felt none of those. On the first morning of my remaining days as a condemned man, what I actually felt was peace. And not just peace; peculiarly, peace and hope. Peace was a feeling I hadn't felt in so long it almost floored me with its intensity. An absence of fear and anger.

Cernus had bestowed something indefinable upon me; or possibly removed it from me.

All I can truly tell you is that the stag snorted very gently and as I felt the warm breath brush my face, all I felt was happiness. Without really understanding why, I returned to the couch and lay down, drifting into a pleasant sleep with a smile on my face.

I dreamt of white stags, of glittering swords and, finally, of Catilina.

Chapter Four

Corda sat in the cohort's small and austere command office within the headquarters building. Behind him, the unit's raven and boar standards and pay chest sat, protected by a thick iron-grille gate to which only three people had a key. There was only one seat in the room, positioned behind a sturdy table commonly used for maps, charts, unit strength reports, rosters, casualty lists and the like. The commanding officer's chair. Corda would habitually, as the cohort's second in command, stand slightly behind and to one side of the seated Varro while the other various sergeants and lower non-commissioned officers would stand at attention while briefed. It seemed wrong to be sitting in Varro's chair. He considered resuming his usual place but quickly put that aside. As temporary commander, he had to be seen to be acting as such, with full authority.

He leaned forward across the table with a sigh. This was not how he had pictured the victorious return from campaign. This morning was going to be difficult for everyone.

A knock at the heavy wooden door was followed a moment later by a click, and the door swung in to admit one of the two fort guard stationed permanently outside this important room.

"Your visitor's here, sir."

Corda nodded solemnly. "Show him in."

The sergeant scratched his full beard and glanced down at the empty desk. It still seemed wrong.

The solid, stocky, youthful figure of Salonius appeared in the doorway, saluted and stepped inside.

"Close the door," Corda said quietly.

As the portal clicked shut, the two men waited a moment for their eyes to adjust to the dimmer interior, lit only by the two small windows high in the outer wall and an oil lamp burning in an alcove opposite.

"You're Salonius." A statement; not a question.

"Yes, sir. Formerly second catapult torsion engineer, currently attached to the command guard," Salonius replied with a clear voice.

Corda's brow furrowed.

"That remains to be seen."

"Sir?" Salonius seemed genuinely surprised, Corda noted. Youth with all its innocence.

The sergeant cleared his throat slowly.

"You had been seconded to the command guard for all of an hour when you became involved in a fistfight with three of your fellow guardsmen. This is not the sort of behaviour we expect from the command guard. What do you have to say?"

Salonius straightened, a hard look flattening his features.

"With respect sir, that was a matter of personal principal and was before I had officially reported for guard duty on my first parade."

"Regardless," Corda pressed, "I want to know what happened. Who initiated the fight?"

Salonius raised his chin and fixed his eyes on a spot high on the rear wall.

"I forget, sir."

Corda sighed.

"I'm not on a witch hunt here, lad, but I can't have the command guard involved in that sort of thing. They are supposed to represent the highest quality of soldiery in the cohort. Tell me something. Just something."

"Sir, I was promoted from a basic green engineer to one of the most prestigious posts in the cohort. There would have to be some 'settling in' if you see what I mean, sergeant."

"Yes," Corda growled. "You settled one of them into the medical tent."

He sighed.

"So you *do* want to stay in the guard, then?"

"Yes sir."

"Why?" Corda leaned forward over the table and steepled his fingers.

"Because it's an honour, sir."

The sergeant frowned and closed his eyes for a moment.

"The problem is, Salonius, that the other guards don't like you. They'll never like you because you came from the engineers, not through the infantry ranks. They will always consider you a young upstart, and the fact that you stood up for yourself could just as easily turn around and make them hate you as make them respect you."

Salonius nodded. "With all due respect, sir, I'm willing to take the risk."

"Well I'm not." Corda sighed and leaned back in the chair. As the young engineer stared at him open-mouthed, he cleared his throat once more.

"Salonius, the captain selected you specifically for a role close to him. There are any number of more qualified men for the post, even if we were short of guards, which we're not. And while he's an exceptionally fair and good man, the captain is not soft in the head and he wouldn't promote someone unfitting without having a good reason. So there seems to me to be an excellent solution presenting itself here."

"Sir?"

"I am temporarily, but for as long as is necessary, assuming full command of the cohort."

Salonius' stiff stance faltered for a moment, and Corda nodded.

"It's true. I don't like it any more than you appear to. But for the time being it's necessary. The captain is currently unable to resume his position, and so it becomes my job. This means that I will now have the command guard assigned to me. In theory I should post a detachment of them to assist and protect the captain, but that's not going to happen."

Corda watched the young man with sharp eyes. He may be little more than a boy, but there was something about him. He was short, but strong and brave enough to take on three bigger and more experienced soldiers and now, as he stood in the low light of the headquarters, Corda could see the lad's mind racing, piecing things together. He smiled.

"Go on, lad…"

"Well sir," Salonius said quietly, "the captain's wound isn't bad enough to keep him away from his post for any length of time, especially while we're in quarters. And, well, I don't like to listen to rumour, but…"

"Go on…"

"Well, I heard the captain was taken to the hospital last night. And that the marshal actually visited his house last night. And I was in the quartermaster's office last night finalising my kit change when you came in asking for a list of all the military salvage from the battlefield."

"And..." Corda prompted.

"I'm not sure sir, and I apologise for my bluntness, but there's something going on; something you're not telling me, and something I think you're keeping from the rest of the cohort too."

Corda nodded.

"Sharp. I can see why the captain wanted you in the guard. But the fact remains that I *don't*. I don't want to spend half my time separating you and the other soldiers. And I don't want you ending up knifed in the latrines one night. But I don't want you to slide back into the engineers either; I suspect you were being wasted there."

Salonius nodded. He could see where this was going.

The sergeant sat up straight and unfolded his arms. "I want you to report to the captain's house. He might want to brief you on the situation straight away, or he might prefer to wait until I get there. I have a few things to do, but I shaln't be far behind you."

He rose from the chair and straightened.

"You'll retain your new rank, pay, uniform and all benefits, but I'm assigning you on detached duty to the captain himself. You know where his house is?"

Salonius shook his head slightly.

"No, sir, but I can find it."

"Good." Corda stepped round the table and reached out, grasping the younger man by the shoulder. "Get going and tell the captain that I'll meet you there when I've got the morning briefing out of the way."

Salonius saluted and, turning, unlatched the door and strode out into the morning sunshine. The captain's house would be close and easy to find. As he stepped between the guards at the door and out into the street, he noted the sergeant of the command guard, followed by all the senior officers of the cohort, marching along the street toward the cohort office.

Stepping respectfully to one side, he hurried across the main square toward the two senior officer's houses that lay between him and the cohort's barrack blocks. A swift glance at the house to his left revealed a tile cemented into the wall next to the door with FC. Fortress command; wrong house. A few steps across the thoroughfare and the tile on the house opposite read IIC; commander of the second cohort. Salonius stepped up to the door and knocked firmly.

The door was opened by the captain's body servant, Martis. The older man gave Salonius a shrewd once-over and then stepped aside without a word. The young guard took a tentative step inside and glanced around. Captain Varro sat in the main room in his tunic and breeches, cradling a bronze cup in his hands and staring down into the contents, seemingly deep in thought. Stepping stiff backed into the room, Salonius came to attention and cleared his throat.

Varro looked up from his cup and frowned.

"Soldier?"

There was something in his tone, Salonius thought, but couldn't identify what it was.

"Reporting under orders of sergeant Corda, sir," he announced.

There was clearly something bothering the captain and Salonius realised he himself had an indescribable itch beneath the skin. Risking breaking his attentive stance, he cast his eyes momentarily about the room and sniffed deeply. The room had a peculiar smell; an old smell that he remembered from the days of his youth all those years ago in that village on the edge of the Northern Woods. A smell of wet forest and disturbed undergrowth had been badly masked with some kind of fragrance. In the old days they'd have burned some herbs over the fire in the centre of the room to remove the smell. Someone... Martis, he suspected, had burned a scented oil throughout the house and then opened the windows to drive the combined thick, cloying scent out on the breeze. It had largely worked, but Salonius knew something Martis didn't.

He smiled nervously.

Varro grunted and took a sip of his heated drink, a wisp of steam wafting up into the air-chilled room. A faint hint of lemon accompanied the steam, adding to the already complex aroma of the room. The captain leaned back.

"Relax, Salonius. I'm off duty for one thing, and for another I actually hold no active rank at all currently."

"Respectfully, sir" the young guard replied, remaining straight, "you are my superior officer and I am reporting under the orders of the acting captain."

Varro smiled. A strange smile that Salonius couldn't quite work out.

"Very well then. At ease, soldier." The captain sighed. "And that can be an order if you like."

Salonius shrugged and settled into a more comfortable stance.

"You seem in an odd mood, if I may say, sir?"

It was impertinent, and he knew it, but something was bothering the captain, and something was bothering him too; the same thing, he was sure. He took a deep breath.

"It may not be possible, sir, but it still happens."

Varro looked up sharply.

"What?"

"A visit? An encounter, sir?"

Varro carefully placed his cup down on the small table and looked past the guard's head.

"Martis. Go to the shop and get me some wine."

The stocky servant nodded silently and, collecting a small bag of coins from a drawer in the cabinet by the door, ducked outside and disappeared out into the morning light, leaving the door to swing shut with a click.

"Tell me what you mean, Salonius. And knock off the inferior officer stuff. This is important…"

Salonius stepped forward and the captain gestured at a seat near the window. The guard placed his helmet on the cabinet and sat carefully, making sure his sword sheath hung neatly to one side of the chair.

"Cernus sir," the young man replied earnestly. "You spoke briefly of him after the battle. It struck me as strange then, you not being one of the folk, if you pardon the expression sir?"

Varro waved that aside and leaned forward, listening intently.

"Well, sir," Salonius went on, "it's almost unheard of for someone outside our people to see Cernus in the flesh, so to speak, sir. I presume you'd seen him before the battle?"

Varro nodded, saying nothing.

"And you saw him again last night, sir?"

"Last night… this morning. When I woke. I thought I was dreaming. But how do you know all this?" the captain queried, his brow furrowing.

Salonius shrugged. "I can smell it. Honestly, sir, I can virtually feel it. I don't know whether any of your servants or friends here would notice, but I know the signs sir. No amount of spiced oil is going to hide that scent."

Varro's frown deepened. "You speak from experience."

The young man nodded.

"Tell me…" the captain urged.

Salonius squared his shoulders.

"I've seen him twice sir. Both times have changed my life. Cernus is a Lord of Portents. To see the stag himself is to be given a portent; a herald of things changing. Something for you will change. I can't speak for what you saw sir, but my first vision was pretty clear."

He smiled, wistfully, his eyes glazing slightly with the memory.

"I was hunting with my brothers in the woods near our village. Somehow we got separated and I ended up deep in the undergrowth on my own. I had a bow, you see, sir? I was after game really, or a coney. Whatever I could find. Other than that I just had a long knife on my belt. I stumbled into a clearing just as a bloody great boar burst out of the other edge. I didn't really have time to react. I dropped the bow and reached for my knife, but I'd have been dead before I'd freed the blade…"

"And?" Varro had moved to the edge of his seat in rapt fascination.

"And the wolf saved me, sir. A big grey wolf came from nowhere and hit the boar in the flank. He tore its throat out as I stood there, then he looked at me just once and settled down to eat his kill. I turned and ran back into the woods and after a dozen steps, there was the white stag. I'd been saved by the wolf, sir. It was clear to me anyway, but I went to see the village healer and he confirmed what it meant. I set off for Vengen the next morning and enlisted to serve the Imperial wolf, sir."

Varro blinked and sat back.

"I don't think your God showed me anything; don't think he told me what to expect. I just remember the feeling; the aura of the place and the thing."

Salonius nodded thoughtfully.

"You're not one of our people, sir. You might not have recognised whatever signs you were given, but rest assured there will have been signs."

"So a visit from Cernus means your life's going to change?" Varro sat back heavily, with a strange smile on his face. "Well, it certainly did. And now I've seen him twice it's going to change again?"

"Not necessarily, sir." Salonius steepled his fingers. "A visit from the Stag Lord is rare enough sir. A second visit is not something that happens very often even in legends. A second visit is… it's sort of a confirmation of destiny, sir. A chance to change things, sir. Something world-shaking."

The captain sighed.

"Your God has, I think, taken something from me. I think that's what our first meeting was. But it's possible that this morning he gave me something in return. I need to tell you the full story, Salonius. But I need you to keep this totally secret at the moment. Not about Cernus; I don't think there's much else to say about that, and most any man you speak to in the army will think you a madman if you start telling them you had a one-on-one with a forest God. I think Corda sent you to me for a specific reason and I need to tell you what's happened over the last twenty four hours."

The young man nodded hesitantly.

Varro drained his now tepid lemon drink and cleared his throat.

"I'm dying, Salonius."

He looked across at his young companion and studied his features.

"You don't seem all that surprised?"

Salonius shook his head slightly.

"I'm sorry about that sir. I really am. But no, I'm not surprised. I knew something was going on and it makes sense, I think. But why and how?"

"Poison, my lad. On the blade that stuck me."

Varro squared his shoulders.

"The larger picture, and the larger problem too, is that this isn't some random viciousness on the part of a barbarian. The sword was an imperial blade and the poison is far too expensive and exotic to have fallen into the lap of a random tribesman. This was done by one of our own; a soldier. And that means I can't trust anyone. Well, hardly anyone."

He narrowed his eyes and focused on his young companion.

"But you're new, you see. I can think of no reason why you can't be trusted. In fact, it may be that your Stag God sent you to me as the only soldier I can trust. Apart from Corda, of course."

Salonius frowned.

"What do you intend to do, sir?"

"What do you think?" the captain smiled coldly. "I'm going to track down the bastard responsible, and I'm going to make him pay. Very painfully. And very slowly."

"Good, sir. And Corda has assigned me to you personally so I'm here to help in any way I can," Salonius nodded in fierce agreement.

'And now something the stag lord showed me falls into place' he thought as he clenched his fists.

Varro nodded gratefully.

"Ok then, while we wait for the serg… the captain, I mean… tell me more about Cernus."

The door opened to Corda's knock and he was surprised to find Salonius admitting him rather than Martis. Of greater surprise was the faint smell of wine on the young soldier's breath. He furrowed his brow in disapproval but issued no comment as he strode past and into the room. Catching sight of Varro on the couch, he saluted and then stood at ease.

"Alright. I've briefed the cohort on the temporary command change. Can't say anyone likes it much though, including me."

The door shut with a click and Salonius returned to the room, stopping momentarily to salute the sergeant before walking over to stand by the window, also at ease.

Varro grunted.

"Can't say I'm too thrilled about it myself, but if these last few hours have taught me anything, it's that time is too precious to spend it messing around feeling sorry for myself. Thank you for assigning Salonius. He'll be of great use."

Corda nodded.

"Until we have a little more information on how this all occurred, we have to be very careful in whom we place our trust. In fact, captain, I would not take it personally were you to dismiss me for now."

Varro laughed.

"Corda, we've been friends for longer than some of our men have been alive. I know I can trust you. Unfortunately, with you taking on command of the cohort, you'll be tied to that job, so I doubt we'll be seeing a lot of you. And really I can't think of anyone else I'd be willing to trust in the cohort at the moment." He sighed and sat back. "Or out of the cohort either, for that matter."

The sergeant took a seat and leaned on his knees.

"So there's just the three of us. And with me busy and you incapacitated it's going to be difficult following anything up."

Varro shook his head.

"Whatever Scortius cooked up for me this time seems to be doing the trick. I'm thinking clearly and I seem to be functioning almost normally. Alright I'm achy and it hurts a bit from time to time, but not enough to stop me. Salonius and I can deal with all this."

Corda nodded.

"Alright Varro. I went through the quartermaster's list of all loot accounted for from the battlefield and there's no sign of a sword anything like your description. Plenty of weapons, but nothing like that." His eyes slipped sideways to Salonius. "Have you briefed this young man yet?"

Varro nodded.

"Well then" the sergeant continued, "I'll have the list delivered to him to go through with you. I'm sure I've been thorough, but it never hurts to have a second set of eyes go over things. So what's the next step?"

Varro shifted in his seat.

"That sword's the key. It's the only link I've got to whoever did this. And it's a good sword. I only saw it briefly, but I'd bet it'd be worth a year's pay for your average soldier. And *nobody's* going to leave that lying in the mud. Someone brought it back, and that means someone in this fort has that sword."

Salonius cleared his throat. "We could approach the fortress command captain. He could organise a complete search of the place with his provosts and be through the whole place in a matter of hours." He frowned. "But that's if you can trust them, sir?"

Varro shook his head.

"No, but I think there's another way around this. We're going to have to inform the prefect and the marshal about the change of command and my removal from duty and, while I don't know about the prefect, Sabian's more trustworthy than any other senior officer I've ever met. He's the most senior officer in the Province, he's trustworthy, and he's here. If I speak to him, he can authorise the search without going through normal fort channels. And he can do it with his own guard, so no one needs to know what they're searching for. It's the only way we're going to get the jump on whoever's responsible."

Corda nodded thoughtfully, stroking his beard.

"Very well. I'll have to get back to the cohort. I don't know how you found time to perform actual command tasks with all the other random shit bureaucracy involved. I've not informed the men of the exact circumstances yet; just that you're under medical care and unable temporarily to carry out your duty. I think it would be better, given the nature of the situation, to keep as many people out of this as possible, particularly the members of your own cohort."

"Agreed." Varro sighed. "Alright, I'm going to have a bite to eat and then Salonius and I will go to headquarters and get things underway."

Corda nodded and, saluting hesitantly, turned on his heel and left the building, the door swinging quietly closed behind him.

Salonius straightened.

"Martis is out getting wine sir. Shall I see if I can get you something to eat?"

Varro smiled.

"Don't worry about it lad. He's already left cold meats, bread and cheese out in the other room. If you could just dash through and get it, there's plenty for both of us."

The two men were seated quietly around the small table munching on hard northern cheeses, lean cuts of pork and bread still warm and freshly baked when the door swung open with a crash.

Startled, Varro dropped a slice of cheese and Salonius leapt to his feet, his hand going immediately for the hilt of the sword at his side before he realised who the lone figure in the doorway was.

Catilina stormed into the room, the door swinging closed behind her. She had an air of haughty anger, somehow heightened by the aroma of eastern oils that followed her, adding to the heady scent already pervading the room. Varro stood, wiping his hands to remove the crumbs.

The marshal's daughter, pale and elegant with fire in her eyes pointed an accusing finger at the captain.

"You!"

"What?" Varro spread his hands out in a supplicant gesture.

"How could you not tell me?" she shrieked at him.

"Catilina, calm down for Gods' sake. You'll burst a blood vessel."

The lady's arm fell back down beside her and she placed her hands on her hips, taking up a defiant stance.

"You get a life-threatening injury and I have to hear it through the bureaucracy?" her voice notched up another octave and her eyes smouldered as she glared at the captain.

"You've heard?" Varro frowned.

"Your doctor gave the prefect the post-battle casualty reports. My father and I were there at the time. What does he mean 'fatality'? You'd better explain this, Varro!"

The captain sighed deeply and gestured to the empty seat to one side.

"I will Catilina, but sit down and calm down."

He turned to Salonius. "I hadn't thought about the casualty reports. Obviously he hasn't released full details then."

"No sir," the young soldier agreed, "but surely he's not reported you as a fatality."

Varro grumbled.

"It'll be 'expected fatality'. Those of us who were wounded and aren't expected to pull through."

Catilina, still standing with her hands on her hips, growled at him.

"He's not reckoned with your tenacity, Varro. You're always getting wounded, but it doesn't take you long to heal" she grumbled at him and then stopped and frowned.

"It's not the wound, is it? I hadn't thought of that. What's happened, then?"

Varro gestured at the seat again.

"Catilina, it's not good. And I can't have the details going round the fort like a brush fire, so I need you to keep this very much to yourself at the moment."

"What?" she barked impatiently.

Varro sighed again and sat back heavily.

"I was stuck with a poisoned blade during the battle."

Finally, Catilina took the seat she had been proffered and stared at the captain.

"Tell me, Varro."

The captain tapped his fingers idly on his knee as he weighed her mood. There was no denying Catilina was an intelligent and resourceful woman, yet her fiery temper sometimes overwhelmed her sense of priority. She would need to be very objective about all this unless the news was to be leaked around the army.

"Catilina, I'm dying. There's no cure and we can't even locate the sword that was used. Scortius is giving me medication to keep me up and about and largely out of pain, but there's nothing he can do in the long run."

The haughty young woman pinched the bridge of her nose and turned to face the window.

"Is the man who did this still among the prisoners?"

"No."

Varro caught her eyes and noticed them beginning to well up. She became aware of his gaze and blinked back the emotion, her face hardening.

"You killed him then?"

Varro shot a quick glance at Salonius whose expression remained unreadable.

"Not exactly." He sighed. "I killed the barbarian who wielded the sword…"

"Yes?"

"But it's the man who gave him the poisoned blade and marked me out that I want to find."

"You mean this was deliberately targeted at you?" She blinked again, this time in surprise.

"It has to have been. The man came looking for me on the battlefield and he had an imperial blade; a very expensive one. Someone from within this fort has had me poisoned. I'm going to die, but I'm going to find out who did this first and why. And I'm going to make them suffer. But you see that's why I can't let you go out and tell people about this. If word gets out that I'm looking into this the culprit will go to ground and I'll never find him."

Catilina was still staring at him, a horrified look on her face and her mouth hanging open.

"Varro, you can't just die?"

"I've no choice, Catilina," Varro smiled weakly. "There's nothing I can do about it."

"There *has* to be!" she yelled at him.

"There *has* to be something we can do. Scortius has missed something."

Varro shook his head sadly. "Scortius is a very thorough man, Catilina. You know that. And he's done everything that can be done. I wish you hadn't come with your father. I'd have spared you this if I could."

"I'll just step out, sir" Salonius said quietly, turning and making for the door.

"Stay here, Salonius." Varro shook his head again. "We're about done. I want you to escort Catilina back to her quarters. I'm fairly sure the marshal will be here soon to see me. And I need to organise a few things with him." He turned to the young woman, who was no longer holding her emotion in check, a single tear snaking down her cheek. "And Catilina: this is going to be hard enough for your father and I without you here."

A hard look impressed itself on her face. Varro sat back slightly. He'd known Catilina long enough to know that look.

"Catilina…"

"No."

She sat back in the seat and folded her arms defiantly.

"Catilina…"

"You can say what you like Varro, but I'm staying. You need people you can trust around you right now. That's me and father and you know that. We need to work out what we're doing next, and preferably before father gets here. He's going to want to do everything by the book and that's clearly not going to work in this case. You're going to need me to persuade him to our way of thinking. No one else can do that. You know that."

"Alright," the captain replied with a resigned nod. "Salonius, sit down and let's work out what we need to do."

The young man stepped away from the window toward the chair and, as he did, there was a heavy knock at the door. He turned to the captain and raised his eyebrows questioningly. Varro nodded at him.

"Best get it. The marshal wasted no time, eh?"

Salonius walked across to the door and opened it, the morning breeze cutting its way into the heady, spiced atmosphere of the front room. He stepped back, startled momentarily. In the street outside the door stood three of the fort provosts, the army's police unit, their black and white striped crests flicking around in the wind and their black cloaks snapping back and forth.

"Show me to captain Varro."

The provost sergeant stepped to the threshold while his two companions took up positions on guard to either side of the door. Blinking in surprise, Salonius stepped back, allowing the soldier into the room.

Varro and Catilina looked up in surprise as the provost sergeant stepped into the room and came smartly to attention.

"Sir."

Varro raised an eyebrow.

"Yes, sergeant?"

"I would be obliged if you would accompany me outside the fort, sir."

Varro's eyes narrowed.

"What?"

The provost reached into the recesses of his cloak and whipped out a parcel. A leather wallet bound with a thong, the corner of a piece of paper poking out at the edge. He reached out and proffered the object to the captain. Varro frowned.

"What is this?"

Slowly, the sergeant turned the parcel over. In a neat script, someone had simply inscribed the front 'Varro IV-II'. Varro reached out to grasp it.

"Provosts delivering letters now?"

The sergeant's face remained straight and unreadable as he withdrew his hand, the parcel remaining out of Varro's reach.

"Hardly, captain. This was found on the body of a soldier about a mile from the fort. The man has been attacked, sir. Brutally."

Chapter Five

Varro pulled his cloak tighter against the biting breeze that whistled across the common near the fortress as he kicked the lazy mare forward again. He'd only had time to throw on a cloak and some boots while the impatient provost sergeant had stood in his doorway, tapping irritably. He felt grateful for the presence of Salonius, fully armoured in his cohort guard uniform. While he had no reason to distrust the provost, these were highly unusual circumstances and he'd thought deeply about the wisdom of this course of action before grabbing his cloak in resignation and stepping forward.

He'd not even reached the door when he realised Catilina was by his side. He'd tried to deter her, unsuccessfully, as he'd expected, and the pair of them had joined the three provosts as soon as Salonius returned with three horses from the stables of the second.

The journey through the town was uneventful. It was now mid to late morning and the locals were going about their own business while the majority of soldiers were on duty within the fort. The growing civilian settlement would liven up considerably as the bulk of the troops were dismissed at sundown.

And almost a mile beyond the township, over wind-blasted heaths on a surprisingly chilly and blustery morning for so late in the season, the small party approached a knot of people clustering beneath a tree in the shelter of a hedgerow.

A gulley ran from near the crest of the hill down alongside the hedgerow and to the stream in the shallow valley. A seasonal stream, the ditch was currently dry and rocky. Beneath the beech tree, two more of the fort provosts stood with three locals, a boy and a girl of perhaps seven years and a man; presumably their father.

As they approached and reined in, the children huddled to their father's knees, partially for warmth, as much for fear of the now seven soldiers around them. As the six riders dismounted, Varro stepped toward the ditch, scrunching up his eyes and peering into the shade of the tree.

A body lay curled up in the bottom of the ditch, his tunic covered in mud but, more disturbingly, blotted with dried blood.

Dried rivulets meandered down the slope in the gulley. The provost sergeant stepped up beside him, clutching the bound leather parcel, as yet still unopened. Varro glared at him in irritation, but the man ignored him and pointed into the ditch.

"My first question, captain, is whether you know this man."

Varro examined the body from the top of the bank, taking in as much detail as he could. The body was dressed in a plain and basic military tunic and breeches, with no armour or insignia. A cloak of plain grey wool lay several yards away up the gully, shredded and stained with mud and blood. Though the face was hidden from view by the body's position, lying where it had either fallen or been thrown, the ruffled brown hair and skin colour were decidedly nondescript.

The cause of death was plain, though. Six holes in the man's tunic spoke eloquently of the vicious stab wounds the man had suffered. In Varro's professional opinion just two of those wounds were fatal alone, so the attacker had been unnecessarily violent. It was one thing for a soldier to die in the height of battle with an enemy spear through his middle, but ambushed and viciously murdered and left in a ditch for the crows was a bad end for any man.

"Can I see his face?"

The sergeant gestured to one of his provosts and the man clambered down into the ditch, along to where the body lay and carefully turned the torso so that the face was visible. His cheek and forehead were marked and cut from the stones in the ditch, but he was a young man, perhaps twenty years old, clean shaven and moon faced. Varro shook his head.

"I don't recognise him, sergeant. But then I see an awful lot of recruits as I'm sure you'll understand. Are these the people who found him?"

The provost nodded.

"They came to the fort to inform us. The man had done a search of the body when they found it and discovered this pouch tucked away beneath his tunic. They should have left well alone, but I'm satisfied their motives were good and they came straight to us, so I see no real reason to detain them. They told us everything they know and they live in the civilian settlement anyway."

Varro nodded.

"And so the next question is 'what was he doing here'?"

"Indeed," the sergeant nodded, withdrawing the leather package from his bag and proffering it to Varro. "Out of deference to your rank, captain, I'll let you read this first, but I will have to have it back and examine the evidence myself."

Varro grumbled and untied the thong around the outside. He carefully unfolded the case and straightened the paper within as Salonius and Catilina made their way across to him. His eyes flicked across the writing as he scanned down the short and obviously hastily written note.

He blinked.

Rubbing his eyes, he straightened the paper once more and squinted as though trying to see through the paper itself.

"What is it?" enquired Catilina quietly as she stopped before him.

Varro stared at the paper a moment longer and then let his arm fall by his side as he rubbed his temple and forehead with the other hand. He looked across at her, a somewhat bewildered look upon his face.

"An impossible letter…"

"What?" Catilina stepped towards him again. Reaching down toward the paper she was momentarily taken aback as Varro's hand twitched away, moving the letter out of reach. Wordlessly she gave him an appraising glance and decided not to push him.

"Not here," the captain muttered, "and not now."

As Catilina stepped back to join Salonius, the provost sergeant reached out his hand.

"Captain?"

"No."

The soldier ground his teeth and snarled through tight lips "Now, captain!"

"No, sergeant." Varro shook his head and folded the paper away inside the leather wallet again.

"Explain yourself, sir" The provost growled. His hand had, probably subconsciously, come to rest on the pommel of his sword. Threatening, however unintentional.

Varro fixed him with a hard stare.

"Not only is this personal, sergeant, it is also very, very confidential."

"I'm afraid I must insist, captain Varro."

Varro stepped back.

"You can insist all you like, sergeant, but you're not having this piece of paper."

The two men stood poised, staring at each other. The air around them almost tingled with the tension. Varro saw the other provosts striding up the hill to join their sergeant and noticed with some satisfaction that Salonius had sidled round and was almost by his side now.

"For Gods' sake!"

Both men started at the anger in Catilina's voice as she stepped between them, shattering the tension.

"Sergeant, you may have authority to make such demands, though I'm not sure about their viability in open areas outside military land. Varro, you may well outrank the sergeant, but you know that this is his job. Now the two of you need to saddle up and we'll all ride back to the fort. My father can decide what to do. I'm assuming both of you will submit to the marshal?"

The provost had gone slightly pale, though Varro would be willing to wager that was through frustrated anger rather than fear. Deliberately turning away from the sergeant to face Catilina, he nodded.

"I will submit to the marshal's judgement."

There was a long, irritated silence, and finally the provost growled "I too" through clenched teeth.

As Varro and his companions returned to their mounts, the sergeant barked orders at his men, his eyes never leaving Varro. Two of his men gathered up the body and laid it carefully across the back of one of the horses.

Taking advantage of the delay, Varro, Catilina and Salonius mounted up and began a brisk walk back toward the fort. As soon as they were far enough away for Catilina to deem it safe, she leaned slightly in her saddle.

"Care to tell me what that was about now?"

Varro glanced back quickly to see the impatient sergeant hustling his men along.

"As I said: an impossible letter. " He frowned. "A letter from an impossible source… or a lie."

"Varro…"

"It's from my cousin Petrus."

Salonius frowned. "Why is that so strange, sir?"

Varro took another quick look behind him and saw that the provosts were hurrying to catch up. He settled into the saddle and growled.

"Because Petrus has been dead for a decade now."

As the party rode slowly in through the gates of the fort, two of the provosts peeled off from the group and made for the hospital with the body of the unfortunate soldier. The sergeant exchanged quick words with another of his men and as the rider trotted off ahead, he pulled alongside Varro and eyed him suspiciously.

"My subordinate has gone ahead to arrange to meet with the marshal and the prefect."

Varro nodded.

"Good for him."

The whole party continued on in silence along the busy main street of the fort, though all the occupants hurriedly shifted out of the way of a senior officer and a noblewoman in the midst of a group of provosts. Two minutes later they reined in at the side of the headquarters building, where the other provost stood waiting. As they dismounted, he remained expressionless and at attention and followed in behind his sergeant as they entered the building. Members of the marshal's guard joined them inside the doorway and escorted them through the colonnaded courtyard and through the main hall, into the main room where Sabian sat at a wide oak table with prefect Cristus on his left.

Salonius came to a halt next to the captain and scanned the room quickly and subtly. It was rare that anyone other than an officer or a guardsman saw the inside of the prefect's office. Office was perhaps an understatement. The room was large enough to mount and fire a catapult in. Bright light streamed in through large leaded dormer windows high in the roof some twenty five feet above him. The floor was decorated in a mosaic depicting the Imperial raven, and maps and trophies adorned the walls all around. To a soldier who'd spent most of his time in a shared barrack block, the effect was quite breathtaking.

"Sergeant." A curt acknowledgement of their presence from Sabian, who was busy studying paperwork on his table, drew Salonius' attention back to the reason for their presence.

Sabian glanced up and Varro assumed he was not the only one who saw the anger in the marshal's eyes or heard the irritation in his voice as he said sharply "Catalina! Join me."

For a moment Catilina looked as though she might argue, but in the end good sense won her over and with a quiet "father," she walked across the room and took the free seat to her father's right. He gave her a quick look that Varro couldn't see, though he was sure he knew what words that look conveyed. Then the marshal pushed the ledger away from him and sat back.

"Sergeant, what's this all about?"

The provost stepped forward.

"Sir, three locals came to the gates this morning to inform us they had found a body. The father, whose name…"

"A succinct version if you please" barked Sabian. Varro sighed. Catilina had clearly put her father in a sharp and uncooperative mood.

The sergeant shifted uneasily.

"They found the body of a soldier in a ditch around a mile away. He'd been stabbed six times. The locals had quickly searched the soldier for any identification and had discovered a sealed leather wallet addressed to Captain Varro. The captain visited the body with us and had confirmed that he does not know the soldier in question, but now refuses to relinquish the item back to the provosts."

"Is this true, Varro?"

The captain nodded.

"You know, captain, that in matters of military law, the provosts have the right to seize and withhold what they consider to be evidence. You may outrank the sergeant, but his authority is clear."

"Ordinarily, sir, I would agree," Varro stated clearly. "However, I feel that in the circumstances, certain aspects need to be considered before I'll agree to let this go."

"What aspects?" Sabian was beginning to look annoyed.

Varro drew himself up straight.

"If I said the wallet was connected with Petrus, would you expect me to relinquish it, sir?"

Sabian sat back heavily.

"Petrus?"

"Yes, marshal."

Sabian waved his hand dismissively at the provosts.

"Sergeant, this is no longer your issue. Take your men back to barracks."

The sergeant blinked in surprise, and then cast an angry glance at Varro before saluting, turning on his heel and marching from the room, followed swiftly by his provosts. Sabian frowned at Varro and the captain cleared his throat meaningfully.

Sabian rubbed his brow wearily and then turned to the fourth army's prefect.

"Cristus, would you be so kind as to allow Varro and myself a little privacy."

The prefect nodded sharply and stood, striding quietly from the room, though Varro couldn't help glimpsing the irritation on the man's face as he walked past the two men standing in the centre of the room.

"Sir?"

He turned to his side and realised that Salonius was awaiting the order to withdraw.

"No, Salonius. I need you to stay here."

Sabian glanced briefly at Catilina and then beckoned to the captain. The room suddenly seemed remarkably large and empty with only four occupants. Varro nodded at Salonius and the two soldiers approached the table. Varro fiddled with the tie on the leather wallet.

"You remember Petrus, sir?"

As Sabian nodded, Salonius cleared his throat.

"Sir, if you'll pardon the question, who is Petrus?"

The marshal leaned forward over the desk and cradled his fingers.

"Do you know the story of your prefect and the defence of Saravis Fork, soldier?"

Salonius nodded respectfully. "I know the story, sir. And Petrus?"

"Was my cousin," Varro stated in a flat voice.

Salonius turned and blinked in surprise as the captain faced him and continued.

"My cousin, and the senior sergeant in Cristus' cohort. We were the same age and both served under the marshal when Velutio ruled, along with Corda. But by the time Cristus pulled back from Saravis Fork, he'd lost three quarters of his men. Petrus had died in the siege."

Sabian turned his gaze to the young soldier by Varro's side.

"Your captain came to see me on Cristus' return. He requested permission to take a scouting party out to the mountains to look for survivors; to look for Petrus, I suppose. I turned down his request. Cristus was already being commissioned to lead a punitive campaign."

He coughed and reached out his hand towards Varro.

"I assume you have no objection to me reading this note."

"Of course not, marshal. There's not actually much to it, but... well I gather you've heard my news?"

Sabian let his hand fall to the table, and patted the rough wood reflectively.

"I have. I was intending to come and see you this afternoon to talk about it, but events seem to have run away with us."

"Well, sir" Varro continued, "I'm fairly sure someone within the fortress is behind this and, given that, I'm doing my best to keep anything that might be remotely relevant under wraps."

The marshal leaned back.

"You fear you have been poisoned by one of our own men?"

"I have reason to believe so, sir. I'm not sure of how all this ties in yet, sir, but I'm pretty sure it does. I was wounded in battle, as you know, but the wound was inflicted using a fine imperial blade coated with poison, albeit wielded by a barbarian. The sword seems to have vanished like a morning mist, but I intend to find it. It's the only connection I had to my enemy... until this morning."

Sabian nodded. "You think someone tried to kill you to prevent you receiving this?"

"Yes sir."

Varro reached out and placed the package on the table.

"Have a look, and I think you'll agree."

Sabian leaned forward again and slowly unwrapped the thong, opening the wallet and smoothing out the paper flat on the wooden surface. He scanned down the brief missive. Scrawled in an almost childlike script were the words:

. . . .

Varro.

I realise this will come as a shock to you, and you will find it hard to believe this is me, but it is true. I am alive. And I am safe. But the same is not true for you.

I urge you. I beg you to meet with me as I have the most dangerous information to share with you. I am at the civilian settlement outside the Saravis Fork fort, in a back room of the inn.

Tell no one, but hurry. It is vital that I see you.

Petrus.

. . . .

Sabian looked up at Varro.

"I see your point. I assume you intend to go?"

The captain nodded.

"Then I'd best send an escort" the marshal said. "Dangerous territory up there. It may be Imperial land, but far too close to the border for comfort."

Varro shook his head.

"No, sir. Considering what's happening, I'm considerably safer on my own than with anyone from the military. Salonius here can ride with me."

Sabian sat back for a moment and then nodded his agreement.

"I suppose so. I assume you intend to leave quickly and quietly?"

"Yes sir. I thought tonight, while it's dark. We'll need time to get supplies together, and I'll have to go see Scortius and get some more medication. It's three days to Saravis even at the fastest pace we can hope for, and I'm on a finite timescale."

He turned to Salonius.

"I trust you'll come along?"

"Of course sir," the young man straightened slightly. Varro faced the marshal again, tapping his finger on his lower lip.

"I'll need to speak to Corda about the sword too."

Sabian stood and waved his hand gently.

"You concentrate on getting ready for the journey. I'll speak to Corda and we'll find your mysterious sword, Varro. And I want updates whenever something happens."

He bent to one side and reached into a heavily bound chest, withdrawing a small bag, which he cast onto the table. It landed with a clink and sagged to one side. Varro raised an eyebrow.

"Around forty corona. Use it wisely. It should buy an awful lot of loyalty from the commoners en route and you can hire some couriers to apprise me of any changes or anything you think I need to know."

Varro reached out and grasped the heavy bag of coins, tying it to his belt for safety.

"I am grateful for your support in this, marshal. It makes a great deal of difference having someone I trust here; there are so few at the moment."

Sabian smiled. "We've known each other a very long time Varro. You know I value good men. Now get going and sort things out. And bear in mind that I want you back here in one piece. I shall be making it absolutely clear to Scortius that he's not to give up on you. Just because no one knows of a cure doesn't mean there isn't one there somewhere."

With a bow, Varro turned and strode from the room, with Salonius at his heel. Catilina watched them go and then turned to her father to find him looking at her with an unreadable expression on his face. She felt involuntary tears well up.

"What is it, father?"

The marshal smiled and gripped her arm reassuringly.

"He'll be back, my dear. And if there is a cure, be certain Scortius will find it. I shall make sure of that."

She smiled weakly.

"It all sounds like a conspiracy. Murders and poisonings and messages from dead people. Not trusting your own men. That's how you used to describe the civil war…"

The marshal nodded sadly and stared past her at some invisible point in the air.

"Strangely, that's how it feels. Makes me wish Caerdin was still around to sort it out. He had that kind of corkscrew mind. I think in too straight lines for intrigue. Fortunately, Varro's clever and resourceful and he remembers the old days too."

Scortius tapped his fingers absentmindedly on his forearm as he stared at his dispensary cabinet with its shelves and compartments stuffed with strange herbs and extractions.

Varro sat impatiently on the bench with Salonius at his side. Glancing round the doctor's office that occupied but a small part of the fort's hospital block, he took in the low, wooden beams, the plain whitewashed walls with a strained hint of pink, the utilitarian wooden floor and the scrolls and charts pinned to most of the open surfaces depicting strange and unpleasant visceral body parts with informative labels. He cleared his throat and opened his mouth to speak, but Scortius waved a hand irritably without turning and made 'tsk' sounds. Finally the doctor found what he was looking for and withdrew a small muslin bag. Tipping a small quantity of powder into the mortar, he ground it into the existing mixture.

The two visitors waited, the captain tapping his fingers on his knee irritably. Scortius returned silently to his shelves and began to peruse them once more. After what felt to Varro like an hour, the doctor located a small bottle of something oily. He held it at an angle above the bowl and watched one of the viscous seeds slide down the glass and drop into the mixture.

"Right," he said as he began to grind once more. "This is your last-ditch mixture."

With a satisfied air, he tipped the mixture in a waterproof bag and carefully tied the top off. Turning back to his visitors, he marked the bag 'III' with an inked stylus.

"So," he announced in a businesslike fashion. "The big bag with the 'I'?"

Varro looked down at the first bag he'd been given almost an hour ago.

"'I' is three times a day, every day regardless of circumstances."

Scortius nodded. "Conditions?"

"Got to have eaten before hand and have something to drink afterwards."

"And effects?"

Varro shifted like a scolded student.

"Symptoms only?"

Scortius' jaw firmed up.

"Not all symptoms, Varro. Three times a day and that'll keep your mind clear. It's purely for your mental state and your wakefulness. But I will warn you right now, the poison's setting in deeper every day. Even with the best medicines I can give you, you'll gradually notice some deterioration in the brain. I've worked out a regime that should keep you going long after you'd normally be 'toes up'. You shouldn't really have more than a couple of days, but you might last two weeks or more on all this."

"You're such an optimistic man to be around, Scortius."

The doctor glared at Varro.

"I'm a doctor, Varro, not a miracle man. If I could cure death, my son would still be around."

The captain sat back and sighed.

"Alright then. The first is to keep me thinking and awake."

Scortius nodded and the captain handed the bag to Salonius, who carefully placed it in the saddle bag on his lap.

"The 'II'? Scortius prompted.

Varro lifted the second large bag off the bench and examined it.

"That's for the pain. Once a day; twice if the pain starts to get too bad."

"Details, man!" barked Scortius. "This stuff's here to keep you alive. You need to keep on top of it!"

"Erm…" Varro looked blankly at the bag.

Scortius reached down and swiped it out of his hand.

"Every morning as you start your day's activity. It's very strong. If you take it and then lie around for a long time the medicine will only affect a small part of your system, but will over-medicate and you risk bringing on a whole slew of new problems. You need to be exercising once you've taken it so that the stuff gets pumped round your entire body. Only that way will it get everywhere it needs to be at the right concentration."

Varro nodded unhappily.

"And..." the doctor went on, "if things get truly unbearable, and I mean unbearable, not if 'it hurts', you take a second dose sometime in the evening. And then you need to spend at least an hour doing enough to make your heart pump it round."

Varro nodded again.

"And the third?" he enquired. "You've not told me that yet."

He hefted the small waterproof bag as Salonius collected the second container from Scortius and put it in the saddle bag.

The doctor leaned back against the cabinet.

"Important. Very important that you remember this." He was clearly speaking to Varro, though his eyes fell on Salonius as he tapped his left index finger into his right hand to emphasise his words."

Varro and Salonius nodded in unison.

"This is one of the strongest mixtures I've ever put together."

Tap.

"That bag holds four doses only."

Tap.

"So make sure you take some scale to *accurately* measure exactly a quarter of that."

Tap.

"Don't take it within an hour either side of your other medicines."

Tap.

"Don't drink anything but water for three hours either side of it."

Tap.

"Don't let it touch an open wound."

Tap.

"And be absolutely sure to take no more than one dose within a day."

He finished tapping and folded his arms.

"And you." He glared at Salonius. "Don't touch it. That mixture misused could kill a healthy bear, let alone a human. It's dangerous for Varro, but then what's he got to lose?"

Varro stared at him but the doctor leaned over to the young guardsman.

"If he has too much, for any reason; or if he seems to be having a reaction to it; if there's signs of a fit or his skin gets a purple tinge to it, make sure he drinks pint after pint after pint of water. Flush him right through. Don't let him stop drinking water until he's pissed himself raw. Do you understand?"

Salonius nodded and Scortius turned back to the captain.

"Good job you've got this sensible lad with you. I have a feeling you'd be dead before you got to the village if he wasn't there to look after you.

"You haven't asked where we're going, Scortius? Aren't you a little curious, given my circumstances?"

The doctor sighed.

"Varro, I haven't got time to mess around. You've got things you need to do? Fair enough. Stick with my medication plan and you should be around long enough to do whatever it is and come back. In the meantime, I've got almost a hundred wounds to track and look after, some of which are life threatening, *and* the marshal's sent word that he wants to see me, so I'm going to be busier than ever."

The captain nodded and stood gently. Reaching out, he placed his hand on Scortius' shoulder and squeezed lightly.

"Thank you. I will be back, hopefully within the week. Look after the men."

The doctor smiled sadly.

"Don't I always? Now get out of my hospital."

As Varro turned stiffly and strode through the door, the doctor grasped Salonius by the arm as he rose to follow suit, hoisting the leather bag over his shoulder. He blinked in surprise and looked up.

"Look after him, young man. Make sure he's careful with that medicine and make sure he gets back to me. I've a few ideas I need to follow up on."

Salonius nodded, saluted and followed his commander out into the cold yet bright afternoon sun.

Varro tied the pouch tight and put it carefully away in the saddle bag draped across his knee once more. Using his index finger, he stirred the mug of lemon and water, mixing the powder thoroughly until fully dissolved, and then drained the contents in one long draught. He peered across at the window and then back at Salonius.

"I think it's time."

Salonius sighed gratefully. The two men had been packed and ready now for three hours waiting for darkness to descend before they made to leave. Slowly he stood, squared his shoulders and stretched hard. Deferentially, he stood quietly to one side to let Varro past and the captain stood, shouldering his bags.

"Salonius, there's something I've got to say…"

The young man raised his eyebrows but said nothing.

"I'm not a serving captain and you're not even serving in an official capacity at the moment. I'm relying heavily on you and you'll likely have to rely on me. We're not going to be in camps, among soldiers or anywhere where rank's going to matter."

"Sir?" Salonius looked unsure.

"I know it seems odd," the captain smiled, "but I'm Varro and you're Salonius and I think that's enough. No ranks. You're not a soldier right now, nor a guard or a bodyguard. You're my travelling companion. You understand?"

The young man nodded and grinned.

"Got it, sir."

"Knock that off!" the captain grumbled.

Still smiling, Salonius followed Varro out of the room, hefting his saddle bag over his shoulder in the same manner as the captain. The two stopped momentarily in the kitchen area to the rear of the house, where Martis stood holding out a bag of prepared food for them. Varro stopped in front of his body servant and smiled sadly.

"This is it Martis. I'll be gone for a week at least, so I doubt I'll see you again."

The stocky man looked up at Varro and cleared his throat.

"I do not need to rush away sir. I will await your return."

Varro's smile faltered for a moment before returning with a slightly forced look.

"I'm not going to be around much longer, Martis. You need to look for new employment. I've informed the fort commander that you have full control of my house in my absence. Stay as long as you need until you can secure a new position, and I've left a few months' wages in a secure pouch. You know where to look."

Salonius was surprised to see tears in the servant's eyes and straightened, realising he himself was close to showing far more unhappiness than was seemly. He stood quietly as Varro clasped hands with the servant and wordlessly turned, striding out of the door to the stable at the rear.

Salonius grasped the bag being proffered by the servant and nodded gratefully at him.

"I hope everything works out for you, Martis."

Casting a last sympathetic look at the suddenly frail looking man, Salonius turned and walked out into the late dusk breeze, across the small garden and into the stable. Martis had arranged for a fine chestnut mare for a very reasonable price from the settlement outside the walls. As an officer, Varro owned his steed, but that assigned to his companion remained the property of the cohort. Their efforts during the afternoon had been thorough, the horses laden with well balanced packs, all done within the privacy of the captain's stable.

As he entered, the captain was just fastening the straps on his saddle bags. He walked round the horse, tugging straps and pulling at bags to test the fastenings as Salonius attached his own saddle bags and made final checks. He looked over at Varro, satisfied with the results, and the captain walked over to the stable doors and peered through the narrow gap.

"Dark enough. Let's go."

The two men led their horses a couple of steps forward and Varro threw back the wooden beam, swinging the doors wide open. The street, as they'd predicted, was all but deserted. Most of the men were now off duty, relaxing in the baths or in their rooms, or making the most of their free time in either the fort's own bar or one of the less reputable drinking and whoring establishments in the civilian settlement.

The pair drew a few interested looks as, fully armoured, they led their mounts along the paved road between the officers' houses and toward the fort's west gate. Their exit had been carefully selected as the only road that passed between nothing but quarters, granaries and workshops, giving them the lowest number of personnel to encounter.

Varro eyed each man they passed with deep suspicion, though apparently unfounded. The few looks they drew were from the ordinary soldiery going about their evening business. Five minutes later they approached the gate with its burning braziers and torches and half dozen guards leaning on their spears until they saw a superior officer approaching and came hurriedly to attention.

The gates stood half open and would do until the evening guard came on duty and these men fell out. The guards saluted as they passed but made no move to question them. Such freedom was a novelty to Salonius, but then why would the guard be expected to question the authority of a senior officer leaving the camp. And then the two men were out in the night, the burning lights behind them making the darkness ahead seem that much deeper.

As soon as they were out of the circle of light from the gate, Varro gestured to his companion and the two of them mounted up and wheeled their horses at a right angle, away from the road and along the line of the fort wall, lit at intervals with braziers and patrolled by now distant shadowy shapes. Ahead the faint lights and brooding shapes of the civilian buildings stood out against the ever darkening skyline.

With another gesture, Varro directed them down the slope and behind a small knot of trees. Wordlessly, listening to the distant murmur of the men on the walls, they removed the crests from their helmets and slid them down into the open bags beside them. Then, removing the helmets altogether, they fastened the chin straps and hung them from the saddle horn in front of them before pulling the hoods of their cloaks up over their heads and drawing the woollen folds tighter around themselves. And no longer displaying openly their rank and position the two now mundane riders returned to the grassy slope and pressed on into the civilian settlement, between the houses and out onto the main north approach road to the fort.

The few figures wandering around in the open were entirely indifferent to the two cloaked figures trotting gently through the town, concerned as they were with making the most of their off-duty time, filling their free hours with cheap wine or beer, women of low moral virtue and games of chance. Reaching the end of the occupied area, Varro and Salonius began their journey north toward the mountains.

As they disappeared from view, shapes detached from the shadows cast by one of the fort's towers and trotted out into the night, taking the northern road at a leisurely pace.

Chapter Six

The sun rose slow and blood red over the hills to the east, casting a strange and eerie light across the plain, punctuated by the shadows of the lonely trees dotted about. The first hungry birds of the day called mournfully from the scant bushes and the undergrowth thronged with rustling creatures. The road from Crow Hill to the mountains passed through a number of native settlements and Varro and Salonius had passed through the first a little after midnight; the only sign of life, a dog barking at the passing riders from behind the gate of a farm.

And now, weary from a long night's ride, Salonius turned his heavy head to the captain and cleared his throat. It had been a strangely quiet night, the two men remaining almost entirely silent throughout by mutual unspoken agreement. Now, riding in the ever brightening sunlight, the quiet seemed less necessary.

"Captain?"

"Varro" the captain reminded him.

"Yes, ok… Varro?"

"What is it, Salonius?"

The young guard shifted slightly, his stiff and achy bones clicking as he moved.

"Are we intending to sleep during the day and ride at night? I'm getting a little tired now."

Varro shook his head.

"I think now that we're this far out, we'll keep going today and stop for the evening." He pointed ahead and Salonius followed his gaze to the distant peaks and the valley snaking up ahead of them, too far yet to pick out any details.

"The valley," Varro said, "is a clear place to stop. There's a village near the entrance with a good inn and we should reach it late this afternoon, allowing for a couple of breaks today to rest and eat. More important, there's an Imperial way station about an hour's ride up the valley from the village and given our position, I really don't want to end up waylaid there. We can stay at the inn and eat there and set off several hours before dawn tomorrow. I want to use the darkness to get well clear of any watchful eyes."

Salonius nodded. Whoever was behind all of this had one officer poisoned and a soldier stabbed. Caution would seem to be the order of the day.

Varro glanced across at his travelling companion and raised an eyebrow.

"Think we should stop and have a break for something to eat then?"

"Oh yes, Varro. I certainly do."

The captain grinned. "Come on then."

Stretching as much as his saddle allowed, Varro steered his horse off the road toward a small enclosure formed by a horseshoe of thick undergrowth and a grassy bank dotted with rabbit burrows. Dismounting in the little dell, they tied the horses to the sturdiest branch of a young elm growing on the edge of the undergrowth, and rummaged in the saddle bags for more of the food packed lovingly by Martis yesterday.

Varro grasped a bag of meat cuts and cheeses and half a loaf of bread and wandered over to a protruding boulder, drawing his belt knife and the bag of Scortius' medicine as he went. Salonius dug deep into the bag, trying to locate a shy bag of fruit. As he worked his fingers between the tightly-packed contents of the bag, the tip of his tongue protruding from the corner of his mouth, he stopped sharply, ducking his head.

"What's up?" Varro called from his seat a few yards away.

Salonius slowly raised his head and peered around the greenery of the small elm.

"Not sure." He raised his hand to shelter his eyes from the glare of the sun. The land was flat for several miles and the early morning sun was burning off the night's dew, creating an eery blanket of pale mist across the fields and streams. Shapes emerged before his eyes, at first glance riders or monsters, which quickly resolved into the shape of harmless trees or large bushes. He sighed and shook his head.

"Nothing. Seeing things. All this riding and no sleep, I suspect."

By the time he turned, Varro was already standing beside him.

"Don't be too quick to dismiss your instincts, Salonius. I had a feeling several hours ago that I saw someone keeping pace with us about half a mile away. If we've been followed all the way from Crow Hill, they're at their most vulnerable today. Tonight they could get to the way-station and send messages if they needed. But at this point they're still too far away from any Imperial outpost. I think we'd best be moving on as soon as we've had a bite to eat."

The younger man frowned.

"D'you think we should try and make it out of the valley unseen and come round the other side of the hill?"

"No point," Varro shook his head. "They obviously know we're here and, unless they saw you duck down, our biggest advantage lies in them not knowing that we know about them."

"Good point. On as though nothing's out of the ordinary then."

The two men sat in thoughtful silence for a few minutes munching on bread and cheese until Varro realised that his companion was watching him with interest.

"What?"

"I can't understand it, sir."

"Can't understand what?" replied the captain patiently.

"Why anyone would want to kill you, I mean." Salonius shuffled nervously on his rock, aware that he was treading dangerous ground. "The high command respects you, the other senior officers all like you and defer to you, you've got the most loyal junior officers in the army and your men love you, sir. I know the engineers are the most isolated and shunned unit in the army, and even the engineers respect you. So who would do this?"

Varro gave a weary laugh.

"If I knew that I don't think we'd be in this position, but I'm afraid I'm probably just a casualty of something a lot bigger than me."

"Your cousin's message" nodded Salonius. "That soldier was killed to prevent the message reaching the fort and you were…" He faltered for a moment. "What happened to you was for the same reason. So…"

"So whatever's behind all this has something to do with Petrus and the Saravis Fork fort. And that means it's possible that prefect Cristus is tied into this somehow, given his connections with Saravis Fork. But we can't rule out anyone just because there's no obvious connection. Whatever you say, I've made a few enemies in my time."

Salonius sat back and folded away the remains of the cheese and meat.

"Well I suppose we'll find out more when we get there."

The two men stood and packed their saddle bags once more, keeping a surreptitious but keen eye out on the landscape as they did so. There was no further sign of movement and the early morning mist was beginning to burn off, leaving verdant green stretching away to the distant hills. Untethering the horses, they mounted and navigated their way out of the undergrowth, back onto the road.

The miles passed by quickly and quietly as the sun climbed steadily higher, picking up a warmth that had been absent the previous day. The sporadic birdsong gave way gradually to a day filled with chirruping, the hum of bees among the flowers by the road, the distant sounds of lowing cattle and other farm noises, and the steady crunch of their hooves on the gravel of the road. Conversation had been occasional and brief, both riders acutely aware of their surroundings and taking pains to notice any and all movement within sight while apparently remaining oblivious to any observer.

As the sun had passed its zenith and begun the slow descent toward the hills and the western ocean, the pair stopped at a ruined barn and consumed a few more chunks of bread and meat in a sheltered and defensible position. Once again finishing their meal and packing away the remains, Salonius was withdrawing his hand from the bag when Varro grasped his hand and pointed out of a window, the glass long gone, frame rotting and sill covered with ivy.

"Look there!"

Salonius followed the direction and spotted two figures on horseback. The riders were perhaps half a mile distant, visible where they'd broken cover of the few sparse trees. There could be little doubt of their unsavoury intentions, given the fact that they moved so swiftly and surreptitiously across open countryside parallel with the road. He squinted but could make out little detail other than their being covered with dark cloaks.

"They're getting ahead of us. Perhaps they lost us?"

Varro shook his head. "They know exactly where we are. They're just taking the opportunity while we're busy to cover the open ground quickly so they can get back in cover and wait for us to pass."

"Then we go on as normal?"

"Yes," Varro nodded.

"What do you plan to do about them?" the young man asked as he tied the thongs on the saddle bag.

"I've been thinking about that. I think we'll have to deal with them tonight. The village is a crossing point for the valley road. It's the only bridge across the river and the water up there's quite fast and deep. The riders could theoretically go round, but it's a little precarious in places and not something you'd try in the dark."

"So they'll have to go through the village?" Salonius frowned.

"Likely. If it were still light they could get ahead round the hillside and off to the Imperial outpost, but then they'd lose track of us, so I think they'll stay within sight. That means we need to slow down slightly. I want to reach the inn as it gets dark, so that they're forced to either cross the bridge where we can see them or camp down somewhere this side of the village."

The young man smiled.

"And whatever they do, we'll know where they are."

Varro nodded.

"But tonight I think we'll probably have to take care of them. I want to get a closer look at who we're dealing with here."

The two mounted up once more and rode on toward the village nestled between steep, protective hillsides and pierced by a swift young river pouring down from the mountains.

Their pace slowed barely noticeably, and Varro and Salonius first caught sight of the village as the last arc of the sun disappeared over the valley side, plunging the floor into gloom. The valley was surprisingly narrow at this point, two rocky spurs jutting out from the hills and almost meeting like pincers. In the gap lay strewn a collection of buildings, mostly constructed in northern Imperial style with a dark grey stone base reaching as high as the windows, surmounted by timber uppers. Some houses consisted of only a single floor, that being the favoured style of many of the northern peoples, but here and there some buildings also had an upper floor like the townhouses and apartment blocks of the more southern Imperial cities. Through the centre of the village flowed the river, not wide, but deep and fast, filling the valley with a background roar.

Salonius took the opportunity to cast a glance behind him but saw no sign of their pursuers. In fact they'd not seen them for several hours now, and the young soldier was beginning to worry they'd gone ahead through the village already.

There were few signs of life as they approached the outermost buildings. These were farms, the continual sound of roaring water now joined with the bleating of sheep and the squawking of chickens in their enclosure. The two men rode slowly across the narrow stone bridge and squinted ahead. Darkness had descended swiftly since the sun set and the grey stone and dark oak constructions loomed as deeper shadows within the gloom. A few houses showed signs of flickering lights within. Tallow candles, Salonius thought. Oil was expensive this far north and a poor hill-farming village would be unlikely to have a regular supply.

The inn stood overlooking the central space of the village, a green with a constantly flowing spring from a boulder pile that fed a small stone trough before trickling down a runnel and into the river. Salonius smiled appreciatively as he took in the welcoming sight of a large, well lit double storey building. The door was of the stable variety, separated into upper and lower panels. The lower was latched shut; the upper standing open and casting a welcoming yellow glow onto the dark ground outside.

Wordlessly the two men dismounted and led their horses to the door. Varro handed the reins to his companion and went inside, disappearing from view for a couple of minutes as he approached the bar. Salonius stood quietly holding the reins, taking the opportunity to look around in a bored fashion and observe his surroundings. The bridge was narrow and of stone. There was little hope of any rider crossing it quietly, so Varro was right. Unless their pursuers had taken the chance to get ahead this afternoon, they would have to stay in the valley for the night, presumably close enough to be able to keep an eye on the village and their quarry. So long as he and Varro alternated sleep they could watch the bridge easily from the inn. He smiled.

"Over here!" Varro's voice called from around the side of the building.

Salonius led the horses at a walk around the building and to the stables where Varro waited with a boy in an apron. The stable hand reached up and took the reins, while the two guests collected their various bags and important belongings from the saddles, after which he led the horses to their accommodation for the night. Varro and Salonius watched him disappear, noting where their mounts would be stabled, and then strode in through the side door, into the inn. Varro stopped by the entrance and spoke to his companion in a hushed voice.

"I've arranged a room at the other side of the inn; the direction we entered the village. I'll explain when we're up there."

The two swiftly passed through the warm, welcoming bar and trotted lightly up the stairs to the rear. At the end of the corridor, Varro stopped and fumbled with a key until the lock released with a click and the door swung open. Salonius crossed the room and dropped the bag on the floor before approaching the window and peering around the side of the frame into the darkness beyond.

The window looked out over the bridge and into the distance down the valley. The advantages of the view were clear. Varro joined him and pointed at an angle down the alley at the inn's side. Salonius peered into the shadowy space and noted the low wooden roof of an outhouse only a few feet away: an easy exit without alerting any of the inn's patrons. He smiled.

"For an unnoticed start in the morning?"

Varro nodded and dropped his kit next to the other bag.

"That and more. As soon as we're settled, we're going out to find our friends and see what they're up to."

The moon was high but partially obscured by scudding clouds as Varro and Salonius slid the table bearing their dirtied dinner plates away from the window and the captain climbed through, surprisingly nimbly, Salonius thought, given both his age and his current state of health. As the younger man approached the window ready to follow suit, he saw Varro swing from the sill and land with a soft thud on the gently-sloping insulated wooden roof of the outhouse.

Salonius climbed through and swung across to the roof quietly and dextrously, landing in a crouch. He glanced down into the alley to see that Varro had dropped lightly to the dirt floor. Following, the young soldier joined him in the shadowy street. Quickly, the pair dusted themselves off and unwrapped the linen scarves they'd bound around the hilts of their swords to prevent unnecessary noise during the descent.

"Are we taking the horses?" he asked in a hoarse whisper.

"No," Varro replied squaring his shoulders. "Too noisy. And they'll be near enough to see the inn, so they can't be far beyond that farm. Follow me."

Salonius nodded and the two moved softly to the rear of the inn. Ducking around the back of the next house they could see a short alleyway that led to a patch of darkness from which came the sounds of rushing water. Taking a deep breath, Varro jogged quietly down the alley and to the bank of the river. Clearly too far to jump and too fast to wade or swim, the only crossing point would still be the bridge. Turning the corner once more, they made their way along the river bank towards the bridge.

"Do you think they'll be watching it?" Salonius whispered as they came to a halt a few yards away in the shadow of the last building.

"Definitely. Certainly one of them will be awake."

"So what's the plan?" the young man queried.

"We've a choice. Least visible route is to climb along the outside." He pointed to a very narrow lip where the tile bonding layer jutted out of the grey stone. "It'll be dangerous, 'coz there's not much of a lip and it's bound to be slippery. The alternative is we take the chance and run across."

"And hope they're looking away at that point? Bit risky."

"The side it is, then" agreed Varro.

Another deep breath in preparation and the captain darted across the small space to the bridge, ducking below the parapet and grasping the capstones tightly. With a last glance back at Salonius, Varro began to shuffle slowly along the side of the bridge with gently scraping noises that were almost completely drowned out by the rushing water.

The young man watched with some trepidation, his breath held and his heart pounding in his chest. He almost jumped out into the open as he saw Varro's foot slip on the narrow lip and for a heart-stopping moment the man hung above the torrent by his fingertips before regaining his hold and shuffling along to the safety of the far bank. As he dropped silently into the long grass and climbed up the bank, he waved across to Salonius.

The young soldier ducked across the gap and dropped down the bank, grasping the top of the wall. With a grunt, he began to pull himself across, relying mostly on the strength of his arms and using the tips of his toes on the ledge mainly for balance. In what felt like hours, yet was really only moments, he reached the far bank and dropped gratefully to the grass next to Varro. The older man slapped him quietly and encouragingly on the shoulder and paused long enough for the pair of them to get their breath back.

With a deep breath, he gestured to Salonius to follow and moved along the outer wall of the farm.

"We'll head round the back and out of the village that way. They'll be concentrating on the inn, the bridge and the road, so we should be safe."

Salonius nodded and joined the captain, slowly creeping along the wall. Somewhere nearby a dog barked and both men stopped for a tense moment before moving on as quietly as possible. A few minutes later they had rounded the back of the farm and were picking their way between a hen run and a rickety wooden shed with slats missing. Passing the last of the net fencing, they reached a gooseberry bush that provided the last cover before open ground.

The two men stopped and scanned their surroundings. Varro turned to face his young companion.

"If you were wanting somewhere to camp down unnoticed and get a good view of the bridge and the inn, where would you be?"

Salonius squinted into the darkness. The valley side was a steep grassy slope, pockmarked with rabbit warrens and punctuated with small rocks. Where the slope began to flatten out was a collection of large boulders that would be perfect were it not for the view was too restrictive to be of use. A wide area of open grass used for grazing goats would offer no protection. Close to the road was a small copse. It would be uncomfortable to camp in, certainly, but offered both cover and a clear view. Across the road much the same land stretched away to the bare slope of the valley side. A messy wooden structure stood in the open ground amid a wide circle of churned mud. He couldn't see it from here, but remembered passing it on the way into the village. A cow byre.

"Two possible locations, sir" the young man frowned. "The copse and the shed."

"Which one, though?"

Salonius shook his head uncertainly. "Could be either. The copse'd be uncomfortable, but no one's going to come across them there and they've a good view. The shed would be warmer and more comfortable, but there's the possibility of the farmer finding them."

Varro nodded.

"But it's night time. All the farm animals are safely tucked up in their beds. Can you hear a cow?"

"No." Salonius frowned. "You mean they've killed all the cows?"

"We're talking about people who've killed at least an officer and a courier. Do you think they'd baulk at removing a farmer and a few cows?"

The young man peered into the darkness, trying to take the measure of the building.

"So what do we do now, sir?"

"If they're watching the bridge and the inn then it's unlikely they can see the rest of the valley. We head to the rocks, then round the trees and down the valley a way before we cross the road and come up behind the shed from the other side."

Without waiting for acknowledgement from the young soldier, Varro jogged quietly and swiftly away from their cover and disappeared in the gloom around the pile of boulders at the foot of the valley side.

His heart beginning to beat faster once more, Salonius followed suit, sprinting and keeping low. Though it had seemed such a distance when he first looked, he reached the boulders in mere moments and disappeared among them, panting. He found the captain also wheezing and clutching his side, leaning on one of the larger stones.

"Are you alright, sir?"

"Hurts a bit. I'll have to dip into the medicines when we get back to the inn."

Without further comment, he took several deep breaths, pushing back his shoulders, and then strode out from the boulders. For several hundred yards their movements would be hidden from the cow byre by the trees and once beyond that they would be far enough away to be masked by the darkness itself. Salonius followed once more, falling in alongside the older man and noting unhappily the way Varro held his side as he walked.

"If the moon comes out from behind the clouds we're going to be a lot more visible," he noted. Varro shrugged.

"If the moon comes out we just have to drop to the grass and wait for another cloud."

The two walked on for a while in silence until Varro judged that they'd gone as far as they needed to, and then as quickly and lightly as they could, they slipped across the road and ran across to the relative cover of the undergrowth on the valley side. Once among the low scrub, they stopped for another rest, leaning forward with their hands on their hips, breathing deeply.

Varro looked across at Salonius and shrugged. The young man nodded and the two began to move toward the byre, now a vague, looming darker shape amid the greater darkness. They moved slowly and carefully. There was little chance the occupants would be watching anywhere but the village, so speed was of far less importance than silence. Picking their way between the scratchy, rustling plants as quietly as possible, they edged closer and closer to the barn, the rough planks from which it was constructed gradually becoming visible in the gloom.

Salonius regarded his superior, three steps ahead, with a worried look. It was clear that all this sudden exercise and movement had stirred up trouble with the captain's wound. Perhaps it had even opened up once again and he could be bleeding to death as they moved. Salonius wouldn't be able to tell until they reached a patch of light. The state of Varro added to his collection of concerns as he moved. What if the cows had been locked up somewhere else and the barn was empty. Where would they look then? What if their pursuers had already gone ahead and were at the Imperial way station? What if, and this one had been nagging at him all afternoon: what if these men turned out to be innocent? Or even allies?

He realised his pace had slowed and he was gaining distance on the captain out ahead.

"Damn it" he muttered under his breath and picked up the pace a little. It was no good surrendering to doubt now.

By the time he'd caught up with Varro, the two were mere yards from the shed. At least one of his fears was allayed as they ducked across the open space, the mud fortunately dry due to the recent lack of rain. As they crouched by the wall of the barn, Salonius could hear the murmur of hushed conversation within. He strained to hear more, but the detail was still indistinct. There were clearly two men talking in very low tones.

Varro shuffled silently along the wall to where low flickers of yellow light shone out through a hole in the boards. He peered through and then beckoned Salonius to join him.

Inside the barn were two men. One, lying on a rough bed of straw, was wrapped tightly in a blanket with a saddle blanket rolled up beneath his head. The other sat at the barn's window, gazing out toward the village in the distance. He was dressed in rough tunic and breeches. Not a military uniform tunic, but that of a civilian, yet on the belt fastened round his waist was a solid Imperial military sword. A quick glance back confirmed that a second sword lay next to the reclining man, within arm's reach. Salonius craned his neck to look further back into the byre and noted with distaste the source of the smell wafting gently through the window. Half a dozen cows lay in various positions to the rear where they'd been led and, without a moment's thought, had their throats cut. Salonius felt unaccountably queasy.

Varro nudged him and pointed to the watcher and then tapped himself quietly on the chest. With two fingers making a walking motion, he mimed moving around the shed to the window and then lightly patted his sword. Salonius nodded his understanding and pointed at the door of the barn. The large door was held shut with only a length of twine, designed, as it was, to be shut from the outside. He mimed cutting the twine with his blade and then pointed at the reclining figure. Varro nodded agreement and held out his hand. Salonius grasped it and shook once before slowly and quietly drawing his sword. Varro did the same and, with a single nod, began to creep slowly and quietly around the wall.

Salonius sloped off in the opposite direction, to the door. There were cracks around the door and he'd have to be careful not to be observed. He took up the best hidden position where he could see the tied twine through a crack which would be wide enough to thrust his sword through. His heart racing, he sought another crack and, finding the best, quietly waited, watching the man at the window. Irritatingly, now he was somewhere he could hear, they'd stopped talking. With bated breath he waited.

His first sign that Varro had made a move startled him. There was an unpleasant 'crunch' and a faint squawk from the man at the window. Even as Salonius thrust his sword between the planks and severed the twine with ease, he watched with fascinated horror as the man at the window slumped slowly backwards and fell to the floor, a gaping hole where his eyes had been and a multicoloured slick of unpleasantness pouring from the wound. He twitched for a moment, gurgling, as Salonius pulled the door open. Varro had appeared at the window now, a grim look of determination on his face and his sword running with the man's blood.

The man lying wrapped in a blanket had grasped his sword and was coming to his feet quickly, his eyes flickering between the messy corpse on the floor and the vision of bloodlust at the window. So intent on Varro was he that he never noticed the door swing open behind him and never saw the stocky young soldier leap across behind him, his sword raised high.

With a grim smiled, Salonius brought down the bronze pommel of his sword hard on the very top of the man's head, knocking him unconscious instantly. The man slumped to the floor.

Varro glared at him.

"You think we've time to take prisoners?"

Salonius shrugged defensively.

"I'd rather know who they are before I kill them, sir."

Growling, Varro rounded the wall of the shed and stormed in through the door. As he leaned down and wiped his sword on the dead man's tunic, he glared up at his companion.

"You think they're innocent men?" he barked. "They're in civilian clothes with no insignia or sign of rank. Yet they're armed like soldiers and following us. You want more?"

Salonius stood silently.

Varro kicked the fallen body.

"This one I don't know but I think he might have been one of the provosts from Crow Hill."

He pointed at the unconscious man.

"That bastard, on the other hand, I know. I know the face. He's one of the prefect's guard."

Salonius shrank back from the force of the captain's anger. Varro walked over and pressed his finger into Salonius' chest.

"You brained him; you carry him."

"Yes, sir."

Sheathing his sword, the young man bent down and lifted the unconscious soldier easily, slinging him across his shoulder. As he settled his burden more comfortably, Varro collected the saddle bags from the pile in the room and shouldered them. With a single angry glance at Salonius, he strode purposefully out of the shed and toward the road that led to the bridge.

The young man hurried after him, giving a worried glance back at the interior.

"Sir?" he called as he jogged to catch up.

"What?" barked Varro furiously.

"What about the mess. Shouldn't we hide the body? And find their horses, sir?"

Varro stopped dead and Salonius almost fell over him. He turned and pointed back at the barn.

"Firstly, if you'd been more aware of your surroundings and less worried about the ethical consequences of what you were doing, you'd have seen that the farmer was lying gutted in the back of the barn behind the cows. No one's going to find that till tomorrow morning; afternoon probably. We'll be long gone by then."

He started to walk again, slowly, and Salonius strode alongside, a contrite expression clouding his features.

"Secondly: we don't need their horses. We've got our own, and I've got their saddle bags. There'll be nothing at the horses that we could use."

He glanced sideways at the younger man.

"Thirdly, you have *got* to stop calling me sir!" He sighed.

Salonius smiled weakly.

"I'm sorry. It's hard. Years as a soldier and these things become ingrained. You know that? I'm finding it hard to stop. Whether you're with the second or on your own, you're still a captain. You're still my superior, and it's wrong."

Varro opened his mouth to speak, but Salonius plunged on.

"I know I've got to. I know we need to be as unobtrusive as possible at the moment and that 'captain' and 'sir' draw attention, and I *am* trying. Time will change things."

"That's part of the problem, Salonius," Varro groused. "I'm running out of time. Every hour that passes for you brings you closer to promotion, or retirement. You might end up owning an inn like that." He pointed across the bridge at their destination.

"That's what I always planned. But every hour that brings you closer to your future brings me closer to a hole in the ground."

He stormed along in silence, his head bowed as he crunched along the gravel leading up to the bridge. There was no need for subtlety now.

"I'm sorry."

The captain turned to Salonius.

"I'm sorry," he repeated. "I'm dealing with this, but sometimes it feels hopeless."

Salonius gave what he hoped was a supportive smiled.

"What you're doing matters. What *we're* doing matters. We're fated for this. The Gods themselves set us on this path and who can argue with the Gods. And the future's unknown to us, for all the Gods might read it. My sergeant says that Scortius is the best doctor in the whole army. If there's a way to cure you, he'll find it. But we've got to pursue this; get to Saravis Fork and find your cousin. If whatever this is is so important people will kill to stop it, then we need to find it."

Varro looked down at his companion and finally his brow unfurrowed and a smile passed briefly across his face.

"You put a lot of faith in this Cernus, don't you?"

"With respect," the young man replied with a grin, "it's because of the Stag Lord you found me. When you were wounded you wanted something to drink. On the way to the hospital tent you must had passed more than a hundred men; sergeants, engineers, archers, infantry and medics. How many of those men know Cernus?"

Varro blinked.

"Perhaps a handful," continued Salonius. "And of that handful of men who'd heard of Cernus out of the hundreds around you, how many do you think had stood in his presence?"

"I never thought of that" replied the captain, blinking again in surprise.

"Fate. Gods. A path." Salonius smiled. "Cernus blessed you because there is something you have to do. Something really important." He grinned. "And because you couldn't do it alone, Cernus blessed me and sent me to you. These events have been rolling forward since before I even joined the army."

Their voices lowered a little as they entered the village square. The light still shone from the front door and window of the inn. It felt like midnight to the two men who hadn't slept in two days, but in truth it was still only mid evening.

"I need a drink." Varro grinned.

Salonius frowned at him.

"Not if you're taking that strong medication though."

"I'll forego that and just take the normal medication and a little of the hard stuff from the shelf behind the bar."

The two of them dipped into the alley beside the inn and Varro looked at Salonius and pointed to the body slumped over his shoulder.

"I'll climb up to the roof and lift him from there."

"Ok." Salonius shifted the weight slightly and stood still, his legs slightly apart, braced ready. Varro grasped a wooden plank that projected slightly from the wall of the outbuilding and hauled himself onto the roof with a grunt. Salonius took the opportunity to study the captain's side as he did so and was surprised to see no blood. Perhaps he was worrying too much about the wound. Bracing himself further, he lifted the body to the roof level and felt the weight lift as Varro grasped it and heaved it onto the roof. A casual whistle caught his attention and he ducked back into the shadows next to the outbuilding, his eyes darting to and fro searching for the source of the noise.

A figure, whistling happily and weaving a drunken path, wandered into the alley from the front of the inn. Salonius held his breath and watched in morbid fascination as the man entered the shadows near the alley entrance and fumbled with his trousers before urinating, mostly on the wall of the next house, but partially on his own feet.

"Bollocks" he muttered as he shook his foot, tying his trousers tight once more. Still shaking the piss off his foot, he left the alley without looking back and started to walk across the green. A moment later and he was gone from sight, the only sign of his presence a distant happy whistle.

Heaving a sigh of relief, Salonius stepped back away from the wall and looked up to see Varro convulsed in a fit of silent hysterics, rocking back and forth. Grinning, the young soldier grasped the plank and pulled himself up to join his captain.

Varro wiped his eyes, burst into muffled laughter again and the stopped with a deep breath. "Precious. Absolutely precious." Clapping his hand on Salonius' back, he reached across from the roof and grasped the windowsill. He hauled himself up, still facing Salonius, and braced himself in the frame.

"Alright. Pass him up."

Salonius stretched with a grunt, thrusting the unconscious body towards the window. Varro grabbed him by the shoulder and hauled him up, swearing under his breath.

"Heavy bastard, this one."

As the body came through the window and Varro was suddenly relieved of the heavy weight, he fell backwards into the room, collapsing to the floor on his back to find himself staring up into eyes shining with curiosity.

He started suddenly and, as his eyes adjusted to the room's darkened interior, found himself staring into the smiling face of Catilina.

"What the hell are you doing here?" he demanded. Behind him there was a scraping noise as Salonius pulled himself through the window and dropped down next to the body where he crouched, staring in surprise at the lady sitting on the edge of the bed.

Catilina looked down at the captain.

"You can't possibly think I was going to let you trot off on your own. Even with your ever-present guardian there."

Varro sat up, shaking his head.

"Your father's going to be furious with you. He'll never let you leave Vengen again. Shit, he'll have me pulled apart by horses when he knows you're with me!"

Catilina sighed and her eyes twinkled mischievously.

"Let me handle father. You know I can. Besides which, he's so busy with everything going on at Crow Hill, he's probably not even noticed I've left yet." She looked at Varro's expression and put her finger on his lips as he opened his mouth, squeezing them gently shut again.

"Just don't bother trying to dissuade me. You know it won't work, so why waste both our time. If your cousin is alive, we're going to see him. Besides," she smiled at him, "if this is some military conspiracy, don't you think I'm safer here than among thousands of potential enemies at the fort?"

Varro stared at her in a mixture of panic and admiration. He was used to dealing with conflicting emotions when it came to Catilina. He also knew that she was right. Once she'd made up her mind, nothing would change it. Not Varro; not her father; probably not even the Gods themselves. Besides, what would he do, send her back on her own? Safer to keep her with him until he returned from Saravis Fork. Safer. Safer away. "Cristus' guard!"

"What?" Catilina stared at him.

"Your father." Varro said, slapping his forehead.

"What are you talking about, Varro?"

"If the prefect's guard are following me and killing farmers, then there's a good chance the prefect himself is involved. And if that's the case and your father's investigating this, every day he stays in Crow Hill, surrounded by Cristus' men, he's in danger."

Catilina narrowed her eyes.

"The men following you are Cristus'?"

"One certainly was. I know his face well." He crouched down and rolled the unconscious body over so she could see his face. "This man had lost money to me in dice games. He's definitely one of them."

"And the others?" Catilina asked, staring into the peaceful face of the unconscious man.

Salonius stepped into the centre of the room.

"Excuse me, my lady, but you knew about them. And what do you mean 'others'?"

Catilina sat back and stretched.

"I saw them leave the fort; four of them all cloaked up and secretive. I've been a mile or so behind them all the way. They're not particularly observant."

"Shit!"

Varro turned to Salonius.

"There's two more somewhere. They could already be at the way station up the valley."

The young man nodded and pointed at the body near the window.

"I suspect our friend will know where they are."

Varro pushed his shoulders back and rubbed his side.

"Well he's not waking up in a hurry. Get him tethered and gagged. Make sure he's absolutely secured and push him under the bed. I doubt he'll wake til the morning anyway, but I don't want to lose him."

He turned to Catilina.

"I think we need to talk. Can I buy you a drink?"

She flashed him a devastating smile.

"It's been a long time since you've said that, my little rabbit."

Varro smiled for a moment and then noticed Salonius grinning in the background.

"And you can stop smirking and get to work on him. When he's secure, come downstairs and join us. I'll get you a drink in."

"With pleasure, sir."

Varro glared at Salonius and then turned to escort the lady in her travelling clothes down the stairs to the bar.

Chapter Seven

Adana awoke feeling unusually sore and disoriented. What had he been drinking last night? He tried to reach up to touch his sore head and realised something was dreadfully wrong with the world. His surroundings slowly swam into focus and it took a moment to realise he was upside down and swinging gently back and forth. He squinted at the figures in front of him. Ah, yes…

Varro grasped the stick he'd been idly tapping his leg with and held it out to stop the man swinging.

"I'm afraid you might be in a little trouble here, my friend."

Next to him, Salonius smiled nastily.

"Care to tell us a little about yourself?" Varro asked in a friendly, sing-sing voice as though speaking to a difficult child.

"Who are you people?" the dangling man asked innocently.

Varro smiled happily and swung the stout, young, green stick he'd been holding at the man's head. The impact made him yelp and left a long red line across his cheek and temple.

"Some bad things have happened to me recently," said Varro in his happy tone, "and this is really beginning to lighten my day. In fact, I daresay the longer you hold out, the happier I'll get!"

"I have no idea what you're talking about!" The man hanging from the tree finally became aware that he was cold and struggled to lift his head enough to see his body. He was naked. "What are you doing with me?"

"Oh, the naked part? That's entirely unnecessary and gratuitous, I'm afraid" Varro laughed. "I just wanted to humiliate you a little. Now tell me who you are."

"My name's Marco. I'm a smith from…"

He was interrupted with another sharp thwack from Varro's switch and yelped again. A sore red line crossed his chest. Varro leaned forward grinning.

"You can skip the most blindingly obvious lies. I can't remember your name but I think it starts with an 'a'. I know you're in the prefect's guard and I know you have appalling luck at dice. How's about you come clean, or do I get to have more fun?"

The man coughed, shaking on his tether.

"Ok, I'm one of Cristus' guard. And yes, my name's Adana. We were sent by the prefect to keep an eye on you. Rumours have reached him that you're on to something important and he sent us to protect you."

"Indeed." Varro grinned and gave a sharp flick of his switch, leaving a nasty line across the man's hip. "Damn. I was aiming for somewhere delicate there but you moved."

"Hey!" the man shouted in pained panic.

"Come on" cajoled Varro. "You haven't even asked about your provost companion who you know damn well I left dead back in that barn. We're not stupid, Adana. Just irritable and armed!"

He gave another swipe, this time across the buttocks and much harder than before. The switch came back down by his side glistening and a drip of blood dropped from the end to the dirt. The man shrieked.

"I've got so much more energy in my arm," grinned Varro, "I could go on like this for hours."

Catilina stepped into view.

"Varro, you may be having fun, but that's all. He's a professional soldier, like you. And a good one, if he made it to the prefect's guard. You need to step this up."

Varro raised an eyebrow. Catilina cleared her throat.

"Adana, tell us where the other two are."

The dangling man frowned. "Other two?"

With a sigh, Catilina crouched down by the undergrowth at the side of the road and broke off a length of sharp, woody plant stem. With a look of concentration, she gritted her teeth and broke the foot-long stem into three pieces. Reaching down under the bemused gaze of Varro and Salonius, she retrieved Varro's belt knife and used it to cut the ends of the three pieces at an angle. As she sheathed the knife again, she shrugged.

"My father made it a rule at Vengen that all ladies needed to be taught how to defend themselves, given the fact that there are such a large number of off-duty soldiers there at any given time, and not all of them are gentlemen. I watched the first class and decided that being able to trip someone up and bite them wasn't good enough. I asked my father's adjutant, Captain Cialo, and he and Mercurias came up with a diagram of what they called pressure points. It's quite fascinating, really."

Catilina held two of the sticks in her left hand and grasped the other tightly in her right. Slowly, she turned the hanging man so that he was facing away from then and crouched down. With one slender, immaculately manicured finger, she traced the line of muscle running from below his ear to his shoulder. Almost teasingly, she stopped half way along and drew a line inwards towards his spine with her nail. A couple of inches in, she stopped, and with a forceful thrust, pushed the sharpened end of stem into the man's muscle. He screamed and jerked around on his rope like a fish on a line.

Salonius' eyes widened and Varro grinned, as the blood started to run in a slow stream down along his neck and into his hair, Catilina gave the end of the stem, sticking out of the flesh, a little tap and then turned him back to face them. The man's eyes were scrunched up tight, tears streaming up his face.

The elegant lady smiled at him.

"Adana, I would very highly recommend you start answering Varro's questions. There are more than a hundred pressure points. I can only remember thirty or so, and we'll run out of points before we run out of sticks, but you really don't want to get that far."

The man shook his head defiantly, his mouth clamped shut and his eyes closed tight.

"Don't say I didn't warn you, soldier."

She turned to Varro. "Care to have a go?"

"Don't mind if I do," he replied lightly. "Where next?"

She spun the dangling figure round again and pointed to a spot on the back of the man's leg, just above the knee. "That's a good one."

Varro nodded, stepped forward and drove the stick in to that spot, point first. The man screamed again.

As Varro turned him around once more and stepped back, he held out the third stick.

"Salonius?"

"Thank you, but I won't. Fascinating to watch though."

Catilina grasped it.

"Time to stop giving him time to breathe and recover. Salonius, cut some more sticks."

She stepped forward and used her fingers to locate a point next to the tendon above the man's heel. Pausing only long enough to take a breath, she drove the stick in, accompanied by new shrieks of pain.

As she returned to Varro's side, she smiled at the weeping soldier.

"Salonius: hurry up with those sticks, I'm getting bored."

Varro gave her a sidelong glance.

"You can be a frightening woman, Catilina."

She shrugged. "No one stirs up trouble for my father. And no one hurts my friends."

She grasped the switch and ripped it out of his hand. Varro momentarily saw the tear trickle down her cheek before she stepped forward and began lashing the man repeatedly with the green rod, causing lines and welts and streams of blood to pour down the man's chest and into his face. It took a few moments to realise that the man was babbling in a panicked voice, amid sobs and the repeated smacks of the rapidly-disintegrating cane.

"Salonius!"

The young man looked up at Varro and saw Catilina thrashing wildly at the man. As Varro stepped forward, grasped the switch and gently, but forcefully removed it from her hand, he turned and led her away, across the grass. Salonius walked over to the babbling man and, crouching down, began to talk to him, all the while grasping a few more sharpened sticks as incentive.

Varro turned Catilina to face him and threw his arms around her shoulders. She buried her face in his chest and began to cry, clutching him so tight he tilted his face upwards and took a deep breath.

"It's alright Catilina. I sent two separate riders back to Crow Hill this morning telling your father he's not safe and that he needs to head back to Vengen."

She shook her head without pulling away from him.

"And I told him you were with me and safe," he added.

"No..." she said, muffled from within the folds of his tunic.

"Don't worry" he replied. "They were well paid and promised a lot more when they deliver. And there's two of them. They'll make it."

"But that won't help you" she shouted, her voice thick with a mix of anger and despair, still muffled by his tunic.

He opened and closed his mouth a few times, unable to find the words he felt he really needed, and finally closed his eyes and held her as tight as he could, as though he'd squeeze the hurt from her. Slowly her sobbing subsided and he loosened his arms. He smiled down at her; a strange smile.

"That was most unlike you."

She gave him a weak smile in return.

"Sometimes you just have to get it out of your system, Varro. Sometimes if you hold yourself together tight you crack like a new pot that cooled too quickly. Soldiers let their emotions out through violent behaviour and debauchery, both of which are frowned upon in a lady."

Varro laughed.

"Whoever said that never saw you with a pointy stick!"

He became aware that Salonius was standing patiently some distance from them, facing tactfully away and apparently studying some point on the horizon. Gently pushing Catilina away from him, he pointed at his young companion. Catilina nodded and, as she wiped he eyes and pinched her cheeks, the two of them wandered over to Salonius.

"So what'd he have to say?" the captain asked casually.

"Nothing too good," the young man turned to face them. He looked troubled. "He says the four of them were sent after us by Cristus. Their orders were to observe us and report back until we reached the way station. After that their orders were to 'deal with us'. The way he said it suggested to me that this is very much 'off the books'. Kill us and dump the bodies somewhere they'd never be found; that kind of thing."

"And the other two?" Catilina queried.

"Already ahead of us and waiting at the post, ma'am."

"That does it then" Varro snorted. "We can't get too close to the place. If the two of them have orders to take us, then they're going to have the garrison of the way station on their side."

"Why's that?" Salonius frowned.

The captain sighed.

"We're on personal business. I currently hold no active rank, you're not officially on the cohort's command guard lists, and the garrison won't be able to identify Catilina. Those men, even if they're perfectly innocent, have absolutely no need to take orders from us or even trust us. You can be pretty sure the two men waiting for us there have letters from Cristus giving them complete authority over the local garrisons. That's what I would do if I were the prefect."

"Then we find another way around" stated Catilina.

"I'm afraid not, my lady," Salonius shook his head and Varro nodded his agreement. "The only reason for an outpost here is because it controls the only viable route."

The captain turned to his companion.

"Unless, that is, you know of anything, being a local…"

Salonius shook his head,

"My home's a good forty miles from here. I don't know these valleys."

"Then there's four choices," Catilina held up her hand and counted off with her fingers as she spoke.

"One: You attack the way station. I don't know how many men they hold, but I presume you do. Very dangerous, but at least you have the initiative and surprise on your side."

She folded down her first finger.

"Two: we ride like the Gods of the underworld are after us and try and just get through on pure speed."

Her second finger folded.

"Three: We sneak up there and just try and get round. We could wait for nightfall for extra cover. The safest way, certainly, but also the slowest."

Folding down the third finger, she tapped the fourth.

"Lastly: we ride up there as bold as iron and try and bluff our way through. If it fails then we either have to fight our way through or ride as fast as the winds will carry us. Either way, the chances aren't good."

Salonius and Varro looked at each other for a long moment and the younger man shrugged. "That's about the size of it, sir. Little or no chance any which way."

Varro's brow furrowed in thought.

"I have number five though." He smiled and tapped her remaining finger. "I can't put you at risk on some mad charge or crazy chase, but we can't afford to waste an entire day here. I'm on a limited time frame. Catilina, I want you to stay here with the horses.

Get them well away from the road, completely out of sight over by those trees and stay there until Salonius and I get back."

She frowned, but nodded her agreement. Salonius kicked at an errant pebble.

"What will we be doing?"

"Distracting. Come on."

Salonius followed him back to the dangling soldier, now silent, blessedly unconscious, though still breathing. Varro pointed at him.

"Cut him down and bring him along."

With a look of uncertainty, Salonius drew his knife, cut the man down and threw him across a shoulder before turning and following the captain away. Varro stopped for a moment and smiled at Catilina.

"We'll be back in less than an hour. Stay out of sight."

"Be careful" she stated flatly.

Answering with just a smile, the two soldiers with their prisoner strode across the grass and away from the secluded knoll. As they made their way to the road and the village came back into sight, Salonius stopped.

"We're going back to the village?"

"Yes."

"With him?"

"Yes."

"After all the trouble we had getting him out without being seen?"

"Yes."

Salonius stared in amazement at the captain, continuing on ahead, and then hurried to catch up.

"But why?"

Varro smiled grimly.

"He's going to be useful. We need to give his friends a reason to leave the way station."

Salonius frowned. He had a horrible suspicion about what was about to happen but, try as he might, he just couldn't think of a better alternative. He started to feel increasingly uncomfortable as they entered the village, passing the outlying houses at the opposite end to where they'd first arrived. But the discomfort he felt heightened as he noticed villagers staring at him lugging a body along the road. The fact that the two men were clearly well armed would deter most ordinary folk from questioning these frightening strangers, but whatever Varro was up to, he'd have to hurry or things could turn ugly very fast.

The captain pointed at the small grassy area beneath the three beech trees in the centre of the village.

"Drop him there and then go pick up his friend and anything of theirs you can find in the barn. Be quick."

Salonius flashed a quick, worried glance at his companion and then nodded and allowed the unconscious man to fall unceremoniously to the turf. Whatever it was that Varro had in mind, Salonius was pretty sure the man wouldn't be walking away at the end of it. As he walked off, he deliberately avoided looking at both the captain and their prisoner. He shut his eyes tight as he heard the captain's next words, then opened them and picked up his pace as he crossed the bridge toward the outlying farm buildings.

"You!" Varro turned and pointed at a group of half a dozen concerned spectators gathered outside the front of the inn. In other circumstances it might have humorous the way the individuals in the crowd automatically shuffled away from the finger, leaving a startled man leaning on a cane in the centre of a widening circle. The man gave Varro a frightened look and spoke, his voice shaking.

"Yes, sir?"

Varro shook his head in irritation.

"Somewhere in this village there are ropes, nails and a hammer. Find me them."

The man turned his head left and right briefly, casting helpless looks at the crowd around him, none of whom met his eye. Quivering slightly, he picked up his stick and turned toward the house next to the inn.

Varro moved his finger and pointed at a young woman nearby.

"You go with him and make sure he finds those things for me. I don't like to be kept waiting, and I'm not the world's most patient man."

As the woman turned and rushed after the absent man, Varro turned to see a lone figure standing across the green. Where the deep, narrow river briefly widened out into a pool, probably used for washing clothes, a fence with a gate had been erected, presumably to prevent children and animals falling into the rushing water. Leaning on the fence was a large, heavy set man with a drooping red moustache and a shiny bald pate, dressed in a huge leather overall. A blacksmith, clearly. And watching Varro with something akin to anger and visibly no fear at all. The captain smiled. Could be trouble; could be useful.

He waved a hand to the smith and wandered over.

"I need a hand to take a rail off this fence. Top rail only; it'll still stop children and animals drowning."

The big man glared at him.

"I have no interest in helping you, brigand!"

Varro smiled unpleasantly.

"I'll let that one pass. I'm no brigand and, as always, what I do is for the good of the Empire." He reached the fence and stood next to the blacksmith, considerably shorter, gazing up at him with a flinty look. His voice dropped to a low growl. "You *will* help me. If you do it without comment, we'll be on our way shortly. You wouldn't want to cause an 'incident'!"

The big man glared at him for a while and then nodded slowly.

"You give me your word you'll move on quietly and not come back and I'll do what I have to in order to speed you on your way."

The two men locked eyes for a moment and then Varro nodded. He gripped one end of the fence rail preparing to heave and blinked in momentary surprise as the large smith casually tore the rail form the fence, accompanied by the tortured shriek of stressed iron nails. He turned with the long piece of wood and walked back across the green.

As the two of them walked, Varro noted with interest the way the smith's grip on the rail changed momentarily. With a smile, he ducked down and drew his belt knife. Even as the smith swung the huge rail at head height, Varro was underneath it and stood once more with the tip of his blade pressing very gently into the big man's side by his kidney.

"Last warning, friend. Go stand with your neighbours." He pointed to the growing crowd outside the inn.

Grunting, the smith dropped the rail to the grass and walked angrily away to join the throng. Varro looked around, stretching his shoulders and neck. Shame about this. Good people these, and the captain disliked looking needlessly cruel. Still, there were greater issues here.

Across the bridge, he saw the stocky figure of Salonius emerge from the cow byre, a body slung over one shoulder and a bag over the other. Back near the inn, the man with the stick and the young woman had reappeared from the house and were milling around at the back of the crowd, blending in. Varro dropped his head and smiled to himself, but then put on a fierce visage as he raised it again and used the knife to gesture to the man.

"Nails! Rope! Hammer!"

The man came hurrying nervously and jerkily with his stick as a third leg around the edge of the crowd with a small bag. He reached the green, stepped nervously around the body on the floor and stopped a few yards from Varro, holding out the bag with a terrified look in his eye. Varro smiled at him, trying not to look too fierce.

"I'm not here to hurt you. Drop the bag and go away!"

The man needed no second telling, scurrying across the grass, barely allowing his stick to touch the ground. Varro hid his smile as he removed the hammer and a long nail from the bag. Picking up the rail, he rested it against the tree at shoulder height and hammered the nail deep, driving it home until it protruded only half an inch and then bending the excess over. Collecting another nail, he grasped the other end of the rail and lifted it so that it rested at shoulder height on one of the other trees. With three efficient strokes of the hammer, he repeated the process. In short order he drove two more nails into each end for good measure and then tugged at and leant on the rail, testing the weight. Satisfied, he stepped back and examined his makeshift frame.

Behind him, panting with the effort, Salonius arrived with his burden.

"Are you sure this is a good idea, sir?"

Varro grunted.

"These men accepted the risks when they signed up. As far as I'm concerned, and you too, they're enemy combatants, spies and assassins. They deserved to die, don't you think?"

"I suppose so, sir, but I can't say I like it."

"Neither do I, Salonius, but sometimes you have to do things you don't like. Sometimes it's our job as officers to be harsh and unyielding for the greater good. And we're not hurting an innocent here."

Salonius nodded and let the mangled corpse drop to the floor. Dropping their kitbag next to the captain, he wandered over to the unconscious prisoner and grasped his wrists. With a deep breath he hauled on them and dragged the body across to the new construction. He glanced briefly at the now surprisingly large crowd outside the inn.

"I realise you're trying to create a distraction, but I'm not sure how this is going to work?"

Varro nodded. "They'll need a little prod, but keep watching. Now lift them up so I can tie them on."

Salonius hauled the body up to the level of the rail and the captain tied the wrists to the wood. As he let go, the faceless, visceral body dropped and sagged, the legs dangling at uncomfortable angles to the floor. Reaching into the bag at his feet, he drew out two more nails. Placing one between his teeth, he held another over the man's wrist, between the two bones and hefted the hammer.

Salonius looked away and ground his teeth, wincing as he heard the first thud. With open sympathy, he began to heft the unconscious man. Another two bangs. He paused and waited without looking. He heard the second nail being positioned and three more bangs. Taking a deep breath, he turned to the grisly scene, lifting the unconscious prisoner to the bar. While the whole idea of what they were doing repulsed him, the captain was right and he knew it. These men deserved this; they deserved worse than this in truth, and Varro was doing nothing needlessly cruel.

He forced himself to watch as the captain tied the man's wrists to the rail. With a glance at the crowd before the inn, he realised that he had to appear as invested in this as the captain. He reached down to the bag and withdrew two nails, grasping the hammer. Varro raised an eyebrow.

"My turn" Salonius rumbled, looking distinctly unhappy. "I assume you've got a speech ready?"

Varro nodded.

"Then go speak" the young man said, holding the nail in position over the wrist. Gritting his teeth, he swung the hammer. Of course, Varro's victim had been dead for quite a few hours and had bled mostly dry. This was a whole different matter. He made sure he stood to one side, grateful that he'd taken the opportunity to give the man a heavy blow to the head on the way over to the tree. Though he wasn't quite dead, the chances of even agony waking him now or ever again were very small. Continuing his grisly work with a professional concealment of his true feelings, he concentrated on Varro's voice and allowed himself the bliss of detaching himself from his work.

"You think we are brigands or murderers. But even out here at the frontier, there is justice in the Empire."

He waited a moment for his words to sink in and then continued.

"These two men are traitors. They have betrayed not only their own unit, but the army and the people of the Empire. I have seen first-hand evidence of their involvement in corruption, murder and intrigue and their fate is clear under Imperial law. As a captain in the fourth army it is my duty to carry out that punishment."

He turned to see Salonius standing back, the blood-soaked hammer hanging in his blood-soaked hand, an unreadable expression on his face. Bending, he retrieved a sword from the kit. He turned, made sure the crowd was watching and then slowly, deliberately, and with great force, drove the blade through the chest of the hanging man. With a sigh he let go of the hilt and left the sword jutting out of the chest of its former owner.

Salonius shuddered and let the hammer drop, speaking in a quiet voice, unheard by the crowd at the inn.

"Are we done? Did we achieve anything?"

Varro nodded.

"While you were busy, I saw three men disappear off up the road toward the way station on horseback. I suspect in an hour or more this village will be filled with panicked guardsmen and two very angry conspirators. We need to get back to Catilina and get ourselves hidden."

The young man nodded and, leaning down, wiped his hands on the grass, taking the opportunity to look up subtly and observe the crowd around the inn. There was a tense silence as the population of the village hovered nervously between the dangers of confrontation and the consequences of inaction.

"Which way?"

Varro nodded toward the road and, stretching, began to walk.

"Same way we came in, bold as iron. Nobody's going to follow us after that. They'll just be glad we left."

Salonius fell in alongside him and tried to keep his face impassive and stare straight ahead as they passed the villagers. As they passed the last house he felt a little of the tension drain from his back and, despite willing himself not to, his pace picked up a little until the pair of them had rounded the first bend in the road and the village had disappeared from view.

"We'd best get off the road," he said, glancing ahead with some trepidation, expecting to see riders bearing down on them round the next corner.

Varro shrugged. "Should have at least a quarter of an hour yet, even if they tried to break their horses."

The pair walked on. Despite Varro's casual comments, Salonius noted that their pace picked up considerably as they rounded the corner. After perhaps half a mile of dusty road, they recognised the small village boundary stone that marked their departure point. Taking a deep breath and a nervous glance up the road, Salonius stepped on to the grass and held up his hand to ward off the thin branches snapping back at his face in the captain's wake.

On springy grass without the constant crunch of gravel beneath their boots, all the sounds of a summer morning flooded in and filled their ears. Birdsong, the buzzing of bees, the splashing of the fast, narrow river in the middle distance and the occasional scurrying noise in the undergrowth all combined to send a flood of calming relief through the two men as Varro finally pushed through the last branches and broke out into the clearing where Catilina sat on a rock. The reins of the three horses were tied to a branch behind her, while she, herself, sat with a hefty Imperial blade between her fingers, point-down on the grass. Salonius raised his eyebrows as he recognised the blade from his saddle. For some odd reason, the lady seemed perfectly natural and happy bearing a heavy military blade.

Varro smiled at her and turned to Salonius, pointing up the slope at the side of the valley.

"Can you climb up there as quietly as you can and find somewhere to hide? As soon as you see horses, get back down here fast."

Salonius nodded and strode across the clearing.

"But for Gods' sake don't get seen coming back down!"

The young man made an affirmative noise and began to clamber up the bank beyond the small knot of trees. Varro wandered across the clearing and sat on a stone near Catilina.

"Shouldn't be long; then we can get going up toward Saravis Fork." He cleared his throat. "I've been thinking; it's dangerous to come back this way, but I really can't see an alternative. There's no Imperial road other than this. I believe there are native trails but even then it could take weeks to get back down. Are you sure you want to risk this? Going to the very border of the Empire and maybe even getting trapped there?"

Catilina nodded and patted him on the wrist in a soothing manner, idly spinning the blade on its point with her other hand.

"I'm quite sure, Varro."

"But…"

"You don't understand" she stated, cutting him off. "It's been a long time since we were together, but you knew I'd wait, surely? I knew you would. There'd always be time for us to be together again, but now…"

Varro lowered his head and Catilina smiled sadly.

"I don't know whether we've got six months or two days. If Scortius is the genius they say he is, we may even have many years. However long you've got, you're spending it with me. On that point there's no give!"

Varro looked across at her and grinned.

"Who does know how long they've got eh?"

Salonius burst through the leaves and ran out into the clearing, trying to arrest his momentum. Coming to a halt in the centre, he put his hands on his knees and breathed deeply, looking up at Varro and Catilina. The two were sitting close together with their hands on their knees. Catilina was smiling a genuine warm smile, while the captain appeared flushed and looked away momentarily.

Salonius grinned at Catilina.

"Hope I'm not interrupting anything my lady?" he muttered very quietly.

"Of course not, Salonius" she replied, almost in a whisper, her smile taking on a mischievous edge. "I take it we're moving?"

The young soldier nodded.

"They should be passing us any moment now."

"How many?" Varro enquired, professionalism once more taking over.

"I counted eight."

Varro nodded with satisfaction.

"Assuming they're a normal outpost garrison, there's only going to be two left up there." He reached up and started to untie his reins from the branch. "And I'm guessing that our two friends are among the riders coming down here we'll just have two lightly armed guards to deal with there."

Salonius reached out and grasped his own reins. He stopped for a moment and then put a finger to his mouth and cupped his hand around his ear. The others fell silent and listened intently. The drumming of hooves was deadened somewhat by the undergrowth between the open clearing and the road around six hundred yards away, but there were clearly several riders pushing their horses as hard as they dare.

Once the sound of the hooves began to recede and the riders were out of sight in the direction of the village, the three slowly made their way out of the bushes and onto the road. There was no sign of the horsemen passing bar the slowly settling dust kicked up by their passage. As they mounted and began to move at a brisk pace up the valley Salonius, with a troubled look on his face, cleared his throat and looked across at Varro.

"I can't do that again, sir."

"What?" Varro replied in confusion.

"I'm a soldier" he said flatly. "It's not fear. I'll fight the enemies of the Empire. I'll go into battle with no regrets, sir. But…"

"What?" the captain repeated, with a trace of irritation.

"I'll fight the Empire's enemies, sir, but I won't execute any more of its men."

Catilina raised an eyebrow and leaned across.

"I know Varro, Salonius. He won't have liked this any more than you, but those men were no longer soldiers of the Empire. They were prepared to kill us. That makes them fair game."

"Yes ma'am, I know. It's just... well I don't think a soldier should be required to torture or execute. That's why we have provosts."

Varro looked down for a moment and then fixed his young companion with a hard look.

"Sometimes you have to be everything from the accuser to the executioner. It's not a nice thing, but it's necessary. If you ever intend to make it as a sergeant or even an officer you have to understand that. It's not easy, and everything about you tells you it's wrong, but you have to push yourself past that and do what needs doing."

"You've done that before, sir?" Salonius asked.

Varro nodded sullenly.

"A couple of years ago we had a problem with supplies. We were campaigning in the mountains about thirty miles west of here and had to drop to half rations for a week or so, to eke out our stores. But the supply trains never came. So we had to drop further, to quarter rations. I sent a request to Vengen for extra supplies but things were almost as bad there."

The young man nodded and risked an interruption.

"I remember the time. Crop failures all over the north. The tribes were starving too."

The Captain smiled sympathetically. "It was a hard time for everyone. Finally we were on emergency rations for more than a week; not really enough to feed a dog, let alone a human being. The men were beginning to lose their fighting strength, but we couldn't afford to leave our position."

He grasped the reins tighter and shared a look with Catilina that Salonius couldn't see.

"Things just kept getting worse and the mood of the men got ugly. We started having to break up fights over food. We even had the occasional desertion, though why's beyond me. If the army had no food, why would a man think he could do better for himself? And then one night the camp guards caught three men stealing food from the commander's supply; from my supplies, you see. Well, it's not as though I had any more spare food than any other man; I was living on the same rations as them, but some men will always think their officers feast on a roast hog while they starve. The thieves attacked the guards when they were spotted and almost killed one of them before they were overcome."

He squared his shoulders.

"Well, what could I do? I know there were extenuating circumstances, but there comes a point when discipline has to be maintained, even at the expense of personal preference."

"What did you do, Sir?"

"We found out who the ringleader was; a promising young soldier called Terentius. He took responsibility straight away. Good man really. It meant he saved his companions."

Varro glanced across at his young audience and let out an explosive sigh.

"I had the other two beat him to death on the parade ground in front of the entire cohort."

Salonius lowered his eyes.

"It's all about discipline, Salonius" the captain added. "You sometimes have to make hard choices and do unpleasant things because, if you don't, you lose control and without control an army turns into a wolf pack."

Salonius nodded.

"I understand that sir; I'm just not sure whether I'd be able to do that."

"Then I hope you're never given the situation."

The young man continued to nod, grimly. "So what do we do when we get to the outpost? Those two men are probably entirely innocent."

"Relax" Varro smiled. "Catilina and I worked that out while you were keeping watch."

The way station was more of a small fortress than a simple outpost. Four walls roughly two hundred feet long enclosed two barracks, a commander's room, garrison office, a small granary and storeroom and a small house to provide accommodation for passing dignitaries, Imperial couriers or men of rank. The single, heavy gate was surmounted by a higher parapet. And yet this small fort seemed strangely quiet and empty as Catilina approached, the gentle breeze that flowed down the valley rippling the rough and basic cloak wrapped around her.

As she walked, she carefully kicked up as much dust as she could, to dirty her clothing and make herself appear more mean and poor than her clothes would normally suggest. Her arm was beginning to ache from the heavy bundle of sticks she carried awkwardly. The gate of the way station stood open, surprisingly. She narrowed her eyes and squinted through the dust she'd created. Two figures stood deep in conversation in the gate's interior.

Salonius and Varro had been careful to stay far enough back that there was no chance of being spotted from the station but, given the soldiers' lack of attention, they could likely have walked up to the gate before being seen. Still, while her father would have the men hauled over the coals for their ineptitude, she had no complaints since it all served their cause so well.

Finally, as she was little more than ten yards away, one of the men spotted her and held his spear point toward her menacingly.

"Who's that?" he barked.

"Sir…" she called back, hurrying, but giving herself a slight shuffling gait.

"I said who goes there?"

Catilina smiled inwardly. Varro had insisted that they'd need a signal, but she'd been sure he'd be able to tell when she'd arrived. She shuffled to a halt and waved her sticks as best she could."

"Magda… from the farm, sir!"

The spear wavered for a moment and the second man stepped out of the gate's shadow and into the sunlight.

"What do you want, woman!"

"Your men…" she broke into a grating cough that positively reeked of serious illness. Her mother had always said that if the family lost their wealth and privilege Catilina had a future on the stage. It was important to both create the right impression and to drag this encounter out as long as she could.

"What!"

The man was quickly getting angry. Balance was required. She couldn't afford to lose his attention, but she also could not have him run and fetch his horse.

"Your men… down to the village."

"What about them!" As the first man grounded his spear, Catilina tried not to smile. The other, more senior, guard reached out and grasped her by the upper arms. Over his shoulder, she watched Varro step like a cat from the bushes beside the fort and creep along the wall toward the relaxing guard's back. She looked up into the commander's eyes.

"Your men are in danger!"

"Why?" He swung his arm up to bring it down in a ringing slap, but at the apex it would not descend. He looked round in surprise and Salonius' face split into a wide grin.

"Morning."

The guard started to open his mouth, but the pommel of Salonius' sword thunked into the back of his head with some force and his eyes glazed over as he slowly collapsed. Salonius caught him by the arm before he could slump too far and lifted him, slinging him over a shoulder. The young man smiled at Catilina and turned with his burden to see Varro dragging the other man, unconscious, toward the gate.

As the two soldiers dropped their prisoners unceremoniously in the first building they found, Catilina searched the store and reappeared with a roll of twine. As she and Salonius busily set about binding the wrists and ankles of the two men, Varro stuffed bundles of cloth into their mouths and gagged them.

Finally the three stepped back to admire their handiwork and Catilina smiled.

"You do realise we've probably only an hour or so before those riders come back. We need to get a good head start."

Varro nodded.

"Leave that to me" he smiled as he ushered them out of the building and closed the door. "You go out and get the horses ready."

As his companions left the fort, Varro stopped behind them and closed and barred the heavy gate. Happy with the result, he ascended the staircase to the wall. Looking down the twenty five feet from the wall walk to the dust, he took a deep breath and swung his legs out over the drop. He heard Catilina draw a sharp breath and, smiling, lowered himself until only his fingertips clutched the wall and let himself drop.

"Let's get going. If we ride hard and through the night, we should be at Saravis Fork by sunset tomorrow."

Chapter Eight

They'd made excellent time. The high saddle of one of the most important passes in the northern mountains opened up to a grand and breathtaking sight. As the three riders and their exhausted mounts crested the high point and looked down, none of them could deny the astonishment they felt. The pass descended slowly and gently, becoming a wide but short valley, bisected at the far end by a spur of land, turning it into the 'Y' from which its name stemmed. A small, fast river ran from the left fork and off down the right, cutting through the centre of a large civilian settlement of stone and wood houses that nestled in the valley at the foot of the spur. On all sides the mountains reared up higher than those through which the riders had passed, protecting the valley from the worst of the weather and making it a haven of lush greenery amid the snowy grey.

And yet, given all this wonder and glory, their eyes were drawn inexorably up to the spur of land towering above the village and bounded on two of its three sides by a steep slope and a fast river. And rising like the Imperial Raven Standard itself, testament to the undying power of the Imperial army, rose the stone walls of the fort of Saravis Fork. Salonius whistled through his teeth as he studied the strong walls with the trained eye of an engineer.

"That got overrun by barbarians?"

Varro nodded.

"The Clianii were a big tribe, and I mean *big*. A cohort's a great fighting machine, but even ours wouldn't be able to hold that from an entire tribe of, what, ten thousand? And the Clianii weren't traditional barbarians. They weren't like the lot we fought the other day, all hair and teeth and bloodlust. The Clianii had learned from the Empire over more than a century. Hell, some of them had even served in our military. They knew how to build your machines, Salonius; machines that could batter those walls from across the valley."

Catilina nodded and pointed at the brooding walls of the fort.

"Cristus held that for five days against odds of almost ten to one. That's why my father likes him. That's why Cristus is your commander."

"How?"

Varro and Catilina turned to face Salonius, who was rubbing his chin thoughtfully.

"What?"

"How did he hold it?" The young man waved his arm expansively at the spur and the valley. "If they had catapults and bolt throwers like ours and the knowledge to use them."

"What do you mean?" Catilina frowned.

"Well without wanting to annoy you, sir," Salonius replied. "You're not an engineer. It looks like a heroic deed, I'm sure. But to an engineer it's quite simply impossible. If you gave me two catapults, I could have one of those walls in rubble inside a day. How does a cohort stand against ten to one odds for four days with no walls?"

Catilina stared at him and shrugged.

"Cristus told me the first time I met him, back at Vengen when I was about twelve, but it was such a self-centred tale of daring and heroism that I can't remember a word of it. Probably mostly lies. I expect we'll find out more when we find Petrus."

The three set off once more at a walk, Salonius with a perpetual frown and rubbing his brow with one hand, clearly troubled.

The road led down through slowly mounting scrub and greenery and finally apple trees and brambles thick with fruit. As they approached the civilian town, the fort on its great promontory became increasingly oppressive. The settlement was extensive, even for one gathered around such an important fort; almost the size of one of the towns of the southern provinces, complete with shops, a mill, granaries, large tavern, and even a temple to the Imperial pantheon. Farms dotted the two valleys as far as the eye could see. As they slowly descended the road to the town Salonius, his brow still tightly knit, glanced across at his captain.

"What sort of man is Petrus, sir, if you don't mind me asking?"

Varro raised his eyebrow and the young man continued.

"Well I think we can all agree that there's no reason to trust prefect Cristus in our current circumstances. And anyone he's got control over is therefore similarly untrustworthy."

"What are you getting at, Salonius?" Varro rumbled.

Catilina leaned forward, riding between her two companions and blocking the line of sight between the two brooding men. She turned her face to Varro.

"What he's skirting around asking you is whether we can trust Petrus. He has a point too, Varro."

The captain shook his head vehemently.

"Petrus and I are like brothers. Always were. Hell, he was the good and trustworthy one of the pair of us."

"He was also to Cristus what Corda is to you" Catilina said flatly. "They were closely tied, Varro. I'm not saying we can't trust him, but don't be distracted by blind loyalty. You haven't seen him in a decade. People change."

Varro continued to shake his head.

"I understand what you're saying, but you're wrong. Petrus served with me under your father. He was one of Sergeant Cialo's men on Isera. He was there when General Caerdin burned the villa and ended the civil war. You don't come with a better pedigree for trust than that. On Petrus' count, you're wrong."

"I hope so."

The three fell silent once more as they crossed the bridge over the fast and deep, clear, cold river and entered the town. Salonius, his face still dark with notions of conspiracy, looked left and right as they passed the first outlying buildings. Varro and Catilina watched him with interest, paying no attention to the occasional locals glancing at them from doorways or windows.

"What *is* it?" Varro finally snapped with a despairing sigh.

Salonius' frown seemed to deepen, if that were possible.

"There was a week long siege here ten years ago?"

Varro nodded. "Actually more like fourteen years ago, I think. But not just a week. Cristus held the place for five days, but the captain who'd been in charge of the garrison beforehand had held out for over a week himself. The whole siege was at least two weeks long."

Salonius shook his head.

"There was never a siege here, sir."

"What?"

The young man pointed up at the fort walls and then gestured around them at the civilian houses.

"It's obvious to me, sir. And to you I think if you look."

Catilina stared at him. "Not to me. What is it?"

"These houses are perfectly stable, ma'am, and the roofing tiles are old and shabby."

"So?" Catilina frowned.

"So if there were siege engines across the valley and in the fort flinging stones back and forth for over a week, the chance of these buildings surviving intact is almost nonexistent. And an invading army needs food, loot and security. All of those things mean the village would be razed and the people raped, killed or enslaved. I know how tribal warfare works, ma'am."

She shook her head.

"So the village got lucky. Or they made a deal."

"No," Salonius shook his head and pointed up at the fort. "And what about the fort's walls, sir."

Varro stared up the hill and suddenly slapped his head.

"He's right. Those towers are square!"

"So what?" Catilina demanded irritably.

"Ever since the civil war and the change in command, new forts are built with rounded towers. It deflects catapult missiles better. Your father's bloody idea!" Varro barked. These walls haven't been changed since before the civil war, what... forty years ago?"

Catilina nodded.

"Then Cristus lies. And we've a reasonable assumption that he's behind at least two deaths. I hope father got safely away."

Varro nodded.

"Your father's not daft, Catilina. The moment he got my note, he'll have been surrounded by his personal guard and rushed off to Vengen."

She shook her head, worried eyes fixing on Varro.

"You know my father. There's every possibility he'll stay just to try and help sort this out." She sighed. "Still, there's no point in panicking now. We'd best find your cousin and see what he has to say."

Salonius turned his ever-present frown on Varro.

"There's another unanswered question yet though."

The captain answered with only a raised eyebrow.

"The garrison commander." Salonius pointed at the fort once more. "Most of the men there will be too young to notice these things; I wouldn't have thought of it myself were it not for my training as an engineer. But the commander up there, he's got to know. He'll be a captain, so he's old enough to remember what happened here. He's commanding one of the most important outposts in the northern Empire, so he's not stupid by any stretch of the imagination. And he's running what appears to be a quiet, settled fort with no qualms. I'm guessing the same man's been in command here since the 'siege'. I'd also guess he was a close friend of prefect Cristus. You know what that means."

Varro nodded.

"Sharp. Yes, it means that we can't trust the soldiers of Saravis Fork. If Cristus really is trying to kill us, then it's a fair bet these men are under similar orders to the men chasing us."

Catilina frowned and spoke through gritted teeth.

"And even if they don't know we're here, as soon as those two other riders get here, we'll have every man in the fort down on us."

"Shit." Varro rubbed his temple wearily. "We'd best get out of sight fast. Where shall we tie the horses?"

Catilina smiled at him.

"Just let them loose, Varro. They're broken after that ride. We'll need new horses when we leave or they'll catch us before we can leave the valley."

The three of them dismounted, removing their pack and gear. Salonius hoisted the saddle bags over his shoulder.

"We just leave them here? Milling around? Seems unfair somehow."

Varro smiled at him. "I think they're in a better position than us, now come on!"

Salonius reached out a heavily muscled arm and relieved Catilina of her heavy saddle and saddle bags. Seriously laden, he walked on into the settlement.

"Strong lad, isn't he" she observed to Varro as they followed on.

The town became busier as they passed from the suburban road into a wider street, bustling with people. Here they hardly raised a glance from the locals; three dusty strangers in travelling cloaks, all on foot. As the wide street opened out into the main square at the centre of the town, a cluster of market stalls came into view, with crowds around them squawking like a flock of birds.

"Should be easy for us to get ourselves lost in." Varro observed.

"Yes," Catilina nodded, "but easy for other people to hide among too."

Salonius frowned.

"Why is there only one inn here? Your cousin said in his note he was at the inn. A place as big as this with a fort so close? There are half a dozen bars outside Crow Hill."

Varro nodded.

"That just means that the soldiers at Crow Hill are off duty outside the camp most nights. This is frontier territory. I'd suspect it requires command authorisation to leave the fort on personal business. There'll be no soldiers down here getting drunk on a night. Means we'll probably stand out a bit, but it also means we're unlikely to bump into any of the garrison."

Salonius nodded his understanding and turned as they entered the square, lightly tapping a young man on the shoulder. Catilina blinked and Varro stopped in surprise as a guttural string of unintelligible chatter issued from their companion. As they watched in fascination, the young man turned to Salonius, replying in the same dialect and beginning a deep and complex conversation that neither of them could understand. Finally, the young man grinned and clasped Salonius' hand briefly before turning away and going about his business. The other two were grinning when he turned back to face them.

"What? You think the tribe I was born into speak your lovely southern tongue normally?"

Varro laughed and Salonius gestured forwards. The three of them pushed on through the crowded square, finally breaking out in the open area between all the stalls.

"What did you two talk about?" Catilina asked with a smile.

"All sorts," Salonius replied. "But firstly, where to find the inn."

He stopped and pointed to a large wooden building with a stone base at the far end of the square. The inn stood proud of the other buildings around the central square by an entire story, matched only by the temple opposite. Three storeys and wide enough to accommodate perhaps four rooms along the front face, it was an impressive piece of architecture for a largely timber-based northern town. The three of them hurried across the square and made for the wide open doorway, surprised to find the interior well lit with windows and heated by a log fire, far from the dingy and shady room Varro had expected.

Salonius gestured at an empty table, the most inconspicuous in the room, tucked away in a corner.

"I'll get us a drink. Wine for you both?"

Catilina nodded but Varro shook his head. "Get me a beer. I need to keep the clearest head possible right now."

"Alright." Salonius joined them for a moment, dropping his heavy load near the wall, and then walked across to the bar to speak to the innkeeper. Catilina and Varro took wooden chairs with their backs to the wall and carefully observed the bar and its patrons. There were less than a dozen folk in the room but, judging by the size of the place and the number of tables, the usual crowd would be considerably larger. There were clearly no soldiers here and most of the conversation was in the guttural speech that Salonius had used in the market. No one seemed to be paying them any attention, which caused a sigh of relief to pass through Varro.

He turned his attention to Salonius at the bar, deep in conversation with the keeper as the man poured wine from a plain bottle into a plain glass and stood it next to the two mugs of beer on the bar top. The stocky soldier finished his conversation and began to carefully gather up the three vessels in his large hands.

"Sight for sore eye!"

Varro started and turned to see the man standing at the table. He'd approached soundlessly and, judging by the indrawn breath to his left, Catilina had been looking at something else too. Cursing himself for his wandering attention, Varro looked up into the face of the man standing opposite him.

Petrus had changed a great deal in the last fourteen years. Plainly the man had not had an easy time of it. His right eye twinkled with some of the intelligent mischief Varro remembered, but his left was white and filmy, the barest hint of a pupil visible within the milky sickness. Three parallel scars crossed his cheek just below the eye, horizontally and so likely unconnected to the eye, terminating in a long-healed wound that had slightly misshapen the nose. Allowing his eyes to draw back and take in the rest of the man, Varro also noticed Petrus' left hand suffered a constant uncontrollable twitch. The man had tucked the hand into his waist band, but that had merely muted the twitching rather than masking it. All in all, Petrus would have been a sorry sight, had that sight not been so welcome. Varro could feel emotion welling up inside him; emotion that he could scarce afford to allow to the surface. With a grunt he forced it down and maintained his grimace. Petrus gave a lopsided smile that displayed more damage, three or four teeth missing from the left on both upper and lower jaw. He turned that disturbing smile on Catilina.

"Varro, you brought a lady with you? Strange choice, though I can see why you'd pick him." He gestured over his shoulder at Salonius who was approaching the table carrying the drinks.

Varro nodded.

"Not just a lady, Petrus. You remember Catilina?"

For a moment a look of genuine surprise crossed that scarred face and the smile broadened.

"Catilina? By all the Gods! Last time I saw you, you couldn't even pronounce my name!"

Varro nodded. "It's been a long time. We might have caught up earlier if you hadn't been dead." The comment had an edge to it and as Petrus recoiled slightly, Salonius stepped round him and placed the four drinks on the table.

Petrus continued to look at Catilina.

"How's your brother, Catilina? He was always hanging around my knees asking to use my sword."

Catilina smiled.

"He's fine, Petrus. Not a soldier though. Never will be. Always buried in a book, my brother."

Salonius took one of the spare seats, his eyes never leaving the stranger, and coughed meaningfully.

Varro shook his head slightly, as if to clear it. "Quite right. More important matters to think about. So, Petrus, I think you need to take a seat and tell us what happened to you and what's so important people are being murdered to stop you saying it!"

Petrus blinked.

"Murdered?"

"Long story," Varro replied. "But let's start…"

His voice tailed off as Salonius put a restraining hand on his arm.

"What?"

"We need to move, now!" the young man said quietly but with force. As he bent and collected up the bags, Catilina frowned and leaned across to him.

"What's happened, Salonius?"

The young man gestured subtly toward the bar.

"That man who just came in. He told the barman to get his best glasses out, coz some new soldiers were on their way."

"Shit!"

The other two quickly shuffled out from behind the table and began gathering up their kit as fast as possible. Petrus grumbled in the background, his hand slipping from his belt and beginning to twitch more violently.

"You were followed? Varro, you idiot!"

"Not like I had a great deal of choice in the matter, Petrus. We need to get somewhere safe right now!"

The man ground his teeth for a moment and then nodded.

"Follow me."

Varro couldn't help noticing the slight limp as his cousin walking surprisingly swiftly and quietly to the door. The three of them caught up with him as he stepped out into the sunshine. Varro carefully scanned the crowd outside with a practiced eye but there was no immediate sign of their pursuers. Petrus limped off along the front of the inn and round the corner. As they followed, he disappeared into an alley and along the side of the building. Rounding the next corner, they found themselves at a single story wooden wall with a single small door.

"Stables. Back entrance." Petrus announced, as he flipped open the latch and entered the building. The smell of horse sweat and leather flooded out of the building and the three of them followed him in to a large stable surrounded by a dozen stalls, many of which were occupied. A large open door stood at the other side, the common entrance to the building, a young boy with a pitchfork leaning against the jamb, chewing on an apple. A second stable door to their right stood solid with the top half open. The sounds of the bar issued from it. Petrus pointed to a fourth door, small and unobtrusive, to the right, in the corner.

As the other three made for that door, Petrus pointed at the boy and the door and threw him a coin. The stable hand nodded his understanding and pocketed the coin, turning his attention to the grassy bank outside.

Petrus wandered over to join the others as they entered the small door one by one. The space beyond was dark and surprisingly cold. After a short corridor, the space ended with a set of wooden steps descending into further darkness.

"What is this place?" Salonius asked.

"Cellar," Petrus replied. "Where they keep the beer barrels and the crates of wine. I'm taking you to the safest place I can think of: my room."

Salonius blinked at him in surprise and then turned and began to follow Catilina down the stairs. Slowly, his eyes became accustomed to the change in light levels. It wasn't actually pitch black in the cellar, just considerably dimmer than the bright day above. The longer they stood in the room, the stone flagged floor covered with a light carpet of rushes, the more they could see in the low light cast by the minute skylights at ceiling height, set into the base of the inn's walls.

The cellar was large, likely half the size of the inn itself, with a huge dividing arch supporting the heavy building above. The centre of the large space was filled with stacked wooden tables and chairs. Along the cellar's outer wall huge beer casks were stacked two deep, kept cool by the natural chill of the cold earth seeping through the stonework. To the other side, wine bottles stood in wooden crates and beyond them a solid set of wooden stairs ascended to the inn's interior.

"You've been staying here?" Catilina asked incredulously. "How have you not been caught by the innkeeper?"

Petrus smiled his unpleasant smile again.

"Arun and I have an understanding. A silver coin every few days buys a lot of understanding. And I don't sleep in here. I have a hidden room. A secret space."

Varro nodded. "Reasonable. Arun will have it for smuggling purposes, out here on the border, but under the watchful eyes of an Imperial garrison."

Petrus crossed to the far wall and pulled a rickety wooden shelf unit aside to reveal a door. Varro shook his head. Had they stood by the unit, he'd have been able to see the door between the shelves.

"That's not hidden. It's just not very obvious!"

Petrus flashed him a sharp look as he unlatched the door and swung it open.

"You'd prefer perhaps to stay out here and get caught?"

Varro shook his head with a cheeky smile.

"No. Let's get ourselves almost hidden in your 'not very obvious' room!"

"Gah!" Petrus disappeared into the darkness within.

Catilina gave Varro a warning glance and then followed their guide within.

Varro shrugged at Salonius and the two entered, closing the door behind them.

"Shit!" Varro's voice called from the darkness.

"Shut up" grunted Petrus in a forceful whisper. "If we…"

The sound of Varro slumping to the floor and breathing as though he'd been punched heavily in the gut stopped him mid-sentence.

"What happened?" whispered Catilina.

Over Varro's laboured breathing, Salonius' concerned voice answered. "I think he caught his side on something sticking out of the wall next to the door. I've just put my hand on it and it's wet. I think it might have opened his wound."

"Uh!" Varro was trying to stand with a great deal of grunting.

"For fuck's sake, shut him up!" whispered Petrus urgently.

There was the sound of a leather flap being unfastened and further rustling.

"What the hell are you doing?" demanded Petrus again, the anger rising in his voice, even as the level remained quiet.

Salonius bit back an angry retort and replied patiently.

"He's got a few doses of medication in case his pain gets too bad. I'm finding that and some water. If he's bleeding badly, it'll have to wait until we can get into the light."

"Not the third… one!" grunted Varro between gasps. "Just… give me some of the ordinary… one for now. Can't afford… to be out of it right now."

Salonius nodded, unseen in the dark and passed over the bag of medication for Varro. "Be careful."

"Huh!"

"What's he got medicine for?" Petrus asked quietly, concern suddenly filling his voice.

"He can tell you when we get out of here later. Wait!"

There was a creak as a door was opened at the far end of the room and heavy footfalls on the wooden stairs. The four refugees fell completely still in the silent darkness, the only sound the faintly laboured breathing of the wounded captain. They could hear voices through the door, but not clearly enough to discern what they were saying. The conversation stopped as the boots of two men rand out on the stone flags. Clearly the two separated at the bottom of the stairs and were searching the cellar.

Varro's voice whispered so quietly the others barely heard the bitter humour in his voice.

"You'd better hope they're blind or stupid or both. Your 'not very obvious' room's not hidden by the shelves anymore!"

Petrus replied just as quietly "Yes it is, now shut up!"

The only sounds for what felt like hours were those of boots thumping around on the cellar floor and crates being pushed aside. Every time one of the searchers began a particularly loud action, Varro took the opportunity to gingerly unwrap the medicine in the bag. During one particularly loud scrape beyond the door, Varro lifted a water flask to his lips and swigged down his medicine.

"There's nothing down here. Come on!"

The welcome sound of receding footsteps brought relief washing over the four hidden figures. Petrus waited around a minute after the sounds of the door closing before striking flint and steel and sparking a small oil lamp into life. The room was small, perhaps ten feet square, cold stone with shelves recessed into three of the walls. A rough straw mattress was covered with a sleeping blanket.

"Lucky for you that you only attract thick pursuers!"

In the flickering light, they could see Varro leaning against the wall, a small patch of blood staining the tunic around his wound.

"What happened to you?" their guide asked.

Varro shook his head.

"No time for that now. I'll tell you when we get out of here. We'll have to go really soon, but we took a very dangerous three day ride to find you. We'll have to give it at least five minutes before we leave here to be sure, so why don't you fill the time with words?"

Petrus smiled.

"You always were a charmer! Alright then."

He settled back against the wall and uncorked a bottle from a narrow stone shelf.

"I've been here a few weeks now."

"Start at the beginning" grumbled Varro. "Like the bit about how you don't die?"

"Oh I should have died," Petrus answered lightly. "That bastard Cristus would be a lot happier. I gather he's some sort of hero for saving the fort from a barbarian horde these days?"

Varro nodded. "Prefect for over a decade now."

Petrus gave a humourless laugh. "Prefect! Indeed. Well even back when he was still *captain* Cristus, there was something going on. The bastard was building up some sort of personal group of supporters inside his cohort. I've the feeling he was thinking he might be able to push for higher office. I saw it happening over weeks, months even; good men being brushed aside and given shit duty while his favourite lackeys got preferential treatment. But there wasn't much I could do about it. You and me were Sabian's men, see? He'd never put his trust in us. But still, what harm could it really do me?"

Varro glanced round at his companions and was surprised to see a look of abject fury pasted across Salonius' features. The young man was incensed. He turned his attention back to his cousin.

"So what happened?"

"You remember the reports of the Clianii attacking Saravis? We were sent to relieve the garrison. When we got here there was no garrison. The fort had been overrun pretty much without a fight. Don't ask me how, but I suspect Cristus had even organised *that* somehow. The garrison was down to a few dozen men hiding out in the land around the fort. There were a couple of small breach points in the walls, but not enough to cause the fort to fall. Cristus put those of us who were out of favour to work on the walls, repairing the structure. As senior sergeant I was left in charge of the work detail."

"And what did his favourites do?" Salonius' voice was thick with contempt.

"He took an honour guard and rode up the valley to meet with the chieftain of the Clianii. He was gone for a whole day. To be honest, those of us busy repairing the fort were hoping they'd dealt with him for good. We were starting to get our spirits back. The next morning we'd pretty much repaired the walls. We were putting the finishing touches to it after a day and a night's exertions. We had guards and pickets out of course…"

"But?"

"But they were looking for barbarians…"

"What?"

"Cristus' personal sycophant army returned early in the morning. They arrived at the camp, with no sign of the captain. Cristus' cohort guard sergeant told me we were dismissed and could get some rest. That annoyed me. I outranked the little weasel. That should have been a warning really. We all turned in for a rest."

He took a deep breath.

"Next think I know, I'm being woken at sword point by some Clianii bastard with a wide grin. They were all over the fort. We were marched out into the open; all of us who'd stayed behind on the work party. We were marched out to the parade ground and chained together like prisoners of war. And all the time it was happening, Cristus was sat there on the wall, with the bloody chieftain, drinking and laughing. And all his favourites lounging around and watching us get marched off."

Salonius' grinding teeth were audible in the quiet as he stopped. Varro sat staring at his cousin in abject shock. Catilina was shaking her head gently.

"You don't believe me, Varro? You think he's some kind of honourable war hero? Why are his men chasing you down then?"

"It's not that I don't believe you," Varro replied slowly. "Really it isn't. I wouldn't put anything past Cristus and the more I learn about him the less I'm inclined to think of him as my superior. So you've been where these past fourteen years? Cristus killed the Clianii off…"

He slapped his head.

"He covered his tracks; and his own arse! He wiped out the tribe. He did a deal with them. Probably got more cash than the

Gods, got his fame and his promotion and then went back and exterminated the whole damn tribe to cover himself!"

"Better than that," Catilina interjected. "He lost more than a cohort during that punitive mission. That nearly cost him his new job, those high casualties. I'd be willing to bet that not a man who'd been at Saravis Fork survived that campaign."

Varro nodded.

"Very neat. He plays half an army off against the other, makes a deal with barbarians, then kills both the barbarians and the army off and walks away rich and clean. If I didn't hate the bastard so much, I'd have to admire him!"

Petrus leaned back and took another swig of wine.

"We were all put to work logging and mining. By the time the winter was over the conditions had killed most of us. There were maybe a score of us left and we were the strong ones. We'd tried to escape many times, but when you're in Clianii lands in the deep mountains where can you run to? Every time we got caught we were tortured. By spring those of us left were too weak to work in the forests or mines, so the Clianii sold us on to another tribe further out. Good thing really, I suppose. Six months later the Clianii had been exterminated and we'd have gone with them if we'd still been there."

"So where have you been since then?"

"I was put in the fields for some smaller tribe along the mountains a ways. I wasn't much use in the fields and I think my time was nearly up pretty quick, but then they discovered I could read. That changed things. Within a year I had my own hut, fire and food. I taught the whole tribe, boys and men and women. They never quite put me in a position where I could run, though. That only came a few weeks ago."

"Well?" Catilina urged.

"That's really not relevant to the main issue, Catilina!"

"I want to know, Petrus."

"Alright, I was sent out with the chieftain's younger son and a couple of guards. We were going to buy paper from another tribe for more lessons, but the boy had something to do while we were there. Well on the way, his horse threw him. Poor sod's back was broken on impact. He'd have been dead in a few minutes. Both the guards ran to help him. Well I didn't. I just ran. Kicked my horse and rode south and west until the beast nearly died of exhaustion. Got back to Saravis to find everything all peaceful and nice. Still had the bag of coins to buy paper. Worth a lot to some of these tribes, so I've been living here for weeks waiting for you."

Varro nodded. "How did you get a soldier to come find me? And why didn't you come?"

"Stupid cousin! I couldn't come on my own! I may have changed a bit, but what do you think would have happened if I turned up at Cristus' fort and knocked on the door asking for you? The soldier was a deserter. He'd been on a four day drinking binge and decided that going back to the fort would be a death sentence. I offered him an alternative. He's not known elsewhere and the money I gave him would have kept him drunk for a few weeks."

Varro shook his head sadly.

"He should have stayed here and taken his punishment. Poor bastard was stabbed half a dozen times near Crow Hill."

"So what do we do now?" Petrus held his cousin's gaze.

"We go see Sabian. He should be safely holed up back at Vengen. He's the man who'll deal with all of this. We need to get to Vengen as fast as we can."

"Agreed." He sighed. "I guess we'll have to steal a few horses then."

Varro nodded and, clutching his bloody waist and wincing, slowly opened the door onto the wide cellar room. The four of them piled out, Varro and Catilina carrying their saddles and personal bags, Salonius following along behind, laden with his own kit and his companions' saddle bags. Petrus watched the stocky young man, under his burden, climb the steps to the stable with surprising ease. He raised an eyebrow but made no comment. As he emerged from the stairway, Petrus walked across the room to the stable boy. The young lad smiled curiously at him and the scarred veteran withdrew a pouch from his tunic. He gave it a shake so that it jingled. There were maybe half a dozen coins still in it of different denominations. Ah well. He tossed the bag to the boy, whose eyes opened wide.

"Take it and piss off for about fifteen minutes lad, eh?"

The boy needed no further encouragement. A swift nod and he disappeared into the building.

Varro and his companions had already taken a quick glance into the stalls and selected three horses. As Petrus chose his own and nonchalantly lifted the owner's saddle from the peg, the other three strapped their own saddles and kit to their stolen steeds. Less than a minute later, the four fugitives led their horses from the stable doorway and onto the grass bank. As they mounted up, Petrus pointed behind the next house.

"If we follow the embankment, it takes you most of the way to the edge of the town without going out onto the streets, but we'll have to do a bit of classy riding. There's back garden fences and two orchards on the route. Still, better than going out onto the street, eh?"

Catilina gave him an encouraging grin and kicked her horse into a trot.

The four riders emerged from among the last houses in the town and dropped out onto the road in relative privacy. Barring three children playing with a dog and a woman hanging out washing they were alone. Varro shaded his eyes from the glare of the sun, now beginning to disappear behind the highest peaks out to the west, and peered into the distance up the road.

"Two men on foot. We could outrun them."

Catilina shook her head.

"Not this time, Varro. They're enemies. Pure and simple."

"Ok then," Varro sighed and drew his sword. "But you're getting out of danger. You and Petrus wait here while Salonius and I deal with them."

The stocky young soldier nodded sagely, but Petrus glared at him.

"I think I've earned this, Varro!"

Salonius looked across at Varro and after a moment's pause, the captain nodded. Salonius passed his sword to Petrus and walked his horse across to join Catilina. The two sat and watched as the cousins kicked their horses into a gallop, swords at their side, ready to swing.

"I'd not be the man to get between Petrus and an enemy," he said to the beautiful woman by his side. I swear I heard him growling as he went.

"He's got good reason. But then I suppose we all have. Come on, let's go…"

Chapter Nine

The four companions rode at a steady speed down the valley as they had done for many hours now, through the night and on into the dawn. They had ridden hard past the Imperial way station at the head of the valley in case enough of the garrison remained on alert to hinder them, though not a sound issued from the walls as they thundered past. Likely a skeleton staff remained there at best.

Salonius glanced across at Petrus with a curious look on his face, something of a mix of awe and horror. The disfigured ex-soldier had dispatched the man at the edge of the village with such awful violence and swift simplicity. The young soldier had given the combat as wide a berth as the road would allow but had been unable to avoid seeing the mess that had been the man's face. Petrus had only delivered two blows, but Salonius would have bet good money that the guard had been dead before the second one landed. He realised he was staring and, focusing, realised that Petrus was looking directly back at him with his one good eye.

"Something the matter, lad?"

"No." Salonius tried to control the shiver as he thought once more of that guard's jaw, hanging loosely from one side of his face.

"You ever been in a fight, lad?"

Salonius ignored the question and sat silently for a moment before turning back to him.

"I don't like the idea of having to kill Imperial soldiers, no matter what the reason. It just seems wrong."

Petrus hauled on his reins and pulled alongside his young companion. Salonius turned once more to face forward. Were they not riding hard to stay ahead of potential enemies from the Saravis Fork fort and headed to Vengen to denounce a traitor in the army, he could have enjoyed this ride. The day was turning out bright and warm, accompanied by the constant hum of bees and chattering of birds and the smell of fragrant wildflowers. The valley was widening all the time as they descended toward the northern plains. Varro and Catilina had peeled off a short while ago and were riding together on the other side of the valley, deep in conversation, leaving the scarred veteran and the young soldier to ride together. At this proximity, Salonius became once more aware of the faint aroma of stale beer that clung to Petrus.

"Try getting screwed and left for dead by them," the scarred man said flatly. "I think you'll change your tune."

"Huh!"

Salonius knew he was being unfair to his new companion. Petrus had every right and every reason in the world to mistrust and hate. The man had lived in hell for a decade because of these traitors. He had been a senior sergeant in the army and was cousin to Varro; a man with a position of power and responsibility. And yet there was something about him that Salonius couldn't quite put his finger on but didn't like; something that made him uneasy. Oh, Petrus wasn't a part of Cristus' conspiracy, for certain; nothing like that. But he was too quick to act with violence, perhaps? A risk? A loose blade that could damage anyone around him? He became aware that Petrus was watching him with that one piercing eye and turned to meet that gaze.

"I know you've been betrayed and hurt by your own. I understand that you must feel hollow and vengeful and I can see why you'd turn to your cousin for help. But I also know that people who are driven by revenge and blood can be dangerous to be around. Varro will tell you a bit about that when we stop, I'm sure, but just remember that when you throw a stone, you cause ripples. And if the ripples are big enough they sink ships."

Petrus continued to stare at him, but the look about his eye had changed; softened somehow. Salonius gave him a sad and weary smile.

"Be careful you don't sink your friends."

Petrus' one eye bored into him for a moment longer and then he turned away.

"Varro was right to choose you, lad. I knew you were strong when I saw you, but you're sharp too."

He scanned the valley as he had done every few minutes since they'd begun their ride and then turned back to Salonius.

"Are your eyes as sharp as your mind?"

"What?" The young man started.

"Behind us. A couple of miles, perhaps?"

Salonius craned his neck and peered into the distance.

"Shit!"

"How many d'you see?" the older man asked, his voice low.

"A dozen at least."

Petrus frowned and turned again.

"You *are* sharp! I'd only seen one group. So: two groups of six riders. One on each side of the valley. And that likely means there'll be more coming behind them on the road. These are just outriders to hem us in."

Salonius nodded.

"I know what they're doing. They'll try and outpace us in the next hour or two."

He pointed to the river rushing and gurgling along to their right.

"That river crosses to the other side of the valley a few miles ahead in a little village. There's a bridge in the square and that's the only safe place to cross unless you ride up the slope. If they can get there ahead of us, they can stop us at the bridge. We won't have time to turn back and get up the slope and that other bunch that you're talking about will come up on us from behind. I thought we were staying way ahead of them, but they're playing us into a trap."

Petrus grumbled and snapped his head round to glance back once again.

"That could work both ways, though."

"What do you mean?" Salonius frowned.

"If a dozen of them try to stop us at the bridge, they'd best be good. They may have us pinned down, but we'll have *them* all in one place too."

"Are you mad?" Salonius glared at him. "I've just got through telling you not to put people in danger!"

Petrus growled and fixed him once again with that unnerving cyclopean stare.

"They're already *in* danger, boy, and you know that. But Varro and I are good at what we do, and I have a feeling that you are, too. And at a bridge they lose their advantage in numbers. I'm guessing they'll not be able to get more than four on the bridge at a time. And if they're just following orders, they've more to lose than us, so we gain the advantage, you see?"

Salonius glared at him for some time and finally, with a sigh, he nodded.

"You're right, of course. Unless we swing out and go up the sides of the valley ourselves."

Petrus shook his head.

"No point. We'd only stay a little ahead of them and they'd still be chasing us. We need to deal with this bunch before any more get here."

He placed his thumb and forefinger in his mouth and let out a shrill whistle. Salonius stared at him.

"They'll hear you!"

"No they won't," the scarred man replied, wiping his fingers on his tunic. "They're riding horses a couple of miles away, and it wasn't *that* loud."

Across the valley, Varro and Catilina had turned their horses and were making for the road at the centre. With a nod to Salonius, Petrus did the same. The four riders converged a few hundred yards further on, just as the floor of the valley crested and took a sudden dip. Laid out before them perhaps five miles away was the village with the narrow stone bridge. An involuntary shudder went through Salonius as he remembered the events that took place there a few days ago.

"Pursuit?" Varro's voice was flat; a statement, not a question. Petrus nodded.

"We reckon about a dozen for now. The lad thinks they're going to cut us off at the village and that more will be coming down from behind."

Salonius bridled at the slight condescension implied by the phrase 'the lad' but kept his tongue. This was not the time for argument.

Varro shaded his eyes and peered back up the valley.

"He's right. There's more than those dozen outriders. Half the damn cohort's coming!"

They followed his pointed finger and squinted into the sun. The two small groups of riders were pushing their mounts hard and were close behind. Given the quality of their cavalry steeds against the four stolen horses, they would easily pass them over the next two miles. But the sight that chilled Salonius' blood was the rising cloud of dust further up the valley; the sort of dust cloud that could only be kicked up by a sizeable cavalry unit travelling at speed.

Varro grunted.

"We're going to have to deal with this lot at the bridge pretty quickly."

Petrus glanced at Salonius and raised an eyebrow provocatively. The younger man ignored him and frowned.

"That cavalry won't take long to catch us. If we survive that, we're going to have to find a way to block the bridge and slow them down."

"I'll block it with bodies!" rumbled Petrus. Varro smiled.

"Salonius'll figure it out. You just concentrate on the fight ahead."

The four of them kicked their horses and raced off toward the village. As they travelled, throwing up clouds of dust, Varro and his companions kept an eye on their pursuers. The outriders, realising they'd been seen, had given up any hope of subterfuge and were racing along the sides of the valley. Quickly it became apparent that their horses were of far superior quality to the civilian steeds the four fugitives had taken from Saravis Fork. In little over a mile, the ambushers were already level with their prey. They would have ample time to position themselves at the bridge.

As they rode, Varro drew his heavy Imperial blade from the sheath by his saddle. A moment later Petrus and Salonius followed suit. As Catilina moved to draw a sword from her pack, however, Varro shook his head.

"Not you!"

Catilina, her hair streaming behind her dramatically, flashed an angry look at him and drew the sword defiantly.

"Your father will kill me anyway if I get you harmed. Put it away!"

"No!" She gritted her teeth. "I need to be able to defend myself anyway, you cretin!"

Varro blinked in surprise and then let out a short laugh.

"Then stay as out of the way as you can, my love!"

Salonius smiled to himself. It was the first time he'd heard Varro refer to the relationship that was clearly blossoming once more between them. He'd have to pray to the Gods that Scortius could find some sort of cure for this incurable poison.

Brandishing their swords, the four rode on, bearing down on the village.

"I'll take the right side" shouted Petrus over the drumming of their hooves. "Peripheral vision problems!"

Varro nodded. "You take the left!" he shouted at Salonius, before turning to Catilina. "And you stay at the back and watch that lot behind us."

Salonius frowned and allowed his horse, currently out front by a neck, to drop back a little until he rode alongside the defiant-looking lady with her blade held low.

"My lady?"

She turned to look at him and raised her eyebrows.

"How's your aim?" he enquired.

The eyebrow dropped into a frown.

"Good. Why?"

Salonius grinned.

"Because I have a sling and a pouch of shot in my bag. For hunting coneys."

She returned his smile.

"Never used a proper slingshot, but I've had plenty of practise with home-made slings and catapults."

Clutching his reins with his sword hand and keeping his eyes on the road ahead, Salonius reached round into a saddle bag and rummaged among its contents. Concentrating, he dug deep through his travelling gear until he finally found what he was looking for and his fingers closed on a leather strap. Hauling it out, the heavy bag of shot came with it, tied to one loose end. Extending his arm, he proffered the weapon to Catilina, who gave it an appraising glance and then sheathed her sword before taking it.

"Heavy stones," she said. "They'll hurt."

"They're not stones," Salonius replied. "That's the proper lead shot that gets issued to all engineers. You can kill quite easily with a well placed blow. But be really careful with where you aim."

"Oh I shall." She replied with a smile, and began to untangle the strap from the fastening on the pouch as she rode. "Believe me, I shall."

As they passed the first houses of the village, it was clear that the population had dispersed the moment they saw trouble approaching. The open space at the centre of the settlement was empty and, Salonius noted, there was no sign remaining of the gruesome mess they had left a few days ago. Even the wooden rail had gone from between the trees. His attention was drawn back to the bridge ahead.

A group of Imperial soldiers from the Saravis Fork garrison blocked the far end of the bridge, four of them standing in front of that same wooden rail that had now been placed across the thoroughfare and wedged in at both ends where the men had bashed out chunks of mortar between the stones. With a smile, Salonius filed that thought away. The other men were gathered behind them, some at the bridge end, the rest to one side, on the top of the steep bank.

"Stop!" a voice called from the bridge, laden with authority. "I'm under orders to take you four to the captain."

Varro reined in his mount, having ruled out the possibility of attacking or evading on horseback. Riding them down would have been a dangerous option at best, but in close combat in such a confined area being mounted would present too many vulnerable spots to the enemy and so many additional risks for the rider. And, of course, the horses would be too tired after travelling speedily through the night to even attempt to jump such a large crowd of people. He nodded at his companions and handed his reins to Catilina. She took them and tied them to her own before reaching out and gesturing to the others.

Salonius and Petrus dismounted and handed over their reins, hefting their swords. Petrus gave his a practise swing, clutching his shoulder where the muscles were not used to such exertion these days.

"Put down the swords and we'll not harm you" the leader of the soldiers called from the bridge.

Varro smiled at Petrus, shrugged, and the two broke into a run, Petrus' slight limp not hampering him at all, and becoming unnoticeable at speed. Salonius gave a startled squawk and then raced after them, veering off to the left as planned.

The dramatic effect of the sudden charge was visible on the faces of the enemy as the running men drew closer. Clearly they had expected this to end without a fight. Some hadn't even unsheathed their weapons yet.

The front line of defenders prepared themselves for a charge in the traditional manner; shields locked in front, four abreast and with the wooden rail supporting them behind. Had they been facing an ordinary foe in a normal military situation, it would have stood them in good stead. Their attackers, however, were far from an ordinary foe.

As they reached the bridge itself, Salonius hefted his sword again, and then noticed with surprise that Varro and Petrus had flipped their swords around so that they were pointing out behind and had turned their bodies slightly to the left so that they were both almost facing him.

Varro winked.

A flash of understanding burst across Salonius' face and he almost laughed as he followed suit, flipping his sword around and turning his body just in time as the three of them, at full speed, ploughed into the shield wall. The sheer force of the blow snapped the rail in the middle, along with the backs and ribs of the two central defenders, who fell away, broken and flailing on top of the men behind, who were widely spaced, not expecting a breach so easily.

The soldier on the right showed a deal more foresight as he ducked out of the way at the last minute and pressed himself against the wall of the bridge. His relief was only momentary, as Petrus' sword, angled perfectly as his charging weight pulled him forward and down, sliced out and caught the man in the narrow gap between his upper body plates and the heavy armoured leather strops that covered his pelvis. He clutched at his middle and gasped as glistening purple tubes started to slide out of his torso. The defender on the left, however, took the full brunt of Salonius' massive and powerful shoulder. The blow lifted his feet from the ground and, as the young man barged him out of the way, he scrabbled desperately at the stone parapet for a moment before disappearing over the side and into the foamy torrent with a diminishing scream.

Two of the men behind the front row immediately collapsed under the falling weight of their fellow soldiers, and a space opened up before the three panting renegades as they turned in unison to face their enemy, changing their grip on their swords menacingly.

Varro surveyed the scene. Four dead and two down had already halved the effective resistance and they were now almost at a ratio of one to one. He smiled the particularly unpleasant smile that Corda used to refer to as his 'tiger smile'. The nearest defenders backed away nervously.

"Ok you bunch of treacherous, cowardly bastards!" he shouted. "Who wants to go shake the Gods' hands first?"

The two downed men began to pick themselves up from the floor, pulling themselves back from this crazy man as fast as they could. The wounded soldier, still trying to hold his innards together, and gasping with horror, fell silent as Petrus reached out with his twitching free hand and pushed him over the parapet and into the churning water.

The enemy soldiers edged forward together, brandishing their swords and began to slowly advance on the renegades, keeping their eyes locked on them.

There was a sudden 'crack' and the rear-most soldier, standing by the steep bank of the river, collapsed like a sack full of rocks and rolled down the slope into the water. Salonius smiled as he heard the telltale 'whoop, whoop, whoop' of the sling readying for a second shot. Catilina was right; she *was* a good shot.

The advancing men faltered momentarily and Varro and Petrus shared a look. The captain turned to Salonius, who nodded soberly.

"The fat one's mine" grinned Petrus, and the faltering soldiers stopped altogether as their attackers stepped slowly forward, Petrus' limp becoming pronounced once more at this inexorable and deliberately slow speed. The whooping noise from behind stopped, and the enemy soldier on the far bank furthest from the combat ducked desperately, barely avoiding a skull-shattering lead missile. As he stood straight again with relief, Catilina's third shot caught him on the chin, breaking his jaw and throwing him back to the ground with a 'crump'.

Petrus stepped around the two groaning broken men lying on the bridge amid the shattered remains of the wooden rail, pausing briefly to allow his blade to drop heavily into the throat of the nearest wounded man, granting him release from his pain. Varro displayed less compassion, walking across the other man and treading heavily on his throat, crushing the life from him with hobnailed boots.

Salonius glanced over the side of the parapet with interest as he stepped forward to fall in line with the other two. The three walked steadily forward, leaving the two dying men behind them silent.

As they neared the remaining five men who, Varro thought, were doing well to retain a disciplined front in the face of such a brutal onslaught, the single man behind his four compatriots called out.

"We still have you outnumbered. You can still surrender."

Salonius sneered, remembering his own cohort in battle. When the Second went into combat, Varro stood in the front line and Corda only a row or two back. That was how to motivate men, he thought. Lead by example, not like this idiot, cowering behind his men. He almost bit off his tongue as a lead bullet whizzed through the air between him and Varro, so close he felt the faint vibration on his ear.

The enemy commander opened his mouth to make another fatuous demand and disappeared instantly from view with a 'crack'. Salonius grinned as he heard Catilina fumbling in the bag for another lead shot. Varro's eyes were wide with shock, the bullet having almost clipped him and Salonius, and having been aimed exquisitely between the helmets of two men in the front line. A shot like that would make a professional hunter green with jealousy.

The four men, again to their credit, set their shoulders and brandished their swords. Varro, Petrus and Salonius fell on them like a tide of bloody fury. The defenders' blades lashed out desperately from between their large shields but the three attackers, unencumbered by heavy armour and large shields, easily avoided the flashing blades. Salonius bent to his left, parried two blows from the end soldier and one from the man next to him, and ducked back out of the way for a second. As the innermost of the two men became distracted once more by Varro's furious onslaught, the end man momentarily looked away. Taking advantage of the pause, Salonius dropped his sword and leapt at the man, diving onto him, far too close for the man to use his sword. As the man's eyes widened and he struggled to stay upright under the weight of the bulky young man, Salonius grasped the man's neck defender with one hand and chin strap with the other and twisted with all his might.

The crunch was audible even over the sounds of steel on steel and, increasingly often, steel on bone. Varro glanced across in surprise, almost falling foul of a well-placed blow, and saw the helmet wobble backwards as the neck broke inside and Salonius and his victim disappeared to the ground with a crash and a cloud of dust.

Moments later, as Salonius stood once more, brushing down his tunic, and went to collect his sword, Varro and Petrus delivered the final blows to the only remaining combatant and turned to survey the scene.

Catilina had tied the slingshot and pouch back together and was leading the horses towards the bridge with a disturbing grin.

The captain gestured wearily at Salonius and the young man wandered over to him.

"We need to do something with this bridge."

Salonius nodded sagely, watching with unhappy fascination as Petrus, in the background, went about the grisly business of dispatching the wounded enemies. Trying to ignore the unpleasant sounds and the death rattles, he tapped the parapet where the wooden rail had been inserted with his forefinger.

"This bridge has been here a long time."

"Solid, then" remarked Varro with a sigh.

"Yes and no" replied Salonius with a thoughtful look. "It was pretty solidly constructed a few hundred years ago, probably by the army when that outpost at the top of the valley was built, but it's not been maintained by the military and I'd assume the locals either don't know what to do or don't care."

"What do you mean?"

"Well", Salonius continued in a tutorial manner, "this was built with mortar and not cement or concrete and it's a fairly basic arch bridge with a keystone."

"And?" Varro sounded frustrated.

"Mortar is not as strong as cement or concrete. That's why we use them now. And with an arch and keystone, all the weight of the bridge rests on the keystones. The more weight, the better the arch, in fact. But the weather up here in the mountains has eroded a lot of the mortar. That's how they could wedge the wood across the bridge, you see? The mortar's so old, you can pull it out with your fingers."

Varro bit his lip. "So you're saying we can loosen the keystones and collapse the bridge?"

"I'm saying it's possible."

"But it could be dangerous. How long will it take, if we can do it?" Varro scratched his chin thoughtfully.

"I honestly have no idea."

"The rest of the garrison are about ten minutes behind us at most, Salonius. Can we do it?"

The young engineer shook his head.

"No. Not enough time."

"Then mount up. We've got to go. You can see their dust through the trees now. "

Salonius blinked.

"Come on!" Varro barked, turning and making for Catilina and the horses.

Salonius jogged along behind him, slowly raising his eyes and catching up as the captain left the bridge.

"Rope."

"What?" Varro grumbled? "What rope?"

"Get lots of rope. We can bring this beech down on the bridge."

Varro sighed and pointed up at the branches.

"It's a young tree; not very heavy. It won't collapse the bridge, Salonius!"

"No," the young man replied, "but it'll block it completely; and it's small enough that four horses should be able to pull it over."

Varro blinked and a slow smile crept over him.

"That'd stop them alright. And the valley's too steep and covered in scree here to get a horse up. They'll have to go back a few miles to get round. Hang on… what's to stop them pulling it back out of the way?"

Salonius smiled. "Firstly, they'll only have access to the delicate, easily breakable branches at the top of the tree. And secondly, we'll drag it at an angle and wedge it."

Varro narrowed his eyes for a moment and then nodded. "Petrus!" he shouted at the disfigured veteran, limping toward them from the bridge.

"What?"

"Ropes! We're pulling the tree over."

"Good idea."

As Varro unhooked a length of rope that had been with the saddle when he stole it, and began to unwind it, fastening it to his horse, he frowned.

"Enough here for me, but that's the only rope we have."

Petrus pointed along the river to a solid looking building on the edge of the village.

"That's a mill. Mills have rope," the scarred veteran shouted.

As Varro ran over toward the mill with him, Salonius unhooked a leather roll on his horse's flank and turned to yell after the others "Just get one. One'll be enough!"

Varro gave him a questioning look for a moment, but shrugged, turned and ran on. Salonius was the engineer, after all.

As the leather roll unfurled, Catilina saw an array of tools; military engineer's tools.

"I wondered what that was for. You always seem to be carrying so much."

"Always be prepared" grinned Salonius as he untied a three foot long shaft from the roll. Examining it for a moment, he grasped it by the narrower end and Catilina realised the haft tapered slightly. Placing the wider end on the ground, he untied a heavy axe blade from the roll and placed the hole in it over the shaft, allowing it to drop to the bottom, where it wedged against the thicker wood. Stamping on the blade with a foot to force it as far as it would go, he lifted his axe and walked over to the tree.

Catilina allowed her attention to wander away from the sound of the axe biting into the young wood, noticing for the first time the frightened eyes of the villagers where they peered out from windows and doors.

And, of course, the growing cloud of dust not far from the village. If she strained she was sure she could hear hooves.

"Hurry up" she said, though quietly and to herself.

By the time Petrus and Varro came running back across the grass with a large coil of rope, Salonius had stopped cutting and was leaning all his weight on the tree with an experimental push. Nodding in satisfaction, he smashed the top of the axe head against the bole a couple of times until the blade began to slide back down the shaft. Dismantling it, he wandered over to his horse and neatly returned it to its place. He tutted in irritation before selecting another instrument; a small hand-pick.

"What's up?" Catilina asked.

"I hate putting it away without cleaning and oiling. That's no way to treat a good tool."

He carefully and neatly rolled up the leather container and fastened it under the lady's faintly amused gaze, while Petrus tied the second rope to his own steed and mounted.

"So, engineer... how best do we do this?" the scarred veteran enquired.

Salonius led his horse over to Catilina, casting a professional eye over the tree and the ropes as he walked.

"Take her across with you," he asked Catilina. She nodded and took the young man's reins, leading the horse ahead and over the bridge.

Salonius turned back to Petrus.

"Catilina and I need to get out ahead. Then you both need to walk forward onto the bridge until the ropes are taught; they're obviously different lengths. Once they're tight, start stepping forward very slowly and in unison. Try not to jerk too much. Very slow but very steady. Constant pressure's what we want. I've given you a good start low on the trunk, so once you reach breaking point, the whole thing will come down very, very quickly."

Petrus and Varro shared a look.

"The ropes are long enough" Salonius went on, "that you'll be well out of the way on the other side of the bridge by then, but you need to stop the moment the tree comes down, or you might drag it into the river or even across the bridge. Got all that?"

"Slowly forward, stop when it goes bang. Think I can just about master that" grumbled Petrus.

Salonius gave him what he hoped was an infuriatingly condescending smile and walked ahead of them onto the bridge. He stopped at the centre, shaded his eyes and carefully judged the length of the ropes, the size and angle of the tree trunk and the location of the cut he'd made. Hoping beyond hope that his calculations were correct, he leaned down low and selected one of the largest stones mortared into the bridge parapet around half way up.

Giving the mortar around the stone an experimental prod, he was pleased to see that a mere poke with a finger brought a flood of crumbled mortar like sand in an hourglass. Quickly and efficiently, he dealt a dozen blows with his pick, removing the mortar around the stone. Satisfied, he leaned out over the parapet and, quickly locating the outer face of the stone, he repeated the process there.

Hanging the pick on his belt, he gave the great stone a heave and grinned as it smoothly slid out of the bridge wall and disappeared into the rushing water with a deep and resounding splash.

Running across the bridge he saw Catilina more than twenty yards from the bank, staying well back. He jogged across to her and, retrieving his reins, vaulted onto the horse. Catilina gave him a friendly smile and then turned to watch the cousins slowly manoeuvring onto the bridge, the ropes raising from the floor behind them and slowly tightening.

Salonius sat fidgeting, tapping his fingers nervously on the pommel of his saddle. He began to worry that the ropes would be too old and weak, or his cut in the tree not deep enough. Perhaps the tree was tougher than he'd anticipated, or the horses too tired. Perhaps...

'CRACK'.

The break came so suddenly and crashed to the ground so noisily that all four horses started. As Salonius and Catilina steadied their startled mounts, the young man watched in mild panic as Petrus and Varro tried to stop their horses bolting, still attached to the tree that lay, still shaking and vibrating on the grass eight feet from the far side of the bridge."

"Shit!" Varro wheeled his horse, bucking and thrashing.

Petrus was having more luck, his horse now merely snorting and the eyes rolling as it craned its neck to see the rustling tree it was still attached to.

"For Gods' sake get him under control!" yelled the young engineer.

"Salonius, look!"

Catilina pointed at the tree and Salonius narrowed his eyes, trying to discern what it was she was indicating, when his eyes refocused and he realised she hadn't meant the tree. She was pointing between the branches at the shapes of riders cresting the hill on the far side of the village.

"Oh, shit!"

He kicked his horse and rode over to the two cousins. Varro had finally stopped his horse bucking and was stroking its mane soothingly as the eyes continued to roll.

"Company!" he yelled, pointing past the tree.

"Alright, the next part needs to be done quickly but just right! Varro? About fifteen feet forward and cut the rope! Petrus, you need to keep going until you feel it pull so tight you can't move any more."

He wheeled his horse and quickly stepped to where he estimated they would need to stop and then pointed at the ground next to him.

Varro and Petrus slowly and soothingly goaded their frightened horses into walking forwards. The few steps seemed to take forever, accompanied by the creak of rope and the scraping and rustling of the tree as it dragged and rolled from the open space into the bridge's aperture and a third of the way across.

Varro reined in his horse and quickly severed the rope. He nodded at Petrus and Salonius and then rode on ahead to join Catilina.

Petrus walked his horse on slowly.

"More..." Salonius encouraged, unnecessarily.

"Further..."

He looked up and, as he saw the look on the older man's face, lowered his own head and voice, though continued to encourage under his breath.

He turned to watch the slow progress of the felled tree across the bridge. With one rope cut, the tree was slowly turning. Trying desperately to ignore the sound of dozens of drumming hooves that were now disturbingly close, he watched with a satisfaction that only an engineer would understand, as the severed beech trunk slid neatly into the hole left by the missing stone in the bridge wall.

"Pull it 'til it's too tight to move."

Petrus glared at him again, but said nothing as he urged his horse forward amid the tremendous straining noises of rope and wood. Finally, with a crunch and a shower of mortar, the tree wedged in the bridge. The figures of horsemen were visible at the far end of the village square beyond the wavering, willowy treetop branches. Salonius grinned at them and then turned the grin on Petrus, who reached around and cut the rope, his horse sidestepping freely, grateful to have the anchor removed.

Petrus sighed and returned the smile.

"Let's just get out of here"

Salonius nodded and, turning his horse, they trotted off to join Varro and Catilina, leaving the soldiers on the far side of the river milling uncertainly and shouting conflicting orders at one another.

"Well done!" Varro commended him as they reined in. "That should give us a few hours' grace."

"Go!" shouted Petrus.

Varro turned in surprise and recognised the telltale hiss just in time to duck. The arrow whizzed through the space where his chest had been a moment before. Petrus had already kicked his horse into action and raced ahead. Salonius and Catilina joined Varro as they rode swiftly to escape the range of the enemy archers.

As they thundered past the barn, Salonius glanced across, remembering the assault they'd made when they first entered the valley. As he realised what they'd managed to get through, he smiled to himself. His eyes wandered across to Catilina, hunched over the horse's neck, riding like the wind.

His smile slowly turned sour as he saw the shaft of the arrow protruding from her back and the red stain running down her cloak. She slipped sideways slightly and her arm dropped and swung freely.

"Oh Gods, no!"

Desperately, he pulled his horse alongside her and grasped her reins, slowing both beasts to a walk and then a complete halt. The quiet thud of arrows some way back indicated that they must now be out of range and safe. He turned his full attention to the lady beside him.

Reaching up, he placed his fingers on her neck below her ear and the jaw line. He almost collapsed in relief. She had a pulse. A little erratic as far as he could tell, but strong enough. The most his medical knowledge could tell him was that she was alive. With a sigh, he craned to look at her back. The arrow was deeply embedded, and had punched through her shoulder blade. Racking his brains, he pictured the charts he'd seen in Salonius' room. Thank Gods he took an interest in things like this. The blow would be too high to have gone near her heart, but might have got her lung.

Heaving her across as gently as he could with his huge, muscular arms, he settled her in front of him, turned slightly so that the arrow couldn't be jogged by anything. He suddenly became aware of Petrus and Varro hovering over him, a looked of horror pasted across the latter's face.

"Don't panic sir. She's wounded, but not badly."

'I hope' he added silently to himself.

Varro opened and closed his mouth a couple of times but no sound emerged.

"We have to go, Varro," said Petrus, tugging at his sleeve. "It's no good buying extra time and then wasting it feeling miserable. The lad's solid and clever and he's got her."

Varro continued to stare.

"She's still with us!" insisted Petrus as he grasped the reins of the now riderless horse. "Now go!"

He grabbed a handful of Varro's shoulder material and hauled him around so that he was face to face with the stricken captain.

"Just go!" he yelled into Varro's face, flecks of spittle dancing on the captain's cheek.

Startled out of his shock, Varro turned and rode off, picking up speed. Petrus turned and locked Salonius with a commanding glare from that one frightening eye.

"Take good care of her and make sure she's alive when we get to Vengen. Varro likes you, so he'll just mope, but I don't know you well enough yet not to break your nose."

Salonius glared back at him. So many retorts flittered around the edge of his consciousness, but his head was filled to bursting point with thoughts of Catilina, some of which he wasn't prepared to admit even to himself. Swallowing hard, he nodded and settled the delicate wounded lady in front of him and set his horse off to a trot so they could catch up with Varro, who had reached the crest of the next undulation in the valley floor.

As he and Petrus rode up to meet Varro, the great, wide scene of the lower valley opened up before them, gently sloping down in the morning sunshine and opening out to become the northern plains. Somewhere in the distant haze, among vineyards and private estates, would be Vengen, fortress of the Northern marshal, home of Sabian, and safety.

But between it and them almost a thousand men filled the valley floor from side to side, green tunics bright in the sun and laminated armour flashing brilliant white, all marching with imperial precision.

"Oh, shit!"

Varro nodded, turning toward them, his face hollow and empty.

"The ram and lightening." He waved at the army. "Cristus brought the Fourth after us!"

Chapter Ten

Varro and Petrus shared a quick glance and a determined look fell across their faces.

"Salonius?" Varro shouted. "Get Catilina away from here. I don't care how or where. Just get her away and to a doctor somewhere."

Salonius nodded and wheeled his horse, holding the unconscious Catilina as delicately as he could. How he would escape an army carrying a wounded lady was beyond him, but he would have to try.

"Stand down, Varro," barked Petrus waving his hand. "I don't know what's going on, but there are officers at the front in black!"

"Black?" Varro blinked, pausing in the process of drawing his sword.

"Yes, black" he replied. "Sabian's guard."

Salonius squinted into the bright sun.

"He's right, Varro. There's at least a squad of the marshal's men there." He sighed with relief.

"And that's sergeant Corda!" he laughed, as he pointed at the mounted figure surrounded by black uniforms amid a sea of green.

With a click, Varro slid his blade back into the sheath at his side and rolled his shoulders with a smile.

"I'm almost tempted to let those bastards from Saravis Fork catch up with us now. I'd love to see their faces as the came over *this* hill!" He sighed and glanced behind him at the limp woman leaning against Salonius' chest. "Still, there's more important things to worry about!"

The riders had obviously come to the attention of the cohort's scouts, as orders were shouted and the tramping feet fell silent in unison. After a minute or so, Corda, accompanied by the black-clad guards, rode out from the front of the army and up the slope towards them. As the small group of soldiers approached the knot of riders on the hill crest, Varro frowned. Though well-hidden by that bushy, black beard, Varro could plainly see the effect that Corda's new command was having on him. His eyes appeared hollowed and dark, speaking volumes on his sleep pattern these last few days. He was pale and drawn and clearly overworked, and yet the smile on his face was genuine and warm.

"Varro, by all the Gods."

"Well by the less reputable ones, anyway" replied the captain with a tight smile.

Corda turned to Catilina and the grin fell from his face.

"My lady?"

Salonius saluted with his free hand, the other wrapped around Catilina's waist and clutching the horse's reins.

"I think she'll be alright, sergeant. She's out from the pain but the arrow seems to have missed anything important and the wound is well sealed. Do you have a doctor with you?"

Corda frowned.

"I've got field medics." He swallowed nervously. "Her father's beside himself with worry."

Petrus cleared his throat, and the acting commander quickly turned to the last rider. "I didn't honestly believe it was really you, Petrus. We must talk as soon as we have time."

Reaching out, the scarred man grasped Corda's hand and shook it. Their eyes met for a long, delayed, moment and Corda looked away to Varro.

"What?" Petrus frowned.

Corda growled at his former captain.

"You haven't *told* him?"

"Never been a right time yet, Corda. We've been a little busy." He growled. "And this is *not* the time! Half the garrison of Saravis Fork are only about an hour behind us and Catilina needs to get to a medic as soon as possible."

Corda nodded and they began to wheel their horses.

"So what happened?" Varro enquired of the acting captain as the black-clad guardsmen assembled in a protective group around them.

"Your messenger arrived at the fort a couple of days ago, demanding to see Sabian and asking for money. It so happens that the gate guards at the time were drawn from our cohort, so they sent for me. I took him to see the marshal and since then it's all moved damn fast. Sabian and his men have returned to Vengen but he sent us to find you. We're to bring all of you to Vengen, so he can speak to Petrus himself."

Varro nodded again.

"So Vengen it is. That'll be, what, five days with the cohort?"

Corda frowned.

"It would be, but you four and I are riding ahead with Sabian's men and my command guard. The rest can catch us up later."

Varro shook his head.

"Catilina needs to travel slowly and with medics."

"For Gods' sake Varro, I *can* think, you know!" Corda turned to the one of the black-clad guards nearby. "Ride on ahead and get two of the field medics up front with full kit. They're coming with us to Vengen ahead of the unit.

Corda turned his horse and he, Varro and Petrus rode slowly down toward the army, deep in conversation, the acting captain occasionally casting concerned glances back at Salonius and his wounded charge. The black-clad elite guardsmen neatly divided, half of them accompanying the three officers, while the others formed up around Salonius and Catilina in a manner the young man found disturbingly reminiscent of a prisoner escort. He glanced down at the lady, pale and swaying in the saddle in front of him. Sabian might well be beside himself now, but that was nothing to what the marshal would feel if Salonius was wrong and Catilina was worse than he thought. In a purely selfish moment for which he instantly chided himself, he decided that if Catilina didn't make it to Vengen, they might as well all throw themselves on their swords. Facing Sabian after getting his daughter killed would likely be fatal anyway.

Still, he thought, forcing himself to smile and relax as much as he could; after days of hardship, flight and mortal danger, they were safe once more within the fold. They had a witness against Cristus and his cadre of betrayers, Catilina was alive and should recover completely, Gods willing, and hopefully Scortius would be able to do something about Varro's condition which, while apparently stable, was still a constant worry hanging over them.

It was hard to believe all this had only been... he stopped and counted on his fingers as he rode... three days after the battle they'd left the fort, three more days after that when they'd met with Petrus, and almost two more days now back down the valley. Just a little over a week and yet it felt like a hundred years since he'd been an engineer, greasing pulleys and tying ropes on the huge war machines of the fourth army. He'd changed his unit and his entire career, been promoted, met war heroes and villains, knew the daughter of the marshal on first name terms, fought in three engagements and here he was riding with some of the most important people in the northern provinces, to the home fortress of the northern marshal, escorted by the marshal's elite guard.

As an engineer he'd trained himself to think in pieces. One part at a time and the machine was assembled, but you couldn't work on the whole machine at once; it was just too big and complex. One bit at a time. And he'd done that with this last week; one piece at a time, but when he tried to look at the events and the effects of the whole week at once, it made his head swim.

He sighed and turned his head to gaze into the woodland occupying the higher slope of the valley's side.

"Cernus… I need more direction. I'm getting lost in all of this."

But there was no sign of the great white stag.

The eaves of the forest glowered at him with what looked like malicious intent.

Vengen was more even than Salonius had expected. Once, long ago, it had been the hilltop fortress of the greatest of the northern tribes; so long ago that even the name of the tribe was considered obscure knowledge. The massive plateau had been carefully flattened and the steep banks on all sides carved and built into a succession of concentric ditches and embankments that would present, on their own, a serious impediment to attackers. Indeed, the innermost ditch even cleaved the hilltop in two, creating two separate zones connected by a bridge.

But where the ancient tribe had carved this monument to their independence, the Empire had done what it did best. Adopted, adapted and improved. Taking Vengen as the centre of military control for the entire northern quarter of the Empire, Imperial engineers had raised high walls with a series of towers around both separate zones. Each tower bore a siege weapon that, given the height of the plateau, would have an astounding range and field of fire.

Pennants bearing the Imperial raven and the wolf snapped in the late afternoon wind and sounds of civic and military life issued from beyond the walls. The young soldier stared up at the high walls and marvelled. Truly, this was a seat of Imperial power.

The riders and their escort slowly made their way among the maze of ridges that formed the slope leading up to the main gate, aware at all times of the number of guards watching over them from the walls above. As they approached, he noted the construction with a trained engineer's eye. There had been several different building phases at Vengen that had left the walls more than twice their original height, with a clear line showing the original parapet where the stonework changed. Indeed, the main gatehouse showed four very obvious stages of building, both upwards and outwards, with the last being an external barbican that added an extra level of defence and would be a brutal killing ground for attackers. And even though such defences were beyond the hope of any besieging army, it would still be easier than traversing the six ridges and ditches full of traps and sharpened stakes, all clearly within sight of the archers on the walls.

Vengen was prepared for any kind of assault, though it was clearly unnecessary. Vengen had never been attacked and, with the strength and control of the Empire, it never would be. Vengen was, without a doubt, the most impressive symbol of strength and control Salonius had ever seen.

They passed beneath the arch of the outer gate, two oak doors almost a foot thick standing open but constantly guarded and greased ready to close in a matter of mere moments. The holes in the ceiling of the outer barbican would rain fire and oil and other deadly missiles, blistering and killing a crush of attackers as they desperately tried to cross the yard to the inner gate. The walls connecting the outer barbican to the inner main gate were crenellated on the inside as well as the outside, giving defenders plenty of cover as they butchered the attackers below.

But all of this detail filtered into Salonius' mind on a subconscious, peripheral level, for from the moment he passed under the outer arch, his attention was seized and gripped tight by the main inner gate: an engineer's dream, be they military or civil.

"The great Golden Gate of Cassius." Whispered Catilina as she leaned toward him. "Impressive, isn't it?"

Salonius opened his mouth to reply, but words failed him. Instead, he turned momentarily to look at the pale and drawn lady beside him. The medics had advised they leave the shaft of the arrow in place until they reach hospital facilities at Vengen. They had confirmed that nothing critical had been pierced and that moving the arrow would cause bleeding and worsen her condition. They had given her some kind of medication for the pain, carefully bandaged her and left her in Salonius' care until she came around, which she'd done some four hours later. Salonius had cradled her gently, his eyes full of concern, and she had turned, looked up at him and smiled broadly.

"Did you arrange all this to get me on your horse?" she'd laughed. "Varro will be jealous!"

Since then, throughout the night and the next day, the lady had regained some of her strength, and certainly all her brightness and humour. That first night when they'd stopped for food she'd eaten ravenously and thanked Salonius for his cares before disappearing out of the circle of firelight with Varro for an hour.

And once they finished their meal and mounted once more, Catilina had taken her own horse back, brushing aside all queries and comments of concern...

"Stop staring at me Salonius. I'm fine!"

The young man felt an irritating blush rise to his cheeks and turned his attention back to the Golden Gate.

The Empire was known for its arches. There were glorious arches in the Imperial capital, or so he'd read, and quite a few out to the east, all celebrating the greatest victories of generals and Emperors, but he'd never seen one outside a sketched drawing. There was only one great triumphal arch in the northern lands, but it was reckoned by those in the know to be one of the best ever constructed.

Cassius had been the great conquering Emperor who, over two centuries ago, had almost doubled the size of the Empire in his short, twelve-year reign. He it was who brought the northern lands into the Empire and who had taken Vengen from the barbarian and made it an Imperial fortress. And to mark the conquest of the north, he had an arch built at Vengen to rival those back in Imperial Velutio. The second plateau of the fort had been retained for the military, but the arch stood at the entrance of what was to be the civilian settlement on the first plateau.

The triumphal arch was constructed of tufa, encased in shining white marble brought almost three hundred miles from the coastal ports solely for this monument. Rows of niches peppered the façade in neat lines. Not enough to destroy the simple elegance of the double-arched gate, but enough to house twenty statues, alternating between the great officers and generals of Cassius' army, and the figures of the barbarian leaders, proud and noble even in defeat. A work of beauty and genius, and one that, while promoting the ideal of the Imperial army, still managed to remind the viewer that the barbarians were an enemy worthy of extreme respect.

And then, atop the arch stood the great bronze statue of Cassius in his chariot, four shining metal horses snorting and stamping in their proud frenzy. The sun gleamed off the bronze that was kept polished at all times.

And the final addition to the arch, through which it had acquired its name: the great doors. Solid wood, two feet thick, reinforced in later years with iron, but faced with solid gold, attached to the wood with gold-plated bolts. The doors dazzled and flashed in the sunlight, a blazing, blinding reminder of the glory of the Empire.

Salonius realised he was holding his breath.

In later years, the arch had been incorporated into the walls of the outer bailey of Vengen when the civilian settlement had received its defensive walls. Few concessions had been made to the defensiveness of the glorious structure. The top had been crenellated, massive 'D' shaped towers had been added to either side, and one of the huge golden doors had been sealed permanently shut to restrict access. None of this had detracted from the arch. Indeed, in a curious way, it added to the beauty.

He was almost sad as they passed within the inner gate and entered the town proper of Vengen. The civilian settlement was quite small by Imperial standards, limited as it was by the dimensions of the plateau, but every inch of space on that hill top had been used to the greatest advantage. The buildings were generally three storeys tall and packed in with little or no yard or garden space and, by edict, all buildings in Vengen were of stone rather than wood, bearing in mind the danger posed by fire within the crowded press of the town.

Salonius was surprised, as they rode through the busy streets as to the makeup of the population. He wasn't sure what he expected; probably a mix between the more civilised northern tribesmen and Imperial settlers from the centre of the Empire. He wasn't expecting the cosmopolitan atmosphere Vengen apparently had.

The moment they entered the main street that ran across the town from the Golden Gate to the bridge across the gorge, a small, dark-skinned Pelasian man stepped out from a side street and started shouting something about a restaurant at him. Two crippled veterans of eastern extraction sat on a doorstep playing dice. The ebony skin of a southern tribesman grabbed his attention before he disappeared into the crowd.

The presence of the black-clad marshal's Guard kept people at bay, though. The beggars stared at them in abject misery from alleyways; street hawkers with their stalls of random goods tried one half-hearted shout and then turned their attention to more likely targets. Five minutes of riding at a slow pace brought them to the other end of Vengen's main street.

A small, yet heavily defensible, gate in the town walls stood open, guarded by four men. Beyond, a bridge arched out over the deep ditch between the two plateaus, wide enough to allow a cart or carriage or, in this case, three riders abreast. Salonius was impressed to note that every defensive effort had been taken even with the bridge. The parapet was smoothly rounded with no lip to allow a grapple hook. The other walls of the bridge sloped inwards as they rose such that, in the unlikely event of an attacker managing to create a stable ladder tall enough to reach, it would not settle comfortably against the stone. Even the stones themselves had been fitted flush and the cement between the blocks smooth and regularly repointed. Not a single handhold was visible anywhere on the bridge.

As they rode across the bridge, some ten yards long, he took in the walls and gate of the military sector of Vengen. Constructed earlier than the walls of the civil town, the military defences of Vengen were no less defensive or inventive. The buttresses of the towers spaced evenly around the plateau's circumference had been cleverly embedded in the rock that formed the bulk of the plateau, carved out to allow a fusion of solid rock and stonework. War machines stood atop each tower, as they had around the town, though the towers were more tightly spaced here.

The gate to the military plateau was the first they'd reached that stood closed. The column reined in on the bridge and the commander of the guard unit accompanying them rode out to the front and announced himself. Moments later the perfectly oiled and balanced gates swung ponderously open and the commander geed his horse and led them forward into the military sector.

Despite the limits imposed by the shape and size of the rocky plateau, the military fortress of Vengen had been very carefully and efficiently organised. Salonius picked out the different sections with an eye for their construction. To the left and right of the road by the bridge stood barrack blocks in neat rows; presumably the accommodation of the standing garrison. Beyond that, two large buildings to the right held the telltale signs of a bathhouse and a hospital. The presence of fountains and water troughs, presumably fed by natural springs, bore out that opinion. Opposite stood a plethora of smaller, more utilitarian buildings: granaries, store houses, workshops and the like.

Beyond them came more barracks. These, however, were set apart from each other in organised clusters with one small office-like building fronting on to the main road. Momentarily Salonius was confused by this, until he noticed the flags and standards proudly displayed outside the small office. The ram and lightening of the Fourth Army; the scorpion and crossed swords of the Fifth; the bull and crown of the Eleventh; the Goat and Star of the First. Of course, it was standard practice for one cohort of each army to be assigned to the marshal at Vengen. The Fourth had been excused for the last few months due to being on active campaign punishing border tribes for incursions and looting. Presumably Corda and the second cohort had now taken on the assignment at Vengen.

Ahead stood the huge complex of the marshal's palace; a mix of civilian comfort, civic government and military austerity. As he focused on it, the column once more came to a halt. Salonius and Catilina caught up with the others as Corda turned in his saddle.

"This is as far as I go for now. I've got to get things prepared for the second cohort when they arrive to take up residence. I expect I'll see you all in the morning."

Varro nodded.

"Don't know whether the marshal's going to want to see us tonight but I, for one, could seriously use a rest."

A chorus of nods answered him and he even raised a small grin from the commander of the marshal's guard. Corda gave them a brief salute, smiled a weary smile and, dismounting, led his horse between the buildings assigned to the Fourth Army.

Salonius watched him go and sighed. It would be good to sleep in a comfortable bed. With a chortle he remembered a conversation only a couple of weeks ago with one of his fellow engineers in which they had complained vociferously about the quality of the bunks in the barracks at Crow Hill. Thinking back, he realised how naïve he'd been. An engineer's bunk would have been immeasurably more comfortable than almost any of the recent places he'd spent the night wrapped in a blanket against the cold and welcoming the smell of the horses, because it meant that the beasts were close and radiating a tiny amount of heat. Bed.

"Salonius!"

He allowed his mind to focus once more and realised he'd almost drifted off wearily in the saddle and the column had begun to walk once more toward the marshal's palace. Looking around guiltily at the waiting guardsmen and with a faint colour rising in his cheek, he walked his horse on and caught up with the others.

The great doors of the palace were only a little less defensive than the entrance to the military compound had been. Guardsmen clad in black stood above the parapet and by the doorway. They saluted as the guard commander approached and dismounted. As his heavy boots hit the ground, he adjusted his armour with the clink of chainmail and handed his reins to his second in command. Turning back to the column, he gestured to the four remaining riders.

"We're on foot from here, gentlemen; my lady."

Varro nodded.

"If we're headed for the guest quarters, I know the way, commander."

"I realise that, Captain," the guardsman replied with a stony face, "but I have orders that you are to have guard protection at all times, and I am not about to exceed my authority just because we are within the palace."

Varro nodded again.

"Fair enough. Feels nice that someone has our back for a change."

They dismounted wearily and Salonius began to unhook his gear from the saddle. One of the escort leaned down.

"You can leave those, sir. We'll have them brought to you once the horses are stabled."

For a moment Salonius considered arguing. He didn't like leaving his few treasured possessions in the care of someone else, no matter who they were. But still, this was a courtesy and courtesy needed repaying in kind.

"Thank you," he replied, continuing to untie the two thongs that kept his tool roll attached. "If you have no objection, I will take this, as the contents need to be cleaned and oiled urgently."

The guard gave him an odd look and then shrugged.

"Of course, sir."

Salonius smiled at him and shouldered the roll, turning back to the others. He cast his eye over Varro's horse and cleared his throat.

"Captain?"

Varro turned. "Yes?"

"You need your medicine with you. You're overdue."

Varro glared at him, but reached into his saddle pack and withdrew his bag of medication.

"Lead on," he urged the guard commander and the four fell into step behind him as the tall man swept off into the palace, his black cloak billowing impressively behind him. The palace corridors continued the mixed theme of civic grandeur and military austerity. Everything was constructed of rare marble and expensive glass; the floors were panelled with black and white marble and occasional mosaics of heroic deeds. The only other decoration evident was statues and busts of Emperors, Gods and generals placed at strategic points.

Salonius noted with interest that a great emphasis had been placed on the last dynasty of Quintus and the architects of the

Empire's rebirth twenty years ago. Of course, Sabian had been a part of those momentous events, and yet no bust of the marshal was visible, evidence of his self-effacing modesty. A shrine to the Emperor at the end of the first main corridor exhibited a statue of Darius the Just, with a bust of marshal Caerdin to his right and some young man Salonius didn't recognise, but who bore a look of infinite sadness.

Turning at the shrine, they strode on past a hall of generals and finally to an octagonal room, lit by a glazed oculus in the ceiling. Doors radiated from the room in four directions, with alcoves between them displaying the symbols of the Empire and of the Dynasty of Quintus. The commander came to a halt and rapped on one of the doors. Two black-clad guardsmen opened the door from within to show a much more utilitarian, whitewashed concrete corridor. The commander gestured to the men.

"These two will escort you to your accommodation for the night and explain where everything is. I'm afraid that we must leave you here. The marshal wishes to see the Lady Catilina and then I have to speak to the hospital and have the surgeons report to the palace."

Salonius winced. Sabian would be furious with his daughter, and worried sick. As the commander saluted and he and Catilina left through a different doorway, the young man was impressed with the pride and confidence with which she held her head high. Watching her disappear, he turned back to the others to find Varro smirking at him.

"What?" he asked irritably.

"She can take care of herself, Salonius," the captain grinned.

One of the guards cleared his throat and the two of them joined Petrus who had already stepped into the corridor. Salonius noticed that the guards were glowering at him with some unreadable negative emotion behind their stony countenances and realised how this must look to professional soldiers. Here he was, a guard himself, answering back a Captain as though they were of an equal rank. He suddenly wondered when it had started to feel comfortable referring to Varro by name and not deferring to him. Curious.

The three travel-worn men walked the corridors with their escort, finally arriving at the guest quarters a few minutes later. One of the guards who accompanied them gestured to a series of doors along the right side of the corridor and cleared his throat.

"These three rooms will be yours. The baths…"

Varro waved a hand to cut him short and smiled.

"I know where everything is, soldier. Been here plenty of times. You two are dismissed."

The guardsman shook his head and stood straight.

"I'm afraid that's not your decision, sir. The marshal has given explicit orders that the three of you are to be under our protection at all times."

Varro glared at him as though the force of his stare would make the guard back down, but Sabian's men were of stronger stuff. The captain sighed and glanced at his two companions, looking them up and down.

"Very well. I presume our gear is being brought here shortly?"

The guardsman nodded.

"Alright then. Would you care to protect us to the bath house?"

As Varro leaned back on the crisp white sheets and allowed his head to sink gratefully into the goose-down pillow, he sighed with happiness. He'd extinguished the small oil lamp that burned on the small table beside the bed almost twenty minutes ago and yet, despite his weariness, sleep was slow in coming. His mind continued to reel and he continually reran the events and revelations of the last week in his head.

He was still on edge over the delay in seeing Sabian. Oh, he could understand tonight, for certain. The marshal would be tearing strips off his daughter, but that was not the reason for the pause. Sabian knew of Varro's condition and, given the exertions of the last few days, he was being careful with them all and allowing them time and space to recover before plunging on into ever deepening circles of treachery, particularly in the case of Varro.

He sighed. Thinking about his condition made him hurt. Either he'd been remarkably lucky with his pain so far or his fortitude was greater than Scortius had estimated. He'd taken the medication for his mental state religiously three times a day but had often wondered whether he could have got away with less; his fuzzy cloudiness had never returned. And only twice had he had to take more than one dose of the pain medication in a single day: once after they had nailed up the two men in the village, when he'd exerted himself too much and wrenched his wound, and once after the crazy ride back down from Saravis Fork. The horse riding had not been kind on him. Though perhaps it was the pain, the insistent, dull, nagging pain that was really keeping him awake tonight?

For a long moment, he weighed the pros and cons of leaving the warm and comfortable bed to take a second dose of pain medication. Eventually he sighed. The pain had won; he needed the sleep. With a groan, he pulled himself slowly upright and his feet fell to the tiled floor with a gentle slap.

Hauling himself upright, he tottered quietly over to the table where his belongings sat, the medication uppermost and easily accessible. He smiled to himself about peoples' priorities. Once they'd returned from the baths, they'd each returned to their rooms with their mind on a single task: Varro to take his medication, Petrus to grab some bread, meat and cheese, and Salonius? He chuckled to himself quietly. Salonius had been itching to finish his bath so that he could go and clean his tool kit!

He reached into the pouch and was feeling around for the three different pouches of medicine, his tongue protruding from the corner of his mouth with the effort, when he fell silent. Why, he couldn't have said, but suddenly the hairs were standing up on the back of his neck. Very slowly and quietly, he reached down beside the table and picked up his sword. Gritting his teeth, he drew the blade from its sheath with agonising slowness, trying to mute the sound as much as possible.

There it was again. Outside the window.

Frowning with concentration, he tried to focus in the dark on the window with its intricate latticework shutters. It must be a cloudy night, for it was almost as dark outside as it was in the room. He concentrated on the window, hefting his sword.

The scudding cloud saved his life.

Momentarily, the moon peeked out from behind the high, wispy cloud, and Varro saw the outline of the man outside the window. His heightened senses as he strained to work out what was happening, caught the sound of the torsion cable at almost breaking point. He threw himself at an angle on to the bed, just as the missile was released with a 'twang'. The delicate wooden latticework exploded into finely carved wooden shards as the small bolt passed through the shutter directly at Varro. Had he not moved swiftly he would now be lying on the floor with a foot-long shaft buried in his heart. As it was, perhaps he'd not moved fast enough anyway; the bolt had torn a piece from his neck muscle and gone on to bury itself in the opposite wall.

With a growl, he pulled himself upright, quickly checking the window before he raised himself over the protective level of the bed. There was no sign of the figure and in the silence he listened but heard nothing. Damn, this man was good!

He rushed over to the window and glanced out in every direction. The small courtyard garden was mostly in shadow. Half a dozen people could have hidden in there, but Varro knew full well the man had already gone. Hand held torsion weapons were not exactly cheap or easy to come by. They were almost exclusively in the employ of Pelasian assassins from that that great sandy land beyond the Empire's eastern border. Since the reunification of the Empire, the treaty with Pelasia had led to there being many thousands of Pelasians within Imperial lands. Good for trade, he reflected; bad for Varro!

Rushing over to the door, he unlocked it and wrenched it open to confirm his suspicions. The two black-clad palace guardsmen lay on the floor of the corridor. They could be dealt with later. Damn Pelasians and their codes and honour. They'd kill their targets, but bystanders were outside the contract. These two had been drugged. He glanced along the corridor, but there was no sign of life. Taking a few quick and quiet steps, he gently tried Petrus' door. Still locked.

Ducking back into his room, he ran across to the window and clambered out of it, wincing at the mixed pains of his old and new wounds. Ten steps across the shadowed courtyard brought him to what he'd feared. Petrus' window had a neat hole in it. That 'twang' had been the first noise that had attracted Varro's attention as he was rummaging in his bag.

Biting his lip in anticipation, he eased the shutters open and peered inside into the dark. Slowly his eyes adjusted to the almost pitch blackness within. Petrus lay on the comfortable bed in a wide glistening pool of his own blood. The tip of a bolt protruded from his chest.

"Shit!"

Varro took a deep breath and stepped back from the window. Time to grieve later. He rubbed his scalp, trying to think what to do next through the growing pain in his side and the throbbing in his neck.

Salonius!

He ran across to the next window and his breath caught in his throat as he saw the small, neat hole in the shutter. The assassin had had time to work quietly on these two, but had been forced to adjust his tactics when he'd seen that Varro was awake and upright. With a sigh, he leaned across and opened the shutters. The shape in the bed was absolutely still with a foot of dark hardwood protruding from the top. He moaned in anguish.

"Salonius, for Gods' sake. You're supposed to have been chosen by Cernus!"

With a deep sigh, he climbed in through the window, landing heavily and with a jarring sensation on the floor by the bed.

He blinked.

Reaching out, he prodded the bed.

Laughing, he prodded it some more and then pulled the top sheet aside. The shape in the bed had clearly not been human, but from outside the window with the faint moonlight to the rear, the shape had been indistinguishable in the darkness.

He laughed out loud, causing himself to choke slightly as the pain in his neck twinged badly. Salonius had carefully laid out all of his pack and goods on the bed, including his saddle bags and sleeping roll. They were all neatly arranged and had been recently cleaned and polished; indeed the cleaning rags, oil and polish sat on the small table by the bed. The industrious little bastard couldn't sleep with the knowledge that he had tools that needed oiling.

Varro laughed again and walked across to the door. Opening it, he peered outside, to see Salonius two doors down, peering around the door frame of Varro's room.

"Varro?"

"Salonius! Gods be damned, there you are. Where did you go?"

The young man walked along the corridor, a sword in his hand. Varro pointed at it and Salonius glanced down and noticed the blade in his hand.

"Took it from one of the guards. I saw them down and your door open and feared the worst."

"Where *were* you?" Varro repeated.

"Couldn't sleep," the young man shrugged. "I went to see if I could find someone who could tell me how Catilina was."

Varro smiled, and a sadness slipped across it. Salonius frowned at him.

"Petrus?" he asked in a small voice.

"Dead. Bastard nearly got me too. And he's put a nice neat hole in your saddle!"

"Did you see him?"

Varro nodded.

"Sort of. Only a shape. Pelasian though, so I doubt we'll find him now."

Salonius shook his head irritably.

"So we've no evidence, and now we can't even produce Petrus' testimony! All we can do is make unfounded accusations about Cristus to the marshal."

"Not exactly," Varro disagreed. "Sabian's now well aware of the problem. We've got the actions of the garrisons of Saravis Fork and the mountain way station backing our story. And what you noticed about the rebuilding of the fort, or lack thereof, stands as some proof anyway."

He took in the sceptical look on Salonius' face and gave an evil smile that contained no humour.

"Anyway, all I need is for Sabian to stay out of the way. This is personal between me and Cristus. I don't care whether he gets demoted or humiliated or even executed. What I want is to hear him admit to his treachery and to hear him beg for his life." His smile became even more predatory. "Which I am not going to allow him. I am going to cut that sack of shit into ribbons so thin you could pass him through a portcullis!"

Salonius opened his mouth as though to raise objections, but stopped after an indrawn breath. He frowned, looked over his shoulder at the two unconscious guards, allowed his gaze to stop for a moment on Petrus' closed door, and then turned a smile on Varro that was so frighteningly wicked and uncharacteristic that Varro actually took a step backwards.

"Good." The young man growled.

Varro clapped his hands together and then rubbed them in a business like fashion.

"Alright. First thing's first. Got to go see Sabian."

Salonius shook his head. He gestured at Varro and waved his hand up and down.

"Not yet. Back to your room first."

"What?"

Salonius sighed. "Your waist is leaking again, you've got a chunk of neck missing, which is pouring blood down your chest and your hand is shaking violently. You need your wounds dressed, to take some of your medicine, and to put something clean on if you're presenting yourself to the marshal in his own fortress."

Varro frowned and opened his mouth to speak, but Salonius clamped his teeth shut defiantly and pointed at the captain's door. Like a scolded school boy, Varro nodded unhappily and walked over to his room. Salonius returned briefly to his own room and retrieved the emergency kit he'd been carrying since they left Crow Hill. By the time he entered Varro's room, the Captain was already sitting on his bed with his bloodied tunic on the floor. Rivulets of already-drying blood snaked down his chest and back and the wound at his side, though now partially healed, oozed a small trickle of blood. Salonius shook his head and pointed at Varro. "Do that."

"What?"

"Shake your head."

Varro tried to shake his head, but as he faced left and the muscle in his neck stretched, blood pumped from the missing chunk of neck muscle.

"Shit! Thanks, Salonius!"

The young man smiled.

"I just wanted to make sure it was just a surface wound and he'd not impaired the muscle."

"Gods," grumbled Varro. "You're starting to sound a lot like Scortius!"

Salonius' smile widened.

"I'm interested in the mechanics of the body. It's not so far removed from engineering really. You'd be amazed."

Varro growled and dabbed at the wound on his neck, wincing.

Salonius reached into the bag he'd brought through from his room and withdrew his clean bandages, fasteners and swabs. Laying everything out on the table, he pointed at the table.

"You need to have some of that medicine too."

Varro nodded and, half standing, reached forward towards the table. With a whimper, he crashed to the floor. Salonius dived to him in a panic and hauled him off the floor.

"What happened?"

Varro shook his head and whimpered again at the added pain that brought.

"Don't know…" he breathed desperately between rasping gasps. "Just lost all strength… Almost blacked out… It felt like I was on fire… All over."

Salonius frowned.

We've got to get you sorted but you're going to see Scortius before we go to the marshal. Scortius is in the palace looking after Catilina, so I heard."

He was a little surprised at the fact that Varro nodded meekly with no resistance. In fact that worried him more than the collapse. Hurrying over to the table, he fished out the small, waterproof bag from Varro's medical supplies. Reaching into his own kit he withdrew a small set of weights and a hand-held scale. Carefully weighing the contents of the bag, he divided it up and selected a quarter of it, sliding it onto a small piece of greased paper.

"Take that!"

"What is it?" Varro focused with some difficulty on the oily mixture the young man proffered him.

"It's the big, bad medicine that Scortius gave you. The stuff to take as a last resort."

Varro turned his furrowed brow on Salonius and the young man sighed.

"I think you've just taken a left turn into the last resort, Varro. Take the medicine."

As Varro gingerly imbibed the mixture, his face undergoing a serious of expressions ranging from curiosity, through disgust to downright horror, Salonius began the task of carefully binding the captain's wounds.

He smiled.

"I should draw three lots of pay: guardsman, engineer and field medic!"

Varro glared at him and tried to say something cutting, but the movement of his tongue in his mouth brought all new nightmare sensations to his taste buds. He settled for giving the young man his least happy glare.

Corruption hides within the light...

Ridiculous, I know. Despite recognising with absolute certainty that Cernus exists and having been face to face with the Great White Stag Lord twice, I'd still largely dismissed him. Not 'dismissed' as such, but shuffled him to the back of my mind, behind the stacks of things that appeared to be more urgent. I think that everything we did was informed in some way by the deep background understanding that Cernus had chosen us; had guided us in some way, but sometimes, in the heat of battle or under the pressure of events, we tended to forget that.

Salonius and I strode at some speed through the corridors of the palace. Although we were in a hurry to get to both Scortius and Sabian, Salonius wouldn't let me run for fear it would cause my wounds to open and bleed further. In actual fact, as we tramped along the corridor, we were deep in some heated argument; I forget now what it was about, but it probably revolved around my declining state of health. I do know that we were so involved in our conversation that we were paying precious little attention to where we were going.

We rounded a corner; I remember that neither of us were paying attention. I was prodding Salonius in the chest with my index finger and shouting in his face, and Salonius was bright red, mouthing argumentative nothings at me.

We both stopped dead.

My finger slowly fell from Salonius' chest and the words died in my mouth. We were at a junction in the corridor. I know my way round the palace at Vengen very well. Behind us lay the main entrance and the guest accommodations. To the left lay the administrative area, including Sabian's office where we'd be heading later. To the right there were other areas, including the very heavily-guarded private quarters of the marshal and his family.

The corridor here was of beautiful marbles; a mixture of golden yellow stone from the harsh, dry quarries of the southern lands and powerful porphyry from the eastern provinces. The floor was a geometric pattern of beautiful shapes and colours. And in the centre of it stood a white stag.

I remember Salonius gripping me suddenly on the shoulder, just below my neck wound, so hard I almost passed out. We stopped and stared at the stag. Not only was the situation so astoundingly surreal, given where we were, but we were together. I learned from conversations with Salonius that Cernus sometimes makes his presence known to his favoured peoples by appearing before an entire tribal army prior to a battle but, barring that incredibly rare event, an encounter with the stag lord is an extremely private thing. And yet here we were; the two of us staring straight into those soulful and unbelievably deep, wise eyes.

I reached up and prised Salonius' fingers from my shoulder and we stood, silent and motionless, staring at that strange forest God. For what seemed like hours, though in truth would have been brief moments, we stood there, and suddenly, without a sound or motion, the stag turned and trotted off down one of the corridors. I remember taking a step forward. I was intrigued as to where he would go. Would he just vanish a few steps further away? But Salonius grasped my shoulder again and pointed at the wall behind the spot where Cernus had stood.

I turned my gaze there, but all that was there was a dirty mark on the marble. I shrugged and enquired what was so interesting, and Salonius' voice was quiet and a little shaky as he replied. He told me of the language the priests of the northern tribes use; the symbols they carve in their holy rocks; he told me of the symbol before us. What would look like a swirl of dirty marks on the wall to the layman bellowed a word in the secret tongue of the northerners, and that word was 'Betrayer'.

I began to argue over what could just as easily be coincidence and actual dirt, but two things stopped me: logic and magic. This was one of the most frequented corridors in the palace of the marshal and there would be no dirty mark of that size here. And, in the presence of Cernus, in whom I now had no doubt, what would normally seem irrelevant or coincidental suddenly took on a new light.

Salonius and I walked slowly and thoughtfully, our argument forgotten.

Chapter Eleven

Varro and Salonius were deep in hushed conversation when they arrived in the corridor outside Catilina's room. Two black-clad guardsmen stood at attention outside. Varro held his hand up to Salonius and their conversation halted for a moment as the captain addressed the guardsmen.

"Varro and Salonius of the Fourth to see the lady and her doctor."

The man saluted. "Just a moment, sir."

While the second guard watched the two of them carefully, the first knocked quietly.

"Yes?" Came a testy male voice from within.

The guard announced the two visitors, and Varro distinctly heard Scortius swearing and Catilina berating him for it. After a brief whispered conversation, the lady spoke clearly.

"Send them in!"

The guardsman opened the door and, stepping to one side, saluted smartly. Varro gave him a sloppy, half-hearted salute that he knew would irritate the man and sauntered in with Salonius hard on his heels. Catilina was sitting upright in her bed, fully clothed, as Scortius arranged what was clearly her medicine on the table close by.

"How are you?" the Captain asked with concern.

She smiled lightly and stretched her right arm out behind her. It swung back until it was out to the side, but as it passed straight and moved behind her, she bit her lip and Varro could clearly see the pain it was causing her.

"Oh, I'll live, Varro. Actually it's not really that bad."

Varro glanced across at Scortius, who nodded absently. Without taking his eyes off the medicines before him, he muttered "Young lad did a good job." Pushing the collection of small parcels towards Catilina, the doctor stood.

"I'll get out of your way."

Varro waved his hand.

"Actually, it was you I wanted to see first, Scortius."

The doctor shook his head.

"Sorry, Varro. I've been researching every text I can find, and experimenting with everything I can think of, but I've found no solution so far."

Varro waved this aside, but Scortius went on "Don't give up, though. Mercurias is here... the Emperor's chief physician, and he's helping me research. He's even brought some eastern works on the subject."

Varro continued to wave at him.

"That's not what I need to see you about. I've got a fresh damn wound!"

As Varro took a seat and removed his tunic, Scortius walked over to him with a look of interest. Catilina frowned.

"What happened?"

Varro growled and began to peel the fresh dressing from his neck.

"Cristus gets to us, even here."

"What?" Catilina swung her legs over the side of the bed.

"Petrus." Varro paused and sighed. "They got Petrus. A Pelasian assassin. Nearly got me too."

Salonius leaned toward the doctor and said quietly "He's just had some of your last-resort intense medicine. Thought you'd want to know before you give him anything else."

Scortius nodded and Salonius returned his attention to Catilina, who was now on her feet, her exquisite face full of concern.

"Not a Pelasian, Varro."

The captain shook his head and winced at the pain.

"I'm pretty sure he was a Pelasian. Dressed all in black, using a Pelasian weapon, quick and quiet, and gone before I could pin him down."

Catilina shook her head defiantly.

"I don't care, Varro, it wasn't a Pelasian. No Pelasians ever come inside Vengen except as ambassadors."

Varro grumbled.

"It's not as secure as you think. Pelasians can get anywhere. It's what they do!"

"Not here," she repeated with infuriating calm. "When Prince Ashar signed his treaties with the Emperor, one of the stipulations of freeing the borders was that Pelasian assassins would

196

never violate certain locations, and the fortresses of the marshals are on that list."

Varro growled.

"I think you're being a little naïve, Catilina. Ouch!"

He glared at Scortius, who merely tutted and turned the patient's head away again.

Catilina bridled.

"No Pelasian would break that accord. You know how they are about Ashar; he's more than a God to them."

Varro frowned. "You're right, of course." He turned to Salonius. "I think we've got a problem."

The young man nodded.

"Someone masquerading as a Pelasian to lay the blame with them," he grumbled.

"Not just that," Varro growled. "That someone was within the Palace. That means he's one of our own again. Maybe a Pelasian could sneak in to Vengen. They train all their lives to do things like that. But if it's not a Pelasian assassin, then it's realistically got to be someone who was already in the military compound of Vengen. And that makes it ninety per cent sure he's a soldier! Either Cristus has friends in the First, the Fifth or the Eleventh, or among Sabian's own men, or…"

Salonius' face hardened. "Or Sergeant Corda brought traitors from the Fourth with him!"

The two shared a look.

"Betrayer" they said in unison.

Catilina walked a few steps and then crouched in front of Varro.

"We have to go see my father straight away."

Varro nodded.

"I agree, but just let Scortius finish here first."

Beside him, the doctor sighed as he cleaned the wound.

Varro, Salonius and Catilina arrived at the office of the marshal just as the great bell in the tower at the edge of the complex tolled eleven times. Salonius had been sceptical that the marshal would be available to see them, but Catilina had assured him that Sabian would still be in his office, deeply involved in his work.

The two guards outside the door moved into a defensive posture as the three figures emerged from the corridor, though as soon as they identified the marshal's daughter, they stood to attention and saluted.

"I take it my father is in?" Catilina asked, idly drumming the fingers of her left hand on the back of her right hand, which rested in a sling to aid the healing of her shoulder wound.

One of the guards cleared his throat.

"The marshal is unavailable, I'm afraid, ma'am, even to yourself. We have strict instructions for total privacy."

Catilina glared at him, and the guard shuffled nervously.

"You will announce me this instant or by morning you will find yourself cleaning latrines on a border post. Do you understand me?"

The guard risked a glance at his counterpart, who stared rigidly ahead with an air of relief.

"Erm… The marshal gave orders…"

Catilina smiled a horribly vengeful smile at him and walked across to the door. The guard fumbled with his sword and dithered, unsure of where he stood in these circumstances. The young lady twisted the handle on the door and swept in regally without a further glance at the guards. As Varro and Salonius followed her in, the captain patted the guard on the shoulder.

"Don't worry. They'll both have too much on their plate shortly to even think about you."

The guard look unconvinced and returned to attention as the door to the marshal's office closed.

Varro walked straight into the back of Catilina, who had stopped immediately inside the door, and Salonius consequently bumped into him too. The pair of them peered around the lady's lustrous black curls and stared for a moment before they remembered where they were and came to attention. Varro had been expecting Sabian to be poring over maps, or perhaps writing furiously. What he hadn't been prepared for was the Marshal being draped over his seat, with a cup in his hand and an almost empty bottle on the table. He recognised the smell of cheap northern spirits from the doorway.

"Father?" Catilina's voice hovered somewhere between prim disgust, worry and anger.

Sabian hauled himself upright with some stiffness of muscles. Varro heaved a sigh of relief; the marshal had been drinking, but was still compos mentis at least.

"Ah, Catilina. I thought of sending for you, but I was sure you'd come once Scortius had finished with you. I thought you'd come alone though. I wasn't planning to see these three until the morning."

Salonius and Varro shared an unspoken look behind the lady as Varro held up three fingers.

"Father, can we put aside your disappointment in me and your anger, and assume that you're not going to punish me in the end anyway. It'll save a lot of time, and this is too important to mess around with family squabbles."

Sabian's face hardened.

"Catilina," he growled, "you are not ingratiating yourself with me."

His daughter merely folded her arms defiantly, thought with some difficulty, given the sling, and gave him a patronising look.

"Catilina," the marshal's voice raised slightly and dangerously, "don't play games with me, girl. I'm not drunk but I *am* angry."

The young lady sighed and allowed her arm to drop back down to her side.

"Very well, father. You can shout at me, withdraw my privileges, restrict my movement or whatever the hell it is you want to do to punish me, but be angry later; there just isn't time now!"

Something about her words sank in and Sabian seemed to deflate slightly. His eyes wandered behind her and rested for a moment on her two companions.

"I assumed Petrus would be with you?"

Varro stepped out beside Catilina.

"That's the problem, sir."

"What? You *can't* have *lost* him?"

Varro sighed.

"Petrus has gone to the Gods. About fifteen minutes ago" he said sadly.

"Nearer twenty, I think," corrected Salonius.

Sabian pushed himself upright, slapping the cup down on the desk and sweeping it aside.

"What happened?"

The three visitors stepped forward and relaxed their posture slightly.

"Assassination," Varro announced bluntly. "Someone killed Petrus and tried the same with Salonius and me; thinks he got Salonius, too."

Sabian blinked. "Assassins? In Vengen? That's outrageous!"

"But true. I saw him in the garden outside the guest wing. He was kitted out like a Pelasian, but your daughter assures me that there's no way he could actually have been a Pelasian?"

The marshal nodded in a distracted fashion.

"Sir?" Varro prompted.

"Hmm?" Sabian turned and focused on the captain again. "What? Oh, yes. She's right. You'll not find a Pelasian here unless he's staying in the guest wing and wearing official regalia. Prince Ashar is a good friend of both mine and the Emperor's."

"Then someone in Vengen is dressed like a Pelasian and using one of their hand bows; someone in the fortress."

The marshal frowned.

"Assuming this is Cristus playing his hand, who could he have his hooks into here?"

Varro shrugged.

"Sadly, just about anyone. I…"

Suddenly the captain groaned as his eyes rolled up into his head and he slumped. Salonius, quick as a flash, grabbed Varro around the torso as he fell, lowering him gently to the floor."

The young man looked up to see Catilina staring in horror and Sabian rushing around the side of his desk towards them.

"It's alright," Salonius reassured them, "he's breathing. It's just a reaction. Scortius warned me about this. About fifteen minutes ago he had some very strong medication. He's supposed to be resting as much as possible anyway, but he's overdone it. Two wounds, running around and, of course, his blood pressure's pretty high even normally."

Catilina's face continued to verge on panic as she knelt beside the unconscious captain. Sabian, approaching, stood above her and looked down on her and the captain with a curious look on his face. The marshal crouched and grasped Varro by a shoulder. With a nod to Salonius, the two men hauled Varro up and dragged him across to Sabian's couch, followed closely by the worried Catilina. They gently lay the captain on the soft velvet and tucked a cushion behind his head.

"He's lucky to have you looking after him," the marshal noted, giving Salonius an appraising glance.

"Just my duty, sir." Replied the young man modestly.

Catilina crouched by the divan and gently mopped Varro's brow with a soft cloth. Sabian gave her a quick concerned look, grasped Salonius' shoulder and guided him away across the room. When they were a considerable distance away from Varro and Catilina, he let go and rubbed his hands together thoughtfully.

"I don't think this is a duty thing, lad. I'm very much under the impression that the only people Varro can trust are in this room right now. We have a problem and we need to work out what we're going to do about it."

Salonius frowned.

"With respect, sir, we need to find this assassin."

"Agreed," Sabian nodded. "The question is: how to go about it?"

Salonius glanced briefly towards the door.

"We could perform a search, sir? The assassin was in Pelasian blacks and carrying a hand bow. I would assume that anyone leaving the military compound will be logged, so there are three possibilities as I see it."

Sabian raised a questioning eyebrow.

"Well, sir," Salonius answered quickly, "either the assassin fled the compound, in which case he'll have been logged by the guards at the gate, or he's still got the equipment stashed somewhere, in which case we can find it, or…"

"Or what?"

"Well, if it was me, sir, I'd have thrown the clothes and weapon over the walls. Removes any link with the guilty party."

"Damn it, your right." Sabian ground his teeth. "I'm going to have my commander organise a search of the compound and of the ditches below the walls, but if he's thrown them away we're going to have serious trouble pinning anyone down."

"Perhaps, sir, but perhaps not. It all depends on what the search turns up."

Sabian glanced back across the room to where his daughter continued her ministrations.

"What's best for Varro right now?"

"If it's alright with you, sir, I think we should leave him where he is for now." Salonius answered. "Perhaps we should send for Scortius?"

Sabian nodded.

"I'll have him and Mercurias both attend." He glanced over at his daughter again. "Catilina? Salonius and I have business to attend to. I'm sending the doctors to have a look at Varro, but I think you should stay with him."

Catilina gave him a weak smile.

"Out of trouble, you mean father?"

It was mid morning when Salonius and the marshal made their careful way along the deep grass ditch below the walls of Vengen. They had spent the morning organising the search, watching the darkness slowly give way to the dawn somewhere in the process. The compound had been sealed with the exception of the particular unit of Sabian's guard that had been given the task of searching below the walls. The names of everyone who had left the compound between the time of the attack and the sealing of the gate had been taken, and each one of those individuals had been tracked down in the civilian settlement and brought back to the military compound. They numbered eight soldiers from the army, three from the First, two from the Fourth, one from the Fifth and two from the Eleventh, four members of Sabian's guard, six of the Vengen garrison, and nine of the ancillary staff. Tracking them down in the crowded town must have been a monumental task, but the marshal's guards had carried it out efficiently and without complaint.

As Salonius and Sabian went about their work throughout the morning, they'd watched with growing impatience as black-clad guards methodically turned the palace upside down, searching every room and corridor systematically, with the exception of Sabian and Catilina's quarters. Once they'd finished with the palace, they moved on like a plague of very organised locusts, tearing apart the barracks of the four army cohorts, moving on to the garrison barracks, the stores, and so on. Even the granaries had been emptied and replaced. Salonius had been impressed at the level of activity and the effort put into this and wondered why Varro was so important that the marshal himself would turn Vengen upside down to aid him.

And finally he had come to the conclusion, as he watched the marshal at work, that Sabian was the kind of man who simply wouldn't allow inefficiency and corruption within his demesne, and the young man found a new level of respect for the older man by his side. Sabian controlled Vengen, and therefore felt himself responsible for anything that happened within its walls. Perhaps he even felt a personal responsibility for Petrus' death.

He simply wouldn't rest until this was put right.

And throughout the morning's activity, that single-minded need had driven him to push his men constantly. And all of it had led to the two of them traipsing through the grass, still damp with morning dew where the high walls had kept the ditch in shadow throughout the morning.

"It's taken you all morning to search this?" Sabian demanded irritably of the black-clad captain who had led the exterior search.

"This ditch and the next outer one, sir, to be certain." Salonius glanced at the guard and was surprised to see a sympathetic half-smile rather than the irritable defensiveness he'd expected. The marshal and his men shared a bond that the had been lacking between Cristus and the Fourth. "We were very much hampered by the conditions sir. The search has been much faster since the sun came properly up.

Sabian sighed and nodded.

"My apologies Captain. It's been a hard night. I understand what you've had to deal with."

The marshal rubbed his tired eyes and straightened his shoulders.

"So tell me about this" he said, gesturing with an outstretched arm toward a knot of black uniforms surrounding a small area.

The captain cleared his throat.

"One of the men found them around fifteen minutes ago sir. The bow had been broken into small pieces and both it and a heavy brick had been wrapped in the clothes, tied with cord and thrown from somewhere up there." He pointed to an area of wall high up.

"Have you examined the items close up?"

The captain nodded.

"It's not good news, sir."

Sabian raised an eyebrow.

The guard cleared his throat. "I believe it was one of the army cohorts, sir.

"Explain?"

"Well, sir, the clothes aren't Pelasian, for certain. What they are is a military tunic and breeches dyed black. The head covering's just a standard soldier's cloak cut into strips and dyed. As for the bow, it's a genuine Pelasian bow, but looking at it closely shows a few anomalies."

"Anomalies?" Salonius asked curiously.

The captain gave the young man a quick appraising look and then answered with a surprisingly deferential tone.

"The bow is made the traditional Pelasian way: a wood core for flexibility with horn and sinew all bound to the wood for strength and birch bark for protection from the elements. The problem is that the condition shows that this bow is an old one. It's got to be three or four decades old if it's a day, sir. On top of that, it's been repaired at least a half dozen times and the string on it is new. This kind of thing appears on the black market every now and then, sir. I've seen it before. This has been nowhere near a Pelasian for decades. Someone bought it and recently restrung it."

Sabian smiled.

"Good work, captain. Pass that along to your men. I'll make my appreciation felt once I've finished dealing with it."

They arrived at the huddled group of guardsmen. As Sabian crouched and began to examine the items, Salonius instead stood with his hand shading his eyes from the glare of the bright sky and stared up at the top of the walls. Briefly he scanned to left and right along the parapet, from the walls facing the civilian settlement to the far end where the ditches curved around the cliff-like walls below Sabian's palace. He frowned and studied the face of the wall.

"Marshal?"

Sabian looked up, the black bundle of cloth in his hands.

"Mmm?"

"Is there any time, say in a change of shift, when the guard presence on the walls is diminished?"

Sabian frowned and look at the captain next to him questioningly.

The soldier cleared his throat.

"No sir. The change of shift is given a five minute overlap for security. In fact, during the change of shift there's briefly twice the number of men on the walls."

Salonius tapped his lip thoughtfully.

"Thank you, captain."

Sabian narrowed his eyes.

"What are you thinking?"

"Well, sir," Salonius replied. "It seems to me that there's no way, even in the middle of the night for a man to get onto the walls and throw anything over without being in clear view of at least one of the sentries."

"You're right." The marshal frowned and followed Salonius' gaze up to the parapets and then allowed his eyes to wander slowly back down.

"You're thinking about the windows."

"Yes, sir." Salonius turned to the marshal, his face dark. "And I've been working it out. That's the quarters of the Fourth."

Sabian stared up at the narrow, defensive windows high above them, and let out a slow groan.

"Varro's not going to like this."

"No, sir."

As the marshal and his young companion strode across the compound with the black-clad captain in their wake, Salonius let out a worried grunt; the latest of many such since they'd decided on their course of action in the ditch below.

"I'm still not sure this is a good idea, sir." He winced and yet was astounded at his own audacity. A week ago he wouldn't have spoken like this to the engineer sergeant, yet here he was questioning the judgement of a man who was probably the second most powerful man in the Empire, and certainly someone who could have Salonius broken on a wheel before he had a chance to blink.

Sabian, however, didn't even bother to turn his head.

"I don't see what other option there is, Salonius. We have to rely on traditional methods for uncovering the culprits."

Salonius deferred to the marshal's judgement, while remaining visibly unconvinced. Sabian sighed and turned to the captain behind him.

"They're all in quarters?"

"Yes, sir," the man replied. "All the officers and men of the cohorts and the garrison were returned to quarters as soon as we began the search. They've all been accounted for by head count."

"Good," Sabian rumbled. "Deploy the men."

"Very good, sir."

The captain turned and called out a string of orders. Three units of the marshal's guard who had been following up some distance behind them reacted instantly, their sergeants relaying appropriate orders. In a matter of a couple of minutes almost a score of black-garbed soldiers hand filed out into a wide circuit surrounding the barracks and quarters of the Fourth Army.

Saddened beyond belief by the necessity of his actions, Salonius accompanied the marshal and the guard captain as they strode toward the door of the command building. Twenty yards from the entrance they stopped. Sabian nodded to Salonius and the captain, who drew his sword and hefted it in his hand.

Salonius, his face bleak and unhappy, reached out and collected the two unit standards bearing the ram and lightning bolt of the Fourth. Stepping back with them, he came to attention like a standard bearer next to the marshal, who cleared his throat.

"Commander and senior officers of the Fourth Army, Second Cohort to the front, *now!*" he shouted, with a great deal of grit and emphasis on the last word.

There was a sudden sound of activity in the command building, and a moment later the door swung open. Sergeant Corda stepped out into the brightening sunshine, followed by the ten squad sergeants, the quartermaster, chief engineer and adjutant. With military precision, they fell into rank in order of seniority and marched out into the dusty ground before the quarters, where they lined out and saluted.

Sabian let out a menacing growl. Salonius glanced at him in surprise and, realising it had been involuntary, hurriedly returned his eyes to the front. Once more, the marshal nodded at him. Salonius feared that his heart might break.

"Officers of the Fourth!" shouted Sabian. "This is Vengen. The office of the marshal of the northern armies and stronghold of Imperial power and justice. For centuries this place has been inviolable. Even in the civil wars, this place remained peaceful in the hands of Velutio. The name Vengen is synonymous with the military, and that link has today been broken!"

Again his voice raised in power at the end. Salonius shivered as, on cue and with deliberate flourish, he cast the standard of the Fourth into the dust at his feet. The knuckles on both of his hands were white as he gripped the remaining standard tight as though his life depended on it.

"The Fourth has been dishonoured!" the marshal shouted. "I choose to believe that the fault lies with an individual or at most a few men and as such am willing to give the Second Cohort the chance to regain its honour."

On cue and with heaviness of heart, Salonius turned the second standard horizontal and, bringing it down hard across his knee, broke it in half before throwing it to the dust next to the other. He stared down at the ram, the lightning bolt, and the 'II' staring accusingly back up at him from among the dirt.

Sabian growled again.

"I give you and your men twenty minutes to deliver to me the men responsible for a cowardly attack in the dark last night that resulted in the death of a respected veteran and the wounding of your senior officer. If this does not occur, I will hold the entire cohort in contempt."

He let this sink in for a second and then went on in a low, menacing tone.

"I will then have set my guards to extracting information from you all, which will not be a pleasant task, but will be considerably nicer for them than it will for you. When I find the responsible parties, they will be dealt with, your second standard will be destroyed, the unit will be disbanded, and every remaining man will be dishonourably discharged with no pension."

Again, a pause for effect, before his voice softened once again.

"But you know that I abhor needless violence, so use the next twenty minutes well and get me those men and you can collect your standard and bear it aloft again."

He turned his back on the officers and Salonius could clearly see the cruel misery in his eyes. The marshal truly hated this.

There was a pregnant pause. Salonius let his eyes fall and stared at his feet once again considered the marshal's course of action, the success of which lay in the belief that the culprit would have retained the self-sacrificing honour that informed the code of military conduct in the Imperial army. It seemed unlikely to the young soldier that anyone cowardly enough to commit an assassination against one of their own was unlikely to be willing to lay down their own life for the good of their unit. And a knock-on effect of that would be the punishment of the second cohort and the disbanding of the unit under dishonourable circumstances. He sighed and raised his eyes once more to see sergeant Corda standing several paces forward clear of the line. The interim commander of the second cohort cleared his throat.

"This is not necessary, marshal."

Sabian turned and stared at the sergeant.

"Corda?"

"I will name the names you need, sir."

Sabian stared at him, his mouth falling open. Corda clamped his teeth together and Salonius blinked. Corda?

Out of the corner of his eye he caught a movement and his eyes slipped behind the proud, defiant sergeant, to the sergeant behind him. Salonius vaguely recognised him. He'd been one of the squad sergeants and, by the looks of it, had been pushed up to Corda's second in command. Perhaps the man was going to stop this madness? And then he noticed the man's arm, hidden in the folds of his military cloak. There was a momentary flash of steel from within the shadows of the green material.

"Shit" he muttered to himself as he noted the absence of a sword hilt projecting from the man's scabbard by his side.

"No names!" shouted the deputy sergeant, suddenly pulling his hand out from his cloak and lunging at Corda for the kill.

The world slipped into slow motion for Salonius. Sabian shouted something; the ring of guardsmen began to move forward;

Corda began slowly, ever so slowly, to turn. There was no time. Corda would die, and any information with him.

With a grunt, Salonius dropped to a crouch, grasping the standard of the second cohort in one large hand. He'd never have the time to stand and do this properly. As the muscles in his powerful arm bunched and rippled, the young ex-engineer pulled the standard back, stirring a small cloud of dust, and slung it forward in a long underarm sweep. Without an ounce of modesty, he realised how few people around this square would have the power for such a throw.

The standard, like all imperial military standards, was really a glorified spear. A wide, leaf shaped blade stood proud eight inches above the cross bar that held the flag. Below that came the decorations of the unit that glittered in the sunlight as the standard hurtled low to the ground, leaving a wake of dust.

The deputy sergeant raised his sword arm and suddenly disappeared in a cloud of dust with a shriek. The standard had been too low and slow to do any serious damage, but the point had ripped through the skin half way up the man's calf and the cross bar hit his ankle with surprising force, enough to bring him down in a painful heap. By the time he recovered his wits and found his feet, one of the junior sergeants of the second cohort had retrieved the standard and, with a vicious and defiant grimace, he brought the iron-shot base of it down on the wounded conspirator's head, knocking him flat and unconscious. The sergeant held the standard aloft with pride and fixed his eyes on the marshal. Sabian stared at him for a moment and then nodded.

A hand grasped Salonius' arm and he looked round to see the captain of the marshal's guard, his black cloak grey with grit, crouching to help him up. Nodding his thanks, Salonius stood again and dusted himself down.

Two of the black clad guardsmen had stepped forward and were standing to either side of Corda now. The sergeant slowly and carefully removed his sword from the sheath on his belt and cast it to the ground in front of Sabian. At a nod from the marshal, the two guards grasped Corda's shoulders and bent his arms behind his back, turning him and marching him from the square, through the circle of guardsmen and toward the palace. Two more men collected the unconscious man from the floor behind him and dragged him, unceremoniously, after the others.

Sabian stared at the other sergeants of the Second.

"Justice will be served, gentlemen, and it will in no way reflect on the rest of the unit. Replace your standard." He glanced at Salonius and the guard captain.

"However, my guards will stay here and you will continued to remain in quarters until I am satisfied that I have all of those responsible in custody."

He straightened and squared his shoulders as the officers of the Second saluted. With a sad sigh, he turned to Salonius and the captain.

"Let's go and find out how deep this goes, eh gentlemen?"

Corda stood in the office of the guard captain, his chin raised and shoulders back in a military stance. Salonius was impressed despite himself. Even in just a tunic and breeches, covered in dust, Corda still looked proud, haughty and thoroughly military.

Behind him stood two of the guardsmen, with another two behind Sabian, Salonius and captain Iasus, as Salonius now knew him. Corda had been stripped of all arms, armour and equipment and stood defenceless and yet so proud. Salonius glared at him. Were it not for the need to determine who else was involved, he could happily strangle Corda himself.

Sabian looked around the office at the guards and gestured to the door.

"I think we can deal with this."

The captain looked less sure, Salonius thought, but nodded at his men anyway and placed the palm of his hand on the pommel of his sword as he stood at the marshal's shoulder. The guards filed out and closed the door behind them.

There was a long silence and finally Sabian sighed.

"Why, Corda?"

The marshal hauled himself out of the captain's chair and walked around the front of the desk, facing the prisoner.

"You go back all the way to the civil wars with Varro and Petrus. Hell you even served in *my* army back then!" He growled. "You're supposed to be one of *us!*"

Salonius rubbed his eyes wearily. He'd not slept since yesterday.

Corda cleared his throat.

"I have no excuses, marshal. I am at fault."

"And yet you give in without a fight? Explain!" Sabian's voice rose an octave.

Corda sighed.

"It wasn't meant to be like this, sir. I found out about Cristus' secret a couple of months ago, quite by accident. I happened to be in the wrong place at the wrong time, and I heard something I wasn't meant to."

The sergeant's eyes dropped to the floor.

"I made a judgment call. Then worst in my life."

"I said: explain!" shouted Sabian. "Stop feeling sorry for yourself and tell me!"

"I didn't see the point in bringing it all out into the open. It would have destroyed the Fourth Army and brought dishonour on all of us. And it would have done no good. Nothing would have changed; those men at Saravis Fork would be just as dead. The prefect pointed out that he would soon be leaving the military and moving into politics. Varro would be next prefect and I'd take Varro's place. Why rock the boat? Surely it was all for the best now."

He sighed sadly.

"Cristus is a persuasive bastard, sir. Before I knew it I was transferring some of his men into my units. He even put me in charge of his honour guard when he came here a couple of weeks ago. I assumed to keep an eye on me, but I suspect now for other reasons. I never expected any of this."

Sabian growled.

"It might just be that misguided foolishness is as bad as open treachery, Corda!"

The sergeant raised his eyes and locked a defiant gaze on the marshal.

"Is that truly always the case, sir? I seem to remember that even you made bad judgement calls once upon a time?"

Salonius stared at the sergeant in shock. Marshal Sabian was known for his sharp mind, his quick wit and his code of ethics. He growled. His hatred of Corda was growing with every comment.

Sabian, however, seemed to take the comment in his stride and captain Iasus, by his side, never even blinked.

"But Varro? And Petrus?"

Corda shook his head.

"I realise it sounds like a feeble excuse sir, but I had nothing to do with either. I wasn't aware of the captain's poisoning until he told me himself, and if I had known I'd have done something about it. Likewise I wasn't aware that the men with me had been sent here as assassins, though I should have guessed. It doesn't surprise me. I have seven men with me that came from Cristus' personal guard, including the sergeant you already have. I will gladly give you their names."

He sighed.

"There was supposed to be no harm done. No harm," he muttered, largely to himself.

Sabian swept a hinged wax tablet and stylus from the table and held them out for Corda.

"Start writing and we might rule against death as a penalty."

The sergeant grasped the writing implement and began to mark down the names of the conspirators on the tablet.

"That won't be necessary, sir. I have no wish to go on with this."

As he concentrated on his writing, Sabian glanced across at Iasus and Salonius. Both men wore hard, unforgiving expressions as they glared at Corda. Sabian sighed inwardly. Somehow, despite everything, there was a tinge of sympathy in him for the sergeant. Twenty five years ago, he might have made the same decision. Finishing scribbling, Corda folded the tablet shut and passed it back with the pen to the marshal.

"I realise that I'm in no position to ask for favours, marshal, and yet I'd still beg two…"

Sabian quickly glanced at the contents of the wax tablet and then passed it on to the captain to deal with. Corda took a deep breath.

"I would ask, sir, that I be allowed to take my own life without the humiliation of a public execution…"

Sabian frowned. He concentrated on the prisoner, aware of what the other two men in the room were thinking. After all, it was standard practice for a traitor to be broken in front of his peers. This decision wasn't going to sit well with Salonius or Iasus.

"Very well."

Corda nodded curtly. "And I'd ask that I be allowed to do it before Varro finds out."

Sabian's piercing stare stayed on Corda. He could almost feel the two men behind him seething.

"Once I confirm these names, I'll make the arrangements."

Sabian turned and nodded to captain Iasus. The captain, an unreadable expression on his face, went to the office door and, opening it, admitted the guard detail once more. The marshal cleared his throat.

"For now, you'll go with these men to be detained."

Corda nodded and gave a final salute.

Chapter Twelve

Varro awoke slowly, like a man climbing from a deep, dark tunnel out into a sunlit world. His head once more felt as though it were full of cotton, much as it had when he was first suffering over a week ago. He groaned and slowly moved his head left and right, almost vomiting with the sudden unpleasant sensations that came with the activity. Slowly he focused and became aware of the two figures in the window seat. Salonius and Catilina. Yes, that figured. He tried to sit up and his head filled with what felt like white-hot lead. He collapsed back with a yelp.

"Rest for a moment."

Varro gritted his teeth against the pain.

Salonius was next to him now.

"I talked to Scortius. He's adamant that you'd either already taken something just before the strong medication, or you'd had a drink. Either way, whatever you had reacted with the medicine and put you right out. You'll be fine in about a half hour. Just wait for your head to clear and your strength'll be back."

Varro tried to nod, but the sensation was too unpleasant. Somewhere back towards the window, Catilina's voice said: "Tell him now. While he's still too fuddled to explode."

Salonius gave her a sharp look.

"Tell me what?" Varro reached out a hand and gripped Salonius' tunic just below the neck. "See... my strength's already coming back..."

Salonius gently detached Varro's fingers and folded his arm back across his chest.

"I want you to do your very best to remain calm. If your blood pounds too fast, you'll pass out all over again. Just listen calmly, and try not to react."

"About what?" growled Varro

"We located the assassins."

"Good. I personally want to tear pieces off them."

Salonius shook his head. "The marshal has them in custody. There's seven of them. Cristus' men that infiltrated the Second Cohort. He won't let you near them, Varro. He's dealing with it in strict military fashion. They're to go on trial tomorrow. Of course, the verdict will be guilty, and they'll be executed, but the marshal wants it all done above board. All correct."

Varro ground his teeth.

"Our *own* cohort! That bastard Cristus stops at nothing. How did the piece of shit get his men in our unit?"

Salonius glanced round at Catilina and swallowed nervously.

"They were transferred in at Corda's request."

Varro stared at him as though he'd changed colour or grown wings, his mouth opening and closing.

Salonius sighed. "Corda's been involved with Cristus for some time, though he claimed not to have known about or been involved in what happened to you or Petrus…"

"Not known?" Varro growled and slowly sat upright, fighting the nausea, his anger giving him greater fortitude now. "Not bloody known? *Corda?*"

"Please sit back, Varro. You're going to hurt yourself."

Varro's growl continued to deepen. He sounded like some sort of great predatory cat stalking its prey among the rocks of the southern lands.

"*Corda?*" His voice rose an octave. "*Corda!* Are you absolutely *positive?* Really *sure?*"

Salonius nodded sadly.

Slowly, menacingly, and with great care, Varro turned his body and slid until his legs bent at the knees and his feet his the floor next to the low couch.

"I am going to go find Corda and beat the living shit out of him."

"Sir…" Salonius said urgently.

"Get out of my way lad, or I'll tear something off you too."

Salonius reached out and gently but firmly restrained the captain. Now Catilina was next to him.

"Varro, you can't punish Corda" she said quietly.

"Care to put a wager on that? I don't care if he's in a cell guarded by your father himself. Corda's one of my oldest friends. We've watched each other's back for thirty years, even through the civil war, and then he does this? I will tear him a new arsehole!"

"No you won't." There was something about Salonius' expression that stopped Varro in his tracks.

"What is it?"

Salonius cleared his throat anxiously.

"Sergeant Corda fell on his sword about an hour ago. He's lying in the cellars at the moment and this afternoon he's being taken out somewhere unknown and being buried somewhere with no marker."

Varro blinked.

"Sabian let him keep his sword?"

Catilina leaned towards him and placed her hand gently on his chest, lowering him back to the couch.

"My father let him take the soldier's way out. There were reasons." She and Salonius shared a look. "Not necessarily a decision we shared, I might add."

"Take me to the marshal."

"You're too weak…" Salonius tried as gently as possible to prevent him from sitting up.

"Weak, bollocks. I can walk. Take me to Sabian."

Again Salonius shared a look with Catilina.

"Alright, but slowly and carefully."

The three of them arrived at Sabian's office ten minutes later, Varro staggering along in the middle like a drunkard, his arms draped over Catilina and Salonius' shoulders. The lady glared at the guard by the door; her best haughty glare.

"Announce us to my father."

"Ma'am…"

"You know who we are. Announce us."

"Yes, ma'am."

The guard turned and knocked gently at the door before opening it a crack.

"Marshal, I have your daughter, Captain Varro and his guard here to see you, sir."

Sabian's tired voice issued from within.

"Let them in."

The three entered the room, where Salonius and Catilina took Varro across to one side of the room and allowed him to slowly sink to the chair. Varro fixed Sabian with a defiant glare while Catilina took the seat next to him and Salonius stood by his shoulder. The marshal narrowed his eyes and cradled his hands as he sized the captain up.

"You're not looking well Varro. You should be resting and getting your strength back."

"Pah!"

Sabian sighed. "I presume this is about Corda and the others?"

Varro nodded.

"You know what's been done to me. You'd no right to take away my revenge. Corda was mine to deal with!"

"Not by military law, Varro. And no matter how much slack I cut you habitually, I am your senior officer and you *will not talk to me like that.*" The marshal's word became quiet and menacing as he finished speaking from between clenched teeth.

Varro nodded to himself and looked up.

"My apologies, marshal. No disrespect was meant."

"Good." Sabian smiled but with little or no humour. "That sounds more like you. Neither you nor I can afford you to go vengeance-mad right now. Corda made some stupid decisions, and he's suffered for them, believe me, but that matter's now done with. However, I have seven men in custody that I still have to play with. I am using them against each other. Iasus is down with them now. After the noon bell tomorrow they'll go on trial. None of them will walk away free, I assure you."

Varro glared, but nodded.

Sabian sighed. "I would estimate that, by the time of the trial, at least half of them will have delivered the others to the headsman and given us every ounce of evidence we will need to bring Cristus to justice. They'll get a custodial sentence, along with loss of all pay and position, with a dishonourable discharge. The others will be a little less lucky. I have men taking the wheels off a cart right now."

Varro grimaced.

"That's all well and good, marshal, but with all the respect and goodwill in the world, I intend to deal with Cristus myself."

Sabian shook his head.

"That's not a good idea, Varro. I can understand how you feel. I've been in a vaguely similar situation of betrayal myself, remember. But we have rules and regulations now and an army worth upholding them for. And besides, if you got into an arena with Cristus, he'd cut you to ribbons."

Varro growled. "I think you underestimate me, marshal. And Cristus is a politician, not a fighter."

"Maybe, Varro; maybe. But you are on the verge of falling to pieces without his help. He doesn't need to fight you. If he breathes too hard at you, you'll fall apart."

He shook his head as Varro opened his mouth to speak once more and cut him off, mid-breath.

"Varro, that's an end to it! They will be judged and punished according to military law. And the information they give us will allow us to remove a traitor from power and all his lackeys. It will be done 'by the book' and I will do it myself. I would rather you were with me, to give evidence, to sit in judgement and to oversee the whole thing." He sighed. "But if you're going to insist on revenge, I'm going to have you locked in your room for the next few days, do you understand me?"

Varro glared at him and finally slumped, sighing.

"Alright, sir. By the book. But I want to be there for every part of it."

"Oh, you will, captain. I shall make sure of that." Sabian looked up at Salonius and then turned to his daughter.

"Get him back to his room and make sure he gets some rest. He's going to need it."

Catilina nodded.

"Yes father."

As she stood and grasped one of Varro's wrists, she saw Salonius' face for the first time during this exchange and she nearly recoiled. Salonius looked furious. Trying not to catch his eyes, she helped Varro upright. The burly young man took the other and together they turned him and walked him out of the office. The guards opened and closed the doors for them and stood to attention as they slowly made their way down the corridor. As soon as they'd turned two corners, Varro struggled. They stopped and he pushed them away from him gently. Catilina stared.

"I thought you were weak as a kitten?"

Varro gave a horrible smile. "Strength's coming back in floods now."

He turned to Salonius.

"You know where they're keeping Petrus and Corda's bodies?"

Salonius nodded.

Varro's grin widened. He resembled a shark.

"Find them. Steal them. Get them to the stable and find our horses and a spare to carry the bodies. We're going prefect hunting!"

Catilina stared at them.

"Wait!"

Varro's smile softened and he laid a hand gently on her shoulder.

"You know I've got to do this, Cat. I can't just let this get bureaucratic. I need to look him in the eye as I skewer him. The best thing you can do for me is to keep quiet and not let anyone know I'm gone until we're well and truly out of the way."

Catilina frowned.

"He's right," added Salonius from between gritted teeth. "Cristus needs to pay in a personal way. Even if Varro didn't want to do it, he's not got a choice. There's a higher power involved in all of this. It's fated. Varro's going to kill Cristus even if he tries not to. And I'll be there to help whether I like it or not."

Catilina stared at the young man.

Varro smiled. "It sounds insane, but he's right, Catilina."

The pale, elegant woman lowered her face and scratched her head for a moment. When she looked up there was a sparkle in her eye that made Varro frown nervously.

"What is it?"

"I know." She smiled. "Fate, yes?"

Varro's brow lowered further and Catilina laughed.

"Sorry, my dear, but I won't be able to keep quiet about your absence." She unpinned her hair and threw her head back, shaking the black curls out. "Because I'll be with you."

Varro shook his head.

"Not this time," Varro stated flatly. "Your father will..."

"What?" she interrupted. "Kill you? Don't be naïve, Varro. I'm coming with you and the quicker you accept that, the quicker we can be gone."

Varro sighed. He looked round at Salonius and was surprised to see the young man's vicious expression had slid back into its habitual good natured smile. "You too?"

"The lady has her mind made up, Varro."

Another sigh, and Varro smiled at her.

"Alright. Salonius, you get those corpses; can you manage both of them?"

Salonius nodded.

"Catilina: you get your things. I'll pick a few things, get the horses ready, and meet you in the stable in about fifteen minutes.

With a last deep breath, the three of them split up in the corridor junction and went their separate ways.

Salonius wandered along the corridor. His analytical mind gave him an edge, he thought, that the over-emotional sometimes lacked, particularly when combined with his alertness which led to him needing only five hours sleep a night, give or take, and remaining fully functional. While the others had slept or bathed for the six hours last night before everything went to hell, Salonius had spent time exploring the palace. Combined with his part in the search this morning and further explorations while Varro had slumbered, he had put together a surprisingly complete mental map of the complex.

He had accompanied captain Iasus to the cellars when the seven traitors had been incarcerated. On the way there he noted that they passed a subterranean chapel to the Goddess of the hearth. Lying on the stone benches in this dark and cool place had been the bodies of Petrus and Corda, safe from wandering folk down here in the cellars beyond locked doors and now black clad guards.

He smiled at the guard by the heavy oak door. It was the very same guard that had been placed on the door three hours ago when he'd been here with the captain. The guard, not much older than Salonius, saluted. He continued to smile, raised his arm to salute, and at the last moment, brought it round in a hammering blow to the man's temple.

The man collapsed in a black heap without a sound. Salonius crouched over him.

"Sorry about that. You'll have a hell of a headache, and I suspect you'll be cleaning latrines for a few weeks, but you'll live."

Carefully, he retrieved the black tunic with its white raven and wolf emblem and slipped it over the top of his own green one. He grunted as the tunic split beneath the arm. Sadly there would be few guardsmen that matched his own large frame. Still, he mused, no one would have time to examine his armpit. With a smile, he threw the black cloak over his back and, scrabbling around, found the man's helmet. That was no good, No way would that go over his head. Oh well, the thought as he retrieved the key ring from the guard's belt. He stood, brushing down and straightening his stolen uniform.

Unlocking the door with the heavy iron key, he pulled it open and stepped through, locking it behind him. He would have to be careful down here. He'd seen some of this massive complex of tunnels, but apart from the chapel and the cellars, there were also the dungeons, some store houses and, presumably at least one guard room somewhere. With a deep breath, he strode off into the dark, dank tunnels, lit only by occasional tiny skylights high in the outer wall.

Holding his breath, he reached the bottom of the first flight of stairs and turned right, deeper into the labyrinth of tunnels.

As he turned the corner at the next junction, the tunnels now lit by guttering oil lamps, he almost walked straight into a servant carrying a sack of something over his shoulder. He stepped aside and the servant made very apologetic sounds and sidled round him before rushing off. Salonius took another deep breath and walked on. Two more corners and the shorter flight of stairs. Ahead he could see the corner he didn't want to get to. Light flickered around the bend and there would be at least a couple of men, if not more, guarding the outer door to the prison area. But before then, just ahead, the doorway to the right led into the small chapel. Hurrying now, he ducked aside. He could clearly hear the voices of the guards round the corner and was glad, for the hundredth time, that he had worn soft leather boots and not the hob-nailed standard military fare he usually wore.

The chapel was lit by a flame on the altar at the far end. A barrel-vaulted room, it was not much larger than one of the guest rooms in the palace above. The walls and curved ceiling were of plain grey stone, with just a touch of nitre glistening. The far end wall was decorated with a mural of the gods of house and family, with the Goddess of the hearth, protector of the home, at the centre. Her altar burned forever with a single flame. It was said that nothing was required to fuel the flame on her altar. Salonius had surreptitiously checked the one at Crow Hill and had discovered that the priests filled a recess in the altar with oil every few hours and a clever spring-loaded mechanism kept the oil at the top of the container to burn visibly.

Shaking his head, he returned his attention to the task at hand.

As if to facilitate their retrieval, the thoughtful priest who'd prepared them on the stone benches had removed all of their armour and accoutrements, leaving them in only tunic and breeches. With only a slight grunt, he lifted Corda from the bench and tested the weight. The sergeant had been a wiry man. Tough, but far from large. Damn. The man's leg was tangled in the black cloak. With another grunt, he dropped the body back to the stone and removed the cloak, casting it away to the side of the chapel.

Stepping to the other block, he tested the weight of Petrus. Just as he'd thought, a decade of deprivation had left the veteran with a spindly light frame and very little muscle. Sheer determination had been driving him where muscle couldn't. He could have carried five Petrus'.

Making sure the scarred body was securely in position on his left shoulder, he stepped sideways and lifted Corda with his massive muscled arms, hauling the man onto his shoulder. Bending his knees a couple of times, he tested the weight and how securely they were held.

Satisfied, he stepped slowly and carefully to the entrance of the chapel and peered around the wall. The laughter continued to issue from the lit area further on, but the corridor was empty. Taking another deep breath, he stepped out and turned the other way, carefully and slowly making his way up the first, short flight of stairs.

Under his breath, he continued to mutter prayers to Cernus and any other God that he could name that he make it to the stables unobserved. In retrospect, he should have asked Varro to come with him. The captain couldn't have carried anything, but he could have acted as lookout.

He reached the top step and turned, peering carefully around the corner. Nothing. He stopped and listened. The now-distant sound of laughter behind him down the stairs. Somewhere up ahead was the sound of tramping military boots. Two pairs by the sound of it. Well he couldn't stay in the stairs. He'd just have to hope they were in some other side tunnel.

He stepped out into the corridor and moved along it as fast as he could, his footfalls soft and delicate for a man his size. For a moment, he uttered a quiet curse, as Corda's body slipped on his shoulder and almost fell. He jerked his shoulder to reposition it and changed his grip on the corpse's wrist.

The corridor seemed to go one forever, but finally, the next junction came into sight. As he approached it, he paused for a moment and listened. Those heavy footsteps were now worryingly close; coming from the other branch to the one he needed, but too close for comfort. He held his breath and sank against the wall of the tunnel in as much shadow as he could manage, given the bulk on his shoulders.

A few moments passed and he let his breath escape with a quiet hiss. The steps were going the other way, disappearing off down the corridor.

He shook his head in amazement. Just over a week ago the most exciting thing he'd ever done was oversee the assembly of a giant bolt thrower while scores of enemy stood on the opposite ridge. Now here he was stealing corpses from the dungeons of the greatest Imperial fortress in the north. Astounding. How the hell had he got himself involved in this?

With another deep breath, he settled the two figures draped over his shoulders and stepped out into the next corridor. Ahead, he could see the pale grey glow of natural light. He was getting close to the stairs. Just one more corner.

Slowly, with breath held, he approached that corner, feeling the seconds pass like hours. There was no sound from ahead, but his heart took no notice of the fact and continued to race, regardless.

He turned the corner.

Nothing there. Just dank stairs leading up into the gloom.

Slowly, he climbed the stairs, pausing every now and then to take a breath. The two bodies may be light, but even so, their weight was beginning to make his sore and short of breath. Finally he reached the top and paused again to listen. Distant sounds; from beyond the door, out in the palace proper. Damn it!

As quietly as he could, he padded along the corridor until he was only around ten paces from the door. Very, very slowly and quietly, he lowered the two corpses to the floor and approached the door. He listened.

Just one man. He was down by the bottom of the door, speaking softly. Salonius retrieved the key from his pocket as he strained to hear.

"I'll have to go report it!"

"Not yet. Let's go find him. If I get another black mark, I'll be sent to a frontier post! It's only one man and we've got the jump on him now."

"No, Marco, I've got to report it!"

"Listen: imagine how good we'll look when we bring him in!"

Salonius smiled as he inserted the key into the lock with incredible slowness and began to turn it, waiting for each new line in the argument to help mask the sound of the key turning. He felt the pressure release as the lock completely opened. With a wide grin, he pictured the scene beyond the door and very slowly turned the handle. As the latch slid free, he almost laughed out loud. Stepping back a few paces, he turned his shoulder toward the door and ran.

The impact made his shoulder feel as though it had exploded, but the effect was much as he'd hoped. The door burst open into the room beyond, hitting the guard crouched behind it with tremendous force and a loud crack. As he sailed on through, Salonius brought himself to a halt as sharply as he could. The new guard had been hit in the forehead by the door and thrown back. The guard who was still recovering from Salonius' entry five or six minutes ago was by the wall behind the door, which had come to a stop as it thumped into his shoulder. Salonius turned the second guard over with his foot. The huge red welt and wound on his forehead suggested he would be out for some time.

The other guard was mouthing things with a frightened look on his face. Salonius gave him a grin that he hoped was as feral as the one he kept seeing on Varro. The guard quailed.

"I'm a little concerned that I've done a bit too much damage to your friend here. So we're going to make a deal, yes?"

The guard nodded, wide eyed and terrified.

"Good," Salonius continued. "I'm not going to knock you out because you need to help your friend. I'm going to collect my things and walk slowly and quietly out of here. You're going to wait at least ten minutes after I've gone, during which time you can do your best to stop his wound bleeding. Once ten minutes is up, you can shout for help, run, or whatever it is you want to do. Just not until I'm away from here. And if I hear anything as I leave, I will come back here and leave you in... let's just say a 'worse' condition, eh?"

The guard gave another frightened nod and from somewhere within found a tiny voice.

"Why are you doing this? You're one of the marshal's men."

Salonius smiled.

"Not quite. I'm under the marshal's command, but I'm one of Varro's men. Not stay quiet."

Biting his lip, hoping he'd done the right thing, Salonius stood and returned to the corridor beyond the portal. There he spent a moment collecting the two corpses and settling them as comfortably as possible on his shoulders. It was not easy. His left shoulder ached painfully. It was possible he'd chipped the bone on the door. There'll be a hell of a bruise.

'Ah well', he thought, as he carried the two bodies through the door and stopped for a moment. He turned to the seated guard and put his finger to his lips.

"Shhhh."

The guard gave another nod, staring with wide eyes at the hulking brute and his grisly burden. Salonius gave the grin again and walked off.

Catilina stopped a few steps from the junction in the corridor. She watched Varro limp off slowly toward the guest quarters and Salonius striding off into the depths of the palace. Putting her finger to her mouth, she tapped her elegantly manicured nail on her ruby lip, deep in thought.

After a moment a smile slowly spread across her face, ending in a broad grin.

Changing her direction, she padded off along the corridor that Salonius had taken, then selected a side-corridor and stepped into it. A few more turns and junctions that she'd known well since childhood, and she arrived at the offices of the garrison clerks. She'd played here often as a girl, since the clerks always had plenty of materials to draw with. Many happy hours had been spent sitting at the desk in these four offices and drawing pictures of animals and cloudy skies. She smiled and glanced up and down the corridor at the four offices. There were four chief clerks of the fortress, each in charge of one aspect of administration, and several lesser clerks beneath them. Each office housed desks for six people, but they were rarely occupied by more than one or two at a time, their duties often taking them elsewhere in the fortress or into the civilian town.

Smiling, she peered at the office doors that stood open or ajar. Two were brightly lit, one with a low light and one dark. Sadly, the empty, dark office was the only one that would be of no use to her. The office at the far left, however, was clearly lit by only one guttering oil lamp. That meant only one occupant. She squared her shoulders and strode along the corridor and boldly through the door.

The young clerk busy at his desk looked up as the figure came through the door. The paperwork he was involved in was suddenly forgotten as he scrambled to his feet and stood straight as a javelin.

"My lady?"

Catilina smiled at him.

"At ease, man. You must be new. Is Tarsus around?"

"Er, no, ma'am" the young man replied. "He's in the town with the council. Can I help, ma'am?"

Catilina shook her head.

"Just here for some supplies. Just ignore me. I'll be out of your hair in just a minute."

The young man continued to stand, torn between two courses of action.

"Er…"

"What?" Catilina asked pleasantly.

"It's rules, ma'am. No one can just help themselves. We've got to keep charge."

Catilina laughed a carefree laugh.

"Oh don't be so silly. I've been taking things out of here since I was four. Just get on with your work. My father's waiting for me, so I have to hurry."

The young man struggled for a moment longer and then gave up and visibly deflated slightly.

"Very well, ma'am. But please leave everything the way you found it, or master Tarsus will hoist me for it."

Catilina nodded and crouched by one of the large wooden cabinets at the back of the office. Unlocking the door with the key that sat jutting out, she scanned the contents. Damn it. Someone had reorganised the office. Closing and locking the door, she moved on to the next large cupboard and opened that. A quick scan and she saw what she was looking for. At the back, a pile of very neat, official looking papers.

She smiled and fished two out. She was about to close the cupboard again when another thought struck her and she had another glance around the interior. With a smile, she fished out a different paper, several sheets of meaningless bureaucratic paperwork and, closing the door, stood straight. As subtly as she could manage, she tucked her four prizes in among the unimportant paper. Smiling, she noted that the young man was going about his work, deliberately not looking in her direction.

Almost laugh, she collected a charcoal stick, a seal-stamp, hammer, lead discs and wax from the rear-most desk and slid them into a pocket in her skirts. With a warm smile she crossed the room and stopped at the door to look back at the clerk.

"Thank you, kind sir. Perhaps I'll be back for more supplies later. I'll be sure to tell Tarsus how accommodating you were."

The clerk gave her a nervous smile and, as she left the room, Catilina felt a little cruel. The lad would probably lose his position for this. Still, he shouldn't have let her have free reign among the office paperwork, should he?

Almost skipping along the corridor, she took three more side turnings and arrived at another door. This door, however, was dark and solid, locked and protected by a guard who stood to attention and almost strained something trying to stand even further to attention as the most important lady in Vengen appeared in front of him. These were ordinary soldiers of the garrison, not the veteran black-clad marshal's guard.

She smiled.

"For Gods' sake man, at ease. You'll rupture something."

The guard gave a brief smile and then fell serious again.

"If you would be so good, I need to retrieve something for my father."

"Ma'am?"

She smiled inwardly.

"I need a sash of office for the marshal's guard. My father's transferring Captain Varro to his own unit. He can collect his uniform later, but we need the sash now."

The guard frowned and opened his mouth but Catilina interrupted.

"Look, you can go in and get it for me if you like. It's only a damn sash."

The guard continued to frown and then gave a curt nod.

"I'll have to find it for you ma'am. If you would kindly wait here."

Catilina nodded and smiled. She folded her arms as the guard turned and fumbled with his keys. Finally finding the correct one, he unlocked the door to the uniform store room.

As he pulled the door open, behind his, Catilina unfolded her arms. In one was the seal hammer; around a foot long, narrow and tapering, with a wooden mallet head, coated in steel for hammering the marshal's seal in lead. The guard began to turn towards her and caught the full force of the seal hammer on his temple. His eyes rolled up into his head and he slumped to the floor. With a smiled, Catilina pocked the hammer once more and climbed over the recumbent guard and into the room. She game a small laugh as she pored over the racks and racks and shelves of clothing by the light of the window on the outer wall, mulling over what sizes she thought might fit Varro and Salonius. The young man might be a problem, she thought, as she retrieved the largest garment in stock.

Finally, her arms full of garments, she put them to one side and, bending down, grasped the wrists of the guard and dragged him slowly into the room. Once he was fully inside, she collected the pile of clothing, closed the door behind her and locked it with the guard's key.

Laughing and almost with a skip to her step, she walked off toward the stables.

Varro ran to his room as soon as they separated, gathered all his things and rolled them up and stuffed them unceremoniously in his kit. He'd carefully selected several large burlap bags rather than the saddle bags they'd arrived with. A little too unsubtle, wandering around with saddle bags. As he left his room, the marshal's guard standing at attention in the corridor coughed.

"What?

"What do you think you're doing, sir?"

Varro gave him an unhappy look.

"It seems we're going to be here for a while and we're involved in the upcoming trials and tribulations. The Marshal wants us to look smart, so we're cleaning and tidying all our kit."

The captain turned his back on the man, who looked distinctly unconvinced, and entered Salonius' room. Damn it. He was no good at deception. He'd carefully prepared his excuse and tried to pass it off to the guard as naturally as he could but, as he thought back over what he'd just said, it sounded more like a prepared speech the more he repeated it in his head. Damn it. Let's hope the guards were as bad at detecting lies as he was at telling them.

He wandered over to Salonius' bed and cupboard and almost laughed out loud at how everything was laid out, neat and clean. Even the folding shovel the engineer carried gleamed like shiny steel. His clothing was stacked in piles: tunics, breeches, socks, underwear, scarves. It was ridiculous. Even his small personal items were arranged by type and size. Varro chuckled as he grasped the two bags from the floor and thoughtlessly stuffed everything messily inside.

As he finally forced the second bag shut with some difficulty, he collected his own bag and picked up Salonius' three.

"Shit!"

He almost buckled under the weight. How could the lad carry this stuff for hours at a time? He must be made of rock and iron, the tough little sod! Shifting the weight to a position that was only slightly less uncomfortable, he let out an explosive breath and left the room, feeling like a pack mule.

The two guards in the corridor, who were now standing together and had obviously been chatting, tried to restrain their laughter as a collection of sacks and bags came fumbling out of the young soldier's room, with a person somewhere underneath, grunting and breathing heavily.

"Would you like a hand with that down to the laundry, sir?"

Varro puffed and panted and tried unsuccessfully to straighten. Natural. That was the key. Be natural! He grumbled.

"No, you're alright. Should have let him come and get his own stuff. We might be a while, looking at the amount of shit he carries. He can carry it back up, while I go to the garrison surgeon for back repairs!"

He turned and stomped off down the corridor toward the laundry and palace bathhouse area, grumbling about the young engineer as loudly and convincingly as he could. He left the corridor with the sound of the guards laughing at his misfortune ringing in his ears. Good. As long as they were concentrating on the humour, they wouldn't think too hard.

Continuing to grumble about Salonius, but this time for real, he turned the corner and, once out of sight, ducked away into a side passage and headed toward the stables.

Varro glared at Salonius as the young engineer stumbled through the doorway into the stable. There was no one here yet, though in an hour the stable hands would be here feeding the horses. Salonius blinked.

"What's up?"

Varro growled and pointed to the large collection of freshly-stolen saddle bags on a nice sleek grey horse near the door.

"How the hell do you carry all…" He stopped mid sentence. It sounded so foolish saying something like that to a person who was carrying two dead bodies at once.

"Never mind."

He gestured around.

"The grey's yours and all loaded up. Let's get these two covered up and secured on that bay over there."

A quiet, lyrical voice from the second doorway said "Don't bother with that."

They turned to Catilina, who strolled in as though they were going about everyday business.

"Good. I see you've got the horses ready. I take it the chestnut's mine?"

Varro coughed.

"Yes. What's all that?" He pointed at the bundle of clothing in her arms.

Catilina smiled like a mother indulging an errant child. When she spoke it was in a slightly condescending tone.

"Boys, did you really think this through? How are you expecting to get out of the fortress? Just ride at the gates and hope they let you through?"

Salonius turned and looked at Varro.

"I presumed you had a plan?"

Varro grinned at him.

"I was expecting that something would turn up. If we're fated to do something, surely, it's going to happen anyway?"

Salonius sighed.

"I'm not sure it works quite like that."

Catilina smiled benignly.

"And that's why you two need me. Here."

She tossed articles of clothing at them one at a time.

Varro stared at the tunic in his hand.

"This is the tunic of a soldier in your father's guard!"

"They both are." Catilina kept throwing items at them. "Full uniforms, in fact. The way I look at it, if you just keep the hoods up, you should be able to move around without being questioned unless you happen to bump into a captain or sergeant, and that's not likely between here and the gate."

Salonius blinked. "That's brilliant."

"Why thank you." Catilina fumbled in her deep pocket, withdrew all the goods she'd stolen from the office and began to write on the two official papers with the charcoal pen. As she wrote, she looked up at the other two.

"Well? Get changed, then!"

As the two of them hurriedly changed into the black uniforms, Catilina finished her writing, placed the two lead discs on the floor and brought the hammer down on them, creating official seals. A moment with her flint and tinder and she melted the wax blobs onto the papers and added the lead seals.

Extinguishing the flame, she blew on the wax and as soon as it was dry enough, passed the two papers to Varro. He examined them.

"How the hell did you get all this?"

"What are they? Enquired Salonius adjusting the black cloak and pulling his boots back on.

"They're dishonourable burial orders. They give us permission to take those two out and bury them in an undisclosed location. Strange, as there's probably one of these papers already floating around somewhere with Corda's name on it. These are really rare. They…"

He stared at the papers and up at Catilina.

"Very clever. No one's going to stop two soldiers escorting bodies for burial with all the appropriate paperwork."

Salonius nodded and, unfastening his tool roll, removed a shovel and a pickaxe. With a grin he tossed the pick to Varro who caught it and examined it.

"You do know that it's not normal for digging tools to gleam that much!"

The young man laughed.

"We've got the uniform, the tools and the paperwork. Varro, we're now a burial detail."

Varro turned to Catilina.

"What about you?"

She smiled.

"I'll meet you at the ford about a mile east. I've got my own papers, and it's a determined guard who questions the daughter of the marshal. Now get going and I'll see you in about an hour."

"At the ford, then." Said Varro as he helped Salonius load their burned onto the spare horse. "Burial detail: forward!"

Chapter Thirteen

The sun was now well past its zenith. Varro clicked his tongue irritably and stared up into the sky trying to estimate the time. Salonius sat astride his horse, stoic as usual.

"No amount of getting irritated is going to bring her here any sooner."

"Shut up."

Varro shaded his eyes and stared off down the wide vale to the distant tortoise-shaped lump that was Vengen.

"Someone's coming."

Salonius shaded his own eyes and followed the captain's gaze.

"Dust," he agreed, "but that could be her or someone else; or even several someone elses. If she's been stopped, the marshal's likely to send some of his men after us. He's going to be pissed at you. I think we should get out of sight."

Varro made growling noises, but nodded and turned his horse.

The two men walked their mounts slowly and quietly between the trees that stood above the river bank. The sound of water rushing over the stones and cobbles of the ford would mask any inadvertent noises the horses or their riders might make. Once they were safely back among the foliage, they halted the two beasts and sat, breathing shallow breaths and waiting tensely for any sounds.

After a couple of minutes, Varro turned to Salonius and cupped his ear dramatically and held up one finger. Salonius strained to hear and then nodded.

"Varro?"

Catilina's voice called out from the road, amid the pattering of hooves on compacted mud as her horse pranced impatiently. The two men looked at one another for a moment and then slowly walked their horses back out into the open.

"You took your bloody time!"

Catilina gave the captain an infuriatingly calm smile.

"Captain Iasus came to find me. He'd been asked by my father to check up on me. You know Iasus: he's efficient and thorough. He followed me for half an hour while I tried to think of things to do. In the end I had to go to the baths to get rid of him."

Salonius smiled.

"I can imagine he thought twice about following you in there…"

Varro gave him a sharp look and then the three of them walked their horses slowly down the slope and into the shallow water. Catilina heaved a satisfied sigh.

"So what's the plan then?"

Varro frowned. He'd been thinking about this for some time and, though many conflicting ideas rattled around in his head about how he could handle this, there was a flaw in every plan he came up with.

"I'm not entirely sure. I need to get to Cristus, but there's more than that. I need to face off against him in a fair and level situation, where I'm not at risk from his men and where there are reliable witnesses. That's not going to be easy."

Salonius furrowed his brow in thought.

"What ideas have you had?"

"Riding straight to the fort was my first thought. He can't have the entire Fourth Army in his pocket. But the problems with that are: getting to Cristus past his personal guard and unreliable witnesses."

Salonius nodded. "Placing your head in the lion's mouth. Always a little on the risky side."

"Then there's luring him out somewhere. We could probably manufacture a situation that would get Cristus to come out, say, to one of the local towns. Plenty of witnesses. No problem there. The problem there is that he'll still be surrounded by his guard."

"True." Salonius sighed. "I'm not sure that Cristus is going to be the type of man who will subject himself to danger without his guards, though."

"So…" Varro growled, as they reached the far side and climbed out of the water onto the dry, dusty road. "That leaves me with the best option of the three: find a way to sneak into his personal quarters and do away with him there. Won't be easy though."

Salonius shook his head.

"Not just that, but also there'd be no witnesses. No one would see him confess and beg, which I presume is your intention."

Varro nodded.

"Perhaps we just can't have everything, eh?" the captain grumbled.

Salonius glanced past him at Catilina. The two of them stared at each other for a moment and then nodded.

"We'll find a way. Let's just concentrate on getting there with you in one piece. How are your wounds now?"

Varro glared at him.

"I'm fine, thank you, mother."

Catilina laughed out loud.

Daylight was beginning to wane as the three riders crested a low hill. Ahead the sky had already turned a deep mauve and only the tops of the trees before them reflected the quickly diminishing rays of the sun.

"We should find somewhere comfortable to camp," Salonius noted, "or perhaps an inn for the lady?"

Varro shook his head.

"Two villages and one town on this road before we get to Crow Hill, but it'll be long after midnight before we reach the nearest one. We'll definitely have to camp."

Salonius frowned.

"There are Imperial courier stations? We've only passed one quite a way back, so there must be another close ahead."

Varro shook his head.

"There are, but at courier stations, all guests must log in and out and non-military or administrative personnel have to provide proof of identity. Sabian would hear about it long before we were safely out of the way, I can assure you of that!"

Catilina sighed and pointed off some way to their left.

"How about there?"

Salonius looked across at Varro and shrugged. Varro pursed his lips.

"That place has been ruined since the civil wars. I used to ride past it on my way to and from Vengen. It's got twenty years of decay about it. Could fall down on our heads."

Salonius nodded.

"True, but it's also got walls for warmth and protection."

Varro continued to look unsure, but Catilina clicked her tongue irritably.

"You two are worse than a pair of old women."

Shaking her reins she turned her horse and rode off toward the dark shell that rose eerily from its bed of scrub and bramble. Varro glared at her retreating form for a moment and then gave a sigh and followed her. Salonius smiled as he left the track himself.

As the ruined shell of the manor loomed closer, more details became apparent. It had been more than a manor house in its time; more even than a great villa. This place had been a fortress of considerable strength, protecting a sumptuous, palatial residence within. This place must have belonged to a strong lord, or perhaps even an Imperial councillor.

Catilina admired the shattered remnants of architectural grandeur as they approached, her eye picking out elegant curls and delicate tracery. The lord of this place must have belonged to a wealthy line. The decoration was old; not four or five decades old, from just before the civil wars, but centuries old, from the early days of Imperial settlement in these cold, northern provinces.

Varro and Salonius cast their own eyes over the ruins, though their assessment was more military in nature. The place had indeed been heavily fortified. The original early palace had been surrounded by stone walls with two gates at an early stage, presumably when the owner had realised how newly settled this area was, and had seen acts of barbarism perpetrated nearby. These defensive walls had been given towers and what Varro liked to call 'decorative defence' some time around a century ago, as was the fashion at the time. But the last defences had been added perhaps forty years ago, early in the civil wars, and these defences were far from decorative. The walls had risen by a further ten feet; the line of the original parapet was clearly visible three quarters of the way up. The bottom half of the towers had been given great, square encasements of tufa for extra strength. One of the double arches of the gate had been blocked to narrow down a point of attack. Finally, as they began to close on the crumbling walls, they could see that the walls had been revetted with a great bank of earth. The lord of this manor had been expecting attacks and had been prepared for them.

Not prepared enough.

The stone facing that remained on the shattered towers and extant stretches of wall showed shattered blocks and great cracks and rents where the defences had been pounded relentlessly by siege engines. Plainly the stretch of wall closest to the gate had been the first area to fall. Salonius shook his head sadly at clear oversights that had been made by the military architect; a wide stretch of wall with no buttressing and no support from towers. No amount of earth embankment was going to help there though. The thoughtful architect had added a ditch that was far to close to the wall to allow for the wall's footings. The first half dozen blows on that wall had probably brought the stonework crashing out into the ditch, handily filling one obstacle whilst collapsing the other and leaving a sloping earth embankment as the only defence. Once inside that wall, the siege would be over in minutes.

Varro's fears of the decayed condition of the building were only partially founded. The military defences of the place were thick and heavy and, though they had fallen to a clever enemy, were withstanding the ravages of time surprisingly intact. The palatial building within, however, had fared less well. Constructed for form rather than for function, the weak and delicate architecture had rotted and crumbled, leaving a mass of sad stone that was now largely held together by ivy and brambles.

"Best stay away from that central building" he called ahead to the others.

Varro turned in his saddle and nodded. As Salonius caught up with them, the three riders dismounted and led their horses to the great gatehouse that retained its strong walls and towers, though the portal itself had long since gone.

Salonius tethered the three horses on the grass nearby and padded off quietly among the ruins with his sling, while Varro began gathering dry sticks and building a fire and Catilina set about excavating food and various necessary items from the kit bags.

Within half an hour they had a pleasant little camp site formed beneath the massive, protective, arched roof of the gatehouse just as the last light of day faded over the horizon, leaving the scene in the shattered ruin dark and eerie. Various timbers that Varro had located had created a screen across both sides of the gatehouse, shielding them from the mounting evening wind and hiding their small fire from view for any passersby on the road. Salonius had returned with two rabbits and was currently turning them on a spit above the flames, watching hungrily as the juices dripped down with a hiss into the fire. A thought occurred to him and he looked up at the captain across the dancing flames.

"You need to take your medicine."

Varro grumbled once more, but nodded. As he wandered off toward the horses, where his medicine bag was still hooked, Salonius turned to Catilina, who was staring off into the dark ruins.

"We need to find a way to get Varro to Cristus without the prefect's guards. And in front of witnesses."

Catilina nodded.

"We need to find a way to get my father there."

"That's a problem," Salonius sighed. "Varro wants to send Cristus to the Gods personally. Your father wants it all done according to military law, with a trial and an execution, if necessary. He's never going to let Varro have Cristus, and Varro's never going to let your father have him."

Catilina frowned.

"So what we need to do is to make sure we get Cristus to a specific place, then Varro a few minutes later, and father a few minutes after that. Tricky…"

Salonius laughed. "Tricky? Impossible, I'd say."

The elegant lady, wrapped up against the night air, pulled her cloak tighter.

"Nothing is impossible, Salonius. It's all in the timing. Father will know we're gone by now. It'll take him perhaps half a day to put everything in order and follow on, and I doubt he'll set forth at sunset, so we've got the best part of a day on him."

"So what do you suggest?"

"Well…"

Catilina stopped, mid-sentence, as Varro came hurtling out of the darkness, crouched almost double.

"Wha..?"

Before she managed to voice her thoughts, Varro clasped his hand over her mouth and, turning to Salonius, raised his eyebrows. Salonius frowned and, very slowly and very quietly, began to draw his sword from its sheath. Catilina pushed the captain's hand away and pointed out into the darkness. Varro nodded and held up three fingers.

Salonius frowned again and tugged out part of his black tunic, pointing at it? Varro shook his head and pointed at the lush, green grass by his feet. Even in the flickering light of the fire, Varro caught the curse his companion silently mouthed. As he slowly drew his own blade, Catilina drew a narrow and wicked-looking dagger from her belt.

Varro held up his hand to indicate that she should stay by the fire and the two soldiers moved off into the darkness at a crouch. Salonius paused for a moment and looked into the darkness. Varro glanced at him and then used his free hand to motion around the back of the villa ruins. The young man nodded and they both moved off once again.

The terrain within the walls was rough and difficult, consisting of the rubble of collapsed or demolished ancillary buildings long overgrown with grass and weeds, all interspaced between hidden rabbit holes that lay in wait for unwary feet and thick brambles and thorns. Some care was required to pick a clear way through the 'open' ground.

Salonius stumbled among the rocks for a moment, almost losing his footing as he felt his ankle wrench, when Varro suddenly grasped his shoulder and hauled him to the ground where he landed painfully among ruined brickwork. The captain pointed ahead and Salonius raised his head to look over a fallen lintel. In the pale moonlight, two men were stepping slowly and deliberately among the tangle in their direction.

Salonius swallowed and held up two fingers. Varro nodded and made indicated that the third figure had likely taken the other direction and was moving around the back of the ruined mansion. All to their advantage, since it gave them even odds; better than even, given that their prey were not expecting them.

At a gesture from Varro, Salonius shuffled as quietly as possible down the mound of rubble, being sure to remain out of the enemy's sight behind the jumbled stonework. The enemy were still around twenty yards away from them and all sounds of movement were somewhat disguised by the twittering of the bats and the shuffling of the ruin's resident wildlife. At the base of the rubble heap, the young man looked up. They were now at the outer wall of the crumbled residence itself; the wall along which the two men were creeping and closing on them.

Here, the residence's outer wall had collapsed in the centre, leaving a 'v' shaped breech. The room beyond had once been magnificent, a grand hall of some kind, colonnaded along both sides and with a decorated façade at the far end, with friezes and carvings above a pair of now long-tarnished bronze doors. The roof had fallen in many years ago and the moonlight playing among the columns of the colonnades created interesting patches of starkly lit faded glory among the stygian gloom.

Varro pointed up to the breech in the wall, back at his own chest, and nodded. Salonius' eyes followed his finger up to the crumbling masonry and went wide. He returned his gaze to the captain, who grinned at him. He mouthed the word 'seriously?'

Varro nodded and slipped over to the fallen wall, grasping the stonework and climbing with care and held breath. Salonius watched nervously as small flecks of plaster and showers of dust dropped to the grass. What the hell was he doing? Swallowing, he shrank back behind the protection of a huge piece of fallen lintel. The two men were getting tremendously close now and both he and Varro were aware that they had to dispose of these soldiers silently and quickly. Sighing gently, he drove his sword point-first into the grass.

He raised his eyes once more and saw Varro about twelve feet from the ground, leaning around the crumbled edge of the wall. He was levering a large, loose stone from the wall. As the stone came away in a small shower of mortar, he grinned in triumph and hefted the heavy block. Moments passed as the two men came ever closer and finally, after what seemed like an age passing in slow motion, they drew level. Salonius glanced up once more and, at a nod from Varro, tensed and leapt.

The captain released his grip on the heavy stone he held and with deadly accuracy, the missile plummeted around ten feet and hit the front most soldier square on the top of the head. There was a quiet but audibly sickening noise and the man's skull exploded under the weight, shattering his spine in multiple locations and killing him instantly. The remains of the body collapsed to the ground with a gently thud.

His companion did not have time to register the impact, let alone scream. As the stone his the first man, so, from his perch among the rocks, Salonius landed on the back of the second man, his left hand going round the man's head and muffling any sounds he might try to issue. The hand was, in the event, unnecessary, as the impact drove the man to the floor and knocked all breath and sense from him. Before the soldier could recover, he placed his right hand on the back of the man's skull and repositioned his left on the jaw. Heaving with all the tremendous strength in his powerful arms, he twisted the man's head through one hundred and eighty degrees with a nasty cracking noise, staring in disgust at the strange sight of the glazed eyes now settled on him accusingly. He dropped the body and, retrieving his blade, stood and walked over to the wall. Varro descended the first few feet slowly and then dropped the last distance to the ground, landing with his knees bent.

"We've got to get that other one before he gets round to Catilina" the young man said quietly, pointing through the ruins of the building to the imagined figure of the third soldier creeping through the undergrowth. Varro nodded and gestured along the wall.

"You go round; I'll go through" he whispered. "Hopefully we can catch him by surprise."

Salonius frowned.

"Do we need surprise all that much now?"

Varro gestured for him to lower his voice.

"There's more out there. If Cristus sent men out to find us, there'll be at least a squad out there; probably more."

Salonius nodded. Of course, he was completely correct. With a last glance and Varro, he began to pick his way quietly along the ruined wall in the direction from which they'd come. Varro watched him go and then turned into the darkness of the ruins.

"You've stayed up for twenty years," he addressed the mouldy walls of the great vestibule quietly. "Try not to fall on me tonight."

With a deep breath, he set off through the wide, colonnaded room. Fragments of masonry and broken roofing tiles lay scattered here and there among the dark grass and shrubs. Picking his way as carefully as he could, he thanked the Gods for the moonlight that made this a less than life-threatening trip. At the far end a set of wide, shallow steps led up to the great bronze doors. Trying to picture the palace as it had once been, he realised that this must have been the grand entry way into the villa itself. The various doorways that led from this room to either side, beneath the arches of the colonnade would open onto waiting rooms, cloakrooms and other public spaces. The façade before him at the top of the steps heralded the entrance to the private areas of the villa.

Climbing the five steps, he was impressed at the quality of the marble used in their creation. The porphyry alone would be worth a year's wage for a merchant of even above-average means. Sadly, many steps were now missing. Any place where marble was going to waste, some enterprising folk would remove it and burn it down for more useful lime.

The doors had, in their time, been magnificent. When burnished they must have shone in the sunlight from the high windows, situated above the colonnade, much like the golden gate of Vengen. Now, sadly, they were decayed and blue-green. One door miraculously remained in position, rusted shut many years ago. The other hung at an awkward angle, the central and lower hinges having long since given way.

Very carefully, Varro stepped between the doors, being certain not to touch the precariously-hanging portal.

The interior was almost pitch black. The roof above this small octagonal chamber had remained largely intact, though the stars were visible here and there in places. Squinting into the dark, he made out the glow of moonlight through the doorway ahead. Stepping as carefully as he could in the darkness, he made his slow way toward the light.

The next room was wide and long. Most of the roof was missing, allowing the moon to clearly light his path now. The grass and weeds here were patchy, leaving areas of rich mosaic faded but clearly visible. This must be a great reception area or dining room. Varro could imagine the parties that had been held in this great space. A shallow granite bowl had been a fountain, clearly once decorated with a number of statues. A peculiar sense of sadness and loss settled on him as he traversed the room, his eyes now locked on the great aperture at the far end that had once been an ornate window.

As he approached the outer wall at the far end, he began to tread lightly and quietly once more. Creeping up to the window, he carefully edged his head past the stonework and glanced left and right. The figure of a man was moving along the wall, almost invisible in the moon shadow.

With a frown, he realised that the man would likely reach the corner before Salonius. Racking his brains, he suddenly grinned. Reach down to the floor, he collected a small pebble and hefted it, testing the weight. Squinting along the wall at the retreating form of the soldier, he swung his arm back and cast the stone out into the undergrowth roughly halfway between them but further out away from the building. He held his breath.

The soldier stopped dead in his tracks and turned. The shadow in which he was standing obscured his face, though Varro could imagine his expression. Very, very slowly, the man began to move away from the walls in a half crouch, toward the source of the unexpected sound. Varro nodded to himself in satisfaction.

Waiting until the man was at a good distance and facing away, Varro quickly and quietly climbed onto the ruined windowsill and dropped lightly to the soft, springy grass in the shadows outside. Something moved out of the corner of his eye and he glanced sharply along the wall to see Salonius echoing his steps from the corner. He nodded toward his companion and pointed at the figure now lurking by the undergrowth and Salonius returned the nod, drawing something from his belt and waving it at the captain.

Varro frowned. What the hell was the lad up to now?

He stopped in the shadows and tried to discern what Salonius was doing as the young man rummaged and fumbled until suddenly he lifted his arm above his head and began to swing it. Varro jumped. What the hell did he think he was doing? He waved his arms frantically, trying to get Salonius' attention. The building 'whoop, whoop' sound of the sling as it completed each circuit would easily attract the attention of the lone figure.

And yet, while he was still trying desperately to get the young man to stop his noisy attack, Salonius let go of the strap and the stone flew with a gentle whistling sound. Sure enough, the man by the undergrowth turned at this new sound, but not fast enough. Before he ever saw the two darker shapes lurking in the shadows by the wall, the lead shot took him in the side of the head and knocked him clean from his feet.

Varro blinked, impressed despite himself.

With a quick glance at the young marksman, he jogged across to the prone soldier. The side of his head had been staved in and was oozing dark matter onto the grass. He wouldn't be crying for help any time soon. The captain jumped at Salonius' quiet voice by his shoulder.

"Bigger than a coney and considerably slower moving."

Varro turned and grinned at him.

"That's some bloody aim you've got there."

"Almost a year assembling and dismantling catapults, bolt throwers and so on. That was my principle job. Every time you do it you have to check the aim and adjust to new conditions. After three months, it's second nature. I could hit a sparrow with a siege engine, given a couple of minutes to sight."

Varro laughed quietly.

"Come on. Let's check the lie of the land."

Catilina sat hunched up against the wall of the gatehouse, staring off into the gloom in the direction Varro and Salonius had taken. Her night vision was being seriously hampered by the dancing flames of their small fire and, after a few moments, she shuffled along the wall so that the fire was behind her. If she really strained her eyes, she could just about make out the shapes of her two companions moving like ghosts among the rubble and ruin near the centre of the complex.

She smiled. The noble women and the other girls she'd grown up with at Vengen and at the Imperial court in Velutio had always treated her with an aloof and distant attitude. It was, of course, no mystery why that was the case. Her brother was studious and interested in politics, history and rhetoric; her mother had been a fascinating woman, though. Catilina was always saddened when she thought of that beautiful, mysterious figure that had passed away when she was still a young girl. She knew what her mother had been like though: a genteel court lady, with hobbies and habits as befitted her station, but with a hidden side that only came out with her husband and children. Her mother had loved to ride and to explore; she had travelled with her husband on campaign in those early days of the Imperial restoration. She was no wilting flower, and neither was her daughter.

That was why the court ladies were never sure what to make of her: she had never settled into the sedate court life. Indeed, the only time she had spent any real length of time in a courtly situation was at Vengen those few years ago, and that had been when she'd met Varro and her life had changed forever. Her father had pleaded and cajoled, then demanded and shouted and finally, in the end, gave up and let her be who she wanted to be. He would never change her and, since he'd obviously come to realise that, she was sure he was just that smallest part more proud of her for it.

She had never been happier that at times like these, living roughly by a campfire with a constant threat of danger and puzzles to solve. Except for the ever-present knowledge that Varro was going to be taken from her. As soon as the thought occurred to her again, she pushed it back out of her mind. Every time she let her guard down, she risked being washed away by the turbulent emotions that pounded her. She was too strong for that. And Varro was refusing to let it get in his way, so she had to be all the more strong to keep him from despair.

The man behind all this...

Something behind her made a snapping sound. Her mind raced for a fraction of a second. Twigs popped and crackled in the flames, but there was something different about this sound. This was not a burning twig.

Gritting her teeth, she held her breath and listened as hard as she could.

Very, very quietly, she heard a footfall. Good. Between the crack and the quiet step, she had enough information to see it all in her mind's eye. The man was directly behind her, and perhaps two paces away. She held her breath a moment longer and heard the next footstep, slow and soft. This one was close enough that she felt the faintest vibration on the ground.

Her eyes hardened as, without moving any other part of her, she swung the needle-pointed knife up with her right arm straight behind her until her arm reached back as far as it could, but not before it met resistance. There was a horrible noise and a trickle of warm liquid down her hand and wrist as she immediately released her grip on the knife handle and, turning, leapt to her feet.

She had only a moment to take in the scene. Her aim had been precise and unfortunate, the height of her seated form having driven the blade as far as the hilt into the man's crotch and up through his bladder. His eyes were wide with shock and his mouth formed an 'O' as he fought to find his voice. The arm out to his side that held his sword twitched and the blade dropped from his fingers.

Panic hit her momentarily. Varro and Salonius had been so careful to remain quiet and this man was about to scream and ruin it all. Instinct took over and, pulling her arm back at the shoulder, she threw a solid punch directly at the man's face. The low groan as he began to howl was cut short and ended in a crunch as the blow broke the man's nose and two of Catilina's fingers simultaneously.

He spun, his eyes rolling up into his head, and collapsed heavily to the ground.

She stared down at him for a long moment, stunned by the sudden violence and then, slowly, the pain in her fingers began to make itself known. Shaking her head to clear it, she stared out into the darkness past the fire. Even with her hampered night vision, she could see the gap where the attacker had removed a single board in their fire shield. He had been alone.

Grimacing, she stepped out of the gatehouse and edged round the corner into the darkness where she would be less visible and scanned the gloom for a further sign of her two friends. After a long moment, she saw Salonius creeping along the wall of the central building and then he disappeared around the far corner and into the darkness. She heaved a slow breath and then settled down to wait, her ears pricked for any sign of movement.

Varro and Salonius clambered to the top of the wall walk. The flight of steps they had found was missing a number of stones and covered with creeping undergrowth, rubble and dust. Slowly and carefully they approached the battlements and peered cautiously around the merlon.

"Shit!"

Instantly, the pair ducked back into the protection of the walls. Below and perhaps fifty yards from the walls scattered soldiers sat astride their horses.

"How many d'you reckon?" Salonius whispered.

Varro shook his head.

"I'd say about ten down there, but you can bet we're surrounded, so we're looking at forty or so. Shit, shit, shit!"

Salonius nodded.

"Shit indeed."

They stood crouched for a moment, deep in thought, and then raised their heads in unison.

"Catilina!" they both whispered.

Moments later they were scrambling down the stairs and running across the rough grass towards the gatehouse, all concerns over being observed forgotten.

As they approached the great defensive structure, Varro's heart leapt into his throat. The archway, lit by the flickering flames, was empty. He and Salonius slid to a halt just as Catilina stepped out from the shadows by the gate.

Varro visibly jumped at her sudden appearance.

"Shit, don't do that!"

Salonius flexed his shoulders.

"Varro…"

The captain turned to find his companion pointing at the blood-soaked body lying next to the fire. He turned to Catilina and raised his eyebrows.

"Lucky." She said, flatly, cradling her sore fingers in her other hand.

"I think our luck might be running out" Varro replied. "Looks like there's several dozen men out there, waiting for us."

Catilina frowned.

"Do you suppose Cristus is there with them?"

"I doubt it," Varro grumbled. "This is dirty work. His sort doesn't do dirty work."

Salonius nodded.

"Then we've got to get away from here" Catilina replied, scratching her neck carefully and noticing once again the blood trails across her hand. "I think we can distract them."

She crouched near the fire and found a patch of dry, dusty ground. Retrieving a stick from the grass with her good hand, she drew a rough square on the floor and marked their location with an 'x'.

"We're here, yes?"

Varro nodded.

She used the stick to draw a line of dots around the square, marking the presumed location of the soldiers.

"I assume they're all round us?"

Salonius sighed. "We haven't actually checked, but they'd be stupid to concentrate on one side and leave the others empty."

"Alright then." Catilina cleared her throat. "Before we do this, you need to check all four walls. We'll need to know all possible ways out, and where their cordon is weakest."

"What's the plan?" Salonius muttered quietly.

"They sent men in here to get us. We need to distract them. I suggest we dress three of them in our clothes, strap them to horses and send them running out of one of the exits."

Varro frowned.

"And what happens if they manage to stop the three 'riders' just outside the walls?"

Catilina shrugged.

"Then we're in the same amount of trouble as we are now."

Varro stared at her and then shrugged.

"I suppose it's better than just fighting our way out. Salonius? We need to check the lay of the land from each wall."

He paused for a moment.

"Salonius?"

Turning at the continued silence, he regarded the young soldier with a raised eyebrow. Salonius was staring off into the distance thoughtfully, his index finger pressed against his chin.

"Salonius?" he repeated, slightly louder.

"Huh?" The young man shook his head and focussed on the captain.

"Sorry… Thinking. There might be a better way."

The other two waited expectantly and after a moment, Salonius removed his finger from his chin and used it to point at the ruins at the centre of the complex.

"What we need is a distraction."

"And?" Varro was becoming frustrated.

Salonius shrugged.

"We need to get them to come here. If most of them are inside, they'll be thinly spread out there and it'll be easier to slip past them."

"Granted," Varro nodded, "but they'll try and cover the perimeter anyway, and with so many of them milling about within the walls, how would we get outside? And what are you planning for your distraction?"

Salonius frowned in concentration.

"It's all nice and logical. There are large sections of the central villa that are on the verge of collapse. A good tug with a rope and we could start around a quarter of the structure imploding, I reckon. That should bring them running. In the meantime, we need to head over to the section of walls near where I used the sling. I checked the wall out while we were over there and there's a postern gate that's caved in. Just off to the side is a section of fallen wall that collapsed inwards. We can hide in the overhang of the postern while they come to investigate. Then, while they're busy, we nip out, over the fallen wall, and off into the countryside."

Varro growled. "And what if we cross the wall and they're covering that spot?"

Salonius shrugged.

"I don't believe they will be. If they're spread thinly, they'll be concentrating on the gateways and the holes in the walls. That section will still have a drop at the other side maybe as high as ten feet. They'll likely assume the inside is equally vertical. We'd be crazy to try leaving there, so they'll write that off."

"You mean we'll have to jump the horses down a ten foot drop?" Catilina queried, staring at him. "You're quite right we'd be crazy!"

"I'm afraid so; maybe even more. But within the next ten feet there's what's left of the defensive ditch too, so if we do it right we can land on the ditch slope and save the horses. It's a long shot, but then that's why I don't think it'll be watched."

Varro and Catilina exchanged glances and their shoulders sagged. Varro cleared his throat. "You really think it's feasible?"

Salonius shrugged. "I believe it's a better option than faking our escape. Whether it'll work depends a little on skill and mostly on luck or whether the Stag Lord is really watching over us."

Varro nodded and the two men focused their thoughts on the task ahead, failing to notice the curious expression that crossed their companion's face as she regarded the young engineer. Catilina allowed her smile to pass and then cleared her throat.

"Alright then. Salonius, you and Varro go and get this 'distraction' of yours organised. I'll pack up and get everything ready then I'll find you."

"We'll take the bodies and leave them among the ruins." Salonius agreed. "They should get a proper burial if all this works. When you've packed away, could you bring the horses over to the ruins?"

Catilina nodded and, as the two men untied their horses, surreptitiously tore a strip from the hem of her dress and broke her drawing stick in half so fashion a splint for her two damaged fingers. Tying the material off tightly with two of her fingers held uncomfortably straight, she set about the task of collecting their gear, carefully and wincing regularly. Damn it. She was still suffering general aches and pains from the wound in her shoulder and even the odd sharp pain when she turned wrong. Chuckling to herself, she realised she was beginning to sound suspiciously a little like Varro.

Varro grasped the reins of his horse and led it away into the darkness alongside Salonius, who checked over the strength and quality of a coil of rope as they walked.

"I hope you know what you're doing" muttered Varro, giving the young man a sidelong glance.

"So do I" muttered Salonius fervently.

A little more than five minutes of frenzied activity later, three figures moved slowly and quietly away from the jagged broken mass of the central range toward the outer wall, leading their horses and stepping carefully to avoid unexpected hazards among the long grass. Catilina and Varro's horses stepped lightly and quietly; Salonius' moved slowly, its rider spending much of his time walking backwards and facing in the direction from which they'd come. Behind him a length of rope snaked out among the grass, one end knotted tightly around the horn of the young man's saddle, the other anchored among the ruins with the precision of a career engineer. The curtain walls were now only twenty yards distant, and the three of them could just make out the shadowy arc that denoted the presence of the postern gate. Varro glanced back once more to check their progress, hoping his young companion's calculations were correct.

Finally, very slowly, the waves of rope on the ground behind them began to straighten. Salonius gestured to Varro and then pointed back down behind them. The two men watched, Varro in relief, Salonius in satisfaction, as the rope gradually pulled tight and started to lift from the grass.

Salonius coaxed his steed onwards as the strain began to show in the horse's manner, stamping its feet in frustration. The rope, having reached shoulder height, strained and creaked and the horse snorted its irritation.

Salonius looked up to find Varro giving him a concerned glare.

"Nothing else I can do now but trust to luck and judgement."

"Huh." Varro turned away and moved ahead, catching up with Catilina. The dark arch of the gateway loomed ahead and, grasping the steed's bridle, he urged her on. The groaning and creaking behind him grew in pitch and volume and for long moments, as he plodded slowly forward one step at a time, he wondered whether he had misjudged the breaking strain of the rope or the condition of the walls.

The result when it came was so sudden and surprising, even for the one who planned it, that Salonius suddenly found himself jogging forward to try and restrain the horse. For a moment, he truly believed he had failed and that the rope had snapped somewhere along the line. The horse had shot forward and the rope whipped away in coils behind it.

He hurriedly brought the horse to a worried stop and turned just in time to see the tallest section of interior wall begin to move. A high section that would have supported the dormer windows at the very centre of the complex, replete with cornice and moulding, swayed for a moment towards him. Very slowly it rocked back to upright and, as Salonius held his breath, he watched it continue on past the vertical and rock out away from him. Once more, the tall spire of shattered wall reached a critical point and swung back with enough momentum that it continued on past the apex, picking up speed and falling with ponderous grace against the lower wall opposite. The domino effect began and, with a grin of sheer satisfaction, Salonius turned his back on the cacophony and jogged with his horse to catch up with the other two, just as they reached the dark archway.

Varro was grinning from ear to ear in the shadows as he turned to face his young companion.

"Nicely done. They probably heard that all the way back at Vengen!"

Salonius nodded. "Now keep your eyes peeled. As soon as they start to gather we need to be up and away."

The three of them mounted ready and lurked in the shadows, keeping their horses as quiet and still as possible while they watched the dust begin to settle in moonlight, a strange and otherworldly sight. Almost unbearably slowly the cloud began to clear and almost immediately they became aware of figures moving around and of dulled conversation.

"Come on." Varro whispered, and very slowly and quietly they walked their horses out of the shadows and into the bright moonlight. It was a gamble, certainly. Three mounted figures would be plainly visible in the moonlight and the wall cast no shadow on this side. Likely, however, the men would be too busy examining the collapsing central range and that, combined with the confusion, the settling dust, and the fact that the three of them only had to cross around twenty yards of open ground, meant discovery was at least not a foregone conclusion.

Nervously, Salonius rode alongside Catilina at a steady walk, with Varro in front, almost at the point where the fallen wall created a steep bank. He held his breath, his eyes locked on the figures moving around at the centre. After what seemed an eternity, they reached the embankment and began to guide their horses slowly and painstakingly up the slope.

Once again, Salonius found himself wondering what in the heavens had given him this idea. The fact that they'd survived even the last ten minutes astounded him. That they might survive the long drop into a ditch, evade a small army and get away seemed such a farfetched proposition that it almost made him laugh.

"Hey!"

A sudden commotion behind them announced that they had finally been spotted.

Varro looked back over his shoulder.

"Run for it!"

The captain kicked his horse into action and ran up the steep slope as fast as the beast could manage. As he reached the top he disappeared from sight with a last cry that tailed off:

"Cernus!"

Racing now for his life, Salonius glanced across at Catilina. A confident rider, she bounded on ahead and over the crest. Swallowing nervously and painfully aware of his own lack of equestrian skill, he followed on, his heart racing. As he reached the top of the embankment of fallen wall, he had to fight the urge to haul on their reins and stop the beast. To stay here would be a death sentence. Forcing himself forwards, instead of slowing he picked up speed and charged ahead into the unknown.

The ground disappeared sharply before him and as he launched into his jump, he unintentionally clamped his eyes tightly shut. His heart skipped a beat and he was almost unhorsed as the beast landed heavily and awkwardly on the slope. His eyes shot open as he panicked, but as he glanced about wide-eyed, he realised that the beast was slowly walking in the shallow ditch. Varro and Catilina sat astride their horses at the top of the other side.

Salonius gave them a shaky smile and, turning, stared in amazement at the wall behind him, at least eight feet tall.

Varro returned the grin, trying not to laugh out loud.

"I hope you don't use that language in front of your mother!"

The young man blushed furiously, grateful for the fact that his colour would not be visible in the darkness.

"No guards nearby, but they'll be here soon enough now we've been seen." He looked up at Varro. "What now?"

Varro set his jaw and rolled his shoulders.

"Now we ride like merry hell for the wood of Phaianis. They'll not follow us in there."

Chapter Fourteen

The ride had been furious and unrelenting for almost three hours. Varro had refused to slacken the pace for even a moment, and even Catilina now wore a concerned look, fearing for her horse. The poor beasts had been slowing through necessity for the last hour and would likely drop from exhaustion at any moment. In the eerie quiet of the night, they could always hear, just on the edge of their range, the sounds of pursuit. They'd been lucky really. It had taken their pursuers a good ten minutes to organise and follow on, the few ready and mounted outriders having kept an eye on the three fugitives as they travelled.

It had occurred to Salonius that perhaps they could have somehow hidden and evaded their pursuers, but Varro had been adamant. These were not only professional soldiers, but the chances were if they went back to Cristus with talk of failure they'd now see another dawn. Besides, the few outriders Varro had seen wore the uniforms and gear of northern barbarian scouts. He'd used such scouts himself on duties and knew they could track a rabbit over twenty miles by smell alone, they were that good.

No. Their only chance was to reach some place of safety, and that, to Varro's mind was the sacred wood of Phaianis. Salonius was sceptical, though only in a background, racial fashion. In fairness, he told himself, his own people had plenty of sacred places, including copses and pools. Phaianis was the Imperial Goddess of the hunt and her places were inviolable, but Salonius' problem was with Imperial pragmatism. His own people would never violate a sacred space, but then none of them would dare choose to seek shelter there either. But his years spent among the Imperial army had led the young northerner to the conclusion that the people of the Empire didn't really believe in their Gods. They just kept them around because it was important to have someone to thank or someone to blame. That Varro was willing to break religious law and violate the sacred space of Phaianis was reason enough to worry that their hunters would do the same.

But Varro's mind was made up and another thing Salonius had learned, though relatively recently, was that Captain Varro's mind was changed with difficulty.

His horse slowed again, enough that he actually felt the change of pace and the shifting of the beast's gait. Slapping the reins and kicking the horse's flanks, he urged what speed was left in her, but with no success. Varro was ahead, but Catilina seemed to be having similar trouble.

"There!"

Varro's voice calling out from ahead was such a relief Salonius actually smiled. The low, dark bulk of the sacred wood loomed on the slope ahead of them. They had ridden for hours through open countryside and Salonius wasn't entirely sure exactly where they were any more. He knew of several shrines to Phaianis that the army's scouts visited to pay homage, but had never been to one himself. He knew the main road to Crow Hill was somewhere off to their right, probably about five miles away, but that was the limit of his geography.

They had just crested a ridge and ahead of them lay a long, grassy slope that descended into a wide valley with a river at the bottom, as evidenced by the ever increasing sound of rushing water. The scene was almost as clear as day, given the bright moonlight and only occasional light, scudding clouds. An owl flew overhead, and Salonius followed its path until his eyes came to rest once more on the woods ahead.

Perhaps half way down the slope, the sacred grove of Phaianis occupied perhaps seventy or eighty acres. It was tightly packed with undergrowth; no human would have trodden paths through the wood, and the only point of ingress would be animal trails. The young man sighed. They would have to leave their horses out in the open. In a way, they had swapped the defensible ruins of the villa for an open wood and no steed. He fervently hoped that Varro knew what he was doing. As they approached the eaves of the wood, Varro finally slowed his shattered horse to a walk and the other two caught up with him.

Off to their right, perhaps twenty yards away, was an altar, ornate and decorative. Salonius couldn't make out the detail from here, but the shallow depression in the top would undoubtedly be stained with long-dried blood from various animal sacrifices to the Huntress. The front face of the stone would detail the soldier or wealthy civilian who had set up the altar, either as a gift of thanksgiving or a plea for future aid. Such altars would ring the wood.

Dismounting, Varro began to remove his kit from the horse. As Salonius and Catilina followed suit, the captain turned to the elegant young lady and stretched.

"We've got at least five or ten minutes before they get here."

"Yes?"

Varro hesitated for a moment.

"I know you're not going to like this, Catilina, but the plain truth is that it's me they're after. They'd hunt young Salonius here too now, but if you get out of here you'll be safe. They'll not do anything to the marshal's daughter if you're not with us. We're going in, but you should saddle back up and head for Vengen again while they're busy with us."

"You idiot."

Varro stared at her.

"You know damn well I'm not leaving the pair of you," Catilina snapped. "I'm as much a witness to all this as you. You think I'll be safe riding back into the darkness? How many more groups do you think Cristus has out there? He'll be watching every road for my father coming. And I expect he'd think it a real shame if I just disappeared in the night and never reappeared. The safest place I can be right now is with you two. Besides, you think in straight military lines and Salonius can only wrap his mind around a problem if it involves building or dismantling something. You need some common sense. Now get going."

Varro opened him mouth and then closed it again with a look of frustrated defeat. As he followed Catilina into the edge of the tree line, Salonius trod quietly behind him, a look of mixed confusion and disappointment on his face.

"You don't think I'm like that do you?"

Varro laughed.

"Salonius, between you and her, the pair of your could outthink the Gods themselves."

The young engineer glanced up to either side warily, regarding the trees of this hallowed space from the narrow deer trail, and imagined the face of the angered Huntress peering from every knot hole in every tree.

"Well that'll be useful."

Varro laughed again.

"If Phaianis has enough time on her hands to worry about three folk wandering among her trees then I'm sure there's better things she could be doing. Besides, I'm almost out of her reach and your people don't even believe in her."

Salonius grumbled.

"She's still there though. If I didn't believe in air, would I stop breathing?"

"Besides," the captain went on jovially, glancing over his shoulder, "we've got the Stag Lord on our side."

Salonius glared at him but walked on silently.

After a few minutes they reached a small, overgrown clearing and Varro judged they had passed far enough into the woods and drew them to a halt.

"I think we'll be safe now. I suggest we sit and wait."

Catilina dropped her pack to the ground at the base of a tree and slumped against it, rubbing her sore hand and adjusting the splint before tightening the knot that had worked itself loose on the ride. Varro frowned and reached out to her wounded hand.

"I hadn't noticed that before? What happened?"

Catilina shrugged. "Just a bit of bruising. Hurt my fingers on a man's jaw."

She sighed.

"I don't wish to sound negative, Varro, but what exactly are you planning next?"

The captain grumbled.

"Next? Hell, I think we're lucky to have got this far! I…"

Without warning the man suddenly collapsed as though his legs had been swept from under him, landing with a crash among thick tree roots. Salonius rushed over to him, bearing a look of extreme concern.

"What is it?" Catilina was suddenly next to his shoulder as he grasped Varro by the shoulders and tried to haul him into a seated position.

"I don't know. Whatever it is, it's not good."

Salonius gently raised the captain's face and a dark gobbet of blood blurted from the older man's mouth and ran down his chin onto his chest, leaving a slick trail. His eyes flickered open and he looked around in confusion.

"I…" He choked on another gob of blood that ran down his chin, following the trail of the first. His look of confusion cleared and he frowned.

"I think I'm getting a little too close to Phaianis for comfort now. Argh!"

He suddenly clutched his side. Salonius pointed back at the captain's bag and addressed the lady beside him.

"Get his medicines. He needs the small bag. The strong one."

As Catilina nodded and spun away to the other packs, Salonius realised she was forcing herself to stay in control. He could see just how close to panic and despair she truly was and wondered just how long she's been hiding that beneath a veneer of optimism. A marvellous woman.

Turning his attention back to Varro, he undid the belt around the man's waist and hauled his tunic up to examine the wound that had begun all this. As the meagre light afforded by the moon shining between the leaves hit the man's pale skin, Salonius recoiled in shock and almost dropped the captain. The wound was no longer a neat and tidy scar. Repeated reopenings had given it a torn, jagged look and the edges of the wound were clearly badly infected. That wasn't what had struck Salonius though. He was aware that the captain had been pushing himself further than he should and that the wound would likely be a mess. What truly frightened him was the area of skin surrounding the wound. Most of the man's side, almost up to the armpit and half way around the torso was a dark purple-green colour and the veins stood out as black lines wriggling among the sickness.

"Shit!"

"What?" Catilina looked up from where she rummaged in the bag for the medicine, hampered by the lack of clear light.

"Er… nothing. His wound's a little infected."

Salonius concentrated on pulling the tunic back down and fastening the belt, unwilling to look at the young lady in case she saw the concern in his face. He had no great knowledge of medicine, but nobody that looked like that was going to last long.

Varro grasped him by the tunic below his neck and drew the young man down to his face level.

"Say nothing to her," he whispered. "Let her hope."

Salonius nodded, suddenly aware that there was a tear in the corner of his own eye. Clearing his throat, he wiped it away and turned to Catilina.

"I think we need to give him a dose of each of the three." He was acutely aware now of the warnings Scortius had given him about the administration of medicines. Under no circumstances was he to allow Varro to take the strong one close to the others. It was a judgement call that wasn't his to make. He leaned over Varro and whispered.

"You know what that means?"

Varro nodded.

"How could it make me worse, eh? You and I both know I'll be lucky to leave this wood now." Varro's voice tailed off from a whisper to nothing.

Catilina approached, undergrowth crunching underfoot.

"Here. I'll return in a moment."

"Where are you going?" Salonius asked with concern.

"Just look after him. I'll be back in a moment. The Huntress might listen. It's her wood after all, and I'm not about to make a sacrifice of him."

Salonius stared at her as she walked across the clearing and began to push her way into the brush.

"Don't go far. And don't be long."

"Yes father!" she called back to him, without a trace of humour.

The young man watched the silent dark trees for a long moment and then drew his eyes back to the captain slumped in his arms. Varro smiled weakly.

"She's gone off to cry. You know Catilina. She won't snap in front of us again."

Salonius shrugged sadly.

"You never know. Perhaps Phaianis is listening after all."

"I wouldn't rely on that." Varro tried unsuccessfully to pull himself upright. "Alright. The three medicines. You're brighter than me, lad. We both know I'm dying and we both know that mixing these three is probably going to place the coins on my eyes for my final journey. The only question I have is how long can you keep me upright. I need to feel strong and healthy for a little longer yet."

"I can't guarantee anything" the young man frowned. "I just don't know what it'll do."

"Shh!"

Varro waved his hand in front of his young companion's face and point out back along the deer trail. As Salonius concentrated, he realised someone was shouting outside the woods. Varro grasped the medicines from him and began to ingest them as fast as his laboured breathing and strength would allow. Salonius stared.

"That's more than a dose of each!"

Varro tried to shrug, but winced in pain.

"Who gives a shit now? Help me up and get me within earshot of that arse."

Salonius gingerly lifted the captain to his feet, aware unhappily that the front of the man's tunic was spattered with his own dark blood and noting also that fresh trickles of blood ran from the corner of his mouth occasionally as he spoke.

Very slowly and endlessly carefully, the two of them limped along the trail for minutes that seemed like days.

"Captain Varro!" the voice came once more from outside; still distant, but now clear.

Varro cleared his throat and wiped the blood from his mouth.

"I can hear you, you traitorous dick shit!"

There was a long pause and Varro grinned at Salonius; a grin that, with the rivulets of blood on his pale, moonlit skin, looked far more frightening than any war paint Salonius had ever seen.

"If you surrender now, I give you my word that the lady will go free. You and your companion are a different matter, but I'm sure you can see that's a generous offer."

Varro frowned.

"Huh."

He took a deep breath and bellowed out of the woods "Very generous. But liars and traitors can afford to sound generous, can't they. Who are you?"

Another pause.

"My name is captain Crino. I'm prefect Cristus' adjutant. I am authorised to speak for him. I given you a promise that Catilina

Sabianus will be escorted to safety. I pledge that by the flag fo the Fourth."

"Piss off." Varro sneered audibly. "I wouldn't trust you to fasten your shoes right now."

"Then we are at an impasse, captain" the soldier called. "I would prefer not to violate the sacred wood to come get you, but I don't think I really need to. How much food and water do you have in your packs? Not a lot I would suspect. We can sit here for days."

Salonius cleared his throat.

"The woods are full of rabbits captain. I expect we'll eat heartily. And there's a stream."

Varro grinned at his young companion and Salonius smiled back.

The voice came once again. "I do have some unscrupulous barbarian scouts with me who don't really believe in Phaianis. One of them already offered to burn the woods down for me. Obviously that would be irreligious and I could bring myself to give that order. But it's possible that if I don't keep them on a tight rein, they might do it anyway. They're very eager to help, you see."

Varro laughed.

"I think your biggest problem, soldier, is the fact that marshal Sabian isn't far behind us and he's really not going to be very happy with you when he gets here. In fact, I think you'd probably be advised to make a miraculous switch and offer your sword to him and give up your boss."

"Very frightening. I don't believe you, Varro. And even if he is, he'll be on the main road. He won't come to the woods."

"I think you'll find," Varro countered, "that Sabian has more and better men than you. Our trail's nice and easy to follow, and the mess you lot have left will make it all the easier. Now shall we stop this pointless banter and get down to business?"

There was a pause again and then Crino's voice.

"You have only two options, Varro: surrender or hold out. If you surrender, we'll make it nice and quick. If you hold out, we'll burn you out."

Varro grumbled and glanced at Salonius, who straightened and called out.

"Option three, captain: get prefect Cristus here in person and we'll sort it all out."

Varro stared at him.

"What?" he asked quietly.

Salonius shrugged.

"You're running out of time. You want Cristus. Problem solved."

The captain continued to stare for a moment, mumbling to himself.

"I guess it's the best chance I'll get. The only question is who gets here first: Sabian or Cristus. Both of them are about a half day away. You need to keep me alive and strong 'til then."

Salonius nodded.

"Alright" the voice called from outside the woods. "Prefect Cristus leaves the fort at first light for Vengen. I'll bring him here on the way."

Varro nodded to himself.

"It's going to be close."

Salonius smiled.

"At least we're safe for the night. Let's get back to the clearing."

Helping the weakened officer along the deer trail, Salonius pushed into the depths of the wood to the small space where Catilina sat waiting for them.

"All went well, I take it?"

Salonius blinked. She seemed so calm; hardly the same person they had seen a few minutes ago leaving the clearing. As Salonius gently lowered his commander to the ground, Varro cleared his throat and smiled.

"Cristus will be here not long after first light."

"And my father will be here around then too, I believe. I hope you have something planned?"

Varro nodded, his teeth clamped together in a feral manner.

"Oh, I do."

Catilina smiled a genuine and surprising smile.

"Then we have the night to ourselves."

Rummaging in the packs once again, she withdrew several blankets and her bedroll and spread them on the ground to create a thick, comfortable mattress. Smiling, she laid upon it as she pulled the largest blanket over the top and rolled the corner back invitingly.

Varro stared at her and she raised a cheeky eyebrow.

He turned to Salonius to find him grinning. The young man hurriedly turned and cleared his throat.

"There's a very small clearing about half way back along the trail. I think I'll keep watch if you don't need me."

Catilina nodded at him, turned to face Varro once again and patted the bed.

"We all know what's happening here, Varro. I'm damned if I'm going to let what might very well be my last chance slip away from me while we sit, cowering, among the trees waiting for the end one way or another. I don't know whether Phaianis will protect you in the morning, but I'm positive you'll last the night. Don't ask me why. Now come here."

Meekly and nervously, the captain crossed the clearing on hands and knees and slowly laid himself down on the thick bed of blankets.

As he gathered his pack and slowly made his way back along the track toward the small hollow he'd seen earlier, Salonius smiled. It was nice. It was right in a way that, for some reason, he couldn't quite identify. But through it all, he couldn't help but notice deep within himself the edges of jealousy roiling around in his gut. Setting his jaw firm, he focussed on the task at hand. Tomorrow morning, one way or another, Varro was going to kill Cristus or vice versa.

Reaching the hollow, he dropped his kit, slumped beside it and pulled a thin blanket over himself.

His task was to make sure Varro was capable of doing this; to keep him as strong as possible and to give him as much of an edge as possible when he needed it. Sadly, while he had a number of ideas of how he could help, a lot of this still depended on Cristus. Salonius found himself wondering what the prefect was actually like and wishing he knew him better.

Tonight would pass slowly. His mind raced with ideas. How could he help his friend? How could he solve this? Catilina was right: he could only solve problems when they involved building or destroying things. Had to got with his strengths. For Varro; and for Catilina.

From back along the track he heard a light-hearted girlish giggle.

Tonight would pass slowly.

Varro fastened his belt around his tunic and looked down at Catilina, lying under the thick blanket and smiling up at him. The faintest rays of the dawn were piercing the deep blue of the darkness and the first birds of the dawn chorus were warning up for their arias. He squared his shoulders and sighed.

Strangely, he felt good; stronger than he had for a long time. Whatever the long-term effects of mixing and overdosing the drugs that Scortius had given him, in the short term, it made him feel like a warrior again. He flexed his bicep and smiled; a smile that faltered as his gaze passed across his tunic and took in the unpleasant blood stains from last night. He would last as long as he needed to. He would last the morning, and that was all he needed.

With a last glance at the young woman lying in the clearing, he sighed contentedly and strode off purposefully along the track.

Perhaps half way along it was a small hollow where Salonius had spent the night. But the hollow wasn't there; or rather it was, but had changed. Now there was a sizeable clearing. Piles of wood and sticks were banked up against the clearing's edge. Tools lay on a low rock, and Salonius sat cross-legged, busily working away at something with his back to the path.

Varro cleared his throat and the young engineer jumped.

"Hell, sir! You gave me a start."

"Deep in concentration, then?" replied the captain as he crouched down next to the young man. Salonius was holding what appeared to be some sort of foot-thick belt and was slowly running it through his fingers, pressing it rhythmically with his thumbs.

"What the hell is that?"

"This," Salonius replied with a smile, holding the item aloft, "is what's going to give you the edge against Cristus. It's not cheating. You're at a disadvantage, since he's fully healthy and you've a badly bruised and wounded abdomen. Take your tunic off."

Varro blinked but, knowing better than to argue, did as he was told. Once he was standing, half naked, in the clearing, with the first light of dawn casting an eerie glow around him, Salonius stepped forward with the item.

"Kneel down and raise your hands above your head."

Varro did so, and Salonius stepped above him and lowered the corset-shape over his arms and gently eased it over his head and chest, down to the wounded abdomen. Varro examined the item as Salonius began to tighten it, pulling cords that were ingeniously worked into the construction.

"Explain?"

Salonius carefully tied off the three cords as he spoke.

"It's essentially a corset. The inner is formed of three thicknesses of my blanket. I used sap resin to attach vertical lengths of willow that I cut into strips. More resin set them into place. Another thickness of blanket attached with sap and the outer is made of stripped of boiled and hardened leather I tacked on. They're from my water skin, pack and so on. But since they're individual strips tacked on, they're nice and flexible. My thought is that it's give you support and protection around your abdomen. Without it, even if he punched you in the side, that'd be the end, I think. I've just got to attach the shoulder pieces to keep it in position."

Varro stared and him and burst out laughing.

"You did this during the night?"

Salonius bridled.

"You need an edge. I'm giving you that edge."

The captain clapped his hand over his young companion's shoulder.

"Oh, I am grateful Salonius. You have no idea how grateful. I think I regret the fact that I'll not live to see the day you command a cohort."

Salonius blinked.

"Sir?"

"Oh come on." Varro laughed. "When this is all over and I'm gone, you and Catilina will be the two who brought down a traitor and save the northern army. And you know the marshal personally and saved his daughter! Great things await you, my friend, and I think the army's going to change when you get your hands on it. More flexible; more adaptable. The army's always been led by brave men, but brave, intelligent and resourceful is rare. I think I'm going to miss you, Salonius."

"Captain…"

Varro shook his head.

"Strangely, the large doses of everything that I took last night seem to have given me the strength and energy of a race horse. I think I'm going to take the same again in the next hour. Damn him, if Cristus shows up here this morning, I'm going to carve bits off him until he begs for mercy."

The young man's jaw set hard.

"Good. Now stay still while I attach the shoulders."

Five minutes later the two men entered the main clearing to find Catilina up and dressed, the blankets folded into low seats and a pot heating over a low fire.

"Plenty of dead wood on the ground. I brought oats. I though we should have some breakfast to strengthen us for the day."

Varro smiled.

"It's like some kind of conspiracy to be helpful! Remember my bad wounded side?"

She nodded uncertainly as she fanned the flames of the small fire.

Varro pick up a stick from the floor and, give the difficulty of the manoeuvre, swung the stick at his wounded side as hard as he could manage. Catilina leapt towards him in shock but stopped as the stick bounced of his tunic with a deep 'clonk'.

"What in the heavens?"

Varro grinned.

"Our engineer friend put his genius to the task at hand again. Hell, at this rate, I could even fight my way through Cristus' guards to get to him."

She laughed.

"I rather hope it doesn't come to that. Now sit down and rest. Time to get the pair of you fed and watered before you start any trouble."

The sun was rising and bright morning light dappled the floor of the woodland as the three packed their gear.

"Phaianis has been good to us," Catilina noted. "I think when this is over I might dedicate an altar to her."

The two men nodded.

"Time to finish this" Varro announced, testing his sword, sliding it an inch or so in and out of the sheath to ease the draw. "Let's go see what we can see."

Salonius reached down for the debris by the captain's pack. The empty wrappers spoke volumes. Cristus had better show up now; Varro had taken every last pinch of the medication he'd been given. The chances of him coming unstuck by noon due to severe overdosing were worryingly high. Gritting his teeth and forcing a casual smile onto his face, he turned and, as he did so, watching Varro's retreating back as the man walked over to the track, he caught sight of Catilina's face as she also gazed after him. There was something about the look on her face. He smiled knowingly.

Pondering on his suspicions, he collected his pack, tipped the pan of water onto the already dead remnants of the fire and followed the others onto the track.

Given the bright daylight, the three were able to position their selves only a few yards from the edge of the woodland and could see the activity outside. A dozen or so men stood to attention in full armour within view, the cordon continuing on out of sight, presumably surrounding the grove. Varro squinted at them and then turned to his companions, lowering his voice.

"They've been on guard all night. Look at them; they're all shattered."

Salonius nodded.

"Good. And they had no sleep the day before. They'll be slow. Don't know what use that'll be when Cristus turns up with fresh men, but it's worth knowing anyway."

Catilina pointed off to the left.

"Looks like were about to find out, boys. Look!"

Away to the side, at the crest of the hill, men were arriving on horseback, bearing the standards of the Fourth Army and marching in Imperial green. Perhaps two dozen men; some senior officers; others members of the prefect's guard. All well equipped and well rested bar one. That one must be Crino, riding alongside his master in deep conversation. Anger flared up inside Salonius as he watched the prefect riding calmly under the Imperial banner as though he were the greatest and most noble soldier of the Empire and not a cowardly, enslaving traitor. He only realised he had half drawn his sword when Varro's hand enclosed his and slowly pushed the hilt back down.

"Later. Whether I kill him or not, I suspect you're going to have to fight your way out and protect Catilina."

Salonius shook his head.

"We have to wait until Sabian arrives. This needs to be witnessed, and then Catilina will be safe."

"No, my friend."

Varro drew his sword.

"I don't know how long I've got. This might be my only chance. You stay here with Catilina when I go out. You'll be safe here for now. You two are the clever ones. I'm sure you'll think of something."

Salonius' face fell.

"Now let's see what we can do" said Varro stepping to the front and leaving the cover of the woods to stand under the eaves.

It took a minute for the weary guards to spot the figure of the captain, standing in the shadows beneath the trees, then suddenly all was commotion. Varro's eyes flicked to the side, to one guard who had unshouldered a bow and was reaching in his quiver for an arrow. Half a dozen men in senior officers' uniforms came striding forward, Cristus and Crino among them. The guard captain gestured to the man with the bow.

"That won't be necessary, soldier."

The small party stopped around twenty yards from the tree line and the prefect, resplendent in his dress uniform and polished breastplate, stepped out to the front.

"Captain Varro. You look tired."

"Cristus." Varro acknowledged him with a faint nod of the head.

"I was told you wanted to meet with me. I am glad. It's time to put all of this unpleasantness behind us."

"Indeed." Varro glared at him.

"Is there some way we can come to an arrangement?"

"What?" Varro looked genuinely baffled.

"An agreement. Some sort of deal. I would always rather talk out a solution than fight one out."

Varro snarled.

"Curious sentiments for a soldier."

"Not really." Cristus smiled and removed his plumed helm. "Any good commander will agree. Fighting should always be a last resort; an end game when diplomacy fails. No general wants to fight unless he has to. It's wasteful and stupid."

He smiled and relaxed his shoulders.

"So... some sort of promotion for you and your man? I don't know what we can do for the lady Catilina, but I'm sure she can be persuaded to see sense. You're dredging up ancient history. I may have made a mistake or two in judgement when I was young, but why rock the boat now? What possible benefit can you reap?"

Varro stopped. The argument was persuasive, he had to admit. He thought for a moment of the trials that were to come; of the sizeable portion of the officers and men of the Fourth who would be brought to justice and many of them executed. It *was* a waste. It *was* all history. And then for another moment, he thought on his own history. Petrus; a cousin he had loved, murdered in the night. Corda, tricked and cajoled into treachery himself. The men who had died these last two weeks on both sides of the game, just because of this man's greed. And finally he thought of his future. The future he didn't have.

"You're a traitor, a liar, a murderer and a monster, Cristus. There can be no deal. Now I know you've always thought of yourself as a swordsman... well here's your chance to prove it. Let the Gods decide and draw their own conclusions. Your men here will respect if you face me, and it'll be real respect; the sort you earn through blood, sweat and sacrifice; not the sort you buy."

Cristus smiled.

"That's your only offer?"

Varro nodded.

"To the death for the honour of the army. I've no fear, because even without divine retribution against lying scum, I know damn well I could gut you like a fish on a slab."

The prefect's hearty laugh rang out again.

"Varro, just look at yourself, man. You're wounded and sick; dying even. You're covered in your own blood. You haven't rested properly in weeks. You're a mess. I don't *need* a sword; I could beat you to death with a tunic for heavens' sake. Just see reason and end this with negotiation. This is my last offer of peace. We can try and get you healed and back to normal."

Varro's feral grin marched across his face.

"Take your offer and jam it up your arse sideways. Are you going to fight me or not?"

Cristus sighed.

"Very well. No armour. Just tunics and swords, yes?"

"Fine by me."

With a growl, Varro hefted his blade and stepped forward.

Cristus unbuckled his cuirass and handed it and his helmet to one of the staff officers beside him. He looked for a moment at the leather bracers on his wrists.

"Would you mind if I keep these on? Personal reasons, you see. Awards for meritorious service. One doesn't like to be without them."

Varro snarled.

"Just get ready."

Cristus smiled again, broad and relaxed.

"You must calm down, captain. Your skills with the sword will be of no avail if you blow a blood vessel and expire before you even reach me."

He stretched his shoulders and drew his sword, giving it a few experimental swings.

"Feel free to invite your young engineer friend and the lady Catilina out. I will guarantee their safety. After you've needlessly thrown yourself away, the young man will certainly have a place with me in the Fourth, and I have nothing but respect and admiration for the lady."

"Just shut up and get ready."

Varro stopped five yards from the prefect who smiled and removed his scarf. With a flamboyant sweep of his arm, he handed it to another officer, who took it silently.

"Now, gentlemen... if you'll all step the requisite twenty paces back and give us some room."

The party of officers retreated up the hill a way and took up position with Crino's men. Cristus flipped his sword around in his hand expertly a few times.

"Isn't it said for the modern military that bravery and stupidity are so often aligned in a man."

He grinned as he began to slowly circle Varro. The captain started to move likewise dropping his shoulders and holding his sword ready.

"I've got to kill you Cristus, just to stop you talking if nothing else!"

He stepped forward with lightning speed and lunged out towards Cristus. The prefect laughed and ducked to one side, knocking the blade out of the way with his own sword.

"Fast, but sloppy and obvious."

Varro smiled and circled once more. After a momentary pause, Cristus suddenly twirled back on himself, bringing his blade out in a wide, flashing arc at shoulder height. Varro ducked, but only just in time. The damn contraption Salonius had made might save his life, but it meant he couldn't bend low enough. Damn it! He would have to adjust. Adapt and adjust, like his friend would.

"Flashy. Does that impress your friends, Cristus?"

The prefect smiled an unpleasant smile.

"Sadly, every move I make tells me something about you. And now I know that you can't duck. Nasty wound and that evil toxin destroying you from within. I'm surprised you can move. Scortius must have done wonders with you to keep you upright."

Varro growled.

"I'm not going to exchange chit chat with you, Petrus, you piece of shit. Just fight me."

"With pleasure."

Almost unbelievably fast, the prefect's sword lashed out and caught Varro a stinging, if minor, blow to the thigh.

"I'm really trying not to kill you, Varro. I'd like to give the men a bit of spectacle first."

"Sir!"

Cristus' head snapped round. For a moment Varro wondered whether to take advantage of the distraction, but decided against it. If this was to be done, it had to be done right."

"What?" Cristus demanded of the young cavalryman who'd just rode close to the combat and reined in.

"Sir, marshal Sabian is on his way. He and his guard have just crossed the stream."

Varro was pleased to see the prefect's smug expression slide for a moment.

"Now we'll get an audience, Cristus!"

Chapter Fifteen

Marshal Sabian arrived on the scene in spectacular fashion. Though a practical and realistic man, the marshal was well aware of the effect that pomp and splendour could have on a situation when used to its maximum effect. The trumpets calling the army to order were clearly audible before a single man became visible. Then, a few moments later, the standard bearers appeared over the slope, their banners fluttering in the light breeze and displaying the insignia of the marshal, the Northern Provinces, and all four armies under his command.

At the first blast of the horn and without the need of a command from Cristus, every soldier on the hillside came to attention, and nervously maintained their posture as the standard bearers hove into view, followed in quick succession by the trumpeters and the drummers, beating out a marching cadence. Behind the musicians came Captain Iasus of the marshal's guard, astride a magnificent black horse that matched his uniform in shade, giving him the appearance of some sorting of avenging spirit from the underworld. Iasus was accompanied by a dozen of his men in full dress uniform who rode in an arrow formation, forming a protective shield around the marshal himself on his white mare. The column went on behind them, with several of Sabian's senior officers, more of his personal guard and two thousand troops split into four columns, representing the northern armies.

It was a spectacular and fearsome force to behold and the effect was not lost on the two men facing each other with drawn blades. Regardless of whether Cristus won their melee, the day was now lost to him. Sabian's force outnumbered the prefect's by hundreds to one, and the sudden glorious reminder of the marshal's power and influence would already be melting away the resolve of even Cristus' most avid supporters. He smiled an odd smile.

"It appears that my options are diminishing at an alarming rate, Varro."

The wounded captain snorted.

"You have no options, Cristus."

"I fear you may be disappointed there, Varro; I make it a point to always have a way out. However, I feel bound to offer you one last time my hand in friendship. We could still walk away today.

The marshal could be persuaded to put aside any animosity were the two of us to stand side by side."

Varro barked a laugh.

"No options, Cristus! No way out today."

The prefect shook his head sadly.

"Were I to find myself at the marshal's mercy today, remember two things, Varro: firstly, I will kill you before I finish. That is not a boast or a threat but a simple statement. I am a better swordsman than you, despite all your frontline experience, and I am fully healthy and rested, while you are dying and weak."

He smiled.

"And secondly, I am a master of politics. I can assure you that when all is done here, I will go on. I shall be leaving the military, of course, but I believe my place in the ruling council is still secure. No matter how sentimental over you Sabian gets and no matter how angry he may be over my dirty little secret, I have tricks up my sleeve and information in hand that will guarantee my safety and my future."

"You lying turd!"

Cristus chuckled.

"Come, Varro. Do you really think I haven't planned for this kind of eventuality? That I did not set wheels in motion to protect myself decades ago? It *will* be a shame to have my commission removed and be mustered out without a triumphal parade and great show, and I daresay one or two of my senior men will have to be sacrificed for the look of the thing, but Sabian is practical and it will be much more trouble to punish me than to promote me, I can assure you."

Varro bared his teeth.

"Then, skill or no skill, I'll just have to make sure you don't leave this field, eh?" he growled.

The two men stood for a long moment, their eyes locked on each other; Cristus' expression an unreadable mix of smugness and satisfaction, Varro's a look of pure hatred. Slowly, distrustfully, the pair tore their gaze from each other and looked up at the approaching column of men. The troops of the four armies had begun to move into position in a wide arc with one tip at the wood's edge and the other at the crest of the hill, enclosing the men on the slope. The standard bearers and musicians had fallen into ranks on either side of the command unit and had ceased their bleating and thumping. In the centre, the black-clad guardsmen settled into a protective cordon behind and alongside their captain and the marshal, who gently walked his steed forward.

Cristus lowered his sword and gave a crisp military salute as the marshal and his men drew up their horses twenty yards from the combat. Varro merely let his sword drop and nodded a casual greeting.

The marshal regarded the scene, allowing his gaze briefly to wander to the edge of the woods and scan the ranks of men on the hillside. He sat comfortably in the saddle, his face a blank mask. Cristus appeared not to read anything into this, but Varro had known the marshal on a personal level long enough to see through the mask and recognise the very dangerous current flowing beneath. Sabian was just about as angry as Varro had ever seen him. The marshal spoke in a flat, dead tone.

"Gentlemen…"

His expression unreadable, Sabian dismounted and passed his horse's reins to one of Cristus' soldiers standing nearby, who took them nervously. Behind him, Captain Iasus and two black-clad sergeants also dismounted and stepped up to join their commander. The marshal clapped his hands together and rubbed them vigorously as he approached the two combatants.

"Speak to me. It would appear that two of my senior officers are ready to cut each other to pieces and I am very much in two minds as to whether to stop this and have you both locked up or to let you kill each other here and now and solve all my problems."

Cristus remained at attention and bowed his head briefly.

"My lord marshal, there are a number of baseless accusations that have been made against me by men driven by greed and jealousy. You will discover that there is no evidence for any of this bar the hearsay and rumour spread by captain Varro and his cronies. I was on my way to Vengen with my officers to bring this distasteful matter to your attention and resolve any questions when I was waylaid by the necessity of confronting the man over his behaviour. As is good and proper by military law, I was about to bring Varro to justice through trial by combat since violence appears to be the only solution that he understands."

Varro let out a mirthful chuckle. Sabian looked across at him and raised an eyebrow.

"Something to add there, captain?" he said in a quiet, yet deadly tone.

Varro's laugh stopped, his smile sliding into a feral grin.

"I believe you're well aware of my opinions concerning this piece of shit, marshal."

Sabian allowed his flat glare to pass across them both before he drew a short breath.

"Prefect Cristus, I think we're beyond denials now, so be quiet and wait." He turned to lay his gaze on the other combatant. "And Varro? I'd need extra hands to count the number of times you've broken rules and deliberately disobeyed my orders. I've given you a great deal of elbow room due to your condition and your past record, but it stops now. I'm thoroughly sick of the sight of both of you. If you're determined to carve each other to pieces, I'm more than happy to accommodate you, but you *will* do it according to military etiquette."

Turning his back on them, he issued quiet orders to captain Iasus. Varro watched him warily, the point of his sword wavering. Iasus saluted and strode off.

"Now," barked Sabian, "Where is my daughter, Varro?"

Varro raised his sword and pointed to the woods with it.

"She and Salonius are watching, sir."

"Catilina!" the marshal bellowed angrily.

The pale, graceful figure of the marshal's daughter appeared at the edge of the wood, followed by Salonius wearing an expression of hopelessness. For just a moment the lady paused at the altar of Phaianis nearby. The gentle depression in the top was stained red with both wine and blood. Reaching up to her neck and wincing at both the dull ache in her shoulder and her broken fingers, Catilina unclasped the necklace that she wore.

Varro breathed in deeply. Even at this distance, he recognised the golden chain and locket; Catilina's most prized possession: a cameo of her mother made the week before she died. Without even a visible hint of regret, she dropped the necklace into the bowl and strode on toward the waiting figure of her father. Salonius stopped for a second to stare at the item and then hurried to catch up.

"Father," the young woman said in a business-like tone as she approached. A greeting; no hint of submission.

"Catilina, look at you. What have they done to you?"

His daughter raised her head, her back straight and proud.

"As they say in taverns the world over, father, if you think this is bad, you should see the other man!"

Varro chuckled for a moment and then clamped his mouth shut.

"Explain!" the marshal barked, glaring at the captain.

She sighed.

"Cristus' men came for us in the night, father, just like they did at Vengen. I defended myself. Valiantly, I would say. I hurt my fingers; they'll heal."

Sabian shifted his glare to Cristus but said nothing. Finally, grinding his teeth, he turned and bellowed back up the slope.

"Surgeon! To me!"

There was a brief commotion among the medical staff and a small group of men came down the slope. Several orderlies ran ahead, coming to a halt at attention close to the marshal. The chief surgeon strode on behind with an air of supreme unconcern and finally sauntered to a halt behind his subordinates.

Mercurias shunned both the white robes common to private medical practitioners within the Empire and the crisp military uniform of their military counterparts, preferring as his standard mode of dress a casual, often worn and creased grey tunic and breeches bearing no insignia. His personal relationship with both Sabian and the Emperor was deep enough that no question would ever be raised over his behaviour, which was, some said, a damned good thing, given the old man's acerbic nature.

"What is it?" he demanded irritably, as though interrupted from a pleasurable pursuit.

Sabian waved his hand at his daughter by manner of an explanation while his eyes remained locked on the two men before him. As the surgeon approached the young lady, Catilina smiled warmly.

"It's been too long, Mercurias."

The grizzled doctor cracked a grin.

"I'd heard about your arrow wound. Now some broken fingers too eh? You trying intentionally to piss your father off?"

She laughed as Mercurias grasped her gently by the wrist and began to unwrap the binding she had used. Sabian raised an eyebrow in question without shifting his gaze. As though by some sixth sense, Mercurias shrugged and reported.

"Looks like two or three fractures on two fingers. She bound them quickly and correctly. She'll be fine, though I'll splint them better."

He cackled.

"But judging by the placement and the depth of the bruising, some well-built young man somewhere is having his dinner fed to him with a spoon."

"In hell" added Catilina with a grin.

Though the doctor continued to cackle, Catilina looked up and caught the expression on her father's face and allowed herself to regain her composure.

A distant pounding noise that had been growing gradually became more insistent and Varro turned to see a large group of men marching down the hill towards them. As they approached, they veered off into two lines and shuffled into position to form a large square around the two men, presenting their shields as an internal wall. Sabian cast his eyes over the makeshift arena and then beckoned to his daughter. The two of them, accompanied by Mercurias, Iasus and Salonius, strode back up the hill a way until they were high enough to obtain a clear view over the double line of infantry forming the arena wall.

Salonius' breathing was becoming tense and short. Sabian glanced across at him and narrowed his eyes. Taking a deep breath, he turned and addressed the assembled masses on the hill.

"I want Cristus' command here to form into a unit at full attention. You may be under suspicion, but you are still soldiers in my army. Act like it!"

Hurriedly the various clusters of men and odd individual soldiers rushed to a position on the hill, where captain Crino bullied them into a semblance of order.

The marshal looked around and nodded with satisfaction. With the masses out of reasonable earshot, he allowed his shoulders to drop a little and relaxed. He glared at the two men in the makeshift arena.

"You two just wait for a minute." He turned to the young engineer close by.

"Salonius," he said in hushed tones,"What's his chances? How bad is he?"

The young man took a deep breath.

"I'm really not sure, sir. Yesterday I wouldn't have pitted him against a sheep with any confidence, but he's dosed himself to critical, probably fatal, levels and he claims to be on top of his game. If he really does feel like he claims to, I think he'll do it."

Sabian pursed his lips and frowned.

"There is another possibility in the event of failure."

"Sir?"

The marshal placed his hand on Salonius' shoulder.

"You have as much right to accuse and challenge Cristus as Varro has. This may sound heartless, but frankly I cannot afford to let Cristus leave this field alive. If Varro can't do it, I need you to go in and finish the job."

Salonius stared at the marshal, but the surprise quickly vanished from his face and was replaced with a mix of determination and distaste.

"It would be my duty and my pleasure, sir. But I still pin my hopes on the captain."

"So do I, soldier. So do I."

The two of them turned their eyes back to Varro and Cristus who stared at each other with open hatred. Sabian squared his shoulders.

"Catilina…"

"I know father. Later."

The marshal watched her for a moment and then nodded, raising his eyes to the arena.

"Let this be official, then. We have an arena. We have two challengers. Military law dictates what must happen here. Both combatants must be on equal terms."

He grumbled something under his breath as he stared at the blood-stained mess that was captain Varro and the clean, limber figure of Cristus.

"We'll agree that this is as equal as you're likely to be, I suppose." He drew a deep breath and announced loudly.

"We have a challenge to trial by combat between prefect Cristus and captain Varro. According to tradition, we need a judge who is impartial. Since that is an impossibility in the circumstances, I shall appoint captain Iasus to arbitrate this dispute. Everyone who knows my guard captain will know of his keen instinct toward law, order and tradition; tradition which, I believe, also requires both parties to have a second?"

Sabian glanced across at Salonius, who nodded.

"Officer Salonius of the captain's guard in the Fourth will second Varro. And Cristus?"

The prefect smiled.

"I nominate captain Crino as my second, though I cannot imagine for a second that I will need him."

Sabian shifted his gaze to the named captain, standing with his unhappy troops, enclosed in a ring of men emanating a low but clearly discernable air of detestation and disapproval. Crino grimaced, clearly unhappy with his lot, and finally nodded reluctantly.

"Very well. Varro and Salonius; Cristus and Crino."

He gestured to Iasus, who adjusted his black cloak and removed his plumed helm. The strict guard captain squared his shoulders and stepped forward, opening a gap in the shield wall and entering the arena.

He called out in an officious tone "Under article fourteen of the codex of Imperial military law, Captain Varro has requested trial by combat."

He turned to the captain.

"State your accusations for the record and be witnessed by all here as representatives of the Emperor and his council."

Varro shrugged wearily.

"This traitorous piece of shit has called on himself the death penalty time and again, according to the standards of military law. He consorted with the enemy at Saravis Fork and sold out a garrison to the barbarians to become slaves or worse... penalty: death."

Some of the weariness seemed to drop from Varro's frame and he pulled himself upright, his voice gaining volume.

"He lied to his commanding officer and his peers, claiming honours and victories that were not his, gaining prestige and position by condemning his own men and covering his tracks with bloodshed and deliberately heavy losses… penalty: death."

His arm shot out and an accusing finger pointed at Cristus.

"He employed assassins and secreted them among the men of the Fourth, with orders to kill myself, sergeant Petrus, Salonius, and possibly even the lady Catilina, succeeding in the death of my cousin Petrus, a hero and survivor of the Saravis Fork massacre… penalty: death."

The captain growled.

"And last night his men besieged us in a ruined villa not far from here. His attack almost killed the marshal's daughter, who was wounded in the process. And now that I think of it, that's the third time we've been attacked by Cristus' men. This is basically a declaration of war against two officers and a civilian… penalty: death."

He stepped back and took a breath.

"If he's allowed to go on, he'll continue to lie, cheat, betray and murder, only in higher levels, on the Imperial ruling council. He has to be stopped now for the good of the Empire."

Captain Iasus waited a long moment to be sure that Varro had finished and then turned to Cristus.

"Prefect? Do you wish to state your case?"

Cristus sighed and gave a sad little smile that he flashed around the crowd of soldiers present.

"Perhaps, if I thought it worthwhile. Captain Varro has fallen under the spell of an unpleasant and thoroughly false rumour concerning my past, spread maliciously by a man who is now conveniently deceased and can no longer confirm or deny it. He has victimised and hounded myself and my officers and, I believe, has already turned most of my peers against me. I fear that in the eyes of my contemporaries, I am already guilty. And so, I am left with only one option: to accept Varro's challenge and leave the proof of my innocence on his body. I have faith in my cause, my Gods and my skill."

He folded his arms, the blade of his sword wavering slightly and catching the rays of the morning sun, flashing them back around the crowd.

Varro coughed, though Salonius saw his face and was sure he heard the word 'arsehole' disguised in there. In other circumstances the juvenile behaviour would have made him laugh.

Iasus took a step back from the arena's edge and glanced up the slope at Sabian, who nodded slightly. Clearing his throat, the guard captain once more addressed the combatants.

"Can there be no peaceable resolution?"

Varro growled "No."

"Very well then." Iasus pointed to two ends of the makeshift arena. "The regulations laid out under military law for this are as follows: The combatants will separate to a distance of thirty paces before we start. Combat will begin when I call the order. There are no restrictions given to the precise nature of combat, and so the employment of certain tactics is down to the conscience of the individual."

He paused to let his words sink in and then took another breath.

"A halt can be called at any time by either party by addressing the adjudicator, that is myself. Equally, I have the right to call a halt at any point. No other party may stop the combat, though they may approach me to do so. Combat will end when only one party remains alive. At that point, the second of the losing combatant may elect to issue their own challenge and step into the arena. The winner of the combat is absolved of any crime for which he stands accused and may return to active service on clearance by the medical staff. The remains of the loser will be dealt with appropriately. Are these regulations clear?"

Varro and Cristus chorused their understanding.

"Then let the parties separate by walking a further ten paces apart from where they currently stand."

Varro crouched and, jabbing his sword in the ground, picked up a handful of dry dirt, rubbing it into his hands before retrieving the blade and standing again. With a quick glance at the retreating figure of Cristus, he spat once on the floor and then turned his back and walked away, counting his paces.

Catilina leaned close to Salonius.

"Can he actually win? Cristus may be more of a politician than a general, but he prides himself on his swordsmanship. He's won competitions."

The young man nodded unsurely.

"I didn't realise Cristus was that good, but Varro's still going to win. Cristus has rigid thinking. He can only see black and white. Varro's cleverer than that. The captain won't win because he's better with a sword; he'll win because he can outthink the prefect."

"I hope you're right."

Salonius continued to nod.

"I am. I know I am."

Catilina swallowed nervously and briefly flicked her eyes toward the eaves of the sacred wood and then focused on Varro, standing poised to one side of the arena, glaring at his opponent, who swung his sword in figure eights with a flourish.

Iasus' sharp voice made her jump.

"Begin!"

Cristus stepped forward, still swinging his blade in elaborate arcs, smiling confidently. Varro pursed his lips, glanced once, quickly at Catilina and mouthed something that Salonius couldn't quite see, and then began to walk forward slowly and purposefully, his sword held straight in his hand and his eyes locked on his adversary.

Salonius tensed and felt Catilina's good hand grasp his wrist. He encompassed her small and delicate hand in his and cast a sidelong glance at her. A single tear ran down her cheek, past her hardened, resolute features.

Varro struck first.

It was a thorough, hard, military blow; backhanded and aimed horizontally at elbow height. As he'd predicted, Cristus suffered a fleeting moment of indecision as to how to block the blow before hurriedly raising his blade and bringing it back down, awkwardly and barely in time to turn the blow away.

Varro took a step back.

"That's your problem, you see, Cristus? You've only ever fought gentlemen under peaceable circumstances. You've never fought anyone who's only goal is to kill you. That's why you'll lose."

Cristus stepped back.

"You're an idiot Varro," he said, quietly enough to be inaudible beyond the pair of them. "You've damaged my reputation almost beyond repair. If I'm to come out of this smelling sweet, I need to make this a show. I need them to think I *deserved* to win. You're just going to look like a thug."

Varro growled and suddenly lunged, thrusting his sword at Cristus' belly. The man laughed and wheeled aside, bringing his own blade down on Varro's theatrically, with a ringing noise. In an almost blinding flash of speed, the prefect's blade flicked across the captain's hand guard and scraped along the wood and leather contraption Salonius had created. Within, Var5ro heaved a sigh of relief. Even that fancy scratch could have ended it. He looked up at Cristus, who was smiling benignly.

"Tut tut, captain. Calmly, now."

Spinning around to face the man again, Varro felt a wrenching in his side. He reached down and grasped his waist, his eyes momentarily blurring.

"Not yet…"

"What was that?" Cristus chuckled. "Your wound and the venom causing trouble. Please rise above it. If I finish this too quickly it's such a wasted opportunity."

Varro suddenly winced and dropped to all fours, making a hacking sound. Cristus sighed as he wandered casually over to the stricken captain.

"Come on, Varro. Get up and die on your feet."

Varro grinned. In a lightning quick move, he rolled onto his side, bringing his sword down to the grass, directly onto Cristus' foot. With satisfaction, he drove the blade through flesh and bone and into the earth, breaking several bones in the middle of the man's foot and pinning him agonisingly to the floor.

Cristus stared down in shock and horror at his maimed foot as Varro rolled back out of reach and slowly and painfully climbed to his feet.

"Never be drawn in by deception, you piece of shit." He tapped his wounded side and smiled at the dull, echoey thudding noise.

Cristus moved ever so slightly and, as the muscles in his foot tore further around the deeply-wedged blade, let out a piercing shriek that cut through the silence of the hillside. Varro laughed.

"You are a good swordsman, Cristus. You're also an idiot, a liar, a traitor and shortly a corpse. Best concentrate on pulling that blade out of your foot. Can't reach me until you do, and the blood's trickling away slowly."

As he spoke, he began slowly to circle Cristus. The prefect attempted to keep his front facing the captain but, as Varro circled behind him, it was impossible. Even the effort made his face contort with the agony shooting up from his foot. Varro stopped directly behind him, smiled, and very, very gently kicked the stricken leg from behind. Cristus shrieked again, so loud that the birds left the canopy of the sacred wood. Combat all but forgotten, the prefect reached down toward the hilt of the sword pinning him, his mouth opening and closing in an 'O' of exquisite horror and agony.

With a calm smile, Varro reached out and gently plucked the man's sword from his hand. The smile deepened as Cristus tried to turn once more and raised a hand to ward off the blow. Almost causally, Varro swung the prefect's sword, cutting the fingers from the raised hand.

Fresh agony rang through Cristus as he stared first at his hand, with only a 'V' of thumb and forefinger remaining, the others lying like uncooked meat on the grass. With a grisly, determined look, Varro took his other arm by the wrist.

Cristus stared at him, repeatedly mouthing the word 'no' through a veil of tears, though no sound issued.

Varro stopped.

"You want *mercy*? *You*? After the deaths you've caused, you have the audacity to ask for mercy. Catilina's wounds? Petrus' death? And that poor messenger too? The soldiers in the valley station who didn't even know what they were dying for? Turning Corda against me? And after all that, my wound and the poison? And you want mercy?"

Cristus stared at him, the pain and shock clearly evident, but another strange look of confusion joining them.

"Poison?"

Varro growled and tightened his grip on the man's wrist.

"Yes. The Ironroot. Very subtle. Much more subtle than the rest of your activities…"

Cristus stared through the tears.

"I've never used Ironroot, Varro. I wouldn't even know where to get it this far north."

Sighing, Varro swung the blade and cut a single finger from Cristus' hand.

"I know that me winning proves your fault anyway, but I'd really appreciate you unburdening yourself of your guilt quite noisily so that everyone else can hear it."

Cristus whimpered, staring at his hand, still in the captain's grip.

"I'll confess to anyone. Just stop torturing me!"

Varro growled again.

"Then tell me how you got the poison to that barbarian!"

"What barbarian? What are you talking about, Varro? Please?"

The captain stopped and frowned.

"The Imperial sword. The nice officer's sword that barbarian stuck me with? Covered in Ironroot? The one that killed me?"

Cristus stopped crying. For a horrible moment, he began to smile. Even through the tears and the pain, the prefect's sides began to shake with laughter.

"What's funny?" Varro barked.

"You!" Cristus coughed out. "You did all this to pay me back for something I didn't do! Priceless. Oh, the Gods like a joke, Varro. They love a good joke, and this one's on both of us. You've ruined me in retaliation for something I didn't do, and now you're going to die without even finding out who really did!"

Varro stared at this laughing maniac and suddenly felt a sharp pain. Staring down, he realise that Cristus had used his two remaining fingers on the other hand to draw a small, slender knife from his belt and thrust it into the captain's side. Still gripping Cristus' wrist, he stared in shock and suddenly collapsed to his knees, bringing the prefect with him. With a tearing noise the disfigured man's foot tore in half around the blade in the floor.

Cristus drew his small knife back in his maimed hand, the blade making curious sounds as it tore back out through the leather support, and laughed again.

"Varro, Ironroot is an ingestive, you idiot. It would probably do you some damage on a blade, but not enough to be fatal. If only I had some on this blade, I could make your last minutes a little more interesting."

He thrust forward with the blade again, going for the chest this time, but Varro's own hand swung up, bearing his opponent's sword and breaking the offending arm at the wrist.

Staring it his limp, broken hand, Cristus giggled.

"Best put me out of my pain Varro. I need to die first or my cause wins and I die a free and honoured soldier. And you'll not even make it to the marshal. I know my anatomy, Varro. That was your liver. See how the blood pooling out at your belt and running down your leg is nice and dark? Darker than mine? That's liver, that is. I…"

Mid sentence, the prefect stopped, his eyes glazing over as the tip of Varro's sword broke through the man's back and out through his tunic with a tearing sound. Cristus slumped over him, a mangled, bleeding mess.

Varro toppled backwards to the ground and looked down at his legs, tangled beneath him.

"Dark."

It was true. The blood running in thick streams down his thigh was dark and wicked.

Clutching at the grass with whitening knuckles, he forced himself to his knees and looked around. Everything was blurred, as though seen through a pain of glass in heavy rain.

Rain.

It has been raining when he'd first met Catilina. He remembered it well. At Vengen. He'd reported to the senior officer in the square before the marshal's palace. The rain was turning the gravel and dirt beneath his feet into a browny-grey mud that clung to his boots. He knew he looked dirty and haggard from a long ride, but then the palace doors had opened and she had appeared in her finery, a young lady; much younger than him, but so beautiful.

He smiled wistfully as he looked down at his knees and thighs, soaked through with deep, dark, red; the colour of Catilina's dress that day, if he remembered correctly.

She had climbed onto her horse and walked it slowly across the square toward the civilian sector, pulling her hood up against the rain. Half way across the square she'd first looked at him. She'd stared and then slowly warmed to a smile. Rummaging in a pocket, she produced a coin and tossed it to him.

"Get indoors somewhere and get some wine while you dry off."

With a lingering look, she'd ridden off.

He'd known that day that they'd be together til death. Curiously it hadn't occurred to him it would happen this soon, but still, he'd known. And he was right, because here she was, his beautiful Catilina, with him in the arena. He couldn't see at all now. Everything was a milky white, but his nose still worked. Even days on the road and nights in the woods hadn't disguised that scent, like roses in the early morning dew. And other hands too; strong hands. He recognised those hands. Who did they belong to again?

There was a pain as he was slowly helped to his feet. He vaguely recognised the heady sensation of standing suddenly; light-headed. The pain was nicely distant. Like something experienced through that same window. If only he could see through the window, but it was so white. And someone was talking to him. He could hear that there were voices, but they were drowned under the surging noises in his ears, like a great torrent of water rushing down a gulley; like the bridge where they'd fought Cristus' men in the mountain village. Such a loud rushing that there was little hope of hearing the voices. Shame, really. Catilina had a lovely voice when she wasn't shouting, and Salonius... that was his name... Salonius... he had such a soft and calm voice for an engineer. He'd miss them.

Oh dear. He couldn't smell Catilina anymore.

Silence.

Salonius gripped the slumped body of his captain with his left arm, holding him upright with all his strength, his right arm clamped tightly around the shoulders of the shuddering woman beside him. Catilina wailed and howled, shaking and snorting. Though only moments passed, it felt like hours to the young man, supporting the two most important people in his life. He waited patiently for the grief to plateau and finally the shaking subsided, the cries turned to sobs and the distraught young lady began to take her own weight once more.

As Catilina stepped back, wiping the tears from her eyes and cheeks with the back of her good wrist, Salonius turned the limp and suddenly light body of the captain to face him. That face; so white. With a sigh, he threw Varro over his shoulder and turned to follow Catilina back out of the arena, pausing only momentarily to deliver a hefty kick to the prone heap that was Cristus.

The arena wall, formed of two rows of men from their own army, stepped respectfully aside as Salonius carried the victor up the slope towards the marshal. As he walked, captain Iasus joined them. Glancing to his other side, he was, as ever, impressed by Catilina. The visual signs of grief had all but fled, leaving her with a resolute and proud look. Salonius tried to match her expression as they reached the marshal.

Sabian's face was blank as they approached.

"Sir," Salonius announced, "I believe since prefect Cristus died first, that this man deserves to be honoured appropriately?"

Sabian took a short breath; then another; then turned to Cristus' second, captain Crino.

"Do you wish to take up the challenge, Crino?"

The relief on the captain's face melted away as he came under scrutiny once more.

"No sir. I believe justice has been served."

"Hmmm." Sabian glared at the captain for a moment and then turned back to the small group before him.

"Iasus? I want you to start working through the Fourth. I want everyone separated into three groups to deal with: those who were a clear part of Cristus' treachery, those who were unwillingly or unwittingly roped in, and those who are innocent. I trust you're able to do this?"

The captain nodded curtly.

"Those with some level of culpability will be placed under guard at Vengen. And those who are innocent, sir?"

Send them to Crow Hill to await the arrival of a new prefect. Let them take their banners and their honours with them. And get the camp commandant and the quartermaster to organise setting up camp here for the night. I doubt we'll be leaving until you've finished your questioning."

Iasus nodded.

"I'll have a palisade erected, sir. I already have pickets and guards out to prevent desertion."

"Good," Sabian waved away toward the wagons. "Get started."

As Iasus stalked away, taking several of the black-clad guards with him, Sabian turned back to Salonius, Catilina, and the wilted body of Varro.

"Sad to see him end so. But a good way for him to go, I think. I suspect he's content, wherever he is."

Salonius smiled sadly.

"We were tasked by the Gods, sir, to achieve something great. I believe we've done so. I think the afterlife is waiting with honours to welcome captain Varro."

Catilina shot him a quick and very strange look.

"It's not quite over for us, Salonius" she said darkly.

And vengeance sends the last goodbye...

The problem with Varro and Salonius is that they both only ever think, or thought, in such limited ways. They had always assumed that the stag God had chosen them to do great works. Them and only them. I didn't like to puncture their bubble of importance. I let them go on dropping to hushed tones when I appeared and whispering secretively like small children who've found a secret place.

I never told them about that night at Crow Hill where Cernus first found me, floundering in my despair; of how the Stag Lord explained to my heart why these things were so; of why Varro was important. They never seemed to wonder why I put my whole world at risk to follow them into the wilderness on their great errand, putting it down to my 'wilfulness'.

And I never told them how Cernus found me again at Vengen; how I was wounded and felt close to the end at times, weak as a kitten from that wound in my shoulder, but how the Stag Lord came to me at that critical moment as my will dissolved and brought me strength to go on, and purpose to do so.

But the strange thing is, that even through my secret clandestine liaisons with Cernus, it never occurred to me that my path was different from theirs. Perhaps that Salonius was the peg that joined our tasks. For I was far from instrumental in their success in bringing down a traitor to the Empire. I played a part, certainly, but they would have arrived at their end without me, I now know. For the Stag Lord had chosen a dying man for his own goals. Cernus is a Lord of the forests and a God of the Northern tribes. What cares he that Imperial justice is served?

No. Quite simply, Cernus chose Varro to right a wrong visited on his own people. Cristus had to die, not for any betrayal of the Empire or his army, but for the violent extinction of the tribe of the Clianii. Varro was his instrument. Salonius was chosen as a son of the northern peoples.

But me? I had no part to play there.

My part was supplementary to the God. My part was to right the wrong done to Varro in return for his efforts.

I was, as so many times before, losing my resolve. We were in the sacred wood of Phaianis. I would never have set foot on such sacred ground under normal circumstances, but the situation demanded it. And beneath those hallowed eaves, I watched the man I loved open the last door to the afterlife. I saw him die once again and knew that his time had come. I doubted he would see another dawn and I broke.

I made some excuse about praying to Phaianis and left them. I just had to be alone to break. I was in the depth of the most hopeless loss I could imagine, and after all that Cernus had done for me, there was nothing I could do for Varro to help him with what he must face. I couldn't understand how I could have come so far, only to be useless now.

And that was the third time the Stag Lord found me. Deep in the woods we associate with Phaianis the huntress, here was that most hunted of creatures, the stag, all unconcerned. To my dying day, I will live in the belief that Phaianis, and probably all of our Gods, are a fiction of our proud minds and that the only true spirits are those that actually touch us.

Cernus found me there in the pit of despair and brought me the knowledge of what I must do. By the time he turned and left me alone in the dark woods, my resolve had returned and I knew that I must harden myself and go on. Varro and Salonius had avenged the Empire.

And now I would avenge Varro.

Chapter Sixteen

Catilina knocked quietly on the doorpost of the tent. The heavy leather flaps were down, but untied. No sound issued from within, and the only windows were holes high up that allowed light to filter within. Her knock was greeted with silence. She paused for a long moment and then rapped once more on the post, this time a little harder, glancing around at the scene.

This area of the makeshift camp was set aside from the rows of accommodation, on the rear slope of the summit on which stood the command tents of the marshal and his various officers. The sky was a bright blue with only the occasional fine cloud wandering aimlessly across the firmament. The commanding view here took in the distant main road and the whole wide vale that lay between Crow Hill and her father's fortress at Vengen.

Somewhere down beyond the rows of tents and the peripheral stockade, she could just make out the funerary detail of the Fourth preparing the pyre in an open patch of cleared ground. Bees buzzed to hide her sadness.

"Come!" called a voice from within the tent.

Biting her lip, she reached out for the leather flap and then stopped. This was not a time to show any uncertainty or weakness. With a deep breath, she brushed the tent flap aside and strode in purposefully.

The interior was a little dull. Small holes cast precious little light into the tent and with the time being only a little after lunch, no lamps or candles had been lit. She allowed the leather flap to drop back behind her and waited for a moment to allow her eyes to adjust to the dim light.

Most of the occupant's goods had remained packed for the return journey to the fort. A cot, a table, a small cupboard and three chairs formed the entire contents of the room.

Scortius sat at the table, papers and a stylus lying in front of him, alongside a goblet and an almost-empty wine jug. Catilina noted with some satisfaction the deep hollows beneath the man's eyes and his haunted expression. He looked up at her and frowned slightly, taking another deep pull from his goblet and then casting it aside, somewhat drunkenly.

"My lady."

His voice was flat; the greeting unwelcoming.

"You find me at perhaps a bad moment."

"Oh I think I find you at the best of all possible moments," replied the young woman coldly as she strode across the room and dropped into the seat opposite him. She cast her eyes around the room once more, taking in every nuance of the place. Pulling her deep burgundy coloured cloak around her as though to ward off a chill, she fixed the doctor with a cold stare.

Scortius gave her an oddly confused look.

"You seem a little distraught, my good doctor?" she enquired her words light; her tone leaden.

Scortius pushed himself back a little in his seat and his shoulders dropped wearily.

"It has been a sad day, my lady Sabianus."

She smiled a horrible, cold smile.

"You have absolutely no idea, Scortius."

Again, confusion passed briefly across the slightly intoxicated features of the Fourth's chief surgeon. Catilina folded her arms.

"A sad day for many; not least for myself. Varro and I were very close; have been since I was an impressionable young girl, I would say. But a good day for the Empire, nonetheless; a traitor brought to light and executed; the army healed of its gangrene."

She took a light breath.

"I just loathe murderers, don't you?"

Scortius' brow furrowed.

"Indeed I do, ma'am. More than you know."

It was Catilina's turn to frown. Could she be wrong? She cleared her throat.

"You knew Varro for many years, didn't you?"

"Since our early days in the army, my lady. We were both there the day Darius was made Emperor. Both kneeled and took the oath the same day. We both signed up to follow Sabian and the new Emperor. And we've served together ever since. I've put him back together like a parent patches their child's favourite toy time and time again."

He sniffed back the emotion coursing through him.

"We travelled and fought from the Western Sea to the mountains and from the swamps in the far north to the cities of the central provinces. He's been my commander all this time, but we only ever paid lip service to the difference. It feels strange. Losing Varro is like losing a limb. I..."

He whimpered slightly and refilled his goblet, taking another heavy slug of dark wine, most of which reached his mouth.

"And now they're all gone. All the men I joined up with: Varro, Petrus and Corda. I'm the last of the old guard now."

He sighed.

"I never realised losing him would hit me this hard."

"You're all compassion" stated Catilina flatly.

"Lady?"

She ran a finger along the edge of the table absently, her eyes never leaving the doctor's.

"I believe I have pieced together the method you used, but it still leaves me wanting for a motive, and everything you say just obscures the motive all the more."

Scortius started, that momentary panic that flashed across his face before his miserable expression set in once again all the confirmation Catilina needed.

"What are you talking about, young lady?"

He pushed himself back upright in his seat, his expression suddenly sobering.

She sighed.

"You must have been planning it for a while. To start with, I thought perhaps that it was an accident, or at least a momentary angry choice, but the more I thought about it, the more I realised you'd carefully planned the whole thing."

Again, Scortius' expression flickered between panic and innocence. She smiled that cold smile again.

"Ironroot is, according to everyone I speak to, almost impossible to lay hands on this far north. Certainly no barbarian would likely ever come across it. But even a doctor, who's used to obtaining unusual substances, must have found it hard to get hold of here."

She leaned forward and steepled her fingers.

"That was something that required some thought. Even though I knew it was you... I just knew it, I couldn't see why you'd have a poison that was so hard to obtain. But then a thought struck me and I enquired with the cohort's clerks as to the last time you were on leave for any length of time."

She smiled at his frown.

"And I was not in the least surprised to find that you took a sojourn of a month to visit relatives down near Serfium on the Southern Sea. Plenty of exotic substances floating around in the dock front markets at Serfium, I'll wager."

She watched a tumult of emotions cross Scortius' face and smiled her unpleasant smile again.

"And I wondered whether you could have a legitimate reason for keeping ironroot. Perhaps there was a sensible explanation? Perhaps ironroot in certain doses worked as a curative, or a paralytic, or some other medical aid. But no. I've done my research now. There's no medical reason for any doctor to keep ironroot. In fact, since the only known use for the substance is to cause pain and death, there's no legitimate cause for anyone to keep it."

She gestured to the medical cabinet at the edge of the room.

"What drawer do you keep your deadly poisons in, doctor?"

Scortius waved his goblet to the side, some of the wine sloshing over the top.

"Pah!"

"Denials, Scortius?"

She laughed. "It must have got to you, waiting for the right circumstances. Varro had to come to you with some wound or illness first. But he was a healthy man, my Varro. Didn't get ill and, with no major wars on, you must have kept that little vial of yours hidden for a long time. Did you even consider making him ill or wounding him so that he had to come to you?"

She laughed. "Lucky there was that little uprising eh? Luckier still that Varro was wounded. You must have been dancing round your tent with joy."

The innocent look on Scortius' face had gradually slid away to be replaced by a mix of anger and sadness.

"You have no idea what you're saying, girl!"

Catilina laughed mirthlessly again.

"Girl? Touched a nerve, have I, doctor?"

She leaned forwards and slammed the flats of her palms down on the table, angrily.

"Save yourself the trouble of denials and feigned innocence! I am in no doubt as to your guilt or the method you employed to kill the man I loved."

Scortius' eyes wobbled uncertainly. He opened his mouth to speak, but Catilina spat out her angry words at him.

"A stroke of genius, really" she barked, slapping her hands on the table. "To soak his medicines in ironroot. I presume that actual compounds were placebos with no real medicinal value? The irony being that he was actually completely healthy and would easily have recovered from his wound had you not administered your care. Every time he took his medication, it would kill him a little more."

She waved a hand angrily.

"From what I understand, the amount he's been ingesting in his medicines would just make him gradually sicker and sicker until he'd consumed enough to seal his fate."

She stopped as a thought struck her.

"Good grief. You must even have carefully prepared the rest of the compounds. They had to keep him feeling ill enough to take them again, but well enough to feel that he was getting some effect from them? What kind of a mind must you have, doctor?"

She shook her head in disbelief.

"Oh, you must have laughed until you were sick over that one. To take away the pain that you were causing him, he effectively killed himself using your remedies for that same pain."

"Shut up!"

Catilina started, surprised by the violent outburst. Throwing his goblet aside angrily, Scortius slammed his hands flat down on the table and half-raised himself from his seat to face her.

"You have no idea, girl. You have no idea. What I did was hard beyond imagining."

"Ha!" she laughed back her retort. "I'm sure it was. All that planning…"

"It was *hard*" he bellowed.

The doctor collapsed back into his seat again.

"It was hard on me. The worst thing I've ever had to do…"

Catilina sighed.

"Forget any pretence, Scortius, or any attempt to obfuscate the reality of it. I know all about ironroot now. Mercurias is not only one of the best doctors in the Empire, but he's a very good friend of my family. It was he who confirmed the presence of the poison on the medicine wrappers I retrieved from Varro's bag. So you can be sure that he knows about it too. It's over."

Scortius' expression sagged, a look of hopeless despair filling him now.

"Still," Catilina said crisply, "since you were under no suspicion until I dug around, I'm pleased to find you so unhappy. Could it be that killing your 'good friend' just wasn't as easy as you'd hoped?"

Scortius grasped his forehead with his hand as though his head pounded.

"Easy?"

Scortius stared at her.

"I never expected it to be easy, Catilina. At best, I'll find release when I go to the Gods, but some things must be done, no matter how much it hurts. If it gives you any satisfaction, what I have done causes me great personal pain. I loved Varro like a brother. We had been through more than most siblings ever do before you'd ever even met him. No, this was far from easy."

Catilina stopped for a moment. The deep emotion behind the man's words spoke of a deep and painful story. She frowned and scrutinised the man before her for a moment before hardening herself again. She'd almost fallen into sympathy and she was damned if she was going to let that happen.

"Then tell me why, doctor."

She growled. "You claim to have loved him so much, so tell me why you killed him!"

She leaned back once more and folded her arms.

Scortius sighed.

"You should count your blessings, really, Catilina."

She laughed a hollow laugh.

"Yes, I feel truly blessed!"

"If I were a cruel man, it would be *you* lying in the priests' tent now, waiting to be burned, and not Varro. He'd be here with me, bemoaning your fate and crying on my shoulder."

"What?" Catilina stared at him.

"I am not as cruel as Varro, though."

As Catilina continued to blink at him in astonishment at the casual tone in which the doctor delivered such brutal words, he relaxed and leaned back in his chair again.

"I dealt *justice* on Varro rather than *revenge*. The great playwrights tell tales of vengeance where deal and pain is traded, like for like. If I had revenged myself on Varro, I would have taken you from him, you see."

He sighed.

"But no... I merely *executed* him for his actions. I could have been much more vicious."

Once more the doctor slumped, the strength leaving him to be replaced once again with grief and pain.

"Varro took from me the thing I loved more than anything else in the world; the thing I loved more than life itself. You see? If I were a vengeful man, I would have deprived him of you."

Catilina blinked.

"Varro took my son." Scortius mumbled, fresh tears streaking down his cheeks as he shuddered with sobs.

"My *son*!" he wailed.

Catilina shook her head, trying to make sense of all of this.

"Varro killed your son?" she demanded incredulously. "Never! He was a good man; a good soldier. Honourable and loving."

Scortius nodded, wiping away his tears again.

" My son... Terentius. A detachment of the cohort were on campaign in the mountains during that year when there was drought and a food shortage. Things became desperate. Even at the fort where we had the granaries men's bellies grumbled and moaned. But up there at Fallowford, there was no hope. Only the meagrest of iron rations."

He sighed. "Terentius and two of his companions snapped in desperation and stole food from the stores, but they were caught. Varro was their commander, you see. Terentius took all the responsibility for their actions. Brave and foolish."

He broke down again for a moment, sobbing and shaking.

"Terentius..."

Catilina cleared her throat.

"I've heard the story. The theft; the punishment. It's a story that's still used to illustrate the need for discipline. And that was your son? The ringleader?"

Scortius nodded again sadly.

"The boy was executed for insurrection" she said plainly, standing and gesturing at him.

"It's harsh, Scortius, but that's regulations. You *know* how a commander has to deal with insurrection and theft!"

She waved her hand expansively. "Would you have expected Varro to go easy on him just because he was your son? What message would that send to other potential rebels? If he'd not carried out that punishment, his own superiors would have broken him in the ranks."

"But the other two lived!" Scortius bellowed.

"Not Terentius though. Oh, no... he had to suffer. Not a quick, honourable death either, but beaten to death by his friends. *Beaten to death!*"

Catilina sighed.

"Varro did what he had to do. What he should have done. It's Terentius that was at fault, you idiot. It is a sad story, Scortius, but not something that justifies premeditated murder!"

Scortius growled.

"How would you know?"

She sighed and stood slowly.

"Truly."

She backed away towards the door.

"Truly, I may just be hypocritical..."

"What?" Scortius frowned at her through his tears. "What are you talking about?"

Catilina sighed.

"I could say I'm sorry, Scortius, but the truth is I'm not. And I may be as bad as you or even worse. You say you dealt out justice, not revenge. I think you're just deluding yourself, but I don't even claim such high morals."

"What?"

The doctor's expression, through the blur of tears, was one of confusion.

"The wine..." she said, pointing at the jug.

Scortius' tears stopped as incredulity swept them away.

"The wine?" he repeated in confusion.

Catilina nodded. "A friend of mine came in and added a little pep to it before you returned. I think you'll find it has a bit of a kick now. I don't have a medical background, you see. I don't know what proportions of ironroot are required for any particular level of effect."

She laughed.

"So we just used it all. I don't think you'll have as long as Varro, though. You see we used everything you had left over, and I think that's rather a lot. And one of the interesting things I found out from Mercurias' investigation is that those medicines of yours were infused with wine, because something in wine disguises both the scent and taste of ironroot."

"Catilina..."

Scortius' eyes were wide and staring now as his gaze flashed back and forth between the cold-faced lady before him and the empty jug nearby.

"I don't think you'll have to keep dosing to make it lethal, Scortius, but perhaps you can tell me. The amount you had left? Would that be fatal, d'you think?"

Scortius' eyes bulged in panic and he forced his finger down his throat, leaning over the arm of the chair and retching.

Catilina gave him an unpleasant smile.

"I shall take that as a yes then. And you know that's a waste of time. You started that jug an hour ago. I know, because I've been waiting outside to make sure you finished it. And that means that by now, with the tremendous quantity you've absorbed this afternoon, it's already deep in your system."

She reached across the table and collected the jug, turning it upside down and smiling at the single drip that slowly collected on the inverted rim and then fell to the table. She replaced the jug and stretched.

"Goodbye, doctor."

Turning her back on the stricken man, she strode from the tent, a strange mix of emotions coursing through her: pity, satisfaction and disgust. She sighed as she looked around herself in the bright morning sun.

Not regret though. Never regret.

Salonius leaned against the outside of the doctor's tent, a long piece of grass hanging from the corner of his mouth where he chewed absently. He raised an eyebrow as the lady appeared outside.

Catilina took a deep, cleansing breath and rolled her shoulders.

"*Now* we're done, Salonius."

The young man looked at her curiously.

"I don't think so."

"What?" she enquired of him. "Why?"

Salonius shrugged.

"Because we *are* better than him; both of us. You know that."

Giving her a sad smile, he patted her on the shoulder gently and affectionately and slipped past her, through the tent flap.

In the dim interior, Scortius was busy searching desperately through the various drawers and shelves of his cabinet, his face white.

"Doctor?"

The man ignored his new guest, his desperation increasing as he searched fruitlessly.

"Doctor?" Salonius repeated as he walked calmly across the tent and took the seat that Catilina had previously occupied.

Again he was ignored. Sighing sadly, he picked up the wine jug and brought it down on the table so hard that the handle sheared off in his grip.

Scortius jumped and stopped his furious searching to turn and stare.

"Good. Sit down doctor."

The stricken man turned once more to his cabinet, but Salonius called to him in a clear, calm voice.

"It's no good trying to find an antidote, doctor. You know there isn't one."

Scortius began to rummage once more. He muttered something in a panicky voice. Salonius didn't catch all the details, but he noticed the word 'emetic' in there.

"Sit down!" This time he bellowed, and Scortius jumped again and stopped.

"I will restrain you if I have to, but we are supposed to be civilised men, doctor, so come here and sit down."

Almost meekly, Scortius turned and wobbled across to his chair, slumping dejectedly into it. Salonius cleared his throat and fixed the doctor with a piercing gaze.

"It seems curiously fitting that I get to give you the same diagnosis you gave captain Varro. Mine's true though. You're going to die, Scortius. There's no cure and the lady Catilina was very thorough. The dosage you've had would have reached lethal more than half an hour ago and no amount of emetics and retching is going to save you now. Varro was enough of a man to face up to what you did to him quickly and nobly. Are you capable of that?"

The doctor stared at him.

"I hope so," Salonius said gently. "Now, Catilina is a little blinded by emotion at the moment. Given free reign, she would stake you out for the carrion feeders and see which killed you first: the poison or the animals."

Scortius' eyes widened at the young man's matter-of-fact tone.

"I, on the other hand, am less emotional. You took a good friend from me; a mentor, even. But from Catilina, you took the man she loved. Now I am here to explain your choices. I'm only going to do this once, and then I go find her and look after her."

Still, the doctor said nothing, but sat open mouthed and staring.

"First choice: Given the quantity I put in your wine, you will be dead before sundown, so you can sit and await your fate. Because I am not a forgiving man, I laced the wine also with strychnine. I realise that ironroot is not a particularly painful way to go, but from what I've read, strychnine will probably kill you an hour or two earlier, but very, very painfully."

Scortius began to gag, making an 'Ack! Ack!' noise. Salonius smiled and went on.

"Second choice: You could try and avenge yourself on me or Catilina. I suppose you could use the time you have left before you double up in pain to go and denounce us. But the problem is, Mercurias is very well aware of what you've done. In fact, he went to report it to the marshal, though Catilina persuaded him to delay a little, but he's probably been by now. I don't think you'll find any support there. In fact it very well might be that the guard are on their way for you right now."

He pushed the chair back and walked past the panicked doctor, to the cot bed at the rear of the tent, where the doctor's uniform lay folded, awaiting the funeral ceremony for Varro. Stooping, the young man collected the doctor's sword in its fancy sheath, likely never used and rarely warn outside ceremonies.

"And your third choice?" he commented lightly as he strode back to the table, unsheathing the sword with a metallic rasp that set the teeth on edge, "Take the noble and least painful way out. As soon as you can. And certainly before the guard get here; they certainly won't give you an opportunity afterwards."

He dropped the sword on the table before the dying man and walked past him to the tent flap. Turning, he smiled.

"Sad that it came to this. But at least *you* have a choice of how to end it. I would hurry though."

Turning his back, he pushed open the flap and walked out into the sunshine.

Catilina stood a few yards away, her arms folded and a cross expression on her face.

"Well?"

Salonius smiled.

"I just gave him something to think about."

She sighed.

"Your heart is too soft for you to be in the revenge business, Salonius."

He laughed and put his arm around her shoulder, turning her away from the tent.

"And you're a very dangerous woman, my lady."

They made a point of taking the more circuitous route to the ceremony below. Exiting the camp's stockade by the west gate, they strode down the hill in no great hurry, coming to a halt a little over half way along the slope, by a heap of fresh earth. They paused for a long moment, side by side and gazed at the shapeless mound that held the unmourned remains of the former prefect of the Fourth army.

As they watched, a crow landed fearlessly in front of them on the summit of the heap and began to investigate the freshly-turned earth for worms. Something about that made Salonius smile.

Walking on, they passed soldiers in full dress uniform, buffing every inch of steel to dazzling brightness. Most were too busy making sure they would meet the requirements of their officers to pay much attention to the two figures strolling amongst them, but those who did look up came to attention and saluted. Salonius returned their salutes as necessary, but still felt vaguely uncomfortable doing so. He was wearing his command guard uniform with the white horsehair crest which meant that he outranked most of the men of the second, but since his elevation to the position a mere two weeks ago, he'd spent little or no time among his peers, or indeed even wearing the uniform.

They came to a halt at the bottom of the slope where, on a slight hummock, the pyre had been constructed. Captain Iasus stood nearby, directing the affair with his familiar, curt and efficient manner. According to tradition, Varro would be sent to his afterlife with full military honours. Once the pyre had burned out and gone cold, his ashes would be placed in the urn that had been paid for by his contributions to the second cohort's funeral club. They would then be escorted back to Crow Hill, where they would be buried in the military graveyard outside the west gate of the fort, under a finely carved tombstone chiselled by one of the cohort's best stonemasons.

Salonius had only served a short time yet in the Imperial military, in a time of relative peace. Those deaths and funerals he had encountered in his time had been of non-ranking engineers. The engineering corps had turned out for them in their best uniforms and for the more notable occasions, a representative officer of the cohort from outside the engineers would attend. Nothing he had seen had come near this scale, though he realised these were somewhat exceptional circumstances. Normally a captain would be honoured only by his own.

Salonius glanced about him. The flags of all four northern armies fluttered in the breeze, carefully sited on a slight rise in order to catch what wind there was, yet far enough to put them out of danger of the flames when they came. The standards of the cohorts of the Fourth stood in rows, jammed into the ground, gleaming and glittering.

The pyre stood fully twice the height of an ordinary man, formed of logs cut from a thicket a quarter of a mile distant, and atop it lay the still figure of Varro, wrapped in Imperial green from head to toe. A sadness touched Salonius. Though Varro had been his captain and his superior, in many ways he had been closer to being a father than a commander. Briefly he wondered if anyone else in the Fourth felt that way or whether it was just the strange circumstances into which they'd been thrown together that had done this. He must remember to have a word with the stonemasons afterwards. Time to raise an altar to Cernus. Strange really. That would undoubtedly be the first altar set up in an Imperial shrine to a purely barbarian God.

He sighed as his mind drifted off into shadowy forests stalked by the stag lord. For a long time they stood, staring at the pyre, lost in their thoughts. At some time during that interminable wait, Catilina had slid her hand into his, though neither of them remembered it happening.

The bleating of the trumpets brought their attention back and they separated, standing proud and quiet. The last few men who were not in position pulled themselves into ranks. Many of the marshal's guard were conspicuously absent as they stood guard over those men deemed to have some level of guilt in the uncovered conspiracy. Varro's guard, resplendent in their white crests, stood positioned around the pyre, it being their task to set the flames. Salonius could have joined them; probably should have, but had elected to stay with Catilina instead.

As the trumpets called out their last note and the echoes rang off the hillsides, marshal Sabian strode into view, accompanied by a number of his senior officers and staff. He came to a halt between his daughter and Iasus, remaining standing and at attention. Mercurias sauntered across to join them, the dress uniform looking strangely inappropriate on the creased old man. The surgeon came to a halt behind them.

"Either of you two seen Scortius? I went to his tent before I came down here and there was no sign of him. I think he'd been drinking though.

Salonius and Catilina exchanged a curious and unreadable look.

"I expect he'll turn up," the young engineer said.

Epilogue

Prefect Salonius slipped off his horse just outside the great stone gate and handed the reins to one of his staff officers. Saravis Fork looked no different despite the decade that had passed. The sleepy town in the valley poured smoke forth into the early evening's mauve sky. Squinting, he could even make out the inn where they'd met Petrus, but everything looked like a child's wooden model from high in the Imperial fort. He smiled as he gave the valley a last, lingering look and tore his gaze away and walked through the gate, across the plateau, and to the wall walk.

Over the years since his rise, some would have said 'meteoric' rise through the ranks, he had found cause to revisit every place they had been during that hectic fortnight that had changed the world for him. Even the ruined villa had been on his list, though it was in a considerably worsened state following his efforts.

He'd been made captain the day following Varro's funeral; quietly and with no ceremony. An officer he'd not known from the First had taken the prefect's position and had done a good job of rebuilding the Fourth and repairing the damage Cristus had done. He'd worked with Salonius to promote the roles of what Cristus had always considered 'support troops' and these days engineers were generally considered a crucial part of any army. Indeed, the military's reliance upon new ideas in both offensive and defensive engineering had been largely down to his own efforts and had led to a summons to Vengen where he had been presented to the Emperor Darius.

He'd not known what to expect of his Emperor in person, but the easy and almost familiar way the great man had dealt with him had further strengthened Salonius' already rock-hard loyalty. How could an Empire fail with men like Darius and Sabian at the helm? It was that meeting, almost six years ago that had seen the reorganisation of the troops in the north and the creation of two new northern armies. It had been sad to leave the Fourth, but the opportunities offered as prefect of the new Twenty First had been great.

Sadly, that week at Vengen was the last time he'd seen Catilina too. She'd been out to visit a number of times early on, including that surprise visit after that first winter, when she'd turned up with Varro's child howling and laughing in her arms.

He sighed. He should have asked her to marry him years ago, but even though he was sure her father would have approved, he knew deep down that he would only ever be a friend to her. And her life was full of her child, with her brother and father taking care of them, so he didn't have to worry about her.

Salonius reached into the pouch that hung beneath his decorative prefect's cloak and, scrabbling around inside, drew out a hand full of fine, grey powder. He smiled at the last of Varro's remains. For over a decade he'd carried that pouch that he'd collected the morning after the funeral, and here, at Saravis Fork, he would make an end of it. Though buried in his urn at Crow Hill, something of captain Varro had been scattered to the wild northern winds everywhere they had been.

With a sad smile, he held up his hand and opened the fingers. The mountain winds immediately picked up the grey dust and whipped it from his hand, hurling it into the valley.

"Rest well, my friend."

The smile still on his face, he stepped slowly back and watched the last grains of dust disappear beneath the flag of the Twenty First: a black banner bearing a white stag and a sword.

END